BOOKS BY MICHELLE MURPHY
Light's Awakening
Light's Lost
Light's Warden

LIGHT'S WARDEN

MICHELLE MURPHY

BOOK 3: ALACORE'S APOTHECARY

The characters and events portrayed in this book are fictitious. Any similarity to real persons, living or dead, is coincidental and completely a byproduct of the reader's overactive imagination. Why are you reading this excerpt when you should be getting a snack to go with your book?

    Alacore's Apothecary, Book 3: Light's Warden

    © Michelle Murphy; D. M. Almond; 2023

    All rights reserved.

1

A manticore is essentially a mythical killing machine. They can be twice the size of an average human, with the muscular body of a lion, mane and all, and the bearded face of a man. Well, not a normal man, because most guys don't sport a mouthful of twelve-inch teeth that could chew the muscles right off my bones. As if that wasn't bad enough, they also have bulbous tails covered with poisonous quills. They use these to sting their prey, causing such happy side effects as convulsions, foaming at the mouth, and paralysis. Apparently, a manticore's favorite pastime is to cripple their victims and force them to watch as they are slowly eaten alive. Reminds me of a few girls I went to boarding school with. Fun times.

To sum that up, encountering a manticore equals rotten luck. If you ever see one, or even hear one might be within a few miles of your location, the sensible thing to do is promptly book it in the opposite direction. Or die. Those are the vast multitude of choices at your disposal. Only someone truly touched in the head would ever go anywhere remotely near a manticore on purpose.

I stood outside the manticore's lair, knowing this full well and wondering why I was doing something so wacked out. Was it really worth risking my life just to become a warden? The jagged mouth of the manticore's lair was a black hole against the rocky mountainside, a stark contrast to the intertwining trunks of the magnolia trees all around me. Their pale pink flowers were so welcoming and fragrant, while the cave in front of me stank of carrion and bad decisions. The rest of the forest was a wonderland—colorful birds chirping in the boughs, flying squirrels zipping among the forest canopy overhead, lush life everywhere the eye could see. I could walk in that forest for hours, drinking up its peaceful abundance.

So why enter a manticore's lair?

The beast's foul musk carried over the stench of rotten bodies. Air hit my face, then sucked away to the rhythm of the behemoth's snoring. It seemed the manticore had fallen for my trap. But if I was wrong, I was dead meat. Literally. I knew I should turn back. I was outmatched and frightened down to my bones. Nothing could be worth such a risk.

Except it was.

I needed to become the Warden of Willow's Edge.

I took a deep breath and stepped forward.

2

A few days earlier...

It had been weeks since the fae trafficking incident. Things moved rapidly once the court ruled in my favor to take the trials to become Warden of Willow's Edge. I scarcely had time to think before I was whisked away from the province and sent to the fae realm. It seems silly now that I was so naïve as to believe the fae would just let me become warden and be done with it.

To become the Warden of Willow's Edge meant following in the footsteps of my grandmother, connecting me to her legacy, which I wanted to uphold. I wanted to live a life of purpose by helping those around me. That was the entire reason for the apothecary's existence. At Alacore's Apothecary I made all sorts of helpful unguents, poultices, and elixirs. I made everything ranging from simple soothing lotions to a remedy for nightmares about spiders. Becoming Warden was just taking that one step further. It meant opening my doors to those in need, those who couldn't get the support they needed through regular channels, whether because they wanted to avoid scandal or because the system had simply failed them.

When they had nowhere else to turn, I could use my unique talents to help them.

"And what talents might those be?" Uriel scoffed, shaking her head. "You can't even tie a proper knot, girl."

Uriel was the gladewarden. A gladewarden was apparently someone who busted your chops and delighted in making you feel ten inches tall. I suppose a more apt description would be an old crone who lived in the forest and went out of her way to make visitors feel as miserable as she was. Or maybe that was just my frustration talking. Uriel was an older woman who perpetually wore shawls and headscarves. Her faerie wings rested, folded against her back, where they protruded from holes in her shawl. She was also overseeing my trials to become a warden. That meant she had the final say in whether I attained the mantle or not. I had been "training" under her since the second day after the court ruled that I could take the trials. I use the word *training* about as loosely as the knot I'd just tied, which was already coming undone. She was right, my knot-tying abilities sucked. It didn't make her disparaging remark any easier to swallow.

"Maybe it would be better quality if you showed me how to do it first instead of just braying at me all the time like a donkey," I said.

Well, that was what I wanted to say, but it came out more like, "I'm sorry, Gladewarden." That's pretty much the same sentence when you think about it.

I was supposed to be weaving a net that we would use to capture gnawing gnats. There was a small cloud of them around a copse of blackberry bushes near Uriel's cottage. I didn't know why Uriel—or anyone else, for that matter—would want some of the nasty little critters. She never explained any of the tasks she assigned me, and I felt far more like an errand boy than a woman training and testing for the mantle of a warden.

She groaned at my apology. I think that was her favorite way of speaking, groaning and muttering beneath her breath. "Give it here, then. We don't have all day." She snatched the tangle of a net I'd weaved with a scowl.

"I mean, we kind of do, though, right?" I teased, trying to lighten the mood.

Uriel rolled her eyes at me. She moved her gnarled fingers as deftly as the legs of a spider, dancing across the twine and unraveling my shoddy work. In seconds she was tying new knots. It was too fast for me to make out the intricacies, but I leaned in close and watched, hoping I might learn something.

"You know, most fae would just use their magic to get the job done," she grumbled.

"Yes, but–"

"You want to learn to do as much as you can without relying on your magic," Uriel said. "I know, I know, you've droned on about it a thousand times."

I wasn't dumb enough to point out that she wasn't using magic to weave the net either. I'd made the mistake of getting snippy with Uriel my

4

first week. That wonderful decision resulted in me chopping wood for *four* hours. My arms felt like cooked spaghetti for two days after that. To be honest, I didn't even know what powers Uriel possessed. She had never used any magic that I could see.

Uriel lived a simple life, tucked away from the town in her stone cottage. Moss blanketed the stone edifice and thatched roof. We generally spent our sessions around the large fire pit in front of the cottage that she used for cooking and crafting. It was dug into the earth and surrounded by heavy stones with runes for the different elements of life etched onto them. She had a weaving loom set up by her front door, a simple rocking chair beside the fire, and a large cauldron set over the crackling flames of the pit. Beside that was a long wooden table, the legs overgrown with vines, that she used to mix her ingredients. I hadn't seen the inside of the cottage, as she'd never invited me in.

"I just think it's better that I not be forced to rely on my magic to do every little thing," I lied.

Uriel had no idea my magic was locked away deep inside me, trapped inside the foul prison of my curse. It had been tricky making up reasons not to use magic to complete my assigned tasks, but so far I'd managed. By *managed* I mean that I was doing very poorly, and I was in a perpetual state of worry that Uriel was going to kick me out of the trials. In truth, I felt it was only a matter of time before she realized I had no magic at all. What would happen then? Who needed a warden that had no magic? What help could they possibly be to the other fae?

I can be helpful, I reassured myself. I had to believe there was value I could bring to the mantle, and I liked to think there were a few others who would agree. The problem was that all of those people were back in Willow's Edge, the province overlapping the human and fae realms. Meanwhile, I was in the fae realm, far away from anyone I knew.

I worried constantly about the state of the apothecary. My good friend Tae had offered to help around the shop part-time to keep Sacha, my business partner, on his toes. Or wings. Sacha's a rather ornery imp with a penchant for complaining and a predilection for lazing about. Uriel and he could have been cousins. It was good knowing Tae was there helping out.

Uriel hadn't made things easy for me, and I was certain she thought me about as useful as a cup with a hole in it.

"Voilà," Uriel proclaimed, lifting the net into the firelight and admiring her handiwork.

"You did that so fast," I complimented.

She gave me a withering look and thrust the handle of the butterfly net into my hands. "Save the ass-kissing and go catch those gnawers. I need exactly four of them."

"Got it," I said. "I'll make sure we have at least four."

Uriel groaned. "Girl, I swear you're daft as a cracked bell. Are you certain you and Rosalie were kin? I said *four*. Not three, not five, four. Exactly four. No need to go ruining a fifth critter's day just cause you're greedy."

Oh, how I'd love to punch this bitch. "As you say, Gladewarden." I bowed and headed off into the forest to collect the gnawing gnats.

"Lanie?" Uriel called.

"Yes, Gladewarden. Four," I called back, already knowing what she was going to ask.

I heard her harrumph her assent just before I disappeared into the woods. The Whispering Woods was an enchanting place that skirted the western side of the Tides. It was fascinating to see a forest untouched by the machinations of humanity. Trees grew wildly, reedy stalks of goldspire between ancient trunks of magnolias that looked like they'd been growing since the dawn of time. Magnolia flowers can grow in pinks, whites, yellows and even green. All those colors and more were represented in the Whispering Woods, with tropical canas, ferns, and orchids blanketing the forest floor. Pockets of sky peeked down through the tangled canopy of the dense woods.

I worked my way down a curving path that wound around a hill and toward the creek where Uriel had shown me the gnawing gnats a few weeks earlier. I distinctly recalled her telling me not to go near them because *"their sting is like getting kicked in the crotch."*

The breeze shifted, and the flowers overhead rustled against the hollow trunks of the magnolias. It sounded like a gathering of fae whispering secrets. Hence the name of the woods. I followed the bend around a massive magnolia, keeping a tight hold of my net. The left side of the path broke off into a steep descent down a red clay cliff, at the bottom of which babbled the creek water. The trail I was on was lovely, a beaten clay path skirted by mounds and mounds of purple elephant ears.

A gap in the canopy let sunlight down onto the expanse of elephant ears, their massive leaves fully open, gathering every ounce of light they could soak in.

A cluster of bushes skirted the creek at the bottom of the sloping path. It was a darned place to grow, as baffling to me as were many things in the fae realm. Berry bushes tended to hate wet soil, but these were lush and overflowing with ripe fruit. I heard the gnawing gnats before I saw their black cloud. Hundreds of them buzzed about the brush, feasting on the berries.

Gnawing gnats are terrible little critters. They're like the fae equivalent of a horsefly. Each one is roughly the size of a marble, with a mouth that takes up half their face. They have rows of teeth that look like bee stingers that they use to gnaw on their food. They preferred the sugary sweetness of fruit but were more than happy to drink some blood if they were disturbed. Unlike horseflies, gnawers have little twig-like arms and claws. They're like flying reverse pincushions, and I shouldn't have been messing with them. Unfortunately, Uriel said to get them, so get them I would.

I stopped to prepare myself for this folly. I pulled my hood up and tugged the strings until it bunched up snug against my ears and cheeks. I wanted as little flesh showing as possible. Next, I tucked the hoodie into my pants and then pulled my socks up over the hem of my jeans. It was a shame I didn't have any gloves. My hands would be completely exposed. I took a deep breath and continued my march down the sloping path. I figured the trick was to fool the gnawers into thinking I was simply taking a stroll. I held my net tucked against my leg on the far side of my body, out of their view.

The cloud of gnats buzzed back and forth, greedily chomping on the berries. They sounded like an army of hornets. I knew a girl in boarding girl who stepped on a hornet nest when she was home for the summer. The hornets stung her so many times she ended up in the hospital. She wasn't allergic to their stings, but after thirty-five of them, anyone's body would go into shock.

Stop thinking about horrible shit, I chastised myself.

My palms felt sweaty as I forced myself to continue my nonchalant pace, staring at every shift of their nasty little swarm through my peripheral vision. Without warning, I spun on my heel sideways and swiped the net across the bushes. The cloud buzzed angrily, shifting away from my paltry attack as I pulled the net back. It caught on a thorny branch.

"Fuck me," I cursed.

The swarm was already regrouping as I tugged on the handle of the net. A stream of gnats escaped as I wrestled the net back and forth, trying to unsnarl it from the bush. Their buzzing grew louder. They were pissed.

"Oh shit." I yanked back as hard as I could. The net ripped free. I fell backward, landing on my ass on the clay path. The swarm was making a beeline for me. I could see their little mouths, row upon row of angry black teeth under beady red eyes.

Time to go, I thought, hopping to my feet.

I ran for dear life. I'm naturally a fast runner. I used to think it was because I walked everywhere, living in the city and all. Now I understood it had more to do with my unicorn bloodline. I hoofed it up the hill, but the snarling gnawers buzzed just behind me. I put my head down and ran full tilt back through the woods. I leapt over a fallen log, slipped coming around a tree too quickly, and kept running until my heart felt ready to burst and my head was pounding. I didn't slow down until I smelled the smoke from Uriel's fire pit.

The cottage was just ahead through the trees. I stopped, realizing the gnawers had given up their pursuit and gone back to their berry feasting. *Why would they give up?* I wondered with a sinking feeling in the pit of my stomach. I never actually looked at the net while I was running like a madwoman through the forest. *Did I even catch any?*

I broke out in a cold sweat. Uriel would kill me if I bungled another assignment. I had already lost the stag horn and broken her rune branch. The latter was from falling out of the tree after I had cut the topmost branch from a four-hundred-year-old birch. Uriel was far more concerned with the damage to the branch than whether I'd been hurt. Most of it was broken, but the very tip was just enough wood for her to make a single rune. She'd scowled at me the whole rest of the night and well into the next week after that one. At this rate, I had to be close to flunking out of the trials.

I panted like a dog needing water as I knelt and wiped the sweat from my forehead. I hadn't even realized how tight I'd been gripping the mouth of the net. The wood Uriel used to form the hoop was elastic, bending without the slightest crack. I carefully opened it to peer inside and had never been so relieved to see vicious little teeth. Little black shapes writhed, pulling against the twine netting. Their teeth were gnawing futilely at the trap. The twine was spun from the reeds of a whispering willow. They could gnaw until their teeth fell out and it wasn't going to cut them free.

"Hey there, fellas," I cooed. "You're stuck in there, huh? Sorry I had to ruin your lunch, but Uriel has plans for ya. Don't worry, though. She's a mean old goat, but I think her bark is worse than her bite." I didn't know who I was lying to, the gnawers or myself. "Let's see now. How many of you did I catch?"

I counted six in total. That put me two above my target.

I tsked. "Well, that won't do." Uriel was very clear about only wanting four of them. Going back with six was just as likely to land me in trouble as if I'd gotten zero. I had to free two gnats.

I reached in for the gnawer closest to the mouth of the net. It felt like trying to pluck a nugget of charcoal free. The gnawer's little body twitched violently as I tugged it loose from the twine. It steadied itself with little claws, delicately laying them flat on my finger and thumb. The gnawer blinked at me with four little red eyes.

"Aw, you're kinda cute when you're not angry, huh?"

The gnawer smiled at me, then promptly chomped down on my finger. I squealed and shook my hand in the air. Its little claws dug into my skin, and it bit me twice more. It felt like getting stung by twelve bees at once. I yelped and slapped my hand down on the ground. The gnawer released me before it hit the dirt and twirled into the air on its little wings. I watched in horror as two more gnats flew past the mouth of the net. All my flailing had shaken them free. I dropped the net in the grass and clapped my hands together in the air.

Yes! I caught one.

I felt the buzz of its body trapped between my palms. The gnawer's compatriots fled into the trees, buzzing their victory as they made their way back to their blackberry bush. My palm stung. The gnawer was living up to its name, chomping on my hand. I shook my cupped hands vigorously back and forth until it released its hold. And then I kept shaking until I didn't feel its buzzing anymore.

I switched the gnawer to my right hand, keeping it cupped as I retrieved the net from the grass. Fortunately, the other three gnats were still trapped in the twine. I dropped the fourth inside the net and immediately pulled the mouth shut like a coin purse. My finger and palm were bleeding from tiny pinpricks of the gnawer's teeth.

I sucked on my finger and made my way back to Uriel's cottage. She was snoring in her rocking chair when I arrived. It made my blood boil. *Of course, she's out like a light while I'm running around getting chewed up for her.*

I stood close to the rocking chair, wondering how anyone could sleep with their mouth open so wide. *What if I flicked one of the gnawing gnats in there? Bet that would take the fire out of the old goat.*

I loudly cleared my throat.

Uriel opened one eye, which was already trained on me.

"I'm back with the gnats," I said.

Uriel sat up and grumbled. She grabbed the cane between her legs and used it to pull herself out of the rocking chair. I felt a pang of guilt for thinking of hurting such a harmless old lady.

"As if the whole forest didn't hear ya yelping like a trapped wolf," Uriel grumbled.

She heard me squealing in pain and just kept sleeping? Ugh, this bitch.

"Stop staring at my bum and let me see what you've brought."

I snapped to attention and quickly followed her to the fire pit. She took the net from me and frowned at my captives. "Kind of a runty little batch," she grunted disapprovingly. "You should have grabbed a couple more."

"Are you fucking serious?"

She looked at me and rolled her eyes. "Well, don't cry about it. They'll probably still get the job done. Just not as strong as I'd like." Uriel muttered something, and a soft tendril of smoke drifted from her palm into the open net.

Whoa, it's her magic! I thought, getting my first glimpse at what the gladewarden was capable of.

The smoke found each gnawer in turn. The air grew colder around us sending goosebumps across my arms. A film of frostbite encircled each of the gnats, and they froze in place, paralyzed except for their eyes darting back and forth.

"Fetch the kettle for me," Uriel ordered.

She kept a pole with a kettle hanging over the side of the fire pit. I used a wool pad to turn the hinged pole out of the fire, where she could reach it. Uriel motioned for me to lift the lid as she plucked the frozen gnawers out of the net. Once she had them all gathered in her palm, she swiftly clapped her hands together. It sounded like grinding seeds in a pestle. I winced at the brutality of it.

Uriel rolled her eyes at me again. "You're too soft, lass," she chided as she rubbed her hands together over the open kettle. What looked like black sand poured from her hands into the water. She rubbed them until every dry speck of the dust was gone. "Add three heads of lavender to the tea."

I gaped. "You're making tea?"

"Nothing escapes you." She turned her back to me and hobbled back to her rocking chair. "Wake me up when it's boiled enough."

I hate her, I hate her, I hate her, I seethed.

"Stop scowling and get to work," she said without looking back.

"Yes, Gladewarden."

I fell to work. I added the lavender and moved the kettle back to the heat. It would be tricky making tea over an open fire. Easy to scald the ingredients. I fell into a rhythm, letting the tea get just hot enough to boil before pulling it back. I stirred to unlock its fragrance, then brought the kettle back to the flames once more. While the tea boiled over the fire, I stared at runes ringing the pit, lost in thought, until the black dust was hard and crystallized. It took a few more rounds of this process, heating, stirring, cooling, and heating again, before I saw what Uriel wanted. The liquid glowed with purple swirling lights, the trails of the black dust. I smiled appreciatively.

"Put it in that bottle over there," Uriel ordered.

I jumped, almost knocking the kettle off its pole. I hadn't even heard her walk up beside me. I can get like that when I'm working at the apothecary too. I kind of fall into a trance, happily working ingredients into healing salves and the like. It's my Zen place.

Uriel had set a glass bottle near the fire, and I used a sifting cup to steadily pour the tea into the bottle.

"What made you think to hold back the lavender?" Uriel asked.

"If it stays in the tea, it'll lose potency and break down that purple glow swirling inside," I said.

"How do you know that?"

I shrugged. "It feels right."

Uriel nodded curtly and pointed to a cork on her table. I brought the bottle over and stoppered it. "Why isn't the glass hot?" I asked.

"I coated the bottle in nelm oil when it was tempered," Uriel said, as if it were obvious. "Go away now. I've got lots of things to do without you tugging at my skirts."

"Yes, Gladewarden." I bowed and gathered my backpack.

"Come back in two days."

There was no rhyme or reason to the span of time between my visits to Uriel's cottage. I was at her beck and call, and that was all there was to it. I bowed and took my leave, eager to soak my aching feet in some hot bathwater back at the lodging house in town.

"Aren't you forgetting something?"

I paused. "Oh, um, thank you for the lesson, Gladewarden." I bowed again.

Uriel scowled at me. "Daft girl. The tea. I told you to take it to Mr. Bukle's smithy."

She had said no such thing. Uriel did that quite a bit. I had learned to just play dumb and move along. "Yes, of course, my bad."

I gathered the bottle and stuffed it into my backpack, then took my leave. I could still feel her scowl even when I was down the hill and through the woods. I loved the view from this hike. Up on the hill you could see clear across the tree line out to the coast, where the ocean waves crashed against the rocky cliffs to the west of the Tides. I could see some of the seashell town from that vantage. My lodging was close to the edge of the woods, at the base of the hill, on the outskirts of town. I could even see my front door from there.

I could also see the man waiting for me in front of it.

3

arly morning light streamed in through the apothecary's only good storefront window. The other window was bandaged over like a sore eye of the building with wooden boards, an unhealed scar from the night of the changeling's murderous assault. Taewyn Śankhinī couldn't look at those boards without reliving the nightmare that had caused them. It made her feel weak in her stomach, a constant reminder of hungry raven eyes peering out at her from the lurking shadows of the apothecary's basement.

The sooner Lanie makes enough money to fix that window, the better, she thought, using a finger to hold her place in her book as she shifted her seat so it angled away from the windows. That was the problem, though. Lanie wasn't exactly making bank running Alacore's Apothecary.

Poor Lanie. She has the worst luck. At every turn, Rosalie's granddaughter had faced new obstacles. To start with, Lanie never got to know her grandmother, the previous owner of the building. Since she'd arrived in the province, the changeling tried to murder her, she lost all the money she made at the bazaar, and then Lobo dumped her. It was a rotten chain of events that Taewyn didn't think someone as awesome as Lanie deserved. *In the end we can only deal with what life throws at us, I suppose.*

The storefront had changed much since Lanie took it over. Rosalie, goddess rest her soul, used to keep her dusty shelves stocked with even dustier antiques, some of them magic relics, others human trash. Most of those shelves were gone now, another casualty of the changeling's attack, smashed to bits during the werewolves' ferocious battle. The broken remains of Rosalie's legacy had been carefully swept up and tossed in the garbage. *They're the purview of the landfill gremlins these days.*

What little remained of the antiques had been sold at the Bazaar. Lanie had turned a pretty profit from that undertaking in just a few hours. And had lost it just as quickly. The money was confiscated by soldiers from the Court of Shadows under the pretense that Lanie was not legally

13

the warden and had no rights to sell goods at the Bazaar. It hurt Taewyn's heart to see Lanie treated so unjustly. That was why, when the opportunity came for Lanie to undertake the trials to become Warden of Willow's Edge, Taewyn had put her life on hold to help out.

Lanie's number one worry had been leaving the apothecary unattended. She didn't trust her partner, Sacha, to stay on top of things and was afraid to lose the small number of regulars she had amassed over the last four months. Taewyn spent most of her days as a fertility and sexual expression counselor. Her primary focus was couples, but she worked with singles as well, teaching them how to experience pleasure and explore the erotic arts. Her succubus magic made her keenly attuned to the sexual auras of other fae, which lent itself to her work as a fertility specialist.

Plus, there was her side gig, the secret one nobody else in her life knew about. Compared to that work, babysitting the apothecary was dreary. But she had made a promise to Lanie, and she intended to keep it.

I just wish these trials weren't taking so bloody long.

Taewyn sighed and forced herself to find her place in the book. She did not fancy herself much of a bookworm, but that afternoon she had her nose buried deep in a dusty old tome that had been specially delivered to her doorstep from the Royal Library of Time. She could understand the attraction humans had to audiobooks. It would have been a much more pleasant morning if she could've simply heard the words spoken while her hands were free to do something more fun. Like crocheting a new blanket. She had a lovely spool of yarn upstairs in her apartment that was practically begging to become a scarf. She shook her head. "Damn, I lost my place again." She needed to stay focused. The book was important to Lanie's freedom.

The storefront bell tinkled as the front door closed behind their latest customer.

"Old coot," Sacha snarled from the other side of the apothecary, behind the counter.

"You could be nicer to Mr. Anders, you know," Tae said, without looking up from her reading.

"He's always in a bad mood. It's so annoying." The red imp fluttered on his small bat-like wings, replacing a jar of ginger root on the top shelf. Lanie liked everything neatly arranged and organized when it came to her ingredients.

Charlie snorted as she came up from the basement. She had a paint can in one hand and a couple of flat brushes in the other. "That's rich, coming from you."

Sacha glided down to his stool and plucked a cigar from the ashtray. He popped it into his mouth and relit the end with a flame from his fingertip. "What's that s'posed to mean?" he said from one side of his mouth.

"She's saying there's a difference between being a grumpy little imp with nothing better to do than complain and an old man whose whole body hurts just from walking the four blocks to this apothecary to get his medicine," Taewyn said. She'd had to reread the last sentence three times to process it over Sacha's complaining.

"Shouldn't you be in school?" Sacha grumbled.

Charlie stopped in the middle of the store, and her shoulders slumped. The school had declared that despite her recent tragic circumstances, she would not be allowed to return until next year, when the new semester began. It was her last year of school. Any friends she had her own age would have moved on by the time she returned. It wasn't fair, not after all she'd been through. Tae opened her mouth to tell Sacha as much.

"Don't you have a third nap to take, old man?" Charlie shot back.

Sacha scrunched his face into a scowl. Tae snorted. It wasn't easy to get under the little daemon's skin, but Charlie was holding her own ever since Lanie had rescued her. The kid had it hard. Besides school expelling her for missing so much time, her own mother had turned her back on the girl. Mrs. Etune was a downright bitch. She had said Charlie "brought all that misery on herself." If Charlie's father were still alive, there was no way the mean brownie would've gotten away with that. And she was wrong. Charlie wasn't a bad kid. She was just curious and a little lost. That was why Lanie had taken her in. She saw the same goodness in Charlie that Taewyn did.

"If she doesn't stay here with me, she'll go back to the Brick," Lanie had said. She never shook the betrayal Charlie had suffered, nor the track marks on Charlie's ex-girlfriend's arms. It would be easy for a kid like her to slip into the abyss of drugs, to numb her pain and slink away from the world. Lanie had done the right thing.

"Did you find all the supplies you need?" Tae asked Charlie, cutting through the tension between the girl and the imp.

Charlie looked down at the brushes. "I'd prefer a paint roller, but these'll do."

"And what makes you think you can use up all our paint for your little project anyhow?" Sacha said, blowing out a plume of cigar smoke that shaped itself into an air balloon. It floated up to the ceiling before dissipating.

"Lanie said I can use whatever I want from the basement," Charlie replied defensively. She set the paint can and brushes down with the rest of the paint cans she'd already brought up, inside a red metal radio flyer wagon she had also found in the basement.

Taewyn tapped her finger on the page, on the word *Sphynx,* and sighed. "Would you get off the girl's back, Sacha?"

Sacha crossed his arms over his chest and chewed on the cap of his cigar indolently. "Fine. What do I care if Lanie goes broke because the kid uses up all her supplies?"

Charlie blanched at that statement. She turned to Tae with a questioning look. Tae rolled her eyes. "Don't listen to him. He's completely full of it." Lanie didn't sell paint. She sold potions and elixirs, lotions and poultices, herbs and oils. Plus, Sacha obviously *did* care about Lanie. The damn imp even died for her once. That wasn't the sort of thing you did for someone you hate. Tae closed her book over one finger to mark her place and moved to the front door. She held it open for Charlie. "Go forth and express yourself, my dear."

Charlie nodded resolutely and headed out the front door with her wagon in tow. The wheels skipped over the threshold, jostling the paint cans about.

Tae let the door shut on its spring hinges. "Now, can you please be quiet so I can read?"

Sacha already had a newspaper lifted over his face. It was from 1928. He didn't respond. Tae eyed him suspiciously as she slowly took her seat. She looked one more time, to be sure he wasn't going to interrupt her, then reopened the book. She scanned the page.

...recesses of the labyrinth, to the Sphynx's lair. This capstone is the pinnacle of the—

"What's that dusty old book about anyhow?" Sacha said from behind his paper.

Tae looked up at the ceiling and groaned. "Please, Sacha, I really do need to read this."

"You should try to focus better. You've been on the same two pages for like thirty minutes now."

Deep inhale through the nose, Tae thought. *Hold it. Slow exhale through the mouth. Whatever you do, do not kill the imp.* She had to block Sacha out. This book could hold the key to unlocking Lanie's curse. Sacha didn't know about the curse. It was a very personal thing to Lanie, something only Tae and Drys knew about. That curse rendered Lanie unable to be intimate with anyone without blacking out. It also kept her magic tied down and impotent. This prevented Lanie from living a free life, true to her emotions. Lanie had such a big heart and so much love to give that it was the cruelest kind of curse Tae could imagine.

Tae had been searching for answers to help Lanie lift the curse ever since she found out about its existence. She'd caught wind that the tome in her hands might have an answer and called in a favor to borrow it from the royal library. If she could only read the damn thing, she might be able to figure out how it could help Lanie.

...call on the Sphynx. Her temple lies at the eye of earthly realms, perched atop snowcapped peaks...

"Sacha," Tae said, "have you ever heard of a person named Sphynx?"

Sacha snorted and turned to the next article of the newspaper. "It's a creature, isn't it, not a person."

"A creature?"

"Keep it down," Sacha said. "I'm trying to read."

Tae set her book down on her lap. "Seriously?"

He flipped to the next page, snapping the paper out as he did so.

Tae put on her best sweet voice. "C'mon, Sacha, help me out."

No response.

"I'll make some of those sausages you like," she teased.

Sacha dropped the paper to the counter and smiled at her. His wings fluttered excitedly. "Sausages?"

Tae nodded. "I have three of them in my icebox."

"What do you want to know?"

"Tell me everything you've heard about these Sphynx."

"Giant creatures, perverts for parents. Angel and a manticore bump uglies and make 'em. Strictly against the rules to mate like that, you know."

Tae shrugged. Nothing consensual and non-manipulative was out of bounds in her mind when it came to love. "Anything else?"

"They get in a lot of trouble if they're born. End up stuck away in temples and what not, to keep 'em from the general population, as it were."

"That's really interesting. What about a *farsteer*? I've never heard that term before, and this book says the Sphynx will bestow *farsteer*."

Sacha turned his head to the side as if listening to something. "Hmm…farsteer. Not sure. Never heard of it." He snapped his fingers together suddenly. "Wait, do you mean flsteer? Yeah, that makes sense. That's like a blessing…um, a gift…"

"Like a *wish*?" Tae asked, hope blooming in her heart.

"Yeah, that's it. Like a wish."

Taewyn's mouth hung open at the possibilities. She leapt out of her seat and squealed as she jumped up and down. Sacha watched her with a wry grin. She ran over and hugged him before he could blink. "You brilliant little devil, you. Do you know what this means?"

Sacha giggled as she set him back on his stool. "Means I get some sausages."

"Yes, absolutely one hundred percent yes." Tae beamed. "In fact, I'm going to cook you *four* of them. But then there's so many things I have to do. I'll have to pack, get tickets, call the cab, reset next week's appointments…"

"Whoa," Sacha said. "What do you mean pack?"

"I must go right away." Tae beamed down at him. "I've finally figured out how I can help Lanie."

4

Stepping off the boat the first day I arrived at the Tides was like being transported to another world. In Willow's Edge, I still saw the remnants of human culture embedded in the fae province. The buildings, paved streets, automobiles—they were all distinctly human in nature. The fae of that province had certainly put their mark on things, but it was familiar enough to feel normal to me. The Tides was a place like nowhere I had ever seen. We were deep in the fae realm, across an ocean of time, and the landscape was both alien and exciting.

The Tides is a coastal town, a quaint hamlet nestled amongst and between the Whispering Woods and the Ocean. The fae don't name their oceans. The idea that you could split up the ever-shifting body of water that covers over seventy percent of our planet into neat little plots is ridiculous to them. The harbor is glorious, with rocky cliffs on either side of the arc-shaped cove.

Human towns are set in parallel rows, neat geometric shapes that are packed with houses and yards and stores and parking lots. The Tides was nothing like that. First off, the buildings themselves were of an otherworldly nature. The material of choice was seashells. Not tiny seashells, but enormous structures the size of human houses and cottages. There were bulbous horse conches, spired horn shells, flat and fanned Venus sunrays. All manner of seashell was represented in colorful majesty, with opalescence, pastel pinks and blues, delicate violets, and vivid purples. The fae would recover the discarded shells from the bottom of the ocean floor. What once was the abode of a dinosaur-sized snail or clam was now home for a fae family.

The bizarre arrangement of the buildings was another anomaly. Instead of neatly set rows with even streets, the houses were placed wherever their owners pleased. One minute I could be walking down a sandy street lined with storefronts and houses, and the next I could find myself in a quiet area surrounded by palm trees and spot a lone shell house nestled between the ancient trunks of magnolias. It all depended on how each fae family preferred to live, either completely on their own or clustered right up against each other to the point of being in a symbiotic relationship. Round holes had been carefully chiseled out of the sides of the shell houses and covered with blown glass, concave bubbles of brilliant craftsmanship. Glass was one of the chief exports of the Tides' economy.

I had been generously put up in a lodging house, a series of conjoined shells near the edge of town. It was a place for visitors or merchants on business to sojourn. I had grown quite fond of the one-room lodging. The sight of that shell made me feel warm inside as I came down the hillside.

However, the man blocking my front door did not.

He was a large man, six foot four, with wide shoulders and a narrow waist. He saw me coming and perked up, rigid as a plank, like a dog that had caught a scent. He had an odd way of standing, with one hand rested on his back and the other near his waist.

"Miss Alacore?" he asked as I approached. His sharp nose and long teeth gave him a rather sharkish appearance.

"What if I am?"

"Ah, you are, then," he deduced. I guessed I wasn't too good at being sly.

"You know, it's pretty creepy skulking outside a girl's room."

The man blanched. He sputtered for a moment, trying to find the right words, and then retorted in the stuffiest indignation. "I can assure you, madame, that I have never *skulked* a single day in my life. I have simply been waiting outside your abode for two hours, anticipating your return."

"Ah, I get it. You're not skulking. You're just a stalker."

The uptight fae's face turned a deep shade of blue. It was unnerving, but I recognized his puffy cheeks and tight lips to indicate he was blushing.

"Listen, fella, whatever you're buying, I'm not selling," I said. "Now kindly step out of the way so I can go inside and relax."

I tried to move around him, but he sidestepped, blocking my path. "Miss Alacore, if you please. My name is Geraldine. I have been sent to inform you that my master would like a word with you."

That was interesting. "No thanks."

Geraldine blinked at me. I didn't think he was used to rejection much.

"That means go away. I'm not following some strange dude skulking around on my doorstep to meet his *master*."

I'd been through enough dangerous situations at that point to knock the naivety out of me. I didn't know this guy, and he seemed like a bit of an ass. I decided I wasn't interested in what his master wanted to speak about. The only thing I cared about was taking off my sneakers and soaking my feet in some hot water. My work at Uriel's had left me feeling achy and tired.

"Oh shit," I said. "I completely forgot." I had to deliver Uriel's gnawer tea to Mr. Bukle. Best to get it done quickly so I could get back and relax.

I turned left and swiftly strode down the sandy path. Geraldine was fast on my heels. At least when he walked alongside me, he stopped doing that weird one-arm-on-the-back-one-on-the-front thing. "Ugh, take a hint, Geraldine. Go away."

"As much as I would relish removing myself from the presence of someone of your rather uncouth disposition, I will not leave your side until such time that you attend my master's meeting."

"That's a long-winded way of saying you're going to annoy me to death." I was getting peeved. "You can follow me, but I'm still not going anywhere with you."

The path circled a cluster of palm trees toward the town center. A fae wearing a straw hat was fishing on the foot bridge. Water is channeled all around the town, some of the waterways going right into buildings. Some of the fae that live under the House of Dawn need to keep themselves properly hydrated with salt water to maintain their health. My own room had the ability to be flooded with water up to the waist, should I need it. My sneakers clapped over the bamboo bridge. The fae casually glanced up at me. He was about to turn away back to his fishing when Geraldine caught his eye. The fisherman promptly snapped his pole up out of the water and bowed to Geraldine.

That's odd. I would've asked Geraldine about it, but I was too annoyed with him for pestering me. He marched alongside me in the stiff gait of a living scarecrow.

The center of town was dominated by a ringed row of seashell houses. Here they were tightly packed, some built right on top of others. I felt comforted by the amount of people out and about. *Maybe I should tell one of them this creep won't leave me alone.*

21

It seemed like a good idea until I noticed that anyone who saw us stopped what they were doing and bowed their head in reverence. The fae that called the Tides home were an interesting assortment. There were the diminutive brownies, bustling about on their daily chores; sparkling sprites that flitted over the lily pads, their wings tinkling like tiny bells; and even some bloody-capped powries getting drunk at the local tavern.

But two fae races dominated the population. They were the droba and the blossoms. The blossoms were water fae, elegant-looking faerie folk with an appearance somewhere between a fae and flower. The droba were an upright walking frog people the size of humans. Many of them reminded me of dart frogs, with brightly patterned colors and glossy skin.

The blossom fae ruled over the House of Dawn. They were the so-called "purebloods" of that great house. The droba worked in town or as soldiers for the House of Dawn. One such droba was seated atop a resting leopard gecko the size of an automobile. She held her pike upright, at attention as she lazily watched a mammoth dragonfly passing overhead. The dragonflies generally kept to their habitat on the coast, but if one decided to descend into town, thinking to make a quick meal out of a fae, the town guardians would strike them down with those pikes.

Mr. Bukle's house was just up ahead. He was the local blacksmith, with his apartments above his workshop. A light drizzle of rain came down as I neared his home. Geraldine was still on my ass. *Enough of this shit. I'll go tell that guard this guy's stalking me.*

I moved off the sandy path toward the guard. The sleeping gecko opened one eye to gaze at me, stopping me in my tracks. The guard looked away from the dragonfly, which was already almost past the town center, and smiled down at me.

"Good day," I said.

Her large bulbous eyes blinked at me, then took in Geraldine. She grew rigid and bowed her head. "Geraldine."

Shit, who is this guy? I looked back at Geraldine. He stood with his strange one-hand-behind-his-back-one-in-front posture and bowed stiffly back to the guard.

"Is there anything I can do for you, sir?" the guard asked.

"Not today, guardian. I am merely accompanying Miss Alacore on her errand."

I stepped back onto the sandy path and squinted at Geraldine. He looked awfully pleased with himself. I rolled my eyes at him and kept walking. I admit I was intrigued at that point. The guy was obviously important if the town guardians were bowing to him. I decided whatever he was selling was too tantalizing to pass up. But he was just so smug. I would rather slap a pie in his face than admit defeat.

"Okay, you've got me interested," I conceded. "I'll go with you, and along the way you can explain just where the hell we're going. But first I need to deliver this tea to Mr. Bukle. Don't be a prick and follow me. Just wait here."

Geraldine turned his nose in the air when I called him a prick. Whatever. He was an uptight jerk wad. But he did stay where he was as I walked up to the smithy. The workshop was closed for the day. A metal gate blocked the wide entrance.

It's awfully early for him to be closed, I thought.

I went around the side of the shell, a rounded conch with a spiral whorl on its sides. I knocked on the door to Mr. Bukle's home. There was some shuffling inside, and then the door opened. Mr. Bukle blinked at me with his large frog eyes until recognition entered them. We had met a few times at the local watering hole. He and his husband were an amiable couple. He always had a brightness in his eyes and a broad froggy smile that was infectious.

When he opened the door, he looked nothing like that. He was troubled and had clearly been crying recently. "Ah, good afternoon, Ms. Alacore. I'm afraid we're closed for the day."

"The gladewarden sent me," I explained, fishing out the bottle of tea. "I have a delivery for you."

Mr. Bukle's eyes lit up with hope, but he was confused. "The gladewarden? But how did she know?"

"Reginald, would you step aside and let the poor girl inside?" It was Jerri, Mr. Bukle's husband.

"Oh, of course, please come in," Mr. Bukle said, stepping aside.

I slipped out of my sneakers and stuffed my socks inside them, then entered their house. Water came up to my knees. Most people think algae smells rotten, but that is usually because there are dying plants around. Algae actually tends to smell rather leafy to me, fresh like a geranium.

That was what their house smelled like as I waded through the den. Large lily pads dotted the living room.

"Oh, thank you, Lanie," Jerri said, folding his hands over his leather apron. "Please, come back this way. She's in her bedroom."

I followed him down a spiraling hall. We passed a room on the right, at the center of the shell, which must have been their bedroom. It looked like a mini terrarium, with ivy-wrapped branches angled against the walls and the dense foliage of tropical plants. It was my first glimpse into how the droba lived, and I would have found it deeply fascinating if not for the pervading sense of anxiety hanging over my two friends like a dark cloud.

Jerri stopped at the doorway to a circular room. Reginald paused just behind me, wringing his hands with worry. A child lay on a hanging bed of reeds by the far wall. She coughed hoarsely and whimpered.

"We've tried everything—hoca root, elderflower, even some dried fendlspin," Jerri explained. "Her fever just won't go down."

"It's endrival," Reginald said gravely.

Jerri started crying, and Reginald moved around me to hold him. They were worried parents with a very sick child. I felt so helpless. I wanted to take their pain away. If I had access to my unicorn magic, I could have surely healed the girl. As it was, I was smothered under that abominable curse.

"Let me give her the tea," I said.

Reginald nodded as he held Jerri close. I crossed the room and leaned over the girl's bed. She opened her little frog eyes and peered at me. Her skin was flaking and ashy. A droba's skin should have a shiny wet sheen, even when they're on land. The luster was gone from her mottled blue spots.

I gently stroked her arm as I spoke. "Hello there, I'm Lanie. I'm a friend of your dads. What's your name?"

"Tinsie," the little girl whispered. Her voice was very weak.

"I love your room." I made a point of looking around. The walls of the shell were dyed an iridescent pink, and she had dolls sitting on a lily pad near her bed. She clutched another one in her arm. It was a seahorse. "It's spectacularly pink. That's my favorite color."

Tinsie smiled feebly. "Mine too."

I grinned at her. I could feel her parents watching us from the hallway.

Her eyes drifted down to the glowing bottle in my hand. "Is that medicine?"

"Yes, I brought it here special, just for you."

"I don't want any more medicine. It tastes yucky."

Oh shoot. I didn't have kids. Weren't they just supposed to do what adults said? I tapped on her seahorse. "Is this your favorite doll?"

Tinsie nodded. "Gigi is my friend." She coughed, hoarse and rough, then groaned. I didn't know anything about droba biology, but I knew Tinsie was very ill. If we didn't get the right medicine in her soon, this was not going to end well.

"Well, Gigi told me they want to play with you. But they can't do that until you drink this tea I brought."

Bella frowned. "Is it gross? That elderberry stuff daddy gave me was yucky."

How to answer that? Elderberry was actually kind of sweet. If she didn't like that, I doubted she was going to enjoy a tea made from crushed gnawing gnats. I decided to be truthful. "I don't know. It's a mystery. But if you drink it, the tea will start to heal you, and then you can splash in the pond and play with Gigi again. Your daddies are very worried about you. Do you think you can show them how brave you are and try a little?"

Bella nodded, and I uncorked the tea. The room instantly filled with the aroma of lavender. I cradled the back of Bella's head with one hand and brought the bottle to her lips. Her little frog tongue came out and tentatively slurped the mouth of the bottle. I tipped it more until the liquid splashed on her lips.

"Mmmm." She snatched the bottle and started drinking, slowly at first, then chugging. Soon she had finished the entire bottle and was handing it back to me. "That was tasty," she said, settling back into her mattress. The bed swayed on its vines.

The change was gradual at first, a shift in her posture as the tension worked its way out of her muscles. Before I knew what was happening, an inner light glowed across her skin. Everywhere it moved became no longer dry and withered but supple and glossy. It spread from her mouth down to her toes, and soon she was snoring peacefully with Gigi pressed against her cheek.

The water splashed around me as Jerri approached. "It worked," he exclaimed in a high whisper, not wanting to wake the child but too excited to contain himself. He hugged me from one side as Reginald hugged me from the other. I could not have been happier for them.

They walked me to the front door. "I told you there was something special about her," Jerri said.

Reginald nodded in agreement. "Jerri did. Ever since we met you at the Watering Hole. You're a very interesting fae, Ms. Alacore. I can see why your province chose to put you up for the warden trials with Gladewarden Uriel."

"Your potion was amazing," Jerri agreed.

I was going to point out that it wasn't my potion. The thanks belonged to Uriel. But then I realized I'd been the one who actually made the tea. Was that what the whole trial today was about? Was Uriel testing my ability to make an effective healing potion? I was astounded by how crafty she could be. But what if I had failed? Was she really willing to gamble on a little girl's life just to test my mettle? But it hadn't failed. The potion I made had certainly healed her. I needed to have more faith in myself.

I bid my farewells, but not before Jerri could stuff a few coins in my hand as gratitude. It felt amazing to help someone in need. I could have been floating on air, I felt so blissful when I left their home.

Then I saw Geraldine waiting for me. *What a nuisance.*

"Ugh, I forgot all about you. Alright, go ahead and speak. Who is your master, and what do they want to talk about? Tell me so I can decide whether a meeting with them is worth my time."

"I can assure you, Miss Alacore, a meeting with Ambrose Amaryllis is certainly worthy of your time."

That was the last name I expected to come out of the pestering man's mouth. My gaze automatically went to the south, to the cliffs overlooking the cove and the towering white tree that watched over the town. That tree was the palace of the leader of the House of Dawn. He was one of the most important, most powerful, most influential fae in all the realm.

And it would seem he wanted to speak with me.

5

The fae realm used to be ruled over by a monarchy. I don't know a heck of a lot about the royals, but I do know there was some big war that engulfed the realm. It was the giantkin against pretty much everyone else. The fae blamed the king and queen for this war, which stemmed from a disagreement between King Oberon and King Thyrm. The monarchy rallied their forces to counteract the giant invasion, but in the end, victory was due to the actions of rogue fae, who slew dragons and stole their power to smite King Thyrm's forces.

After the dust settled, Queen Titania and King Oberon made a deal with four of the firstborn races to decentralize power and spread it out amongst them. Thus rose the four great houses that ruled over the fae realm: the Court of Shadows, the House of Amber, the Summer Court, and Ambrose Amaryllis's House of Dawn.

The Tides was only one of the lands the House of Dawn claimed dominion over. It is considered their smallest settlement, with a population of twenty thousand or so fae. The House of Dawn also rules over an underwater city aptly named the Deep and an archipelago called the Gales.

To think that I was walking up the stepped cliffs to meet a man who oversaw the lives and well-being of so many people was intimidating, to say the least. I gave it a lot of thought as we hiked up the cliffside. Why would someone like Ambrose Amaryllis want to meet me?

Geraldine had been tight lipped after I finally agreed to follow him. We walked in silence for an hour, through the town and up the windy cliffs on shale steps. A mist from the ocean spray covered the stone, making it slick. Geraldine seemed to have an inexhaustible energy, effortlessly climbing the steps. The town sprawled beneath us, lights twinkling to life as the sun set over the horizon. It was a spectacular view, one I wished I had thought to visit before. Seen from on high, the town looked like a miniature diorama, something fanciful I could have bought at a renaissance festival and put in my garden for the "fairy folk." The massive conche buildings looked regular-sized, with tiny frogs and motes of lightbugs fluttering about them. Even the swarming dragonflies on the coast, each of which was as long as a city bus, looked almost normal from that height.

I was sad to give up that view once we reached the top of the plateau. The white tree towered over me, even though it was still several acres up the walkway. When I'd first heard the tree referred to as Ambrose's home, I assumed that meant his palace was nearby or on the same grounds. Looking at it now, I realized the tree literally was a palace. I could see tiny windows glowing with light in its trunk. The setting sun reflecting off its gleaming white boughs stung my eyes.

Geraldine cleared his throat. "This way, if you will, Miss Alacore." He stood to one side of a tall hedgerow. There was an opening between hedges, carefully and finely manicured into a perfect rectangle.

I was too lost in wonder to feel shame over gawking at the palace. "Is this a labyrinth?" I asked as I entered the hedges.

"I'm sure you do not mean to suggest that the House of Dawn is in the habit of imprisoning minotaurs," Geraldine said stuffily as he retook the lead.

It surprised me that a fae would know about old human mythology, but I hid it, refusing to rise to his goading. The path was wide and led us by a rectangular pond bordered with white stones. The water inside was clear, yet something floated just beneath the surface. It was translucent, like looking through a piece of plastic wrap. I couldn't believe someone would throw trash into such beautiful water. It was a sacrilege to desecrate something so pure. I reached down to pluck the plastic out of the still pond.

Geraldine's hand clamped around my wrist, halting my hand just above the surface of the calm water. "It would not be wise to enter Lady Eloriil's water."

The plastic shifted, twisting inside itself and then back out, flowing like a graceful jellyfish. A rainbow of neon lights blinked in concentric lines down Lady Eloriil's body as she swirled just beneath the surface.

"A water syren?"

The syren was a beautiful creature, the first of her kind I'd seen in real life. I recalled stories of how they lured men into the sea to have sex. Based on Geraldine's reaction, I was willing to bet the syren had more in store for her visitors than some cunnilingus.

"As I said, it would not be wise," Geraldine confirmed. "Shall we move along? Master Ambrose is waiting for you, and the day is growing long."

Geraldine waited until I nodded my understanding before he released my wrist. We followed the long pond down the hedgerow path until finally Geraldine veered left. The rectangular pond kept going all the way to the tree palace up the hill. We moved firmly in the opposite direction, striding through the hedge maze until we finally came to an opening.

And what a grand opening it was. The clearing before us was at the tip of the plateau, overlooking the crashing waves of the ocean three thousand feet below us. A crystal gazebo dominated the clearing. Every piece of it was formed from a clear quartz—the posts, the balusters, even the joists and domed rooftop. The gazebo was surrounded by different varieties of conebush. The galpini silver balls looked like twirling stars caught in time, a stark contrast to the burgundy bracts and vibrant reds of the azaleas bordering those. Large red sunflowers leaned over the rail of the gazebo, as if their heads were craning to listen to its sole occupant.

Geraldine stopped at the base of the gazebo, folding one arm behind his back and bowing. "Miss Alacore, my lord."

The head of the House of Dawn waited for me to join him. I didn't know what to expect from Ambrose Amaryllis. He was seated at floor level on a wide cushion. He gestured to the white cushion across from him, and I felt a moment of panic. I had spent the morning tumbling around in the dirt and then the afternoon wading through water at Mr. Bukle's. The cushion was as ivory and pristine as his palace.

But it would be rude for me to stand, right? What was the proper decorum?

"Miss Alacore," Geraldine urged in a low voice.

I looked at him. He stared pointedly to the side of the gazebo steps. There was a wooden pail of water with a ladle hanging off the side of the bucket. Beside this was a pair of wooden sandals.

My eyes lit up. Ambrose wasn't wearing shoes. I took off my sneakers and set them beside the sandals, tucking my socks into them for the second time that day. I used the wooden ladle to wash my feet and shins. Geraldine cleared his throat. He had a towel ready for me. I thanked him sheepishly and dried myself off. He had saved me from calamity twice that day, and I was beginning to feel guilty for treating him so poorly on my doorstep.

Once I was clean, I made my way up the crystal steps. I expected them to be cold, as glass might be, but the surface was delightfully warm on my aching soles. I took a seat opposite Ambrose, crossing my legs as he did. Once I was seated, Ambrose nodded to Geraldine. The sharp-nosed man made his way to the entrance of the hedgerow that fenced in the clearing and stood at attention.

What do I do now? Was I supposed to say something to begin the conversation? Was it polite to speak before a king? *Wait, is he a king or…? Lucien's father is a king. He's the head of the Court of Shadows. Does the House of Dawn operate the same way?*

"You are wondering why I sent for you," Ambrose said. He was soft-spoken and yet his voice conveyed confidence.

I nodded. "Have I done something to upset you, sir?"

"I am sure a great many things you have done upset a great many people," Ambrose said plainly. "Though I cannot claim to be one of them."

What did that mean? Who could I have upset besides some lowlifes who wanted to murder or kidnap other fae? I scoured my memory for some snippet of offense I might have caused to the people of the Tides.

"I understand you have had quite a long day undertaking your trials with Gladewarden Uriel. Would you care for some tea?" He gestured to a bamboo platter on the floor between us. A ceramic teapot and cups steamed on the platter.

My mouth *was* awfully dry. "That would be awesome, thanks." I winced as the words came out of my mouth. It was a very human expression.

Ambrose chuckled. He was an interesting-looking fae. The blossoms were both plantlike and humanoid in appearance. They had glossy skin like the waxy leaves of a begonia. Except for around their joints, where their skin more closely resembled a plant that had grown in overlapping layers. That was typically where their coloring changed too. Ambrose's coloring was like the plants around the gazebo. In fact, a conebush is exactly what he reminded me of, with a rich burnt umber that shifted to the deep red of currants. His eyebrows and hair were long and densely packed waxy leaves, a creamy dappled tangerine hue that ended in brilliantly fluorescent magentas and crimson.

He was a small man, unassuming if you saw him in a crowd of fae. He wore a long black coat with pointed shoulder pads over robes. Cherry blossoms weren't just printed on the fabric. They were growing from it. The delicate petals looked vividly pink against the strange black cloth, their branches running from waist to shoulders. I'd seen the droba guardians around town wearing a simpler version of this, with high cut pants and without the flowers growing from the robes.

"I've been wondering, why do some of the fae around here wear Japanese-style clothing?"

Ambrose paused pouring the tea and furrowed his brow. *Oh crap, did I just insult this guy?* Geraldine coughed from his place beside the hedgerow entrance. *Is he listening to us? How sharp are that guy's ears?*

Ambrose resumed pouring the tea. "I see my sources are correct. You are every bit as inquisitive as your grandmother was." He carefully set down the teapot, using a cloth to wipe the spigot, then handed me a steaming cup.

The head of the House of Dawn knew Rosalie?

"You grew up around humans. Your perspective will long be twisted by that lens. You see our attire, and your brain forms the logical connection to what it knows. However, there is always more to the story. Nothing is as one-dimensional as it seems. Even paper can be brought to life by the perspective of the artist."

What was he trying to say? I felt in over my head. Ambrose was speaking in circles and yet clear as day. I felt the same way in college, when we were going over our reading assignments. I would plow through a story and enjoy it. Then we would get to class, and the professor would bring up all these allegorical meanings to every nuance of what the writer truly meant versus what was simply on the page. I always found it frustrating. I read to lose myself in a story, to enjoy the time in that world with those characters. It made me feel small to be unable to analyze the words for their "true" meaning. But art was subjective right? And fashion was a form of art.

"I have noticed many of the fae have had an impact on the human realm, artistically speaking," I said carefully. "Could it be that the House of Dawn has had past influences on human cultures?"

"It is to be expected. My lands do border human Asian cultures."

"But the humans don't behave the same way as the fae," I countered.

"Of course not. As you said, you will see the fae influences in the human realm where we crossover. It is a subtle thing—fashion, artistic expression, dance. One does not outweigh the other. Much to the displeasure of some, we cannot dictate the way that humans choose to live. Their cultures are wholly their own, and ours the same."

"I am sorry if I have offended you," I said.

"To the contrary. It is for this very reason I have sought your company today. I have a proposition for you, one which will require that very same inquisitive nature. But first, let us enjoy our tea."

Ambrose lifted his cup to me. I did the same, and he nodded. I mimicked his actions. He first smelled the tea with a deep inhale and held the aroma before exhaling.

My mouth watered when I smelled it. The aroma was apples and cinnamon, a simple and yet delicious combination. Next Ambrose took a tentative sip of his tea. I did the same, letting it sift around my palate. The flavor was intense, apples at first, then cranberries and pineapple, shifting into warm nutmeg. That tea was every bit as complex as the mead Drys served in Free House. I grinned at my cup and slurped up some more before I caught myself. I peered out of the corner of my eye to see if Ambrose had noticed. If he had, he wasn't showing it.

We sat in silence, slowly drinking and watching the sun slink below the horizon of the endless ocean below us. I finished well before Ambrose, but I kept my cup in my hand, too embarrassed to set it down.

"That was refreshing," I said.

"I am glad you enjoyed the tea." Ambrose set his cup down on the platter. "It is a special blend Chef Henri prepares for me every day. Come walk with me a moment as we speak."

Ambrose moved like an unfolding bird, effortlessly rising. He might have looked ancient, but he was clearly in better shape than me. I groaned as I stood, feeling the ache in my knees and hips from sitting in that position for so long. I followed him down the steps and quickly stuffed my socks in my pockets then slipped on my sneakers as he slid into his wooden sandals. The sandals had planks on the bottom, lifting him up to my height.

"Why is it you believe you are here with me in this moment?"

I narrowed my eyes, searching his face for a clue. His grey eyes were impenetrable. Was this another of those deeper-meaning conversations? "You have a job for me?"

"As I have explained. But why you?"

"I don't know what you want me to say. You asked me to come up here, so I did. A man as powerful as you can afford to hire anyone for a job that needs doing. Why ask a nobody like me?"

"I have heard about your recent exploits, Miss Alacore," Ambrose explained. "Taking on a changeling was no small feat. I know many a seasoned soldier who could not accomplish such a task. Then taking on a fae-trafficking ring and stopping a serial killer in the same evening? These are not the deeds of a nobody. These are the accomplishments of a very capable person."

"But more importantly an outsider," I deduced.

It was the first time Ambrose smiled. It was a small thing, but enough to tell me I'd hit the nail on the head. Whatever job Ambrose had planned for me, it was important that I was an outsider. His smile melted back into that placid seriousness. He gazed out over the cliffs to the cove to the west, to his town and all the people below who relied on him for their survival. "Ah, Lamina's Light. They are beautiful this time of day, are they not?"

He was referring to the structures that bordered the harbor. There were a dozen or so crystal stalks shaped as stiff seaweed, each easily six stories high. The locals called them Lamina's Light for the optical illusion they created as the setting sunlight hit them. The seaweed was translucent and created prisms of rainbow light that danced across the seashell houses of the Tides. Many of the locals gathered that light into jars or buckets, like colored water, and used it to charge their magical lanterns.

"They are the epitome of beauty," I agreed.

"Miss Alacore, let me speak plainly. I need to know if you will agree to take on this job that I am offering you."

"But I don't even know what you want me to do."

"I'm afraid there are details I cannot share until I know that you are in my confidence. What I have to say is only known by three people, two of whom stand before you in my garden. You would be the fourth. It is of the utmost importance that what I tell you next remains a secret."

Ambrose was being as earnest as they came. "I can understand that. You are an important person. Thousands of fae depend on your rule. If your secrets were let out, it could damage more than just your pride." I mulled over the possibilities. "I can't let anything interfere with my trials to become warden."

"I will need your assistance for the next three days. In that time, you will stay here at the palace as my honored guest. Of course, you are free to come and go as you please, and I would not dream of interfering with your trials under Gladewarden Uriel."

"Are you sure you have the right person for this?"

"I am positive."

I nibbled my lower lip as I thought it through. What I needed more than anything else was money. If I had enough cash, I could repair my storefront window and plant an herb garden behind the shop. I might even be able to stop living on ramen noodles every day. "I'll need to be paid for my time."

"I can offer you eighty thousand American dollars for your service."

That set me on my heels. It was a staggering sum of money to someone who had been living off a few hundred a month for the last half a year. I blinked at Ambrose in disbelief and stuck out my hand. "You've got a deal."

He took my hand and shook it. "I am pleased you have agreed. Understand that our contract is binding."

"Okay, sure. Now tell me what I need to do."

"Well, Miss Alacore, sometime over the course of the next three days, I will be murdered. I want you to find out who the murderer is."

6

was still numb with shock from Ambrose's words an hour later. Say what you will about humans, but none of them had ever tried to kill or eat me. At least, not that I knew of. Yet I was not even a year into living with the fae and already on my fourth perilous case.

I thought over this predicament as Geraldine led me away from Ambrose's private garden and up the hill to the palace. The shifting of seasons was of great importance to fae. It played a major role in the fluctuations of faerie magic, something I feared would take me years to understand. Each fae house would throw a magnificent celebration at the apex of their appointed season, with the House of Dawn representing Spring. The celebration would be so large that everyone in town would stop working for the week that it happened.

I had already learned all of this while living in the Tides. What I hadn't known until that day was that dignitaries from every corner of the realm would be in attendance. The higher-ranking nobility would stay at the palace. And among them was someone intent on murdering Ambrose Amaryllis.

"Why not go to the authorities with this?" I had asked Ambrose. "Why hire me?"

"If news of my pending assassination were to leak, it would ruin the spring festival."

"So what? Are you saying some big party is more important than your life?"

Ambrose looked at me with the weight and gravity of a dying man. "Spring is the dawn of our being. The coming of the dawn is not simply some *big party*. Dawn is a celebration of rebirth, it is the revival of life, the beginning of new things. Each new dawn is hope. My life cannot be balanced against the hopes and dreams of my people."

They were lofty words, a grand declaration that I did not relate to in the slightest. Had things been reversed, if the looming specter of death hung over me, I would have canceled the party without hesitation. It was obvious Ambrose was going to do no such thing.

"But that's not your only reason," I said. "You don't trust your own people. Otherwise, you never would have called for me."

Ambrose didn't deny it. "You are your grandmother's heir in more than just blood. I have faith you will root out my murderer and bring them to justice, before or after the deed has transpired."

I didn't like the eventuality of that statement, as if it were a predetermined outcome that Ambrose would be murdered. This man wielded more power than 99.99% of fae. He should have been someone I sneered at and blamed for all my financial woes. Except I had heard much of Ambrose and his kind deeds since arriving at the Tides. This was a man who dedicated himself to the care of his people. Everyone in the Tides was cared for and showed great reverence for the House of Dawn. They owed their health and good fortune to his House.

"It's unfathomable that someone would want to hurt a harmless old man like him," I said to Geraldine as we neared the palace steps. The white tree towered over us, its ivory bark gleaming even as night took root.

Geraldine spun on his heel directly in front of me. "There is nothing weak about Ambrose Amaryllis," he insisted with a scowl that showed off his sharkish teeth. I flinched and took a step back, ready to bolt. Geraldine's composure softened, and he frowned. "Please, I apologize for my poor behavior. It's just—"

"You care for him," I said.

Geraldine nodded once.

"I can understand not wanting to see someone you care about come to harm."

"I do not believe you can fully understand how I feel, Miss Alacore. Forgive me for saying so, but I do not believe you should have accepted my master's offer."

"Because you don't think I'm cut out to help him."

Geraldine closed his eyes and nodded again. He was an interesting fellow, as stuffy as any butler I'd ever seen on television and yet ashamed of himself for his own snobbery. *Perhaps it's not snobbery. Maybe he's just speaking plainly. I mean what qualifications do I have to solve an attempted murder?*

"You don't need to apologize for worrying about him," I said.

Geraldine studied me with a frown, then suddenly looked up at the sky. "My, it is getting rather late. Come now, there is much to do, and so little time left."

I followed him up the steps. Well, they weren't stairs as much as part of the tree that had decided to shape itself into pristine steps.

"Tell me something. Why doesn't he get his own lawmen to help with this?"

"I counseled that Master Ambrose should inform them," Geraldine said as the front doors opened of their own volition. "Any number of them would be far better equipped to handle this torrid affair than you. However, it is the nature of Master's information that brought us to our present circumstance. The warning we received was not just that an attempt would be made, but that it would be a traitor who carried out the act."

"Oh snap." So, someone Ambrose trusted was the would-be assassin.

"Indeed." Geraldine bid me follow him inside.

We walked through the trunk of the tree for a solid five minutes. The entrance hall was wide enough to fit a marching band. Ivy-like branches with golden leaves stretched across the ceiling. Translucent seashell lamps hung on the walls, their flickering green light illuminating the hall. I recognized the source of the light as immaru bugs. Many of the droba in town used them to light the inside of their homes, where open fire might be less safe. They fed off the flowers that grew inside their shells, forming a closed loop symbiotic system.

"These walls are so smooth," I said, running my fingers across the white bark as we walked.

"Starfire was a gift from her majesty, the venerable Queen Titania," Geraldine proudly explained.

Queen Titania. She was the one who had intervened in my court proceedings, channeling herself through the Arbiter to force the court's hand. Lobo had warned me not to take that lightly.

"Will the Queen be at your big spring shindig?"

Geraldine snorted. "Your ignorance to our ways is mind-boggling."

The way he talks, you'd think he was the one the Queen hooked up. I decided to ignore his condescension. "Either way, this tree is pretty amazing. Starfire, huh? I like that name. It's almost as beautiful as her."

Leaves rustled as if a whisper of a breeze stirred though them. A sense of approval from the palace hit me. Geraldine raised a brow and peered at me out of the corner of his eye.

A flash of color caught my eye. A large ball of yarn rolled down the entrance hall toward us. It was a chunky fabric Tae would've loved to use to knit a scarf. I didn't see who'd tossed the yarn, and it didn't seem to be slowing. In fact, it was speeding up as it got closer. I was about to ask Geraldine about it when the ball suddenly sprang open and leapt at me. I screamed and threw my arms up.

What I thought was a ball of yarn was actually a creature. It had six legs and was rubbing its furry face into my shins. "Ah, get it away," I screamed.

Geraldine took a deep breath. "Gizmitt is Master Ambrose's pet. He is merely expressing his exuberant welcome at your arrival."

"Gizmitt…?"

I looked down at the creature nuzzling my ankles. His back was armored with thick fur that indeed resembled yarn. He had six legs with big furry paws and large round eyes that gazed up at me warmly. He was like a cross between an armadillo and a cat.

"Oh, you are a cute one, aren't you?" I said as I knelt and stroked Gizmitt's back. His whole body vibrated as he purred and pressed harder against my legs. "What kind of a creature is he?"

"Gizmitt is a ferillo," Geraldine said impatiently. "If you please, Lady Alacore, we really must get moving."

"Sorry, little guy, we have to go," I said to Gizmitt. "Mr. Grumpy Pants has a lot to do."

As if he perfectly understood me, Gizmitt mewled and hopped into the air. When he landed, he was a giant ball of yarn rolling past us toward the palace entrance.

I followed Geraldine deeper into the palace, wondering what other wonders I would behold. Soon we came to a doorway on our left. The wood parted down the center and opened inward, admitting us into a large room replete with sofas, a hanging chandelier, and a mirror-backed bar laden with colorful bottles.

"If you will please wait in the lounge, I shall be back shortly," Geraldine said, waving his arm toward the seating area.

"You're leaving me here alone?"

He nodded. "It will not be long, I assure you. There are certain matters to attend to, and of course, I will need to check that your room has been properly prepared for your stay."

"My room? Whoa, hold up. Nobody said anything about me staying here overnight."

Geraldine looked confused. "Miss Alacore has accepted the master's contract for employment. He expects you to stay here at the palace. I believe he said as much in your presence."

Maybe he was right. Things had been a whirlwind since I arrived. I still felt caught up in the storm. "Well, I can't stay here without any of my stuff. I'll need to at least go back to town and pack."

"All of this is being taken care of, I assure you."

"You like to assure me about an awful lot."

Geraldine waved toward the seating area once more. "Please, Miss Alacore. I shall be back shortly."

I looked around the room. It was certainly the most elegant place I'd ever seen. *I could do a lot worse than staying at a palace. With a killer,* I reminded myself. "Fine." I admitted defeat with all the grace of a pouting teenager, with crossed arms and a tapping foot.

Geraldine bowed and left through a door to the right of the bar. The sofas were as chic and elegant as they came. They were all sorts of shapes and sizes—round cushioned seating with a raised back in the center; a row of massive flower heads growing from one wall, their petals opened and stuffed with fluffy pillows; small swings hanging from the ceiling for sprites to sit on; one growing directly from the floor, a swooping piece of wood that bent back on itself to form a bench. There were enough seats in the lounge to fit a score of fae. There were no hanging pictures, no murals or banners like you'd expect to find in a palace. Instead, the décor was the geometric patterns of the seats. The twist of the ceiling where it came down like reaching branches to enfold its leaves in swirls around dangling orchids. I heard the faint buzz of the immaru wings as the bugs fluttered about their seashell lanterns, softly lighting up the lounge with their glow. It was no surprise that a fae race named the blossom would adorn their house with so many flowers.

I was feeling too chagrined to sit on any of the lovely seats. The bar looked more inviting anyhow. I stalked over to it like a stubborn child. I could feel the silliness of my ire, yet it refused to release me.

Another fine mess I've gotten myself in.

The bar was another piece of wood grown directly upward from the floor. A mossy garden clung to the front of it, with elongated stems as thick as my arm that curved out and upward, ending in broad leaves.

Those are the coolest bar stools I've ever seen.

I'm a curious person, so the bottles behind the bar were begging for me to take a closer look. I found myself behind the counter, eyeing them. I took one down off the shelves. The liquid inside looked like creamy gold paint. I tilted the bottle and was surprised to see the liquid did not cling to the glass. It wasn't oily and dense like paint. I removed the glass stopper and gave it a sniff.

"Whoa," I exclaimed. One sniff was like getting kicked in the head. Except instead of pain, it left me with a pleasant dizziness. My eyes lit up. If smelling it was that potent, what would it be like to drink?

"You shouldn't be touching that," a woman informed me in a very monotone voice.

I'm prone to overreacting when I'm startled. It's something my best friend Deedee has teased me about on numerous occasions, but I can't help it. I nearly dropped the bottle, juggling it a few times before I finally caught a good hold once more. My face heated with embarrassment as I spun around. "Oh, I'm so sorry," I stammered. "I was just looking."

"Well, perhaps it would be better if you *looked* elsewhere?" She said it as a question, but it wasn't. It was a clear command. She abruptly turned away and strode over to the sofas. Her business with me was concluded. There was a cold and clinical indifference about her. I could see it in her commanding gait, in her high cheekbones that stayed taut and her thin lips in a perpetual grimace.

"My family will be arriving tonight. I ask that you keep your eyes and ears open around them." Ambrose had told me to expect his family and given me a brief rundown of each one. I didn't realize it would be so soon.

There was a commotion in the hall. The rest of the Amaryllis siblings were coming. I felt butterflies in my belly as their voices approached the lounge.

The woman who had chided me chose a chair on the edge of the room. *She must be one of his daughters,* I thought. Her skin looked very much like Ambrose's, with the overlapping sections around her exposed elbows and knees a rich burnt umber that ended in magenta at their leafy tips. She had her dark hair pulled back and wore frameless spectacles over her charcoal eyes that were secured around her neck by a gold chain. The only place her skin differed from Ambrose's was in the flowers growing from her leafy hair, with vanilla and pink glowing petals.

"Alegra, how do you walk so quickly on those stumpy little legs of yours?" a woman trilled loudly as she entered the lounge. She was at the center of a group of fae.

Alegra smoothed out her pencil skirt. She sat rigid as a board instead of leaning back into the padded chair. She ignored her sister's barb and purposefully opened the book she had been carrying.

The woman who had insulted Alegra was her younger sister, Cyan. She was loud, braggadocious, and starved for attention. She was also very glamorous. Her clothes were loud and flamboyant, the pinnacle of fae fashion. She seemed to go out of her way to distinguish herself from her sister. They could not have been more opposite.

Where Alegra was quiet and composed, Cyan was loud and erratic. Alegra wore sensible attire, dark subdued colors that contrasted with the vivid red of Cyan's ribbon dress, draped tight against her shoulders but flaring wider to a pointed V between her legs. Her sleeves were tight along the arm, but flared around her fingers, which were covered up to the knuckles. Her skin was a lustrous ebony, and her hair was made of golden tinted vines, the undersides of the leaves a rich purple among vanilla bean flowers. She towered over the other fae, not because of her height but because she wore knee-length platform boots with five-inch wooden soles. The fae arriving in her entourage were all similarly dressed in high fashion.

A young woman broke off from the back of their group. She was a blossom fae, but unlike the others she was dressed in a pink robe with sleeves that flared at the wrist. Ivy circled her waist, keeping the robe closed, and emerald-blue moss phlox grew from the fabric down the lengths of her sleeves and along the front of her robe. The tiny flowers contrasted with the reddish-brown conebush flowers growing from her ivy hair, which were similar to Ambrose's. She pulled a suitcase on wheels to the edge of the room, where she stood looking very timid.

Cyan waltzed straight up to the bar and handed me her handbag. "Be sure this gets to my room before I do."

Five droba marched into the lounge just behind her fae entourage. The poor things looked overwhelmed by the armloads of luggage they had just lugged up the cliffside. The droba scampered to the bar and started setting down the parcels, hat boxes, shopping bags, satchels, and suitcases in an orderly pile.

"I'm thirsty, Cyan," a woman said before I could inform Cyan that not only did I have no clue where her room was, but I was not her maid. The woman grabbed Cyan's arm and flashed doe eyes at me. She wasn't a blossom but a pureblood of some other race. Tiny, delicate, nearly undetectable scales covered her body like a fish. Her faerie wings fluttered as she pouted, and her skin shimmered in the light.

"Of course, Isabo," Cyan said. "Drum up a couple pollen fizzies for me and my wife."

It took me a moment to realize Cyan was speaking to me. *But why would she think I know how to make drinks? Oh.*

I remembered that I was standing behind the bar. An interesting sensation washed over me. Only seconds before I had been ready to give the pushy Cyan a piece of my mind. But as I stood there gazing into Isabo's almond eyes, smelling the rich vanilla perfume of her skin, I felt intoxicated by her beauty. Instead of wanting to cuss her out, I felt an urge to stare at her. This woman was a goddess. No wonder she wore such fashionable attire. I wanted to please her, to satisfy her every whim, if it meant she might smile at me.

"Absolutely," I said.

Cyan smiled at Isabo, then leaned down to give her wife a butterfly kiss, nose to nose, and they giggled. Meanwhile her entourage had moved on to the sofas. There were five of them, draping themselves across the seats as if they were the most bored fae in the world. They reminded me very much of a colorful version of Prince Lucien's entourage.

I found two high glasses and set them on the bar, then surveyed the bottles before realizing I had no idea what I was doing.

"Which liquor is it?" I asked Cyan.

She looked at me as if I were a talking foot that had just sprouted wings. I felt as if I'd been crumpled up into a wad of paper under her horrid gaze. Cyan flared her nostrils and tugged Isabo away from the bar.

"Wait, I don't know—"

"It's the bottle on the second shelf, with the green liquor," a soft voice offered. "Just add a little soda water and ice to the glass then garnish it with a starflower."

I spun about to find the bottle, eager to please Cyan. *How could I have let her down like that? I am such a fool. I'm so rotten and disgusting. I should have—I should...*

I came to my senses holding the bottle of green liquor and staring at the woman who had helped me. "What am I doing?" I shook my head and blinked. "I feel weird."

The woman looked sideways. She was the quiet fae who had been standing near the back of the room. "That's Isabo's magic getting in your head."

Isabo's magic?

"She has the power to charm others," she added.

I took another look at Cyan's wife and realized why she'd felt familiar to me. "She enchanted me," I said.

The young woman nodded, then turned away. The droba finished piling the luggage by the bar. She quietly handed them a few coins and bowed. One of them grinned at his partners as the group of them padded out of the lounge.

She turned back to me, still holding her own suitcase with one hand, and whispered. "Her magic is visual. Just don't make eye contact with her when you bring the drinks over, and her glamour won't make you dizzy."

"Persa," a red-faced man barked as he entered the lounge, followed by another droba lugging baggage. He wore an unkempt business suit that was at least one size too large and hung wrongly off his shoulders.

"Oh, there you are, Artur," Cyan said loudly. "I thought you'd given up and decided to go back down to the ship."

"I'd rather assumed I'd leave the running away to you, dear sister," Artur replied indignantly.

No love lost between these two, I thought.

Cyan didn't miss a beat. "That's a shame." She patted her flat stomach. "You look like a little run would do you well." Her entourage giggled at her jibe.

Artur frowned down at his waistline.

"Oh, stop picking on him," Alegra said without looking up from her book. "Can't you see how much he's dreading speaking with father as it is?"

"Stick your nose back in that book," Artur snapped. "I don't need your help dealing with this sad painted clown."

Cyan responded with a throaty over-the-top laugh. "Oh Artur, you do amuse me. I would practically gag if you weren't such a washed-up dud. Tell me, how much of our family's holdings have you lost *this* week?"

Artur's cheeks were puffed and red. His mouth opened and closed, unable to articulate his anger. He looked ready to blow a gasket.

The blossom fae who had been speaking to me put a comforting hand on his shoulder. "Father—"

He recoiled from her touch and scowled. "Oh, leave it alone, *Persa*." He emphasized her name as if it were a dirty word. Cyan snickered at his outburst.

Persa's shoulders slumped, and she looked down at the floor. She quickly shuffled back to the wall, and I thought she might cry.

"Persa, I've been meaning to ask you," Cyan said, "what in nature's bounty are you wearing?"

"It's a kaunake," Persa answered quietly.

Cyan's entourage laughed. She smiled wickedly. "It's obviously a kaunake." She shook her head in mock wonder. "You're your father's daughter, all right. Didn't you wear that same robe to the banquet in Gelhal? Artur, dear, we've all heard times are tough for you, but I had no idea they were *that* bad." The words were okay, but the way she said them made it clear Cyan was not concerned as much as mean-spirited.

I hate bullies, I thought.

"Here are your pollen fizzies." I handed one glass to Isabo, careful not to look at her face. My eyes remained fixed on Cyan. She reached for the glass without taking her wicked grin off her distressed niece, and I promptly poured the drink in her lap, then dropped the glass.

Cyan screamed as if I'd just scalded her with boiling water. She leapt to her feet on the cushions. Her gaggle of fae swooped to her rescue. Alegra looked up from her book with a raised eyebrow.

Artur snarled at me. "Stupid cow, don't just stand there. Go get a towel."

"You careless oaf," Cyan shrieked. "Look what you've done to my dress! Who taught you how to serve?"

"Lady Cyan!" Geraldine's voice boomed over the commotion.

Everyone stopped speaking to stare at him. Geraldine stood beside the pile of suitcases; one arm folded behind his back. "What in the Queen's good grace is happening here?" he asked.

"Oh, thank heavens you're here, Geraldine," Cyan whined. "This foolish sop got feral and ruined my dress."

"Would you grow up, Cyan?" Alegra rolled her eyes. "It's just a little liquor."

"I hope you will accept my sincerest apologies," Geraldine said earnestly. "I take full responsibility for neglecting my duties. We had not expected your arrival for another hour. Had I known, I would have had the footmen ready to take your things and the lounge staffed." He clapped his hands and a puff of smoke ignited by his shoulder. When it dissipated, there was a monkey flapping its wings. "Lady Cyan requires assistance."

The monkey zipped over to her and twirled its tail around the wet spot of her dress. The sound of a delightful musical note followed, and the stain completely disappeared.

"That was cool," I said without thinking.

"Indeed, Lady Alacore," Geraldine agreed. "Please, in the future, leave the libation service to my staff."

Cyan didn't hear him. She was talking to her gaggle of fashionistas, who were fawning over her as if she'd just suffered some great trauma.

"Now, ladies and gentlemen, if you will," Geraldine announced, "I will ensure your rooms are ready promptly. Until then, Olif will tend to your needs."

"I don't see why we should have to be stuck here together," Artur protested.

"Yes, our feet hurt from carrying our things all the way up the cliffside," Cyan whined.

"I understand," Geraldine bowed. He looked at me. "Lady Alacore, if you will, your room is ready."

"Lady?" Cyan gawked.

You could hear a pin drop. I feel petty for it, but I seized that moment of vindictive satisfaction and promptly put my back to them. I followed Geraldine out of the lounge, feeling their eyes like knives pointed at my back before realizing the mistake I'd made. I was supposed to blend into the background to see what I could find. Instead, I'd called attention to my presence to every person in the room. And likely one of them was the person who planned to murder Ambrose Amaryllis.

I let the events in the lounge sink in as Geraldine led me through the serpentine halls of the palace. If Ambrose's family was any indication, I had a strange week ahead of me. I tried to stay focused on the moment, needing to process as much as possible so I could find my feet.

We came out of the hall into a wide atrium. The tree was far bigger than I had imagined, if that was possible. It felt like standing in the center of a shopping mall, one with smooth white bark walls rising all around me. I followed the walls upward until my neck was craned all the way back. The palace soared to staggering heights. It was alive with the sounds of birds and running water, of rustling leaves and hushed voices. Mystical light streamed down through an inner canopy of leaves and branches that crisscrossed the center of the atrium.

"How many floors are there?" I gaped at the view. Blue jays fluttered among the branches overhead. A balcony ran around the perimeter of each floor, in an ever upward spiral. There were some interior windows in the tree, overlooking the atrium. The ground level was interlaced with steady flowing streams of water.

"Welcome to the hollow," Geraldine stiffly announced as he cut through the open space. We crossed a foot bridge grown from the floor of the tree, an overzealous arch that seemed unnecessary for the stream it crossed, which I could easily have hopped across. "Most of the Spring Festival will occur in this area. Master Ambrose shall give his speeches from the balcony. We have cast an enchantment so that no weapons may be allowed to enter the palace."

There was a double staircase on either side of the balcony that overlooked the atrium. A waterfall spilled from the center of that wall, just beneath the balcony, into a koi pond. The koi were as large as dogs, their colors a dazzling sparkle beneath the frothy surface. All around the pond were bushes, flowers, and miniature trees. Juicy-looking plums and star-shaped fruits hung from some of the trees. One of the plums plopped into the water and was promptly gobbled up by several koi.

"If you would please follow me upstairs." Geraldine led me up one side of the curving double staircase. A group of six brownies met us at the top. They saw Geraldine and promptly stood at attention. They wore smart tailcoats and trousers, but their oversized hairy feet were bare.

"Just in time," Geraldine said, stopping to face them. "Excellent punctuality, gentlemen. The master's children have arrived. See that their luggage is brought up and the beds are turned down."

"Very good, sir." The first brownie in line nodded.

Geraldine nodded back, and we resumed our march through the palace. The wide hall shot forth a good distance, marked by a red-and-gold runner that contrasted vividly with the white bark flooring and walls.

We left the hall and walked briskly through an art gallery. There were glorious oil paintings and statues everywhere I looked. I feasted on the artwork as we passed through. There was a highly detailed map of the Tides, a painting of two centaurs playing chess in a garden, and another of ballet dancers.

"This place could put the Met to shame," I said.

"The Dawn Gallery is open to all palace visitors. Master Ambrose will be displaying a few of his favorite pieces in the ballroom during the closing ceremony."

I stayed close on his heels as we rounded a corner and left the gallery behind. After a few more turns we entered a library. I gasped. There were mahogany shelves from the floor all the way to the edge of the domed ceiling. Ladders were affixed to rollers halfway up the wall on either side. It was larger than the library I'd worked at during college.

"Were these all written by fae?" I asked.

A pink pixie was dusting tomes on the top shelf. She wore a dress with a jagged hemline tied at the waist with a wide belt. She heard us enter the library, quicky stopped what she was doing, and fluttered down on shimmery wings to land just before Geraldine.

"I see we have company," she tittered in a voice that could have come from a certain bow-wearing mouse.

Geraldine bowed reverently. "Good evening, Nuala. Allow me to introduce Lady Alacore. The lady will be staying with us for a few days."

Nuala's yellow eyes lit up, and she clapped her hands together. "How wonderful. Are you excited for the spring celebration, dear? We're a bit gassed for it ourselves." She was the sort of person I could not help smiling around.

Geraldine turned to me. "Nuala is the palace librarian. If you need anything, she can get it for you."

"Pleased to meet you," I said. "You have a lovely library."

Nuala giggled. "Oh, you're a kindly one. I like you already. Not that I wouldn't like any guest of Master Amaryllis, of course."

"Naturally," I said.

Nuala clipped her duster to her belt and opened a leather pouch slung over her shoulders. She pulled out an enormous tome. The mouth of the pouch stretched as if giving birth. Once the book was fully out, the weight settled in her tiny hands, forcing her to lean to brace its girth. "Here is the volume the master asked for, Geraldine."

Geraldine took it in his large hand and bowed to her. "Thank you, Nuala. Miss Alacore, if you will, we must be on our way."

"It was nice meeting you," I said as I hurried to catch up with Geraldine.

"The master will meet you either in the library or his private gazebo for your daily check ins," Geraldine told me.

"The palace is so large," I said. "How do all these rooms fit inside Starfire? I mean, the tree's huge, don't get me wrong, but I'm getting the feeling the palace is even bigger on the inside. I'm pretty sure that's not how buildings are supposed to be."

"Perhaps you've just been around too many mundane human domiciles," Geraldine remarked snidely.

Ugh.

I followed him in silence. We left the library and found ourselves back out in the main hall.

"Wait, this doesn't make any sense. We just walked in a straight line through the gallery and into the library, but now we're coming out that same door, which was behind us." I didn't know what to think. Of course I'd seen magic. Free House was a good example of a building that was larger inside than out. But this was magic on a whole other scale.

Geraldine sighed. "Starfire possesses a different magic than you are likely used to. Suffice to say that space can be a fickle thing inside her walls."

Whatever that means. Either way it was all the explanation I was going to get.

We followed the sloping balcony to the third floor. On the way, Geraldine periodically stopped to instruct his army of workers. There was a fellow repairing a door, two brownie maids carrying folded blankets, a droba watering the immaru habitats, and an under butler who passed him a sealed envelope. Not one of those instances seemed happenstance. Geraldine was checking on his people's work at precisely the time he intended, and each of them was prepared for his arrival.

This guy is punctual to a fault. There was nothing happening inside the tree that he didn't seem to know about. *I'm starting to think it was no accident that he left me alone with Ambrose's children.*

I decided to call him out on it. "You knew the Amaryllis family was arriving early."

That caught Geraldine off guard. He snapped his head around to look at me with surprise.

Ah, caught you Mr. Uppity.

The door to the right of us opened, and a man stepped out. We bumped into each other, and I bounced off him. Thankfully, he caught my arms before I fell flat on my bottom.

"I'm so sorry," I laughed, trying to hide my embarrassment. "I'm a clumsy oaf."

I gazed up to see the most gorgeous man staring down at me. He had strong high cheekbones and dazzling blue eyes. He smirked at me with cupid bow lips. "Nonsense, I'm the one who should apologize. I wasn't looking where I was going."

I could only grin stupidly at him. *Fuck, he's hot.*

"Geraldine, aren't you going to introduce me to your new friend?" the man asked as he let go of my arms.

Geraldine lifted one brow. "Lord Silas, meet the Lady Alacore."

Silas lifted my hand and gave it a delicate kiss. "Charmed."

I felt butterflies in my stomach at the graze of his lips on my flesh and blushed.

Geraldine cleared his throat. "Lord Silas, your family is gathered in the lounge if you would like to greet them. I beg your pardon, but we must be going."

Silas smirked as Geraldine whisked me away. I looked over my shoulder, but Silas was already swaggering his way downstairs.

We finally stopped at a door on our right. "Your room is through here," Geraldine announced. "The gala will begin tomorrow afternoon at midday. Please remember that while you are here, you represent Master Ambrose's house."

"No. I represent myself. Taking this job doesn't make me Ambrose's slave." I put my hand up before Geraldine could interrupt me. "No, you don't get to interrupt me. You dropped me in that room on purpose. I don't know what your game is, but I don't like being used like that, so don't try it again. I know you don't think I belong here, but Ambrose hired me for a reason. While I'm here, I will conduct my business professionally."

Geraldine digested my words. He bowed. "I would expect nothing less."

"Good." For once, I was more fired up than my voice was letting on. Although, my hands were shaking from the confrontation.

"Miss Alacore, I will not tell you how to conduct your business."

"Really? That's all you've been doing since I met you."

"Indeed. I won't tell you what to do, but my unsolicited advice would be to steer clear of Lord Silas. For your own good. Now, please allow me to show you around your room."

"That won't be necessary," I said. "And at least you're correct about one thing."

Geraldine arched his brow. "Oh?"

"You won't tell me what to do." I closed the door in his face.

It felt good to tell Geraldine off. I floated on that high for an hour afterward. I'd been pushed around all my life. In boarding school it was by the rich kids, in college the mean sorority girls, and since I'd entered the world of the fae, it had been one demented weirdo after another. To have Geraldine lecturing me like I was some street urchin on the heels of spending the last few weeks with the ever-condescending Uriel was too much. So, for that hour I reveled in my newfound confidence. Spilling the drink on Cyan had been fun too. She deserved it. She was just another bully.

And then it was over. The taste of victory turned bitter in my mouth over the most mundane of things. I could not figure out how to turn on the bathwater.

My room was a magnificent open space, with curved walls and a domed ceiling all formed from the white tree. There was a glass vanity with a birch stool. A plush bench at the foot of the silk-curtained poster bed. The sheer curtains were soft, and the room smelled like a mixture of grapefruit and jasmine. My luggage sat beside the bench. The worn *I ♥NY* sticker on my suitcase couldn't have looked more out of place in that lavish faerie palace.

A calla lily the size of my head grew from a patch of tuberous vines that networked the surface of one wall. Tiny clusters of pink and white flowers grew along their tuberous covering. The calla lily itself emitted a soft glow, lighting the area to the side of the bed. There were two more callas growing in the room, one on the opposite wall and one behind the vanity. However, those weren't glowing.

I wonder why, I thought, my botanist brain's curiosity piqued. *They look like the same species…*

I tentatively stroked the surface of the lower petal. It was dewy and smooth. When I touched the lily, it pulsated, first from the stem, then moving upward to the center. The petals glowed with a brilliant light that stung my eyes. I blinked a few times as my eyes adjusted to it, then stroked the petal again. The light dimmed to a medium glow. *Whoa, that's so cool. It's like a living dimmer bulb.* I stroked it twice more to test my theory. The light dimmed to a soft glow and then went out completely.

It wasn't the first time I'd wondered why the fae kept such things to themselves. How many lives could be changed for the better if the fae shared these discoveries with humans? That was the dreamer Lanie speaking. She was a hopeful, naïve girl. Humans would likely kill all the fae out of superstitious fear and then steal their lands. After all, they didn't have the best track record of playing well with others.

There was an open window on the other wall. I was delighted to find my view looked out from high up in the tree. It was dizzying at first, like looking out the window of a plane as the wings tilted and seeing the world below from the wrong angle. I should have been on the third floor, but my room looked out from far higher on the tree. *I need to get used to this place.*

There was heavy spatial magic at play inside Starfire's boughs. That was going to throw me off for a while.

I could see the cove from that vantage. The lights of the town twinkled at the base of the cliffs. I wondered how Tinsie was doing. She'd seemed on the mend when I left. It felt good to have done something useful. The last few weeks with Uriel seemed like a never-ending exercise in boredom.

That and chores. Cut Uriel's wood, sort her fabrics, gather mushrooms, get told how they're not large enough, sew a tear in her dress and be told the stitching isn't right.

None of it had anything to do with being a warden. What did how well I could fold her laundry have to do with making people's lives better? That was all I wanted to do, really. To live a good life filled with laughter and happiness. To feel that my accomplishments meant something to the world around me.

Then why am I once again hunting down a murderer? Why did I say yes to Ambrose? I could have backed out when he told me what the job was. We had signed no contracts. I wasn't committed to him in any tangible way, no matter what he claimed about our agreement being binding.

Ambrose was so calm when he told me he was going to be murdered. Who could be chill at a time like that? I would be freaking the fuck out. Perhaps that was part of why I hadn't backed out. Besides, I was getting good at stopping killers. It seemed like a natural talent.

Is it, though? Or have I just gotten unbelievably lucky? Geraldine certainly seems to think it's ludicrous for Ambrose to hire me. Maybe the problem isn't as dire as Ambrose believes if his own butler thinks that way.

I had learned to trust my gut instinct by now, and that instinct was shouting from the rooftops that something stank in the House of Dawn. Ambrose didn't strike me as someone who made knee-jerk decisions. He needed my help. I wasn't going to stand by and let something horrible happen to him. *I need to play this one smart, though. Heck, if I can root out the culprit before they do any serious damage, maybe I can avoid the whole choke-me-until-I-knock-you-into-a-buzzsaw thing.*

But where to start? I didn't know the first thing about detective work. I'd done a slapdash job of it in the past, but this was a little more serious. There was always a question mark hanging above my past problems. Was

Charlie actually in danger? Would the changeling come after me next? This time it was more certain. Ambrose said he was to be murdered sometime in the next three days. *Think, Lanie. Where do we start?* I wracked my brain for inspiration, but my thoughts kept coming full circle.

Ugh, I don't know.

What I did know was that I was tired, grimy, and sore. What I needed more than anything was to stop thinking about my problems and lose myself in a nice bath.

A transparent silk curtain marked the bathroom alcove. Thicker mossy curtains had been pulled to either side. The bathroom was a hollowed bubble of a room. The tub was the size of a jacuzzi, set waist-deep into the floor. There were fluffy towels hanging on hooks beside the tub. Cannas grew around the perimeter, along with a bamboo chute that resembled a faucet and a wooden bucket filled halfway with clear water. The bottom of the tub was lined with river-smoothed rocks. There was a small window behind the tub, with open shutters letting in a warm evening breeze. Starfire's leaves rustled outside. It was a calming sound that soothed my nerves. *This looks like my own personal spa. A little time in this tub, listening to the breeze rustle through the boughs, will get my head right.*

There was just one problem. I had no idea how to fill the tub.

I spent twenty minutes trying to decipher that riddle.

Finally, I tried touching the cannas, hoping they worked like the light lilies. I received a mocking laugh for my efforts. A tiny sprite fluttered out of the canna leaves. I shooed the little troublesome faerie away. She laughed all the harder and spun up to the ceiling. I tried rubbing the faucet. She did a somersault, holding her belly and laughing even harder.

"You're not being very helpful," I snapped, then folded my arms across my chest. I knew I was pouting but I couldn't help it. I was mad and annoyed, and I just needed a stinking bath. *That's what snapping at Geraldine earned me. I should have had Sharktooth give me the tour of the room. I'm sure he would have made a point of showing me how to use the tub.* I couldn't very well ask him now, not after the way I'd bitten his head off and declared I was my own woman.

The sprite sat up and tilted her head at me. Her voice was a tinkling sound, like glittering stardust tiptoeing over a xylophone. "Don't be sad big faerie girl," she said.

"I can't help it," I replied, trying to hold back tears of frustration. "I'm just sick and tired of always doing the wrong thing. I mess everything up and get myself in worse and worse situations. It's been a rotten day. I just want to take a stupid bath, and I can't even figure that out."

"Alright, you twist my arm. Bella will help."

"Really?"

The sprite zipped around my head leaving a dusting of glittery powder in her wake. "Sing, big faerie girl. All you have to do is sing."

Seriously? Why did I have to sing to the faucet? Of all the annoying faerie things in existence. I leaned close to the bamboo chute and hummed. Gibberish came out at first but then I shifted to a Yeah Yeah Yeahs song I liked. The bamboo was bone dry.

"Nothing is happening," I said.

Bella circled me again. "Not hum. Sing!"

"Ugh, really? Fine." I sat on the opposite side of the tub, facing the faucet. I cleared my throat. Singing in the shower was one thing, but I had an audience. Albeit a tiny glittery one, but a listener all the same. I felt very self-conscious. I cleared my throat and sang loud and clear about people losing their heads and dancing until they were dead.

Bella fell on her back beside the faucet in a fit of hysteria. She kicked her feet in the air and clutched her belly, rolling side to side. "Can't believe you fell for that."

"Why you rotten little—" I grabbed the wooden bucket from the edge of the tub and tossed it at her.

The bucket bounced off the rim of the tub where she'd been, and its contents splattered everywhere. When the water from the bucket splashed the canna, it triggered the faucet. Steaming water poured from the bamboo chute, rapidly filling the tub with soapy hot goodness.

Bella was still giggling at her prank as she whizzed past the silk curtains out of the bathroom area. I couldn't stay mad at her for long. The water was hot and refreshing. It smelled like eucalyptus and peppermint. I soaked in it for a long time, listening to the breeze outside as I had planned, until finally I started nodding off in the tub. By the time I jumped into bed, I was primed for sleep. Lying in that bed was like sinking into a cloud. I welcomed the promise of dreams that swallowed me, eager to forget my troubles for one evening. It felt self-indulgent in the face of Ambrose's looming problem, but I deserved that reprieve. After all, the next morning I would have to face Ambrose's rotten children once more.

Anyhow, I already had a hunch who the murderer was.

8

I slept well that night. When I woke the next morning, I found the little sprite curled up on my chest, snoring. Bella looked so innocent when she was asleep. Gone was the irksome prankster of the previous evening, replaced by the peaceful miniature woman with her arms cuddled around my night shirt as if it were her teddy bear.

Aw, she looks so cute like that, I thought.

I flicked her off my chest.

Bella yelped as she hit the comforter in a puff of glitter. "Now we're even," I snickered.

The sun shone through my open windows, and I could smell the morning dew in the air. I was refreshed and ready for anything.

I have one day before I need to go back to Uriel's cottage. That leaves me twenty-four hours to gather as much information as I can about Ambrose's family.

I needed to make the most of my time at the palace. From everything I'd heard about Ambrose, he was well-loved and respected in the community. The first thing to figure out was why anyone would want to harm him in the first place. If I had learned anything in life, it was that no one became as powerful as Ambrose Amaryllis by being a nice guy. Revenge was a strong motive for murder. Somewhere along the line, he had to have crossed the wrong person, and that was who I needed to find.

Geraldine told me to wear something nice for the events. I had packed mostly sensible clothes for my trip to the Tides, but since I'd met Tae, she'd been helping me update my fashion sense. I rummaged through my suitcase and chose a white V-neck blouse. It had large green buttons I thought would pair well with the dark green A-line skirt I picked out. I loved that skirt because it had a wide green belt attached to it that made my waistline feel less frumpy. It was a shame I only had sneakers. Heels would have been more appropriate for a day in the palace. At least my Vans looked decent enough with the skirt and blouse.

I sat at the glass vanity and tried a couple different hairstyles. Normally, I couldn't care less what my hair looked like. But that afternoon, the House of Dawn would be kicking off the spring celebration with a banquet. Everyone in the Dawn territories was invited. All business around the Tides would be on hiatus, so there was sure to be a lot of fae in attendance. This was an important holiday event for them, and it felt appropriate to try to put some effort in.

I'd seen families with their kids around Easter all in their Sunday best. Dresses and suits, ties and fancy hairdos, all of them laughing gaily on their way to spend time with loved ones. I never had experiences like that myself. Most of my childhood was spent alone in boarding school. While other kids excitedly readied for their parents to pick them up for holidays, I settled into a book, hoping to lose myself in some imaginary world where mothers didn't abandon their children.

Thacinda Alacore. Her name made my blood boil. I hadn't spoken to my mother in years. I didn't even know how to get in touch with her if I wanted to. She had made it clear long ago that she wasn't interested in my life. She rarely visited me in boarding school, and when she did, she was always cold and distant, focused more on her work than spending a few measly moments with a daughter she could only complain about. When I moved to the city, I decided to make things easy for her. I never told Thacinda where I was moving. In a big city like New York, she'd never know where to find me. I mean, she could have if she wanted to. Thacinda was a wealthy businesswoman. She certainly had the resources to track me down. But I knew she wouldn't bother. And I was right. At least this way I was in control of our relationship. *I* was the one who made the decision not to speak to *her*.

Still, recently I'd expected her to show up. Ever since I'd discovered the fae and learned that Thacinda had cast a dweomer over me to stop me from knowing they existed. But she hadn't.

It wasn't disappointing. It was more of the same treatment she had given me for the first eighteen years of my life, before I cut her off. Why was my mind wandering to that cold bitch? *Oh right, people looking their best for celebrations. Put in some effort, Lanie.*

It was hopeless. No matter what I did with my hair, it looked like a hot mess. In the end I decided to simply braid my sides and tuck them behind my ears. It was past time I headed downstairs anyhow. The event would be underway, and I wanted to make the most of my time there.

I stood and headed for the door. I made it one whole step before tumbling to the floor. My elbow hit the wood and sent a sharp pain up my arm.

"What the—?" I was sprawled on the floor. Someone had tied my sneakers together! I heard Bella's fit of laughter before her twinkling light zipped over me.

She hovered in the air, pointing and laughing. "Now we're even," she mimicked my voice and shook her butt in the air.

"Yeah, ha ha, chuck it up," I said as I sat up and inspected my elbow. There was no cut. The only thing wounded was my pride. "I'm going to have to pay you back for that."

Bella stopped laughing and looked overly alarmed. She zipped away in a stream of glitter. *Great, I get stuck in the one room in the palace with a pranking sprite.*

I made my way downstairs, stopping at the balcony that overlooked the atrium. The transformation was remarkable. Last night, if someone had told me the atrium could get any more impressive, I would have scoffed at them. The buzz of hundreds of voices filled the air. Long tables laden with food were set up all over the wide space. Starfire felt radiant in the sunlight that streamed down through its hollow trunk, reflecting off the pure white bark and lighting up the area as surely as if we were outside. Some of the tree boughs crisscrossed inside the building, showcasing thickets of healthy silver leaves, each larger than my hand.

Topiary displays were arranged between tables, near the koi pond, and on either side of the open terrace doors. They were impressive sculptures that towered over the guests, carved and grown from boxwood shrubs, ficus trees, and azaleas. There was a leaping dolphin with a spray of water beneath it grown from lush hydrangeas. A pair of winged fairies in full bloom on either side of the terrace doors, their hands reaching for one another. The topiary was so intricate that I could see the details of their faces, eyes filled with bliss, lips parted slightly as if they were speaking words across the span of time. It was mesmerizing.

I could see the terrace clearly from that vantage. The House of Dawn had set up a score of tents large enough to fit a three-ring circus on the palace grounds. There were even more fae outside. They had come from all over the realm for the House of Dawn's celebration. There were horned satyrs, chuckling pixies, pink-skinned mirages, and gnomes wearing their droopy pointed hats mingling with large-nosed dwarves. A three-armed tephyr juggled while goat-faced children danced around them. The frog-like droba laughed as they drank honeywine.

Three blue jays swooped over the crowd of people. They chirped back and forth as they flew higher, past my balcony and upward through Starfire's boughs. I watched them ascend and realized there was a whole flock of birds in attendance. Doves perched on the rail of the third-floor balcony. Hummingbirds zipped in and out of the banquet hall. Parakeets whistled around the waterfall that fed the koi pond.

"Where does all the bird shit go?" I wondered aloud.

"There's a dweomer set up around the atrium," a soft voice answered. It was Persa, the timid woman from the lounge. The one Cyan had been picking on. She wore a lovely pale violet robe with white trim. Woody vines overlapped around her waist with clusters of red berries dangling from them. Yellow phlox grew from the fabric down the front of her robe and along the hem of the belled sleeves. She pointed to the edges of the atrium level with our balcony. "If you look closely, you can see where it meets Starfire."

"You're Persa, right?" I said, offering my hand for her to shake. "I don't think we got a chance to introduce ourselves. I'm Lanie."

Persa eyed my hand as if it were a snake that might bite her before tentatively shaking it. I forget sometimes what a human and cultural-centric gesture it is to shake hands. Her skin felt wet, as if she'd just come from the pool. That was the condition of water faeries, being surrounded by and thriving on their natural element, water. "It is a pleasure to meet you, Lady Alacore."

"Not Lady Alacore, just Lanie," I corrected. But wait, would that be a mistake? From the view, there were a score of purebloods below, mingling at the afternoon banquet. What would stick out more, if I went by *lady* as they expected, or bucked that tradition to insist on them calling me Lanie? It was an odd quandary.

Persa looked at her feet. *She's nervous about talking to me,* I realized. "Thank you for sticking up for me last night. That was a very kind thing to do."

"Oh, sure thing. I mean, your aunt is kind of a bully, huh?" I wondered if it was a good idea to openly admit I'd spilled the drink in Cyan's lap on purpose.

Persa quickly hid her smirk behind one hand. "Please forgive my family. They may seem like horrible people, but they are good at heart. These have been trying times, and I fear that has brought out the worst in some of them."

The idea that Cyan was normally a kind-hearted patron of charity made me snort. "I know a bully when I meet one. I'm an expert at it at this point. You don't have to apologize for their behavior. Each person has the ability to decide what actions they take in this world."

Persa shifted her feet. She looked around, worried someone might overhear our conversation. *She's a delicate little thing. I better tread more lightly. I bet she has some information to share, and I'm not going to get at it by lecturing her on the graces of virtue.*

"You're right, though," I conceded. "Maybe I overreacted. After all, everyone has a bad day now and then."

Persa perked up, lifting her chin to gaze at me hopefully. What was she hoping to get out of this conversation? Was it just mere forgiveness for her family's rude transgression? For some families, honor can be just as important as life, even more so. The idea that this timid woman needed to atone for the selfish antics of her aunt made my blood boil. It had another effect on me as well.

I instantly liked Persa Amaryllis. In her I saw a reflection of myself. That Lanie that spent her life trying to please others and excusing the rude behavior of my mother. Thacinda was a far worse tyrant than the petty socialite Cyan aspired to be.

"Though you have to admit it was worth it to see that look on her face." I made a horrified expression, mimicking Cyan's reaction.

Persa's laugh carried over the balcony and the music below. Several fae turned their heads in our direction. She slapped a hand over her mouth, her cheeks suddenly bright red, but still giggling nervously.

I laughed along with her. "You have a great laugh. You shouldn't hide it."

She looked surprised. "You think so?"

"Sure thing."

"Lady Alacore—er, *Lanie*—"

She started to ask me something, but the loud rumbling of my stomach interrupted our conversation. It was my turn to blush.

Persa smiled. "Are you hungry?"

"I'm ravenous."

"I am too. Let's go see what treats Chef Henri's prepared for the banquet."

I eagerly followed her down to the atrium, grateful to have someone I could enter the banquet with. A few curious heads turned our way, but we were as anonymous as any other group in attendance. I'm nervous enough going to parties. I don't have the best track record at social events, and I've had enough mishaps at parties to give me a healthy fear of them.

I embraced Persa's company as the armor I needed to shield me against my own fears. A hundred percent of my focus was aimed at not tripping over my own feet. If I could keep upright and choose my words carefully, I could avoid making an ass of myself.

This isn't a party, I corrected myself. *It's a banquet.* I snorted at my own delusion. *Semantics. Anything with this many people and that much food is a party. Great, if I can't even lie to myself, how am I going to fool these uppity nobles into letting their guard down?*

My eyes nearly fell out of my head when we reached the first table. A delectable display was spread out before me. There were so many different dishes it made me dizzy to look up and down the table. There was roasted eggplant, caramelized to perfection, then sprinkled with sunflower seeds and thyme. The chef had created a waterfall of glazed cinnamon rolls, each one larger than my hand, shingled from a tall platter to a lower one. There were eclairs, pink glazed crème puffs, ambrosia salad, pancakes shaped like fish, crepes wrapped like cones and stuffed with crème and berries. Kiwis were cut like little flowers beside bowls of fresh fruit and above skillets of spinach, plum tomatoes, sweet potatoes, and shitake mushrooms with over-easy eggs on top. My mouth was watering.

"Oh, it looks like they're still set up for brunch," Persa said delightedly.

"That's alright by me. Everything looks so tasty. I don't even know where to begin."

Persa had a shy smile. "Maybe with a plate?" She handed me a dish from the end of the table. She looked very nervous to be around me, and for some reason that helped ease my own insecurity.

I wonder if this is how Deedee used to feel when I was acting skittish.

I forced myself not to think about my best friend before the melancholy could smother me. I needed to stay focused on gathering information. Thoughts of Deedee lying in her coma, alone in Willow's Edge, could render me useless at times. Many nights I'd laid in bed, staring at the ceiling, crying over how helpless I felt that she was in so much pain and there was nothing I could do to help her.

I was saved from my melancholy by a purring against my leg. I looked down to find furry Gizmitt wrapping his little feline armadillo body around my ankles.

"Hello, Gizmitt," I said as I petted the little ferillo.

"Oh, Gizzie," Persa squealed. She knelt and petted his furry ears. "Are you hungry too, buddy?"

Persa looked around to be sure nobody was watching, then snatched a pastry from the table and handed it to Gizmitt. He grabbed it with his front paws and chomped down. I took his mewling as approval. Then, without warning, he hopped in the air with the pastry tucked close to his chest, landed in his rolled-up form, then zipped away.

I shook my head, laughing as I rose. Gizmitt had the right idea. I needed to eat too.

"What in the name of the food gods is that?" I asked, trying not to drool.

"Have you never had ogre toast, Lady Alacore?"

"*Ogre* toast?" The toast in question was the size of Persa's plate, with a layer of roasted asparagus and topped by a poached egg slathered in an orange sauce with flecks of scallions. A fae noble walked around me and snatched one of them off the platter, adding it to a pile of food on his plate and moving on.

Persa giggled. I realized I must have been making quite the face. "Don't worry, the sauce isn't made from ogres. It's just what chef calls them."

I looked at her uncertainly. She didn't strike me as the type to pull a prank. I took one of the large toasts and sniffed it. Ogre or not, the sauce had a pleasing lemony-pepper aroma that made my mouth water. I took a bite. The toast crunched perfectly and assaulted my taste buds with a creamy buttery sauce that was indeed lemon, pepper, and egg. The rich flavors paired well with the crunch of asparagus. "This is delicious," I said between chewing.

"I'm craving something a little different this morning." Persa snatched one of the long eclairs and stuffed it in her mouth with a big bite.

"Well, you certainly know how to get your mouth around one," I teased.

Persa stopped mid-bite, a look of shock widening her eyes.

What was wrong with me? How could I have said something so crude to this woman I'd just met? Months of hanging around Tae had lulled me into a false sense of security. Now, instead of making friends with the one decent person in Ambrose's family, I had completely insulted her like some bonehead. I was mortified.

Persa choked on her mouthful of éclair; chocolate icing smeared down her lips.

"Oh god, that's not what I meant," I insisted.

I quickly patted her back as she bent over coughing. The rest of the pastry in her hand hit my blouse. Chocolate and white blouses don't mix. I leapt away from it as if it were a bomb and backed into a satyr enjoying his food. His fork went flying out of his hand and onto the plate of his partner.

"I'm so sorry," I pleaded as I regained my balance, then raced back to Persa where she was bent over with her hands gripping the table.

"Oh no, are you crying? I'm so sorry, Persa, that's not what I meant at all," I lied.

Except Persa wasn't crying. She was laughing. She turned to me, tears streaming from her eyes, chocolate smeared across her cheek, and grabbed my shoulder with one hand, the other slapping the table as she laughed hysterically. "You said... you... and then you fell into..."

She couldn't get her words out between laughs. I found myself laughing along with her. *The party curse strikes again.* I had made a spectacle of myself at yet another one. The satyr wiped crumbs from his lapel as he walked away, he and his partner shaking their heads at us. That only made us laugh all the harder as I dabbed the chocolate from Persa's cheek with a napkin.

"What is the gaff, ladies?"

I sobered up in an instant as Silas popped his gorgeous face between us. He looked even better than the night before, and his dazzling blue eyes and strong shoulders took my breath away. He wore his blonde hair in a carefree quaff that matched his Italian designer suit, the whole of him exuding aloofness and ease.

"Silas!" It was the loudest I'd heard Persa speak since meeting her. She beamed and threw her arms around him. Despite myself, I felt a twinge of jealousy.

Silas side-hugged her. "Hey, cuz, it's so good to see you."

Ah, that's right. They're related. I sighed and hoped they didn't notice my unwarranted anxiety. *Last night Geraldine said Silas was a member of the family. Still, that doesn't mean there's nothing between them.* It wasn't uncommon for fae nobility to marry third or even second cousins. In fact, some considered it a way to maintain the purity of their bloodline. Human nobility used to do similarly in medieval times for power and prestige.

"When did you get in? I expected to see you on the *Midnight Voyager*." Persa finished wiping the chocolate icing from her face.

"And sit through a three-hour flight surrounded by Cyan's entourage?" Silas snickered. "I caught a ride with the performers the night before last. When I came down to the lounge last evening, you'd already gone to bed. Cyan was in a rough mood, though. You wouldn't happen to know anything about that, would you?"

Persa blanched. She turned away to gather the other half of her éclair from the floor and set it on her plate. "I needed a little quiet time. As you said, it's a long way from the Gale."

"That bad, huh?" Silas waved a hand dismissively, ready to move the conversation along. "Ah, well, I suppose some things never change. Anyhow, where are my manners?" He turned to me.

"This is my new friend Lanie… err, *Lady* Alacore," Persa said. "Lady Alacore, meet my cousin Silas Amaryllis."

Silas bowed his head to me in greeting. "We've already met, if you know what I mean." He nudged Persa and scandalously danced his eyebrows up and down.

"You have?" Persa asked, surprised and blushing.

"I bumped into your cousin last night in the hall as Geraldine showed me to my room," I explained. He was a naughty one, but somehow the way he joked made it a tease and not at all offensive. In fact, I found myself smiling at his jest.

"Oh, you're no fun. The least you could do is pretend I could possibly have had a shot," Silas said, wearing a lopsided grin.

Persa slapped his arm playfully. "I'm sorry, Lady Alacore. I'm afraid my cousin is somewhat of a shameless flirt."

"And a lost cause," Silas added.

"Don't say such dreadful things," Persa admonished.

Silas shrugged. "You know it's true. The family would rather I faded away than embarrass them at a social event of this standing." He winked at me. "Which is exactly why I'm here. Nothing better than ruffling a bit of uptight feathers, eh?"

I snickered back at him. "They do make funny sounds when they scream."

"Oh, she's going to be fun," Silas insisted. Persa waved him off and rolled her eyes. "Tell me, though, Lady Alacore—I know the motives behind my arrival and of course my dutiful cousin Persa's. But why are you here?"

The question caught me off-guard and put me on my heels.

"Grandfather invited her," Persa said as if that were all the explanation necessary. Yet there was a tinge of curiosity in her eyes that didn't escape me.

Silas beamed. "Ah, the great and powerful Ambrose Amaryllis." He waved his hands theatrically as he spoke. "Naturally Ambrose invited our guest. Grandfather has invited the four corners of fae to this little soiree. Yet only a handful of them are staying in the palace."

"I see your wit is as on point as that ridiculous hairstyle, Silas." Alegra arrived, cutting between us as she dropped the remark offhandedly. She carried herself with the same no-nonsense air as the previous night, wearing a black pencil skirt and white blouse. There was a pencil stuck in her hair and a book tucked beneath the arm she used to hold her plate. She ignored me and put a cucumber sandwich on her plate.

"Cousin Alegra." Silas smiled sardonically. "How wonderful that you've graced us with your ever sunny presence."

Alegra shot daggers at him with her large chestnut eyes. If anyone ever wanted to perfect the art of resting bitch face, they need look no further than Alegra Amaryllis for a mentor. Her whole persona was the epitome of *fuck off*. "There's that masterful wit again. How will I ever sleep tonight with such a scathing indictment of my character rattling around in my head?" she deadpanned, then added two shortbread cookies to her plate.

"You're a very rude lady," I said.

"How would you know the first thing about me?" Alegra asked with her back to us as she continued filling her plate with food. "And why should I listen to anything you have to say, for that matter? You're not a *Lady* at all. Geraldine purports you to be, at Ambrose's behest, but you were not born and bred as such. You don't even have wings. I would think twice about my own life before sticking my nose in other people's business if I were you, *Miss* Alacore."

Oh, someone wants me to back off. My blood pressure spiked, and my hands were trembling. Alegra's emphasis on *Miss* shouldn't have bothered me as much as it did. It was the condescending way she spoke about my very existence that rattled me. *This woman's dangerous,* I thought. *She's got a natural talent for getting under my skin, but I can't lose my cool. It's interesting that she's attacking my character out of the blue, though. That's not suspicious at all.*

"That's enough, Alegra," Silas said firmly.

Alegra turned to face us. The food on her plate was tidily arranged in sections, the sweets in one corner, breakfast taking up half the plate, and fruit sorted by color in the other quarter. "You want me to stop? Whatever for? You were the one to broach the question that's on all of our minds," Alegra said to Silas. "Why is a girl who is taking the trials to become Warden of Willow's Edge traipsing around the palace calling herself *Lady* as she pours drinks on my sister's lap?"

Her eyes penetrated me questioningly. *Ah, I see her game. She wanted to rattle me and then disarm me with that statement.* She was appraising me, hoping her dirty trick would make me spill my secrets. I was unnerved by her demeanor, mostly because she was more right than wrong. I was in way over my head with these people. They were sharks, and I was chum. I did feel like an outsider who didn't belong. But she was wrong about one thing. I wasn't going to tell her shit. "Any business I have here is between me and your father alone. In other words, go eat your breakfast in some dark corner and bury your nose in that book." I smiled curtly and curtsied.

Alegra lifted her brow. *Ah, you didn't expect that one, did you?* "Crass and crude, as I suspected." She frowned. "It will be interesting to see how poorly you bungle the task set before you."

Now that did disarm me.

What the—? Does she know why I'm really here? Before I could respond, Alegra briskly marched away from us with her head held high. I gaped after her, but she was swallowed by the growing crowd of fae.

Silas chuckled. "Another classic Alegra drive-by assassination attempt. You would think I'd be used to the spectacle by now."

"Please forgive my aunt, Lady Alacore." Persa bowed, red-faced. It made me angry to see her groveling because of her aunt's rude behavior.

"Stop apologizing for your family," I said. "It's not your fault they're such horrible creatures. What's her deal anyhow?"

Silas shrugged. "Alegra's always had a stick up her—"

Persa cleared her throat. "My aunt has led a tough life that few could understand unless they had walked in her shoes."

"C'mon, Persie, that woman has been picking on us since we were sproutlings," Silas countered.

Persa looked troubled by his remark. I was in awe of her. Persa was a truly kind-hearted flower among a field of vipers. How she kept her sunny disposition was a marvel.

A man called her name from the crowd. It was her father. Artur beckoned impatiently for her to join him and the two fae he was with.

"If you'll excuse me, I must attend to my father." Persa bowed to me.

"Of course," I replied. I wasn't sure whether I should bow or curtsy, so I ended up doing an awkward amalgamation of both that made Silas snicker.

Persa took a few steps away and then turned back. "Perhaps we can spend some more time speaking during the spring festival."

"I would like that," I said.

Persa joined her father. He said something to her and then scowled at me over her shoulder.

"Well, it appears good old Artur doesn't approve of you either. You must have made some impression on them last night."

I had nearly forgotten Silas was standing there with me. I glanced back at him. He had both hands in his pockets and leaned to one side. Fuck me, he looked like a model from a Guess ad. He smirked as if he could read my mind, and I flinched.

Suddenly I panicked. Persa had been my lifeline to entering the banquet. Without her, I suddenly felt exposed. What the heck was I supposed to say to this guy I didn't even know? *And why is he looking at me like I'm chocolate he wants to unwrap and eat?*

"Have fun at the banquet," I said as I abruptly retreated.

Silas snickered.

I left my unfinished plate of food at the end of the table, where brownie waiters were gathering them then cut through the crowd, wanting to be anywhere except there. Soon I came to the waterfall. A shimmering light swam just beneath the surface of the pond it fed into. I peered at it in wonder. It looked almost like a stingray. Or maybe a jellyfish.

A familiar laugh cut through my thoughts. I snapped my head up and looked all around for the source. There was a cluster of fae gathered in a circle, their attention rapt on the center of the group. I have seen men do that many times, usually in clubs or bars, circling around Deedee as if she were a prize hen. Deedee was remarkable like that. She could command a room's attention with ease. She would have known exactly what to say to Alegra too. Then again, if she was around, Silas wouldn't have paid any attention to me. Men couldn't help themselves around Deedee. And who could blame them? She was everything I'm not—beautiful, graceful, sophisticated, fashionable, and fearless. It shamed me to feel jealous over how Silas might react to her presence. I love Deedee. In fact, the only person I'd met in my life who could compare was…

"Tae?" I gawked as the fae group parted.

Taewyn stood at the center of the gathering, wearing a high-waisted pair of trousers that flared from knee to ankle along with a crop top in matching red and gold. A dupatta draped over her bare shoulder, tucked through a sash at her waist and against her curvaceous hips. She looked radiant. She turned to face me and smiled from ear to ear.

"Lanie! I've been looking for you everywhere."

9

"What are you doing here?" I asked as we hugged.

Tae's gathering scattered as soon as she left them with a goodbye wave. She leaned back to take me in. "I looked for you in town, but your landlady said House of Dawn soldiers carted all your stuff away yesterday." She leaned forward and whispered, "I thought you'd been arrested."

"Probably only a matter of time, based on the way I've been pissing off some of these uptight assholes," I teased.

Tae furrowed her brow. She was wearing chunky eyeliner that made her cobalt contact lenses pop in the most pleasing way.

"Ambrose Amaryllis hired me to do a job," I confided as quietly as I could. We shared a conspiratorial grimace, and then I explained everything to her.

I thought Tae would be intrigued. Instead, she looked disturbed. "Lanie, this is serious stuff you're dipping your toes in. The House of Dawn is one of the most powerful forces in the fae realm. Are you sure you should be sticking your nose in their business? Some of these people can be downright dangerous."

She sounded like Alegra telling me to mind my own business. "I don't need your permission to take a job."

Tae put a hand on my back with a disappointed frown. "Lanie, you know I'm always on your side. I just don't want to see anything bad happen to you."

I took a deep breath. "I'm sorry. I just feel so on edge lately, and it's not your fault at all. I think I've been on my own for too long. I used to relish that type of life, but these days it's hard to tell if I'm coming or going. Sometimes it feels like I'm just hanging on by a thread and praying it can hold the weight. You're right, I'm in deep, and I don't know what to do. I took this insane job from Ambrose on top of having to pass my trials with the gladewarden. And she's a real peach too, I'll tell you. I feel overwhelmed. What if I can't do this and something happens to Ambrose?"

"Well, now that I'm here, I'm not leaving. We'll face this together," Tae promised.

I didn't know what I'd done to deserve a friend like her. Once again, I saw the parallels between Tae and Deedee. "Really?" I said, trying to hold back tears of relief. We hugged again. A passing fae grinned lasciviously at the sight of us, and I rolled my eyes at him.

"Wait." I gently pushed away from Tae and wiped the corners of my eyes. "What are you doing here anyhow?"

"I have something awesome to tell you." She looked around as if to be sure nobody was listening, then leaned in. "But not here. It's about your you-know-what." Tae looked pointedly at my belly. That was always where it felt like the curse seized hold of me and where Tae saw it when she worked through my aura. She was right, there was no way I wanted to discuss anything to do with my curse in public.

"Okay, we can talk in my room after the banquet. But first I need to gather my thoughts. I can't understand why anyone would want to hurt Ambrose. If I get a better handle on that, it might help. Didn't you grow up with the water fae? Do you know anything about his family?"

Tae shot me one of her patented "do you know who you're talking" to looks. She sidled up beside me and searched around the atrium until her eyes landed on Ambrose. He was at the top of the stairs, listening to another well-dressed fae couple. "Okay, what do you know about Ambrose so far?"

I shrugged. "He's pretty old, the head of the House of Dawn, and he's spawned spoiled rich kids. Oh, and so far everyone I've talked to since I've come to the Tides has had nothing but good things to say about him."

"Good things like what?"

"He's supposed to be really kind, always taking care of things, that sort of stuff."

"Hmm, that's interesting," Tae said.

"Why? Is he not actually a good person?"

Tae considered it. "Who is to say what is good or bad?"

"C'mon, Tae, seriously, don't fall into one of your waxing philosophical rants. Is he a good guy or not?"

"Ambrose Amaryllis has been the head of the House of Dawn since the four great houses first entered their compact with the royal family. That man has done and seen more than most of us will in a lifetime. Fae have long memories, with passions that run just as deep. I couldn't say if he has ever wronged someone." She held a hand up to stop me from interrupting. "What I can say for certain is that I've always seen him to be a magnanimous ruler. You're right about that. The lands of the water fae are well-tended, its denizens treated with care and respect. There are not a heck of a lot of bullies among his troops, neither the droba guardians nor the pureblood knights."

I chewed on my lip. "Darn."

Tae raised an eyebrow. "You sound as if you wanted there to be something wrong."

"Not that. It's just, if Ambrose isn't some sort of evil dictator, what other reason would someone have for murdering him?"

"Did you ask him that question when he hired you?"

"He said that's what he hired me to find out." I snorted. "Because why make it easy to help you when your life is on the line, right?"

"There's certainly been problems with the House of Dawn since Ambrose went into mourning. Maybe that's the answer."

"Mourning?"

"You didn't know? Ambrose's wife passed away a little over thirty years ago."

"How horrible," I said, looking up at Ambrose. *Ambrose has been in mourning for over thirty years? That's an entire lifetime for some humans.* "He must have loved her dearly. What happened?"

"From what I heard, Criscilla was tending her garden one morning when she was bitten by an hourglass spider. The bite was lethal. By the time Ambrose found her, it was already too late."

"Nature's calling," I whispered.

There is a very common trend among people to find blame when things go bad. There must be a reason things happen. There must be some cause to rationalize the why of things. There was a morbid yet unavoidable instinct to figure out how someone died, the reaction in a human brain being, *"ah, okay, I don't smoke so that won't happen to me"* or *"cancer, well, I don't eat meat so I'm good to go."* In a way such thoughts can provide insulation against the cold reality of death.

Many fae have a contrary belief, that some things in nature are unavoidable. The bite of a spider would be a blameless tragedy. Where a human might say that they should've sprayed the garden for pests, or Criscilla should've worn gloves while gardening, a fae would say it's simply the hourglass spider's natural instinct to protect itself. The spider felt threatened and reacted true to its being. Seen through that lens, Criscilla's death was the balance of nature, an unavoidable outcome. It was *nature's calling*, a blameless event that was inevitable. I had not decided which side of the line I fell on.

Tae nodded. "Ambrose used to be known as a pretty tough cookie. Since his wife died, I've heard plenty of gossip that the old man's gone soft."

"How so?" I thought about the piercing intensity of Ambrose's stare and couldn't picture anyone thinking that man soft.

"Well, for instance, recently the House of Dawn lost a big chunk of their economy to the Court of Shadows."

The Court of Shadows was one of the other great houses that ruled over the fae realm. "That's not good. Tell me more."

"Where's Artur?" Tae looked around the atrium until she found him. He was speaking quite earnestly with a pair of water fae. Persa stood behind him, her head down and hands folded at her waist. She looked very sad and lonely.

What a jerk. He made her come to him just so she could stand there like some prop.

"Have you met him yet?" Tae asked. "From what I understand, he's the reason they lost their holdings. Signed over half of Ambrose's silk trade to the Shadows."

I sucked in my breath. "Bet daddy wasn't too thrilled about that."

"No bets needed. Ambrose publicly shamed Artur a few months ago, right after it happened. Everyone around Willow's Edge was talking about the scandal. And get this, the rumor is that Prince Lucien's little friend, Valia Medi'tu, was involved in the acquisition."

I hated Valia. She was the snobby fae Lucien had been sitting with at the lunar party. She went out of her way to treat me like dirt that night.

"Sounds like a motive," I said.

It wouldn't be the first revenge rooted in ego. Artur struck me as someone with a rotten temper. I couldn't picture him taking a public browbeating from Ambrose without harboring some resentment. The question was whether that resentment was strong enough to commit patricide. It was certainly worth looking into. Also, I wouldn't deny I felt a certain dislike toward the man for how he treated Persa. I wanted nothing more than to waltz over there and take her away from him.

"Ambrose's kids suck," I said.

Tae shrugged. "Maybe. Have you met the rest of them?"

"Yeah, Cyan and her wife, Isabo, and Alegra, his other daughter."

Tae thoughtfully tapped her lip with one finger. "Hmm, I haven't heard too much about Alegra."

"You seem to know a lot about the rest of them," I remarked. "Why is that?"

"Don't humans keep tabs on their royal families?"

"Good point." Whether it was a prime minister, a president, or the royal family, humans loved to learn more about the famous, from actors to heads of state. Shoot, I knew some people who made it their job to learn everything they could about their favorite content creators. Put in that perspective, the fae knowing a lot about their rulers didn't seem such an odd thing.

"Okay, what *do* you know about Alegra?" I asked. She was nowhere to be seen. Probably off in a corner somewhere with her pointy nose buried in a book.

"Not much," Tae said. "She's been an enigma ever since they shipped her off to Queen Titania. Ah, right, you don't know about that. So, the way the compact works is that the firstborn of every Great House is given over to the queen."

That revelation was bitter to swallow. "Are you saying she's like a slave to the queen?"

I spoke a little too loudly and noticed some heads turn in our direction. The atrium was crowded with guests and steadily filling up with more.

Tae winced. "Keep your voice down." She flashed a smile at one of the fae looking our way, who promptly turned away. "She's not a *slave*. Alegra Dawn is the royal librarian."

"Fuck's sake, they changed her last name too?" I hissed in a lower voice.

"The firstborn doesn't just go into service to the monarchy. When they come of age they become a part of the royal family, but they keep the name of their house. It's way more prestigious than you're making it sound. There's plenty of fae who would give their left tit for such an opportunity."

I choked on my tea at her statement.

Tae tossed me a napkin. "Would you stop?" she giggled.

I wiped the tea off my chin. "Royal librarian does sound like a badass job. I worked in the school library back at university. It was really cool. I loved being surrounded by all those books. Just really missed sunlight and plants, ya know? Anyhow, that explains why she's so organized." I caught Tae's questioning glance. "Earlier, when she got her food, she had it perfectly sectioned off on her plate, even down to sorting the fruits by color."

"I'm not sure all librarians do that."

"Yeah, probably not. She is a right bitch, though, and she did threaten me earlier."

"What? Lanie, that's something you lead with, not how she organizes fruit."

I told Tae how Alegra had sharply warned me to stay out of her family's affairs.

"That doesn't mean she's planning on killing her pops," Tae said. "Plenty of people are protective of their families."

"Not this family." I shook my head. "You should see how they interact. They hate each other. Either way, I think we should keep our eyes on her."

"Right, no one is ruled out as a suspect," Tae agreed. "That just leaves us with—" She turned in a circle until she found her last target. Cyan was fake-laughing in the center of a gathering. The water fae around her were all young and dressed in high street fashion with outlandish outfits. Isabo clung to her side. "Cyan Amaryllis."

"The CEO of the mean girl's club," I said.

"Not a fan?"

Cyan caught us watching her and shot me a scathing sneer. She said something to her entourage. Many heads turned our way, and then the laughing began.

"Oh, she's not a fan of you either, huh? Geez, for someone who's supposed to be lying low, you sure have ruffled a lot of feathers in one night."

I winced. "I sort of poured a drink in her lap."

Tae laughed so loudly that Cyan snapped her head back around. Her face reddened as if she knew what Tae was laughing about. Her entourage circled her like a living shield as they shuffled off toward the food tables together.

"I couldn't help it. She was picking on Persa."

"Artur's daughter? That girl's sweet as a ripe peach," Tae said. "Cyan is the only one of them I've interacted with. She's always had this saccharine quality, very fake and twice that venomous. She is, however, one of the most influential moguls of the fashion industry. You'd do well not to make an enemy out of that one unless you know with absolute certainty that she's the culprit. Which she probably isn't."

"But she's such a bitch," I whined.

"And a very successful businesswoman. Cyan's got money galore. Besides which, she's daddy's little girl. Cyan Amaryllis dotes over her father as if he were the second coming."

I raised my brow. That was a scandalous thing for Tae to say. The fae viewed talk of Jesus and God as distasteful human propaganda. It wasn't something I agreed with, but most fae were quite cantankerous about it. "You can't think of any reason she might want to hurt Ambrose?"

"None," Tae said with conviction.

I wasn't buying it. Cyan was a bully. Knowing she was some fashion mogul only meant she was a cunning bully. "Then we'll just have to probe deeper."

A massive blast of air cut through our conversation. It flooded the atrium with a sound like the keening of a whale. All heads turned toward the double staircase. "Oh, the banquet is about to begin," Tae said excitedly.

A looked around questioningly. "Haven't we been in the banquet all this time?"

Tae grinned at me like a mischievous kitten. "This was just the warmup, silly."

"We need to find an insider willing to talk with us," I said. "The more I can learn about the House of Dawn, the better."

The whale's song cut across the atrium once more, and with it came what I sought. It was both a blessing and a curse.

A voice boomed over the gathering. "The spring festival is about to begin. Please join us in welcoming our guests of honor."

A familiar face appeared at the top of the stairs, and I felt my stomach twist in knots.

"Announcing the first of our esteemed guests, Malachai and Minerva Erlkönig, the king and queen regent of the Court of Shadows, accompanied by their son—"

"Oh shit," I gasped. "It's Lucien."

10

P rince Lucien was at the spring festival. I didn't know why it had never dawned on me that he might attend. All four Great Houses were to be represented. It was only natural that the prince of the Erlkönig family would be in attendance. He looked handsome as ever in his slim-fit suit, the black fabric a stark contrast to skin so pale it bordered on icy blue.

My belly fluttered to see him again after these few weeks away. I was confused by my feelings. Was I mad at Lucien for ignoring me all this time or excited to see him? My wonder turned sour when I saw the woman draped on his arm. It was Valia, the rude woman who'd antagonized me the night of the lunar party. I almost didn't recognize her without her thick goth makeup. Gone were the fishnet stockings and leather skirt, replaced by a royal-blue dress that clung to her perfect body like a second skin. The pouting bitch I'd seen on the sofa was now a woman fit for nobility.

Tae ran a hand down my arm as we watched them descend the white stairs into the banquet. "Are you okay?"

I realized I hadn't breathed since I saw Valia glued to the prince's arm. I shook my head and shuffled my feet. My palm stung from clenching a fist so tightly that my nails were digging in. "Yeah, it's fine. I was just surprised to see them, that's all."

"It is our honor to welcome the Court of Shadows to our celebration," the voice boomed over the atrium.

A ripple of excitement ran through the bustling crowd of fae around us. Lucien's father wasn't at all what I expected. Someone needed to inform his body that it was hundreds of years old, because other than a slightly high hairline, he didn't look a day over forty. Malachai was tall and elegantly poised, with a sturdy build. He exuded a menacing presence to me. His eyes were like twin coals, darting across the crowd above his grimace. There was something militaristic about his outfit. Perhaps it was the extra silver buttons to one side of his sharply folded lapel or the squared shoulders of his black suit jacket. Or maybe it was the black leather gloves he wore and the matching leather belt running diagonally across his torso.

"I've never seen anyone wear rings over their gloves before," I said offhandedly.

"He does have an odd fashion sense," Tae agreed. "His wife on the other hand...*yum.*"

Queen Regent Minerva linked arms with her husband. She was drop-dead gorgeous. High angled cheekbones, softly rounded shoulders, flawless skin that made me want to die. Her dress was cut in a sharp V down the center, ending just below her breasts. The dress was black, yet when she moved, I could see hints of crimson ripple over the material. She wore a choker around her long throat. Her eyes were like twin rubies that swept over the crowd with a pride and confidence that bespoke her position. This was a woman who commanded every room she entered, and this banquet would be no different. The back of her dress was open all the way down to her waist, just above her ass. Her faerie wings stood fully erect for all to see, as if daring someone to try to touch one.

"That's Lucien's mother?" I whispered in disbelief. "She looks younger than me."

Tae snickered. "Minerva's a good deal older than you or me. Besides, you're still just a guppy. And technically speaking, she's the prince's stepmother. His birth mother died a long time ago. Strange, though, I don't see her daughter Hellebore. Daddy must've made her sit this one out. She's the youngest of the family, their precious jewel."

Something slithered under Malachai's cape, startling me. The fabric rippled with a sanguine fluidness that reminded me of a living creature. I shuddered. "His cape...bothers me."

"It should. That's the Mantle of Nightmare. That single piece of fabric is responsible for Malachai's dominance over his court. It was his father's, the founder of their great house. There are all sorts of rumors about where the cape came from, but I only know one thing that's true. That cape is one of the most powerful relics in all the realm."

Icy fingers ran down my spine. I shuddered. What kind of power must a cape possess to be named the Mantle of Nightmare? I sure as hell didn't want to find out firsthand.

Then I noticed the pommel of a sword sticking out from the side of his cape.

"Wait, how did he get a sword in here? Geraldine told me no weapons would be allowed inside the festival."

"Try telling that to the leader of the Court of Shadows," Tae scoffed. "No doubt your lover, prince Lucien, has that famous sword of his, *Iceshadow,* on him too."

That wasn't good. If Malachai could get weapons into the palace, so could my murderer. I looked back at Lucien, thinking of the ice sword that was magically kept hidden at his waist as well. I hadn't known it was named Iceshadow until then. He and Valia were reaching the bottom of the steps when his gaze found me. I suddenly found it hard to breathe as we locked eyes. It had been weeks since we spoke. My heart was racing. The last time I saw him, he was sticking his neck out for me in court. He looked devilishly handsome as ever.

I smiled at him. Lucien quickly looked away, but not before Valia noticed. She swiveled her head to see what had caught his attention and met my gaze with a crooked grin, every bit as malicious as it was condescending.

Uncomfortable, I turned back to the balcony. A group of hollow-eyed men and women trailed Malachai and Minerva. There was something stiff and yet overly quick about their movements that I found disturbing. It was like watching an old movie that skipped a few frames. Their eyes darted back and forth across the crowd, jittering unnaturally left to right.

"Ugh, vampires," Tae said with great disdain.

I was shocked. I'd heard vampires mentioned several times since meeting the fae, but this was my first experience seeing any in the flesh. "Why would they be here?" I asked in dread.

"Most of 'em are mercenaries these days, ever since the freedom act. The Court of Shadows created vampires aeons ago. They used to work solely for their court, assassins stalking their prey from the shadows, but that all changed when the vampires sued for freedom. Many deemed being immortal *and* stuck in servitude to be too cruel a punishment." Tae squinted, studying the vampire entourage. "These look like they're wearing the Court of Shadows emblem. They must be royal guards, not mercs."

"They're awfully good-looking." Maybe all those romance books were right.

Tae snickered. "That's just what they want you to see. Pray you never get trapped in a room with one trying to drain you dry."

A nearby water fae sighed and spoke to his friend. "Leave it to King Malachai to bring vamps to the House of Dawn."

His friend snorted. "We get it, you're a tough guy. Yawn."

The way he said the word *yawn* made me giggle. I tried to look for Lucien again, but his group had already disappeared into the bustling crowd.

"Allow us to introduce the Summer Court," the voice boomed over the crowd.

Gazing at the Summer Court was like looking at the horizon as the sun rose for the morning and cast its brilliance over the land. The entire atrium warmed as the first members of the Court emerged.

"It is our great honor to welcome the Royal Twins, Isthir and Duma."

A roar of applause shook the room. The twins were apparently very popular. Draped in robes of gold and white, they were perfectly poised specimens floating inches above the floor with their fluttering faerie wings. Isthir's skin looked like it had been dipped in gold. A light radiated from her, making it difficult to gaze at her for too long. But she was so achingly beautiful I couldn't help but endure the stinging in my eyes to continue gaping at her. Her ears were longer than a human's and pointed. Her eyes were mismatched, the left one yellow and right silver, and set off vividly against her iridescent tallow-and-white wings, which looked like the world's most delicate stained glass. Her chestnut locks draped over her exposed shoulders, and a silver tiara sat atop her head. A star jewel gleamed at its center.

Duma was her twin in all ways, his golden features just as exquisite, except that his mismatched eyes were a mirror of hers, with silver on the left and yellow on the right. Instead of a tiara, he wore laurels, with a twin star floating in the center of his forehead. His robes were draped over his shoulders but parted in the center all the way down in a V that ended at his naked pelvis. His skin shimmered as he beamed over the crowd and waved.

They were an androgynous pair, neither too masculine nor too feminine. I couldn't help thinking, *this must be what angels look like.* I basked in their light as they smiled magnanimously and worked their way down the steps.

Then a familiar face came over the balcony.

"Please welcome the great and benevolent Jarl Olan Sumarr."

Olan looked much the same as the last time I saw him. He was a wizened old man who acted as the Court of Summer's representative for the court proceedings in Willow's Edge. I was pleasantly surprised to see him in attendance on behalf of his great house. He held a twinkle in his eyes, as if he'd just heard a good joke and was eager to share his mirth with everyone around. There was something very Santa Claus about his appearance, whether it was the great white beard or the jolly rosiness to his cheeks and flat nose. Olan waved to the crowd. His eyes somehow locked on mine, and I saw recognition pass through them. He nodded to me and gave a half bow. I was startled to be recognized, and several people around us looked my way. The whispers flowed as I quickly bowed back. Olan beamed with his cherubic smile and made his way down the steps, waving to more of the crowd as he went.

"Looks like you made a good impression on Olan," Tae said.

"What is he doing here?"

"Same as everyone else—he came to enjoy the festival," Tae said as if it were obvious.

"Then why didn't the Court of Shadows representative come?" I asked. "Plus, isn't there a representative for each Great House in every province? Why aren't they all here?"

"I expect some of them will be. Their arrival just didn't get announced. Olan's unlike them. He's on equal ground in the council chambers, but out here, beyond the courthouse, he holds more power than the bulk of this room. Olan is second only to the Twins of his Great House."

"Oh, wow. I had no idea he was so important."

Tae whistled appreciatively. "Would you look at that dress."

"Please join us in welcoming the House of Amber. The radiant Winonal—"

As beautiful and interesting as the new arrivals were, I couldn't keep my focus on the balcony. A commotion had broken out nearby. The Court of Shadows was congregating a few yards to my right, close to the koi ponds. Cyan and her entourage had swooped in to greet them, and she was speaking animatedly to Minerva. Malachai stared impassively at their conversation, the height of disinterested nobility. Lucien was laughing at

81

something one of Cyan's cronies had just said. Valia was on his arm like a leech, already holding a fluted glass of champagne.

Kind of early to be drinking, I thought glumly.

I was hoping he would look back my way. If even for the tiniest bit of acknowledgement. Why was he ignoring me? Surely Lucien saw me when he was coming down the stairs. That couldn't have been my imagination. If he would just glance my way and give me some sort of sign. Was it his family? Was he embarrassed by me?

"Friends, please gather your attention. Our host Ambrose Amaryllis, head of the House of Dawn, leader of the water realms, will now speak."

Voices died down all around us, all eyes respectfully turned toward the balcony. Lucien caught my gaze, and I flinched, quickly turning away. My face felt like it was on fire. Did he think I was pining after him like some lovesick schoolgirl? I forced myself to focus on Ambrose as he moved to the center of the balcony.

Ambrose raised his hands, palms facing the crowd, in greeting. "A good afternoon I welcome you with, my fae brethren." His voice was calm and soft yet carried over the proceedings with the weight of authority. This was a leader of one of the Great Houses come to speak before his people. "Water is life. It is the infinitesimal drop that awakens the seed, the wide oceans, streaming rivers, and great lakes that make up over seventy percent of our planet. We are here to celebrate the spring, and with it the arrival of water, the arrival of new life. The blooming season is upon us. We are but one piece of an ever-flowing river, the bonds between our Houses forever in balance."

Geraldine handed Ambrose a crystal pitcher of liquid. He lifted it high over the balcony for all to see as he spoke beneath his breath in a murmuring hymn. We all watched in silence as the water rapidly shifted to a glowing pink color.

"I offer this water, the gift of life and rebirth, as the House of Dawn honors the balance of the compact." Ambrose spoke loudly and clearly over the crowd. He lowered his hands and slowly poured the water over the edge of the balcony. A collective gasp arose from the people. For a moment it appeared that he had slighted the compact by pouring out the water he had just offered.

Then we saw it. The water hit an angled sheet of smooth white wood that had been placed just beneath the balcony. When it had arrived, I could not say. It was as if the wooden sheet appeared out of thin air—one second there was just air, the next the wood.

The water traced a circuitous line down the panel. Everywhere it traveled, it lit up grooves in the wood with an inner light. Soon shapes were formed. They were the sigils of the Great Houses, all four set in a circle, all four connected by the water. When the last drop of water poured from the pitcher, the circle was complete. All houses were represented and in balance.

A roar of applause shook the atrium. Ambrose's voice carried above all the others.

"I declare the opening of the spring festival."

I turned to look over my shoulder. Lucien was laughing and speaking with Cyan's entourage again. Valia had positioned herself between Minerva and Cyan. They were wrapped in a delightful conversation with each other.

"How can he ignore me like this?" I grumbled. "Not even a hello?"

Just then a waiter came up to us with a tray of drinks. Tae took one and thanked them then saw where I was staring. "Lanie, let it go," Tae warned. "He's always been a prick."

I knew that. Lucien's slight shouldn't have bothered me as much as it did. The fact that his ignoring me made me feel anything at all caused my blood to boil. I opened and closed my fists, trying to shake off the agitation.

Just then Lucien caught me looking and rolled his eyes at something the fae said to him. That did it.

"This isn't how you treat other people," I insisted. I shook Tae off me and snatched a drink from the waiter's tray. "I'm going over there right now and giving that jerk a piece of my mind."

11

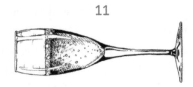

I was a few steps away from Lucien's gathering of fae nobility when my bravado started to wear off. What was I doing, acting like some slighted lover anyhow? Lucien and I had never made any promises. I didn't even want that sort of relationship from him. To me he was just a fun friend with benefits. Benefits I unfortunately couldn't partake of anywhere else due to my curse. So why was I getting all hot and bothered over him not waving at me? Lucien was a prince. There was no reason he should be consorting with me in the first place.

I realized the gravity of my error too late. I was already standing just inside the circle of fae. All conversation had faltered as eyes were pointed in my direction. Lucien's face was an unreadable blank slate. Valia openly sneered at me. Cyan's smile crumpled into something else. *Is that fear? What could someone like Cyan have to fear from me?*

It was Minerva who spoke first. "Can we help you, dear?" Her perfect smile made me feel even smaller. How could I have considered reaming out Lucien in front of his parents? I bet they'd love to hear how annoyed I was that the guy I'm hooking up with didn't run right over to say hello.

Oh shit. How long have I been standing here not talking? Don't be a weirdo, Lanie. Say something! I panicked and took a deep draught of my drink. Liquid courage, as they say.

"Lanie, no!" Tae warned as she cut across the banquet behind me.

Little late to warn me. I'm already here. Now, what to say? Why are they staring at me like that? Just say hello. Start with hello and then walk away. Just wanted to say hello...and then walk away. Okay, that's a good plan.

I opened my mouth to speak. Fire, and I mean fire from the lower planes of hell, scorched my throat. I grabbed my neck in confusion as the burning sensation billowed out through my mouth and my nostrils flared like a bellowing dragon. I was more amazed that no actual flames came out of my open mouth than I was at the quickly budding tears blurring my vision. I clutched my throat, trying to breathe, and bent over.

"Cyan, I do believe your maid is feeling ill," Minerva said with a touch of concern.

What is happening to me? I had to cough so badly, but I was afraid if I did, I might get sick. My stomach lurched and sweat broke out in my armpits. I had to wash down the blazing heat scorching my tongue and clogging my throat.

I lifted my glass to take another swig.

"Don't drink that!" Tae practically slammed into me. She wrenched the glass from my hands. There was a startled gasp from the fae around us. I would've asked her if she'd lost it if I had any sort of voice to speak with. Tae dangled the glass in front of my face, sloshing the drink.

When I turned to the people around me, I found Malachai. He had put himself between Minerva and me, his hand on the pommel of the saber poking out from his Mantle of Nightmare. Two of his vampires had moved in front of Lucien and Valia as well. Malachai's charcoal eyes studied me with a stony impassiveness that was unnerving.

Cyan gawked. "What in the name of Queen Minerva are you doing?"

Tae lifted the glass for them to see. It was a fluted crystal goblet meant for lighter drinks. The liquid inside was straw-yellow, like champagne. Something floated at the very bottom of the glass. It was a curled black pepper the size of my thumbnail.

"I tried to warn you," Tae said to me. "A little mischievous sprite dropped something in your drink when you were walking. It looks like a firecorn."

Minerva giggled. The sound of it was light as air, gay and filled with delight. Cyan shared her laugh at my expense, as did several others. Malachai moved to his wife's side once more, but I noticed his hand stayed near his belt. The vampires that had formed a barricade between me and Lucien were gone, slipping into the murky background once more.

Meanwhile, the firecorn continued to wreak havoc on my throat like an enslaved dragon trying to escape. A flittering tinkle of light zipped over my head. Bella twirled around Cyan, giggling like a cat's bell. She whispered something in Cyan's ear that made her split with laughter. One of Cyan's entourage handed Tae a glass of butterfly milk, which she helped me sip down.

It seemed I had bitten off more than I could chew with Bella. Perhaps it wasn't wise to start a feud with the sprite after all. I downed the milk as fast as I could. It cooled my throat immediately. I opened my mouth to speak, and a puff of smoke came out. Bella grabbed her belly and rolled in the air as she giggled.

I threw a hand over my mouth in embarrassment. Lucien was laughing too. Valia placed an overly familiar hand on his chest as she joined in. I felt queasy. Suddenly I was back in boarding school being picked on by the upper classmen all over again.

I glowered at Bella. The sprite stopped in her tracks and looked alarmed before promptly retreating. She zipped over the heads of nearby fae like a hurtling comet and disappeared into the crowd.

"Lady Alacore, don't get so offended," Cyan cooed. "Bella has been pulling pranks like that since the day she arrived at Starfire."

"You allow sprites to live in your palace?" Valia said with open disdain.

Cyan waved her hand dismissively. "You know how my father dotes on the lesser races."

"Speaking of lesser races," Valia said, looking pointedly at me. I wasn't an imbecile. It was clear she was handing me my cue to leave.

Cyan surprised me with a look of embarrassment. "Where are my manners? Queen Minerva, King Malachai, Lady Alacore is a guest staying at Starfire for the time being."

Minerva looked me up and down as if I were candy. "*You* are a guest of the House of Dawn?"

"Yes, though you'd hardly guess it with that"—Cyan circled her finger, trying to find the right words— "*outfit* she has on. Lady Alacore is not a maid but an esteemed guest of my father's."

Their scrutinous eyes bored into me. I could feel them exploring every inch of my clothing. Each of them wore the finest fabrics in the most fashionable cuts. My outfit cost a fraction of what Minerva must have paid for her ensemble. Add in the chocolate stain Persa's eclair had left on my blouse and I felt ten inches tall.

Cyan towered over me. Her golden vines and purple leafy hair were draped over her shoulders, showing off the vanilla bean flowers growing from them. She looked like a fashion goddess, and I was a mouse among angels. The worst part was the way Minerva, oh-so-friendly and compassionate Minerva, stared openly at my back. I doubt she cared what the back of my blouse looked like. What was more of interest to her was my lack of faerie wings.

The implication in her glare was evident. How could any fae without wings be invited to stay as a guest inside a royal palace?

Tae nudged me in the side. I finally found my senses. "It is a pleasure to meet all of you," I hurriedly blurted out. "I thought I would introduce myself since I'm going to be the new Warden of Willow's Edge." I took another quick swig of the butterfly milk to dull my burning tongue.

A look of recognition passed over Minerva's eyes. She squealed with delight. "Ah, so this is the woman our Prince Lucien spoke up for in court."

"I've been known to make worse decisions." Lucien's comment punctured me as surely as a blade through the ribs. I felt my body slowly deflating.

"Come now, son," Malachai intoned. I expected his voice to be harsh and deep, but it was the intonation of a seasoned orator. "Surely a guest of our host deserves a little more respect. We should be wishing her luck in her warden trials. I was saddened when news of your grandmother's death reached me, Miss Alacore."

"Oh, I…didn't know you were familiar with Rosalie," I said.

"We make it a point to know all those of the realm who help serve the needs of the people," Minerva answered for him.

"No matter how insignificant," Valia murmured.

"What was that?" I threw on a cheery smile. I've found the best way to cut through a bully's bullshit is to play dumb. "I'm sorry, I didn't hear you. That pepper must have really rattled me."

"I was simply agreeing with the queen." Valia flashed her false smile back.

"Well, I appreciate the notion, Your Majesty." I turned the conversation back to the king. "I'm honored you think I can live up to my grandmother's good name."

"Let us not leap to conclusions," Malachai said quite plainly. "I merely wished you luck on your endeavors. Luck which you will surely need, given your inferior upbringing among the humans."

It was a brutally honest thing to say and hit me like a slap in the face. Even Cyan looked astonished at the king's callous snipe.

"Don't look so surprised, dear girl," Minerva said with a beaming smile. "There are many suitable candidates for the wardenship of Willow's

Edge. You must realize this. Each house would like the honor to be represented in that esteemed position, and you, an outsider, have swooped in out of…well, out of nowhere. You who have no official allegiances to any great house. It is no wonder that Ambrose invited you to be his guest at the spring festival."

They think I'm only staying in the palace because Ambrose wants to curry favor with the new warden. Because that's how their minds work.

I saw Minerva's smile and kind demeanor for what it really was, a brand to be sold. *"Look at us, we are the happy successful ones. Join us and you too can be happy."* Which led me to the source of Malachai's hostility.

"And you think I wouldn't have had a shot at becoming warden if Lucien hadn't stuck up for me in court," I deduced aloud.

Lucien winced.

Malachai glowered at me.

Minerva's smile grew wider. Her teeth reminded me of a cunning panther, ready to pounce when I turned away. An uncomfortable silence hung between us, me and her too-white, too-perfect teeth. I needed some way out of this conversation.

"It is good to see you, *Prince* Lucien," I said more sheepishly than I would have liked. "Have you been enjoying the banquet?"

Lucien blinked at me emotionlessly. "That's a silly question, seeing as how we've not been here twenty minutes yet."

Cyan, Minerva, and Valia took great delight in his barb. It made me mad. Why was he speaking to me as if we hardly knew each other? It was one thing to throw on airs for his family's benefit, but it felt like he was being intentionally cruel.

"We mustn't laugh at Lanie's expense," Valia said. "I imagine she's trying her best. It must be a shock to find herself around so many civilized folk. She was raised by humans, after all." They shared another laugh at my expense.

"Oh my lord. Valia, is that you?" I said, feigning astonishment. "Why, I didn't even recognize you without your fishnets and bubble gum."

Their laughter died down at that. Valia turned red-faced. It was clear someone of her stature, as duchess to the Court of Shadows, wasn't supposed to be parading around provinces in goth attire. To them that was slumming it. I actually dug the goth vibe, but Valia was a bitch.

Malachai stared down at her in consternation. He didn't approve. An uncomfortable silence hung in the air.

Cyan cleared her throat. "Yes, well, Queen Minerva, have you seen the latest designs to come out of Ruby City?"

They fell into a group discussion on the latest fashions. Even Lucien joined in. They were all ignoring me, but I didn't care. Something else had caught my attention, and their conversation fell to the background.

It was a woman.

She shouldn't have stood out to me, but there was something about the way she moved through the crowd that I found odd. She was surrounded by fae, yet no one seemed to notice her. She cut through the crowd as if she were pantomiming the stealthy movements of a ninja. She took no action to greet anyone she slipped past, even when she slid between talking couples, and they didn't so much as blink at her presence.

What the hell am I looking at? Her gaze was singularly focused on something at the far end of the atrium. I followed her line of vision, and my breath caught in the back of my throat.

The object of her intense scrutiny was none other than Ambrose Amaryllis.

"Bye now," I murmured offhandedly as I quickly broke away from their gathering.

"What an odd girl," I heard Minerva say as I walked away.

"More like crude," Valia countered.

"Well, it can't be helped, you know," Cyan said. "Father opens his doors to all fae, deserving or not."

Their words slid off me like oil on water. I couldn't be bothered with their hoity-toity barbs. Why should I care if some queen or fashion mogul thought I mattered? I had bigger problems. Like why that woman was zeroing in on Ambrose. And what I was going to do to stop her.

At that moment she froze in place. I picked up my pace, hoping to close the distance between us.

Why did she stop? I looked for Ambrose. He was still standing near the waterfall, finishing a conversation with another water fae, but then he began heading back up to the balcony.

I looked back to where the woman had stopped.

And found her staring directly at me.

12

"**A**re you okay, Lanie?"

Tae's voice was tender. She thought the Court of Shadows royals had gotten under my skin. And in some ways, they had, but that wasn't the focus of my concern.

"Did you see where that woman went?" I asked, scanning the crowd to find her.

"Woman? What woman?" Tae looked back at Cyan and Minerva. They continued their conversation without a care for how their words may have stung me.

"Not them," I said offhandedly. "There was this woman. She was walking through the crowd."

"Shit," Tae said. "Did that evil little bitch put more than a pepper in your drink? If I get my hands on her—"

"I'm not seeing things," I insisted. "There was this lady. She was wearing a green dress, and she moved through the crowd like a ninja." I heard how it sounded and stopped talking. Maybe Tae was right. I was awfully stressed out.

A sound as loud as a gong rang out over the crowd. Ambrose was back on the balcony, facing his guests.

"The House of Dawn is honored to have so many of our brethren in attendance this grand afternoon. Each year we hope to bring a little light to your life. To help us celebrate this year's festival, we have the honor of presenting the vocal mastery of Lady Eloriil." He pointed to the koi ponds.

A jubilant ruckus broke out at the mention of the singer's name.

"Lady Eloriil is really here?" Tae squealed.

Geraldine stood at the top of the waterfall overlooking the koi ponds. Birds flitted around the leaves of Starfire's smaller interior branches. A hush fell over the crowd. Their anticipation was palpable, a collective hunger to hear the majestic melody of Ambrose's guest singer.

Ambrose lifted something for all to see. He held his palm flat, facing us, with a shard of ametrine balanced between his thumb and pointer finger. Light prismed through it, a beam of purple and yellow angled directly at the center of the koi pond at the base of the waterfall. The surface bubbled, a frothy churning white eruption that grew higher and higher in a column of water. It was an impossibility of physics, a straight column that rose fifteen feet from the pond. Along with that movement came the growing intensity of a single note.

The note struck me in its purity. It was the truest sound of music I had ever heard. Its resonance was deep and somber, with the liquid intensity of whales calling to one another across the wide ocean depths. It was the gasp of a child drawing its first breath and also the rumbling at the precipice of a volcano. It was a mysterious note that enveloped me until I no longer saw the column of water. I became nothing. Any trace of where I ended and the song began had vanished.

This was how Lady Eloriil began her ballad, by pulling us into her vision through the power of her voice. I shook my head as I realized what was happening. The fae around me were standing still, their eyes closed and heads craning toward her song. She was a vibrant light that resembled a mix of jellyfish and manta ray floating inside the column, which had now grown to be a curtain of water stretching the length of the pond. Koi swam around the base of the curtain, their own eyes glazed over as they too were lost in the power of her music.

Tae's hand squeezed mine. "Just close your eyes," she reassured me.

I trusted Tae. I shut my eyes and let myself fall into the water syren's spell. The song wrapped around me, penetrating every inch of my flesh. This was more than just seeing images that weren't there. I was immersed in the vision, lost in the depths of the ocean, overlooking a city of splendor. Seashell towers, crystal monoliths, coral palaces—it was an underwater civilization. A dome covered sections of the city, where the air-breathers lived in harmony with their water brethren. Lights from a million souls touched me from the fae below as they sang a harmonious song of unity.

To be touched by that music was a feeling of bliss unlike any other I'd experienced. This was community. This was the balance between the fae and nature. It felt so right.

The music shifted. I was now inside the city, as one of the revelers. We were taking part in a celebration of spring.

A shadow loomed over the city from above.

Screams. Everywhere there was screaming.

The enemy was there above us, massive and serpentine, the leviathan of our destruction. The giants had sent their kraken to punish the fae. That evil descended like a falling redwood, smashing through the dome as easily as tearing through paper. I was terrified to the point where I thought I must be going insane. My death was upon me. The ocean roared as it burst through the opening. The mouth of the leviathan fell over us, growing larger and larger, until gnashing teeth and raging waters were all I could see.

The music pulled back.

I gasped for air.

My bare knees were freezing where I knelt in the snow. I was somewhere else, a city atop a mountain. I held a child in my arms. She was dying. Oh Goddess no, my child was dying. My tears were salty, freezing on my cheeks. All around me the world was chaos. Giants were destroying the city. Clubs which were no more than stripped trunks of trees smashed through rooftops. Eager hands stole fae from their beds. Mouths gnashed on their flesh. A shadow loomed over me. I gazed into the face of terror.

Why was the syren showing me this? I did not want to feel this terror. I did not want to see these horrors.

A giant foot slammed down over me.

Then the bursting of sound, a cacophony of music as if a full orchestra had arrived.

I was too lost in the spell to escape. I could only let it carry me through Lady Eloriil's story. Bursting colors like fireworks went off directly in the center of the giant's breast. The behemoth howled in agony and fell backward away from me. The earth shook as he collapsed into the baker's shop.

They were coming to save us, flying through the sky on black ravens, barbed lances ready to skewer the giants. The spell had come from a man who looked like an older, more alien version of Malachai. This was his father, the great war general Machius.

The scene shifted back to the ocean. Fae and droba sped through the waters on the backs of dolphins. The leviathan was running away, its body riddled with spears and hooked lances.

Then I was back in the mountain city. The constant transporting was making me dizzy. The ground was burned, scarred by war. A drop of blood spilled into the center of the cracked earth. I moved closer, a sprite shaking my wings to release the magic they harbored. The glittery dust twinkled. A small sapling peeked out at the sun. The music grew to a crescendo and I was spinning in the air. The world changed rapidly; the passage of time accelerated. The scarred land was restored, a forest budding where so many brave souls had laid down their lives.

I held a baby in my arms, looking over the landscape as the fae in the city below turned their heads toward the sun and rejoiced.

As the song faded, I stood dumbfounded, surrounded by fae who were still in the trance. The syren's message was clear. The giantkin war had taken a massive toll on all of fae kind. It would be indelibly imprinted into their DNA from now until the end of days. But through that tragedy there was something else. There was rebirth.

I wiped tears from my cheeks and marveled as I came out of the trance. Something about my unicorn blood helped me form a resistance to other magic. I'd realized it after breaking Charlie's captor's illusion.

That was when I saw the woman once more. She was halfway up the steps toward Ambrose, except she was standing still. Cyan blocked her path, the two of them in the middle of a heated discussion. I gazed around to see if anyone else had noticed them. The only other person out of the trance was Valia. She didn't notice me. Her eyes were filled with vehemence and locked on Ambrose.

The syren's song ended on a drawn-out note that fell over the span of two minutes to a soft whisper. In fact, I wasn't certain when it was over because the ghost of her song lingered on in the air around us.

Tae squeezed my hand. She had tears in her eyes, but she was smiling at me.

"That was beautiful," she said.

"The woman," I said. "She's there on the steps."

But the woman was gone. Just like earlier, she had disappeared without a trace. I looked back at Valia. Cyan was standing beside her, calmly speaking with Minerva about the syren's rendition.

Valia, however, was still staring at Ambrose with a look I knew only too well. It was the same look I had seen in Brom's eyes the night he stalked me through the shadows of my grandmother's basement. It could only mean one thing.

Valia wanted to murder Ambrose Amaryllis.

"Valia Medi'tu is not trying to murder the patriarch of the House of Dawn," Tae said. I had searched for the mysterious woman Cyan was arguing with but hadn't seen her again that night. So, we'd gone back to my room after the banquet ended.

"I'm telling you, she was staring daggers at Ambrose," I insisted, setting the glass of wine I'd brought up from the banquet on the vanity.

"That doesn't mean she's going to assassinate him," Tae said. "Lots of people have given someone a dirty look before. It doesn't mean they're all killing each other. Oh, this is a beautiful wall garden. The House of Dawn knows how to live it up. I always wondered what the inside of Starfire looks like. This room is magnificent."

I fished some solavi petals I'd plucked from Ambrose's garden out of my skirt pocket. There were three of them. I snapped them to release their juices like an aloe plant and dropped them in my wine. "No, it was different than that. You didn't see her, Tae. I'm telling you, there's something off with that girl."

Tae stroked a finger across the lily lamp. Her eyes twinkled when the light grew brighter. She was like a kid in a candy shop. "Are you sure your mistrust doesn't stem from something else?"

I scrunched up my face in disgust. "What? Lucien? I couldn't care less about that pompous egotistical jerkwad." I stirred my finger in the wine to mix it with the petals, ignoring Tae's giggle. "Did it bother me that after not seeing or hearing from him in weeks, when I finally bumped into the asshole, he totally snubbed me? Of course. But am I going to pine after him like some wounded lamb?"

"Shit no," Tae answered for me. "Especially when you've got the hots for someone else."

"Ouch," I said, turning to face her. "I'm over Lobo. I barely even think about him."

Tae arched her brow at me and smirked. "I was talking about a certain tall studly bachelor named Silas."

Heat rushed to my cheeks. I cut across the room to the bathtub and wiped my wet finger on a towel. "You saw me with him? But, I don't even know anything about Silas."

"You do agree he's yummy though, right?"

I grinned to myself. I felt a flutter in my belly when I thought of him kissing my hand in greeting the night before. I had to admit the idea of being with him was exhilarating. "I can't be with anyone but Lucien, since I have this damn curse."

A week after leaving Willow's Edge, I'd come up with a theory why I could have sex with Lucien. My curse kept me from being intimate with literally anyone else. At first I wondered if maybe that was because he was supposed to be my one true love or some bullshit. However, that notion felt too naïve even for me. The answer had to be something simpler. Then it hit me. Many fae have different magical abilities. Usually those are defined by their genealogy, but in some cases other powers manifest. I believed Lucien was one of those cases and that he had the ability to negate magic.

It made sense. If he could dampen magical abilities, that could potentially muffle my curse.

"But if you could…?" Tae left the question floating in the air. "Mmm, this smells good. What, are you a bartender now?"

I spun around. Tae had my wine glass to her lips. "That's mine!"

She almost dropped the glass she was so startled. I cut back across the room in a dash and snatched the glass from her fingers.

"Sorry," she said. "We share drinks all the time. I didn't think you'd mind."

"I don't," I quickly said. "I just…don't want *anyone* but me touching this drink." I said it loudly and clearly. "Don't worry about it, just tell me more about Silas."

Tae frowned at me. The evening breeze came through the window and tossed her dark locks across her face. She scanned the room suspiciously, then continued speaking. "Everyone knows Silas Amaryllis. He's a prominent playboy. I don't blame you for wanting to jump his bones. I would too. He mostly hangs out in the human realm, lives in a palazzo in Capri."

"That explains the Italian fashion sense," I said, setting the drink back down on the vanity. "So he's just another spoiled rich boy, huh?"

"I guess. I heard he was kinda kicked out of the family when he was just a kid. He's always been up to shenanigans that a 'high and mighty' man like Ambrose would frown upon. Huge parties, gambling, sordid affairs, getting himself arrested for public drunkenness, even vandalizing the town square."

I snorted, picturing the slick Silas getting a mugshot. "Sounds like a human frat boy."

"Exactly." Tae snapped her fingers and pointed at me. "And as you can imagine, that sort of thing doesn't play well when you're part of one of the four Great Houses. Reputations and all."

That sounded like a lame reason to exile Silas from his family. "How come he doesn't look more like the others? Like all *planty* and stuff? He's a blossom fae, right?"

"It's a glamour. Most fae use them in one way or another. I bet Silas made himself look less like a blossom to peeve off Ambrose."

I kept replaying Valia's face in my mind. "I'm going to have to skip my meeting with Uriel tomorrow. I know you don't think there's anything to it, but I need to trail Valia and see what she's up to. Plus, there was that other woman who was arguing with Cyan.... You know, now that I think about it Cyan seemed pretty chummy with Valia. What if the three of them are in it together?"

Tae looked doubtful. "It sounds like a weak lead to miss a day with the gladewarden over."

"I can't risk Ambrose's life on your doubt."

"You can't afford to get kicked out of the warden trials either," Tae said. "Look, if you believe Valia's a suspect that much, I'll keep my eye on her tomorrow morning while you're gone."

"Really?"

"If it'll give you peace of mind so you can focus on the trials, then yes."

I grabbed Tae and hugged her. "You're the best."

She laughed and hugged me back. It felt good to know there was someone else I could count on. I hadn't even realized how unmoored I'd been feeling until Tae arrived.

Our happy moment was disrupted by a choking sound.

Bella was holding her throat with both hands, coughing in a sputtering fit as she tried to spit out the drink she'd just stolen from my wine glass. Her teeth and lips were stained purple from my concoction.

I laughed at her. "I knew she wouldn't be able to resist stealing my drink," I said to Tae. "That's the thing about solavi flowers. The juice from their leaves smells like honey, but it's sour as an unripe lemon's ass and it stains your mouth."

Bella stuck out her tongue. "Blech, big faerie's drink is gross juice." She shot me a pouting look and zipped straight past us out the open window. I laughed so hard tears rolled down my cheeks.

"You really shouldn't mess with sprites," Tae said as her laughter died down. "They can be pretty devious."

"Either way, I still got rid of the little troublemaker." I closed the slatted window shutters and locked the latch in place. "Wait, what was it you wanted to talk to me about?"

"I think I found the answer to getting rid of your curse." The soft glow of the lily lamp lit Tae's face from the side as she grinned. "It's called the Sphynx."

13

had a restless night of sleep. Not because of Bella. I believed the sprite had taken her leave of my room, but the next morning I found her curled up on my chest again. I gently shifted her to the blanket and sat up on the edge of the bed. I tried to recall the nightmares that had plagued me through the night, but they were already slipping away like dust on the wind.

Butterflies rested among the ivy and flowers of my room's wall garden. It was a new day, filled with possibilities, even if I was exhausted.

Tae's revelation had my gears spinning in overdrive. A Sphynx. It was a mystical creature that would grant one wish to anyone clever enough to seek it out.

I snorted. It sounded like the stuff of fairy tales. Then again, what about my life hadn't lately? If I could discover the location of the Sphynx's temple, there was a chance it could lift my curse. I imagined a world where I was no longer bound by that insidious blight. How would my life be different if I was free to be with whoever I chose? Sex with Lucien was delicious and certainly scratched that itch, but he wasn't exactly my first choice. I could bare it all to Lobo, in all senses of the word. Fully open myself to him with no reason to hide the truth. Would it make a difference? Try as I might to think of that possibility, my mind kept wandering to Silas. I imagined the things we could do if I was freed.

Get your mind out of the gutter. I have to figure out who's trying to murder Ambrose. Nobody was going to hurt that old man so long as I was breathing. Then, instead of the bounty, I'd ask Ambrose to reveal the location of the Sphynx. Tae was certain he would know the answer.

And if he doesn't? I worried. I couldn't think like that. I at least had to try. Besides, the most important thing was to make sure no one laid a finger on Ambrose. That trumped any warden title or Sphynx wishes. *After that I'll ask him to reveal the Sphynx's location, and if he can't, then the money we originally agreed on will still be useful.*

I mulled it over as I made the long walk to Uriel's cottage for my next trial. A heavy rain had blown in off the coast, and I was soaked by the time I arrived. Through the rain and my morning chores I couldn't shake the idea of the Sphynx from my mind.

"Are you daydreaming again?" Uriel snarled.

I flinched. She'd had me spend the morning setting up a canopy near her fire pit. I was still soaked from the rain and trying to dry off, rubbing my frigid hands together over the fire pit.

"I wasn't daydreaming."

Uriel didn't look up from her carving. Her bony fingers moved deftly as she whittled a piece of wood into a roaring effigy. She didn't bother explaining what she was carving it for. It was none of my business, much like the rest of her life. The rain pitter-pattered on the stretched canopy over our heads.

"Oh, my mistake. I'm just a foolish old woman who doesn't know any better," Uriel said sweetly. "Surely you can prove me wrong by repeating what I was just saying."

"You were saying that you're a sweet old lady," I tried for levity.

"Do you take pleasure in wasting my time?"

There was no sense in trying to lie to her. I bowed my head in shame. "I'm sorry, Gladewarden. I didn't get much sleep last night."

Uriel scoffed, flicking a peeled section of the wood into the fire. "I'd imagine not, with you gallivanting around the royal court all day."

"You knew I was at the palace?" I hadn't seen Uriel at the banquet. That wasn't saying much, considering there had to be a thousand or more fae in attendance. Still, I had a hard time picturing Uriel leaving her stone cottage in the woods to attend some fancy spring celebration banquet and hobnobbing with elite fae nobility. I could just picture her grabbing someone like Cyan by the ear and bringing her down to her level to scold her.

"It's not what it looks like," I said. "I've only moved up there to help someone in need."

"The only thing that lot of pompous blowhards *need* is a swift kick in the arse," Uriel said.

I shook my head and remained adamant. "He needs my help."

"Hmm," Uriel grumbled. "Well…listen up, I'm not going to say it a third time."

I sat up and forced my wandering thoughts to the back of my mind.

"For your next trial, you will retrieve a chŏra," Uriel said offhandedly.

The wind whipped up, sizzling raindrops in the fire. "That must be a fae flower. I've never heard of a chŏra before. Where can I find one?"

"The chŏra is a rare quill that only grows once every fifteen years. I can make good use of it for the betterment of the Tides. One will bloom tomorrow morning. You have less than eighteen hours to formulate a plan for how you will retrieve the quill and deliver it to me. If you fail in this task, you will prove that you are unfit to take on the mantle of Warden and will have failed the trials."

What the ever-loving fuck? No pressure, lady. My stomach felt tied in knots. This was serious. "I won't fail," I said earnestly. Plants were my thing. If there was a chŏra quill out there ready to bloom on some flower, I would deliver it safely to Uriel's withered hands. "Where can I find this blossom?"

"There is only one place a chŏra quill can grow." Uriel set the carved effigy on her lap. The flickering fire threw grotesque shadows across her face. "You must retrieve it from the tail of a manticore."

Has she completely lost her mind? I wondered as I walked through the quiet halls of the palace. It seemed Geraldine's entire staff had moved to the atrium, swarming like an army of ants in preparation for that evening's Wyld Hunt. The House of Dawn had planned a scavenger hunt for day two of the spring festival, and their guests would be arriving in less than two hours. I should have been in my room getting ready. Unfortunately, thanks to the bomb Uriel dropped on my plans, I was searching for the library instead.

I felt overwhelmed. I already had my hands full trying to prevent Ambrose's murder. This would hopefully have the added benefit of providing me with the whereabouts of the Sphynx to lift my curse. Now I had to add outwitting a manticore to that list? It was enough to make me scream. The most I knew about manticores was that they were fearsome predators with the body of a lion and the face of a man. The idea of sneaking into the lair of a creature I barely knew anything about struck me as about as smart as running headfirst into a wall. At least Uriel had charted the way to the manticore's lair for me on a folded parchment.

"You're not going to tell me anything else about the manticore?" I had asked.

"A warden will oft find themselves thrown into dangerous situations with only their cunning and perseverance to guide them."

It wasn't much of an answer. In fact, it sounded like some sanctimonious bullshit. "And what if the manticore catches me?"

"You will either deliver the chŏra to me or you will fail your trials," Uriel said calmly.

All I could do was shrug. There wasn't much left to say. I knew trying to reason with her was pointless. She spent the rest of our time together explaining how to safely transport the chŏra quill once I retrieved it from the manticore's tail. After that, I ran all the way back to the palace. There was no time to spare.

She's just doing this because she thinks my attention is wavering. She imagines I'm up here hobnobbing with nobles and eating figgy pudding.

My only real hope was to find the library and pray Nuala had a book on manticores. A familiar archway caught my eye. I hustled through it and found myself in Ambrose's art gallery. Drapes covered the windows, obscuring the statues and paintings in shadows.

They do that to keep the sunlight from aging the paintings, I thought, remembering my many trips through the Metropolitan Museum. Paints used to be made by hand. These days, in human societies, premade paints were typically purchased at a store. But before shopping malls and discount art supply stores were a thing, if you wanted to express yourself on canvas, you had to learn how to make the medium yourself. A color like green was typically laced with copper. You expose copper to UV, and over time it'll become a brownish hue. Not too bad if you wanted your spring meadow to turn into a dying field of dried straw, but otherwise not so great.

Either way it's good I found the gallery. If I remember correctly, the library is close by.

Dim light from the hallway behind me illuminated the room enough for me to move through it. The map I'd eyed the first day was all grey without the light. I stopped to study it. The surface was crinkled parchment. If I looked closely, I could see watercolors had been used to stain the ocean in blues and greens. There was the Tides. And to the west, the Whispering Woods. I found the general area Uriel had plotted out for me. A tiny scrawl caught my eye, and I had to squint to make it out in the dark. It was the outline of a lion with jagged teeth.

Shit. Even the map showed where the manticore lived.

Something moved in the corner of my eye. I twisted around quickly and gasped. The silhouettes of statues looked like gathered visitors. I couldn't make out their faces in the shadows, and their unreadable expressions stared blankly into the void. I found it unnerving how they silently watched me. I moved further down the gallery, wanting to put distance between me and their lurking forms. I passed painting after painting, trying to recall if I had seen them before.

Am I lost? I thought this gallery was a straight shot. Last time we were in and out of here in a couple minutes. It seemed like the gallery stretched on forever, and I was starting to get nervous. I gradually became paranoid and began to think someone was following me. I could feel eyes tracking my movement through the gallery. Every so often, I would stop and peer over my shoulder, certain someone was going to be standing there. All I found were more statues masked in darkness. I picked up my pace, eager to return to the lighted hallways.

How long have I been in this damn gallery? It feels like hours.

I yelped when I came around a corner and found myself face to face with a mermaid statue in the center of the walkway. It shouldn't have startled me so. The statue itself was beautiful, her scales gilded with gold, but I was feeling overly anxious.

Perfect, I saw this when Geraldine took me through. I must be close to the exit now. Not that I'll have any time to hit the library anymore. I was certain too much time had elapsed. The hunt would be underway soon. How was I going to learn anything about the manticore *and* go on a silly scavenger hunt?

I could skip it... No, I have to attend the hunt. What if I'm not there and that weird woman shows up again? Nobody but me seemed to be able to see her before. If something happens to Ambrose while I've got my nose buried in a book...

Something moved behind me.

Stop being so jumpy, you big baby.

I turned around to show myself that no one was there. A statue of a small girl was just behind me in a row of sculptures. She had her hands behind her back as if playfully hiding something. Light from the exit cut a diagonal slit across her serene smile. Her face was the height of innocence.

However, the tall form beside her was not.

The figure shifted slightly, trying to slip behind the neighboring statue.

"Oh shit," I gasped.

The shape burst from behind the sculptures, headed directly for me. I spun and bolted through the exit. I ran as fast as my legs could carry me. Something crashed into a wall behind me, followed by a curse. I kept running. There was no looking back. I couldn't think. All I could do was dash wildly through the halls of the palace.

I blindly turned a corner, through an open door. I didn't recognize this path. I was lost! The hall I entered was as dark as the gallery had been. There was no time to double back the way I had come. I could hear labored breathing fast on my heels. I had to keep moving forward and pray that I would find my way to safety.

There was a set of stairs on my right. I sprinted down them and tripped. My body flew forward, arms outstretched. There wasn't even time to brace for the impact. I saw the floor rising up to meet me, heard the clapping footsteps above.

Something green plucked me from the air. It was hideous. Yellow eyes, long hooked nose, stringy black hair. It was a troll!

For a moment I was convinced I was back in Droll's cabin. *I never escaped. I've been here the whole time. Everything I thought happened in the last few weeks—the Tides, the Whispering Woods, Uriel—it's all been a dream he forced me to live through with that wicked hand mirror of his.*

But the troll's hat wasn't the same as Droll's crooked crown. It was a white chef's cap that flopped to one side. Also, this troll was much younger than Droll. He held me firmly, my feet dangling in the air.

"You almost took a bad spill there, missus," the troll said.

I screamed for help and beat his chest with my fists. "Let me down, let me go!"

The troll looked shocked. "Please don't scream," he begged.

I kicked my legs and tried to grab his hair.

The troll set me down on the ground. "I didn't mean to scare you," he insisted.

"Get away from me, you ugly horrible monster," I screamed as I darted around him and bolted down the hall. I left the troll standing there, gaping at me, as I turned the corner.

I continued to run blindly through the halls, running to get away from the troll, running to get away from the man in the shadows, running out of my mind with terror. I knew deep inside the troll couldn't have been the one who chased me. He was too big to be the shape that had been huddled behind the statue of the little girl in the gallery. The troll saved me from my tumble down the stairs. I felt ashamed of how I had treated him. But it didn't matter. The wounds in my mind were too raw for me to behave rationally.

I finally saw a familiar face. It was Persa. I ran up to her in a fervor.

"Oh, Lady Alacore," Persa said as I stopped in front of her. "What in the world has happened to you?"

I tried to explain but all I could do was sob. I realized how I must look, my hair disheveled, tears staining my face, my hands trembling.

Persa wrapped her arms around me and let me cry on her pretty dress. "There, there. It's okay," she said. "Just breathe. I've got you. Nothing's going to happen to you."

"Lost…" I managed between uncontrollable gasps as I fought to regain my composure.

"Starfire can be a tricky place to navigate," Persa explained with sympathy.

It wasn't just that I was lost. I wouldn't be a sobbing mess over losing my way in a palace. I needed her to understand everything that had happened. "There was…in the shadows…and…the troll." Damn it, why couldn't I catch my breath?

"Did Henri spook you?" Persa asked. "He's a harmless troll, I promise. Henri is grandfather's chef. He's the one who made the ogre toast you liked so much yesterday. I know he looks dreadful, but he really is very sweet."

"I was so mean to him," I sobbed, ashamed of myself.

Persa frowned sympathetically. She produced a handkerchief from somewhere and handed it to me so I could clean up my face. A footman appeared. The color drained from his face when he saw me clinging to Persa and sobbing.

"Lady Alacore has had a fright," Persa explained. The footman offered to help me to my room, but I clung to Persa. I wanted to stop shaking. I didn't want to stand there making a fool of myself, but I kept seeing that shape coming for me from the shadows.

"Thank you, Falduin, but I think it would be better if I escort Lady Alacore to her room myself." Persa rubbed my back as she leaned down to look me in the eye. "Does that sound good?"

I didn't know what I'd done to deserve people like Tae and Persa in my life, but I couldn't have been more grateful for her offer.

So much for my quick trip to the library. I knew the troll wasn't the one chasing me. He'd definitely saved me from a pretty nasty tumble down the stairs. But that left me with a problem. If Henri wasn't the bad guy, then who was chasing me through the palace?

And what do they want from me?

ae thought the streets on the northern side of town looked awfully desolate. Every fae that lived in the Tides would be headed up to the palace by now. Opening ceremonies for the Wyld Hunt would be kicking off soon, and those not present from the beginning would be disqualified. It was a shame to miss it. The House of Dawn threw some of the best scavenger hunts she'd ever been to.

Even better than the Summer Court's famed Crystal Dash, she thought. *Oh well, no fun for me tonight.* She'd given Lanie her word that she'd keep an eye on Valia. A promise she'd thought pointless until around an hour ago, when the daughter of the Medi'tu dynasty suddenly slipped out of the palace.

At first Tae had followed her out of a sheer sense of duty. But as they neared town, Valia's behavior became more and more suspicious. It was the way she lifted her heavy cowl over her head, hiding her face from passersby on the cliff steps. And the way she kept checking over her shoulder, as if to be sure she wasn't being followed. These weren't the actions of someone on a casual stroll through town.

It can't be because she senses me following her, Tae knew.

Decades working on her side gig had made sure of that. She had been on more espionage missions than she could count, and not once in all her years had her quarry suspected her. Well, maybe once. There was the Borloff affair. But she'd been dealing with a werewolf that time. Those bastards could smell a mile away, and that afternoon the storm winds had shifted against her. But Valia Medi'tu was no wolf. She was a spoiled shadow fae who just happened to be from a militaristic family of oppressors.

No, she's up to something. Wouldn't you know it, one of Lanie's hunches proves fruitful yet again.

Tae snorted, ducking behind the corner of a seashell building as she let Valia gain more distance from her. Lanie was such an odd duck. She reminded Tae a lot of her late grandmother. *Rosalie was the same way. She never would have left Ambrose's side if she thought he was in danger.* You could have been the worst fiend or the brightest angel, and it wouldn't have mattered to her. Rosalie would help in any way she could to turn someone's life around or save them from catastrophe. Just like she'd done for Tae once upon a time. When Taewyn had given up on the world and hit rock bottom, it was Rosalie who was there to pull her back from the abyss. One day she'd have to tell Lanie the story of how she met her grandmother.

She could fill volumes with what Lanie Alacore didn't know about her. It had never bothered Tae that she had to keep her spy work a secret from the people in her life, so why was it different with Lanie Alacore? Somehow it felt like a betrayal, keeping Lanie in the dark about her other life.

She'd thought briefly, when they first met, that she must be in love with the girl. Lanie was certainly attractive enough, even if she didn't think so of herself. In the end Tae had decided that wasn't it at all. She liked Lanie a lot, but not in that way. Though she wouldn't mind a casual romp now and again.

Tae had no family. Like Rosalie before her, Lanie had become the closest thing to family Tae knew. She was like the sister Tae had always wanted, or maybe a best friend. It was confusing to care about someone so much in such a short time. She wondered if it had anything to do with their near-death at the changeling's hands. Such experiences were known to bring people closer together, a shared bond formed in survival.

Tae let the thoughts slide away to focus on the task at hand. She checked to be sure her bracelet was clasped around her wrist. With it, she would be unrecognizable. The bracelet was enchanted to cast a glamour over her, a vision of a different woman. It was a gift from her masters. This way, if anyone ever did spot Tae tailing them, they'd be unable to give an accurate description of her.

She waited a full minute before slipping across the street, then deftly beat a path down another alleyway between two conch shell buildings and peeked around the corner.

The ocean's salty spray lingered in the air and on her lips. They were close to the docks. Valia was nearby. Tae could feel the heat of her body. It was one of the few talents succubi possessed. Tae found her quarry across the street, standing in front of a large wooden building at the mouth of the harbor.

The droning of insect wings came from the south. Tae instinctively tucked herself against the building. Valia slipped beside a stack of crates. There were no guardians in town this afternoon. All the gecko riders had gone up to the palace for the festivities. Without fae in town, there was no need for guardians to protect against dragonfly attacks.

Tae remained perfectly still as the fifteen-foot-long insect flew overhead. Dragonflies reacted to movement. They were deadly hunters, and even the overly confident Valia knew better than to stay out in the open where it might spot her. The dragonfly scoured the land for food with its compound eyes as it zipped overhead.

Tae waited until she no longer heard its wings before peering around the corner again. Valia had moved up the front steps of the building in front of a wooden door.

The long building was a warehouse, probably used to store cargo coming in from ships. It blended into the nautical structures around it, with lichen growing on its ocean face. The wooden panels were dyed a cerulean blue that matched the sky. Wood wasn't the material of choice among the homes in the Tides, but seashells large enough to be a warehouse were in short supply. And the lumber used for such a structure would have come from the depths of the ocean, in the forests of the trench. Underwater trees were very rare, their wood more impervious than some stones. It was the perfect material for a storehouse.

But what was Valia doing at a warehouse in the first place? She was the daughter of a nobleman. The Medi'tu family controlled one of the largest military forces in the Court of Shadows. They weren't merchants who needed to catalog inventory before it was loaded on a ship and sent to the bazaar.

For that matter, no ships would be running today, with the entire town focused on the spring festival.

As Tae pondered the oddity, someone opened the door of the warehouse from within. Valia checked up and down the deserted street. Her eyes swept past Tae's hiding spot. Tae tucked herself behind the crates in a flash, catching her breath. When she poked her head back up a few seconds later, Valia was entering the warehouse.

Tae dashed out of the alley and cut across the street. She dipped around the side of the long building, down another alley. More barrels and crates were stacked against this building. She navigated around them until she found a window. She was careful peeking inside, lifting her head up slowly. A fast movement would draw even the laziest of eyes.

I was wrong, this isn't a storehouse at all.

It was a shipyard. Mast sails were stretched across wooden pilings. The sails would generally be repaired on their ships, but these were meant to be sold as new sails. They would be prepared with solar oils and enchanted by the finest spellsmiths so they could carry their ship far over the clouds.

There was also a masthead close by in the figure of a paladin, her wooden mace raised to point the way of the bow. Half of her smooth features were pitted with fresh markings, the carving spools looking like pitted clay. She was unfinished, the work of sculpting her set aside for the festival.

Valia stood in front of the masthead, engaged with a tall man. He wore her family crest on the shoulder of his jacket, the symbols of a closed fist crossed with a blade. *That's odd. The Medi'tu people tend to wear their military gear openly.* They were quite proud of their military heritage. However, where most of them generally wore black armor, the man Valia spoke to was wearing a duster. The black jacket draped down to his knees and matched a wide-brimmed hat that did a good job of hiding his eyes.

Damn, I can't hear anything they're saying from here. Dawn glass was renowned for its beauty as well as its durability. Unfortunately, that durability also made it nearly soundproof. *I should really learn how to read lips.* She had thought the same thing many times in the past. Reading lips would give her an edge on these little spying escapades. But when would she find the time? And who could she trust to teach her? If anyone suspected she was capable of reading lips, it might draw too many questions, attention she could ill afford.

Valia looked hostile, but that was nothing new. *She always looks like someone just stole her favorite toy.*

The man shuffled his feet. He stooped his shoulders and trained his eyes on the floor. His body language said he was being berated. Valia curled her lips in disgust. She opened her cloak and produced a wrapped box, then handed the package to the man while continuing to berate him. He slipped it inside his duster and bowed. Tae wished she could make out what they were saying. Valia was already headed for the front door.

Tae ducked down behind the barrels, watching the road all the while.

"…and don't fuck it up this time," Valia scolded as the front door opened. Tae couldn't see the entrance from her hiding spot, but a few seconds later, Valia crossed in front of the alleyway as she marched back up the street the way she had come.

That left Tae with a serious dilemma. Was it better to keep trailing Valia as she'd promised Lanie? Or should she try and track the man in the duster to glean some insight into what Valia had delivered to him?

What if he's a hitman she's hired to assassinate Ambrose? Tae felt a moment of panic. Whatever she was going to do, she needed to act fast. Valia would already be far up the road, and in a few minutes the man would be gone too.

Tae stood up, slowly peeking back inside the warehouse. The man was still where she'd last seen him. He had his back to the window and was smoking a pipe. *Probably needs to calm his nerves after his run-in with Miss Perfect. Good, I'll wait until he leaves and then trail the fucker.*

"Hmm, there's a little peeping Tom out here, Rovio," a man's voice called over the crashing waves.

Tae spun to find a shadow fae towering over her in the alleyway. He was a broad-shouldered brute. She cursed herself for not checking the perimeter. Naturally Valia's man would have a lookout for any reasonable sort of operation. Tae had underestimated Valia's capability.

She glanced back at the road. If she moved fast enough, maybe she could outrun him.

"Oh, it's a little lost sparrow," the man with the duster said as he blocked her escape route.

What the hell? How did he hear his partner through that glass? And how the heck did he get out here so quick?

Rovio looked Tae up and down, then made a show of cracking his knuckles. "Fexil, let's see if we can't get our birdie to sing for us, eh?"

After Persa escorted me back to my room, it took me a while to recover from my anxiety attack. She offered to stay with me, but I assured her I was better at dealing with stuff like that on my own. It was a relief to find Bella wasn't there.

Tae had left a black dress for me in my room. It was gorgeous, with spaghetti straps and an open corset back. I felt a little silly that all I had to wear on my feet were sneakers, but hopefully nobody would notice. I had just enough time to gather myself and slip into the dress with before Geraldine came to fetch me for my check in with Ambrose. The private garden looked even lovelier in the full afternoon sunlight, which caught in the crystal gazebo and laid a beam of rainbow light across my lap. Ambrose sat across from me, thoughtfully drinking his tea while Gizmitt lay on the cushion, pressing his back against Ambrose's thigh as he purred, perfectly content with the world. The ceramic cup he'd filled for me was warming my hands.

"I understand you've been having a tricky time dealing with one of Starfire's sprites?" he asked.

It caught me off guard to have Bella brought up. When Geraldine had summoned me from my room, I naturally assumed Ambrose was looking for a report on my progress. "Bella's nothing I can't handle," I said, tossing aside the problem.

"That is good." He was such a somber man. "And of our little problem? Have you any success to report?"

I sucked in the air. Was Ambrose expecting results this quickly? Though I'd spent the last day and a half in his palace, I felt like I'd gotten nowhere. "I watched your guests closely yesterday and tried to speak with some of them as well."

He gave a short nod of acknowledgment. "And have you any leads?"

My insides felt like they were being stretched in all the wrong ways. *What am I supposed to say to him?* "Yeah, I think your daughter might be the one who wants to kill you. Either that or her chum Valia."

No way, I can't say that. If I decided that someone of his own blood was responsible, I'd better have some damn good evidence to back up my claim. What I needed was definitive proof. If I could figure out who Cyan's mysterious ally was, then I was certain I could uncover the truth. Then there was also Valia. *Tae just thinks I'm being jealous, but she didn't see the way Valia looked at Ambrose. That wasn't a casual dirty look between rival houses.*

"There were a few things that jumped out to me," I finally said. "I'm going to chase down those leads tonight and try to get to the heart of the matter."

"I see." Ambrose sounded resigned. My answer wasn't what he was hoping for. Everyone saw him as this powerhouse head of state. All I saw was a deeply distraught old man doing his best to keep his emotions in check. It was frustrating that anyone could feel such a heavy burden of responsibility toward their people that they would put their own life in jeopardy.

"Why don't you just cancel the spring festival?" I blurted.

I knew it was the wrong thing to say when I saw Geraldine's face drop in an aghast scowl from his place by the garden entrance. Ambrose, however, remained poised. The only hint that he found my remark distasteful was a tiny twitch at the corner of his mouth. He took a small sip from his cup. He always drank his tea as if he savored every drop on his palate before swallowing.

His thoughtful eyes found my own. "Did you enjoy Lady Eloriil's performance yesterday?"

"She has a beautiful voice."

"Agreed. Tell me, Lady Alacore, what did you make of her song?"

I shrank in on myself. I hadn't spoken to anyone about the things I'd seen while the syren performed her epic ballad. A part of me was scared to talk about it even with Tae. What if she hadn't seen the horrible things I had? Certainly nobody in attendance looked horrified when I fell out of my trance. What if I only saw those things because of the malign curse hanging over me? I was hesitant to speak about the experience with Ambrose. If he discovered the truth, that my magic was locked away where I could scarcely access it, then he might banish me from his grounds. Without this job, I had no chance of finding the Sphynx.

"Does everyone see the same thing when she sings?" I asked, carefully choosing my words.

"The listener can only see what their heart can make room for. Lady Eloriil paints the picture well, as fluid as a living dream."

What kind of answer was that? I gulped down some of the tea. It warmed my insides and matched the heat of my face. Ambrose waited patiently. He wasn't going to let me off the hook.

"The giants…I don't know much about our history. I don't know the full story of why they attacked the fae or why the Great Houses decentralized power from Queen Titania and King Oberon. I know the main theme of her song was rebirth and perseverance through hard times, but it seemed to me that Lady Eloriil was also trying to remind the people that there are greater threats out there than those we create through petty rivalry amongst our own kind."

Ambrose studied me for a moment. I wondered what was going on behind those pale grey eyes. He smiled with a serenity I'd only seen in the faces of Buddhist monks. "You are a very insightful person, Lady Alacore. I am pleased to have your brain working on my case. Go now. The Wyld Hunt will soon begin, and I will need that mind of yours in attendance, watching and listening. And please, try not to scare anymore chefs today."

I wilted. *He already heard about that?* Ambrose was so dialed in to everything in his palace, I found it unnerving that he thought he needed me at all.

"I feel horrible for the way I treated that poor man," I admitted.

"Perhaps you will have a chance to explain that to him yourself."

I nodded. I owed Henri an apology, and I would need to find time to deliver it. I set down my tea and rose. I bowed clumsily to Ambrose, retrieved my sneakers, and walked over to Geraldine.

"There's just one more thing," I said as I slipped into them. "It's about the details of our agreement."

"Your contract with Master Ambrose has already been sealed," Geraldine snapped indignantly.

Ambrose held up a hand for his butler to be silent. "What part of our agreement would you care to discuss?"

I put on a brave face. Asking to change the terms of our agreement was no small thing. "Instead of being paid for my services in money, I want you to tell me the location of the Sphynx."

"You would be better served to take the money," Ambrose said.

"But you can change the payment to tell me all you know of the Sphynx?"

Ambrose frowned. "If it is truly what your heart desires."

113

"Excellent, thank you." I turned to go.

"Oh, and Lady Alacore," Ambrose called. "About your friend, the succubus?"

I paused to frown at him over my shoulder. "What about Tae?"

"How much have you told her about our business?"

"I tell Tae everything," I said truthfully.

"And you're certain this succubus is someone you can rely on for discretion?"

"I trust Tae with my life, sir," I said definitively.

"Ah, that is all very well to say. But I would remind you, Lady Alacore, that it is not in fact your life which is at stake. It is mine."

15

𝕴 left Ambrose, feeling guilty. Perhaps I had no right to share his secret with Tae. Was it her business what dangers his house faced? I was certain he saw it as the naïve action of an amateur. It never occurred to me to keep secrets from her. Despite his misgivings, I trusted Taewyn with all my heart, as she did me. We didn't keep secrets from each other, and it was a good thing I'd included her, as Tae was a valuable ally to help discern where Ambrose's danger came from.

I was wondering if she had uncovered anything on Valia when I came around the corner of the hedge maze and almost walked directly into Persa.

"Oh goodness," she said, startled. "I found you." She was dressed in a crème-colored robe with accents of sea blue on the raised collar and along a belt of overlapping petunias. Her twining vine hair was pulled up in a bun, the conebush flowers basking in the afternoon sun. It was bewildering how human the blossom fae could look while simultaneously possessing an unnerving plantlike quality. "I thought we could go down to the festival together. I went to your room, but you were gone already."

"How did you know I would be here?" I asked. It came out sounding more suspicious than I'd intended.

Persa blushed. "I didn't. I only hoped you might be. Grandfather takes his afternoon tea in the garden, and since you're here working for him—"

"Right, sorry. I'm still a little on edge," I explained. "That's very thoughtful of you. I would love the company."

Persa offered me her arm. We walked through the hedge maze with our arms interlocked. Between the hedges and her elaborate attire, I felt as if I'd slipped into a period drama on BBC. One with elves and faeries instead of aristocrats and butlers. It was awe-inspiring how much my life had changed in such a short time.

I was fortunate to have befriended Persa. She was such a gentle soul. It was a marvel she came from the same family that spawned the likes of Artur and Cyan.

And Silas, I reminded myself with a secret grin.

I couldn't imagine what she thought of me, given my earlier emotional outburst. That she had still sought my company moved me.

Gizmitt burst between our legs, racing past us like a rolled-up ball of yarn. We laughed as the ferillo cut around the corner ahead of us.

"Looks like Gizmitt can't wait to get to the party either," Persa laughed.

"I made a fool of myself earlier," I said. Better to get the conversation out of the way now.

"Nonsense." Persa waved her petite hand. "Silas told me all about your recent run-ins with danger back in Willow's Edge. Changelings and fae traffickers. I can't imagine what you went through."

Silas was talking about me, huh? That's intriguing. I filed that revelation for later. "Something else happened. Just before I came to the Tides for my trials, I had an encounter with a troll. I thought he was my friend. He was always so nice to everyone. But it turned out he was…*eating* people."

Persa's hair paled. It was the first time I'd seen such a reaction. I didn't have a lot of experience with blossom fae, but it was obvious her horror bled the color from her vines and leaves as surely as a human might pale when the blood drained from their face. "How ghastly. But…cannibalism was outlawed centuries ago."

"I guess he didn't get the memo."

Persa appraised me with a sideward glance. "You're an incredibly brave woman, Lady Alacore."

We skirted the water pond, and I peeked over the edge, half expecting to see the siren swim by. *Brave? If Persa knew how terrified I am all the time, she'd never call me that.*

I saw a strange look play out on her face. Her eyes were distant, recalling some past memory with a frown. How many times had I wallowed in exactly that sort of melancholy? Then it hit me. I understood why I felt so comfortable around Persa. She reminded me of myself. All my life I'd cowed to those louder and more braggadocious around me, desperately trying to slip into the background because I never felt worthy enough. Persa was much the same, afraid of her own shadow. I thought over how hard she'd tried to placate her family in the little time I'd known her. It mirrored my own life in boarding school, at university, and even at the flower shop.

I could hear the crowd gathering around the tents of the outdoor festival as we neared the palace. "I'm not as brave as you think."

"Nonsense. I wish I could be more like you. The way you tossed that drink on Aunt Cyan." Her eyes sparkled. "You were so fearless."

"She was being cruel to you. I couldn't help myself."

Persa covered her mouth to hide her giggle, as if it were a scandalous act. "Aunt Cyan's not like that all the time," she insisted.

My bullshit meter went off, but I kept my mouth shut. Most people didn't wake up on the wrong side of the bed and magically turn into a bully. Persa's aunts were both jerks. Even her father seemed like an ass.

"Things have just been tense lately," Persa added.

"Since your father lost the silk holdings?" I asked, forgetting myself.

Persa was startled, then hung her head in shame. "Then everyone knows..."

I felt queasy that I'd just embarrassed her. We exited the hedge maze and stopped near the cliff to gaze out at the cove below. The giant dragonflies were milling off the coast, by Lamina's Light. The Tides, usually so bustling with life, was as quiet as an empty stage.

"Ever since grandmother passed away, things have gotten progressively worse. When my grandfather was in his prime, he was a force to be reckoned with. I used to watch him when I was a child, how he hustled to and fro, a commander with quick orders and a sharp mind. He was this larger than life figurehead, the core of the House of Dawn. Back then I believed nothing could shake him from his path. Just look below us. Do you see everything the House of Dawn has brought to this land, to our people? The Tides is a safe haven, free of goblins, free of crime, free of poverty. This is a land where fae can pursue their desires, with honest and fulfilling work, arts, trade, love, passion..."

Her voice faltered.

She had a lofty impression of the Tides. It was a wonderful place to live, but no town could be entirely devoid of crime. Could it?

"Depression is a cruel disease," I said.

"*Depression.* This is a human term I'm familiar with. We blossoms are no strangers to sorrow. But to allow things to spiral so wildly out of control..." She shook her head.

I didn't agree with her definition. Depression was a wretched thing that could rip the rug out from underneath someone. It was far more powerful than she seemed to believe.

She shook her head. "My father never should have been given such important responsibilities. The truth is, he isn't a very capable man. Not like my grandfather used to be." She cupped her mouth and trembled, as if speaking the words aloud made her a traitor.

"They say we don't get to choose our family." I could well understand feeling let down by a parent. I placed a comforting hand on Persa's arm. She looked at my hand as if it were an alien artifact. How long had it been since someone showed her compassion? From what I'd seen, other than Silas, everyone in her family used Persa as a punching bag. "They don't deserve you."

She smiled as if she wasn't sure if she was happy or sad. I think it was a little of both. "You are a very special person, Lady Alacore."

"Oh, don't go back to that. It's Lanie." It felt in that moment, with the rawness of our selves exposed, silly to continue the pretense of my appointed moniker. And I felt an affinity to Persa. I wanted her to know there was someone else out there on her side.

She nodded. "Lanie, then." She plucked a handkerchief from her robes and dabbed the corners of her eyes. "It would seem it's my turn to get emotional today. I apologize, I am not usually so candid." She paused and glanced sideways. "Also, the things we spoke about—"

I stopped her and mimed locking my lips and throwing away a key. She giggled, and it warmed my heart to see her smiling again. Persa was a gentle dove who lived under the trampling feet of lions. I couldn't imagine what would happen to her if I failed in my role to prevent Ambrose's murder. I had an image of her simply lying down to die from heartache.

"Now then, we should head inside. The hunt will begin soon," Persa said.

This time it was I who offered her my arm. Scores of fae crowded the grounds outside the palace.

"What are today's festivities? My friend Tae said it's like a scavenger hunt."

"Oh, this is your first time at the Wyld Hunt," Persa squealed. "I'm so excited for you. There will be a series of fun games that you will need to use your wits to solve. The first event today is a tea party!"

I frowned. We paused as a group of children cut across our path, clashing with wooden toy swords in a mock battle. "Does it take a lot of wit to brew tea?"

"Not the making of the tea, silly. You'll be randomly paired with other players. Among them, you must pass three answers and three questions. Each answer must be about yourself and either the truth or a lie. If the other player says you are lying when you are telling the truth, then they are disqualified, and vice versa. But you must not attempt to purposefully trick them, nor should you lead them to the correct answer. Once you have both answered and asked three questions successfully, you will move on to the next round."

"That sounds more like truth or dare than a scavenger hunt," I remarked. The children moved on. A three-armed tephyr juggled eight pins as we cut across the lawn. A group of fae, already drinking, were cheering them on.

"There are no dares," Persa corrected. "It is meant to be fun. If you pass the first challenge, you will then drink the rest of your tea. In the bottom of your cup, you will discover a sigil for your partner. You will have to find them amongst the rest of the festival guests before you can proceed to the following challenge."

"Okay, so it's supposed to be like an icebreaker," I surmised. "This forces us to talk to other guests."

We entered the atrium. The air shifted inside. Starfire's warmth wrapped around us like a mother's warm embrace. The long banquet tables were laden with food just as they had been the previous day, but the streamers were gone. They were replaced by bursts of flowers as large as my body floating above the gathering. They were mirages, transparent like virtual holograms. My breath caught when I saw them.

"Do you like the bouquets?" Persa asked, noting my reaction.

"That's one of the most beautiful things I've ever seen," I whispered.

Persa smiled wide and clapped her delicate hands together. "Thank you! It was my idea to add them to the hunt. And the jack-o-lanterns were a gift from the House of Amber."

"I don't see any pumpkins."

"You will," she giggled.

"Persa!"

Artur waved impatiently for his daughter to join him at the top of the steps. Ambrose was already on the balcony with Geraldine at his side, Cyan milling with her wife behind him. "Looks like I have to go," Persa lamented. She turned to me and tried to put on a brave front. "I think you know all I can tell you to get started on the hunt. Good luck today. I hope you have fun!"

She turned to leave but something popped into my head. "Oh, Persa, wait."

She looked at me curiously.

"What do you know about manticores?"

Persa frowned. The crowd was swelling around us. Alegra appeared behind Ambrose, looking as coldly clinical as ever. "I don't know what you heard about the hunt, but there won't be any monsters waiting to eat lost children. That's just an old maid's tale told to children to make them behave."

"So manticores aren't real?"

"Persa, we're ready to begin!" Artur's face looked fit to burst. He shot me a scathing scowl.

"Lanie, I'm sorry, I really must go. Are you sure you're going to be alright?"

I smiled at her and shook my head. "Never mind. It was just something silly I was thinking about."

Persa looked relieved. She patted my hand and quickly made her way through the crowd just as Ambrose put his hands to the rail of the balcony.

The Wyld Hunt was about to begin.

16

The event kicked off after a short welcoming speech by Ambrose. It was fortunate that I'd run into Persa, as no other instructions were given during Ambrose's speech. It was to be a trial by fire for the participants. I realized that the information Persa had given me was a gift and not to be squandered.

A droba came by, handing out teacups to each fae he encountered.

"Lady Alacore." The droba bowed. A frog in cufflinks and a tailcoat was something to behold. He studied the tray of teacups through tiny spectacles perched on the edge of his froggy mouth. He turned a few cups until he found mine. "Ah, yes, here it is, Lady Alacore." He repeated my name as if it were printed on the teacup, but I could see no distinguishing features on the white porcelain.

"Thank you, good sir," I replied cordially, feeling like a princess in a faery tale.

The droba smirked and moved along. When I looked back down at my cup, I saw it was undergoing a transformation. A repeating pattern originated where my fingers held the saucer, seeping across the plain white surface of the plate and around the cup. Ivy intertwined with orange ranunculus flowers. They were exquisitely detailed, every petal intricately stenciled below the steamy tea.

Persa's decorations! I thought, putting the first part of the puzzle together.

The spinning flower mirages overhead were all different flowers and no two were alike. It only took me a few seconds to find the ranunculus. I quickly made a beeline through the crowd, careful not to spill any of my tea as I walked. Sure enough, other fae were doing likewise, heading toward their respective flowers. A small gathering was already congregating beneath the ranunculus when I arrived.

What was it Persa said I needed to do? Answer questions? I watched a fire faerie swoop into the crowd and immediately confront a snow faerie with a question. I couldn't hear the words they spoke, but a few seconds later the fire fae laughed loudly and confidently proclaimed, "That was a lie."

Suddenly a jack-o'-lantern appeared above the fire fae. The pumpkin head floated above her and began laughing. She snapped her fingers and cursed. She was disqualified.

"That's a bummer," I said to myself as the fire faerie left the gathering.

"Must sting to get cut so early," Silas said jovially.

For once in my life, I didn't jump or yelp when I was surprised. I had been so preoccupied watching the exchange that I hadn't noticed Silas come up to me. He wore a sharply cut suit with riding pants that hugged his muscular thighs. He was avidly watching me with those dazzling blue eyes that looked like they were mentally undressing me. Or maybe that was just what I wanted to imagine he was doing. I had a flash of myself standing naked before him and blushed.

"Oh, hello, Silas," I said, trying to hide my fluster.

"Ah, I'm right, then." He grinned, studying my eyes intently. "We're a match."

"We are?" *Fuck yeah we are.*

He smirked and showed me his teacup. It had an orange ranunculus on it. I was excited and mortified at the same time. What I wanted more than anything was not to make an ass out of myself in front of another hot guy.

"Oh, right, the cups," I said. "So, how does this work exactly?"

Silas squinted at me as if he didn't believe me for a second. "Now that you've found your flower, you'll need to search for the other guests who have the orange ranunculus. The flowers above are meant to draw players toward their assigned groups. You must ask three questions and provide three answers. When asking your three questions, you will have to determine if the other player is telling the truth or lying. If you guess correctly, you stay in the hunt. Guess wrong and you're out. Once you've asked three questions and answered three as well, you'll drink your tea and move on to the next challenge."

"It sounds intimidating to ask questions and bare yourself to so many strangers," I said.

"It's more fun than it sounds. I actually love this part. It's a good chance to meet new people. I believe most people have something

122

interesting to say, even if they normally never get to show it. I mean, without it I might not have had a chance to talk to you today."

I felt the blood rushing to my face as it burned scarlet. Silas noticed my reaction and grinned. *How embarrassing. At least he's not annoyed. If anything, he looks infatuated.*

"I must say, that dress looks awfully flattering on you."

I slapped his chest playfully. "You're trouble, aren't you?" *Ugh, did I really just do that? That's right, Lanie, why don't you just kick him in the shin like he's your kindergarten crush?*

Silas held up a warning finger. "Uh-uh, you already got your question. Now you'll need to decide whether I told the truth or lied."

What was he talking about? I thought it over for a moment. "You jerk, you tricked me," I teased. In explaining to me the rules of the hunt, Silas had indeed answered my first question.

That's what I get for playing dumb, I thought. Although, it did give me one advantage. Comparing Persa's explanation to Silas's, I could easily see that he'd told me the truth. I felt a little guilty, as if I'd cheated the game, but I took the win.

"You answered truthfully," I said.

Silas waggled his eyebrows at me like a dope. It was so lame, it was cute.

I giggled. "Now you get to ask me a question, right?"

"Alas, no. You can only exchange one question or answer with each of the six partners you come across under our flower."

That was a bummer.

"You're off to a solid start for your first hunt though. Not too bad for your first time. I hope you make it through to the next challenge. Maybe we'll get lucky and end up together." He shot me a conspiratorial wink.

My stomach fluttered under his gaze.

"Excuse me, Lady Alacore." It was Olan, the Summer Court's representative for Willow's Edge. His cherubic eyes twinkled as they took me in. "I believe your time with Sir Amaryllis has already born ripe fruit."

Olan bowed cordially to Silas. It was clearly a dismissal, but a very well-mannered one.

"Good luck, Lady Alacore," Silas said with a bow. He bumped into me from behind as he left and ran his finger down my spine. I felt a shiver of pleasure.

Did he do that on purpose, or am I imagining things?

Olan didn't seem to notice. "I do believe I spotted the orange ranunculus in your hand."

"Good day, Jarl Olan," I said, showing him that indeed our teacups matched. "I'm so happy to bump into you. I wanted to thank you for the kindness you showed me during my court hearing."

Olan's beard twitched playfully. He was tickled pink to be acknowledged. "Of course, any outcome of that case was purely based on the facts," he insisted in earnest. "Though, I should say, it did not hurt to have Prince Lucien in attendance vouching for you. What a stir that caused."

"I'm sorry about that. I didn't mean to cause a big scene and disrupt the court."

"On the contrary, it was exhilarating." Olan's laugh was as jolly as ever. The ivory circlet he wore had a gleaming gemstone that emitted light as if it were a tiny star, twinkling to the pattern of his laugh. "Court in the provinces is typically a monotonous affair of petitions for recompense. It's usually more about who owes who what for services rendered or contracts broken. It's a dreary business that could be better handled if the parties in question would only have an honest conversation with one another." He leaned in close. "Plus, it was a truly tantalizing treat to see Shadow get his dander up in a tizzy."

I raised my eyebrows in shock. Olan laughed scandalously, and it was impossible not to join in. "He is an ornery fellow," I agreed. Shadow was the court representative from the Court of Shadows. He had struck me as a man used to garnering respect from his title rather than earning it through his actions. Prince Lucien had given him his comeuppance in front of the entire courtroom. I wasn't one for embarrassing others—unless of course they were bullies. Then, fuck 'em.

Olan took my hand and gave it a warm squeeze then leaned back and appraised me like a proud grandfather. "If only Rosalie could see you now, how proud she would be."

That caught me off guard. It was a more personal insight than I'd expected from this conversation. "You were friends with my grandmother," I realized.

"I first met Rosalie when we were both very young and foolish." There was something about Olan's body language that bespoke a deeper intimacy.

They were lovers! Everything made more sense—how eagerly Olan had risen to my defense in the courtroom, how patient he'd been with my inexperience. Even that twinkle in his eye. Could this man be related to me in some way? Dared I ask such a thing?

As if reading my mind, he lowered his voice. "Perhaps we'd best leave such conversations to occur without the trappings of the hunt."

It was sage advice, but I still found myself reluctant to pull back from the topic. "I guess it's a more serious question than this grand festival demands," I conceded.

Olan nodded. "I think the spirit of the event is to ask questions about others like their favorite flower or whether they enjoy ballet. Which brings me to my question for you. Do you, Lady Alacore, like to dance?"

His question was formally asked. I had to decide whether to tell the truth or lie. "I don't like to dance. I'm no good at it and look silly when I do."

Olan tapped a finger to his lips, then stroked his salt and pepper beard. After some deliberation, he nodded. "You are lying. Though dancing does make you feel very self-conscious, you enjoy the feeling of your feet gliding over the floor, the rhythm of music coming to life in your blood. You would like others to think that you don't like to dance because you are scared to do so, but once you are on the dance floor with a partner, you feel alive and giddy."

His answer hung between us. It was a far more elaborate introspection than a simple *you are lying.* His shaggy head shrank between his shoulders in anticipation as he watched the air overhead for a laughing jack-o'-lantern.

"You are correct," I said, freeing him of his anticipation. We laughed together. "That was quite an answer."

I spotted Artur over Olan's shoulder. He was talking with another blossom fae. This would be a great opportunity to question him.

Olan took my hand again affectionately. "It was a wild gamble. Rosalie was the same way. You know, you even laugh like her. Ah, how her laugh could light up the room."

"I'd love to hear more about her sometime." I hoped Olan didn't hear the urgency that had entered my voice. I tried to maintain eye contact with him, but my gaze kept wandering over his shoulder to Artur.

"Well, I shan't want to keep you," Olan chuckled.

"Oh, you're not at all," I said.

"No need to pretend. I can see how eager you are to overcome the first challenge. These events can be exciting after all." Olan smiled with that cherubic glow on his cheeks and twinkle in his eye. I felt a twinge of guilt in my guts. "Off you go to your next partner. Although, you must promise you'll spare me a little more of your time during the festival so we can chat further."

"That would truly be my honor." I smiled, grateful for his grace, before I broke away and made a beeline for Artur.

Malachai cut in front of my path. His dead charcoal eyes beat through my soul. I stopped in my tracks just before him. He seemed taller than the previous day, more menacing, like a simmering rage hid just beneath the surface of his placid calm. He wore a similar militaristic suit, black and festooned with decorative gold buttons and badges on his breast. His Mantle of Nightmare was thrown over one shoulder, draping down his side and barely concealing the hilt of his sword.

"You look prepared for battle, King Malachai," I noted.

"Life is a blade looking for an opening." The fae around us were laughing with one another, a stark contrast to his words. "Ask your question." It was a command.

He doesn't like having to speak to me, I realized. *Does he know about me and Lucien hooking up? Is that where this disapproval stems from?* I studied his rigid glare. It didn't feel personal. *He hates everyone. Me probably more so because I'm not a pureblood. I wonder what he'd say if I told him what was actually in my veins,* I gloated privately.

I almost toyed with asking if he knew. I'd love to see his face when he got that answer wrong. *Stop that, no one can know that secret.* I searched for where that feeling had come from and saw his cloak ripple, as if hands crawled across his shoulder beneath its surface. I shuddered.

"We haven't got all day, Miss Alacore," Malachai snarled. He was right, the crowd was rapidly thinning as players passed the first challenge. And I wanted to get away from this horrible man. He frightened me like no one I'd ever been around.

"Do you like flowers?" I blurted before I could think. It was one of the examples Olan had just given me and also an incredibly stupid thing to ask someone I hardly knew.

"I detest flowers," Malachai said, curling his lips. His eyes moved over a nearby blossom faerie.

I knew my answer before those cold eyes found their way back to me. "You're lying."

"How can you be certain?"

"Your daughter's name is Hellebore. If you hated flowers, you would never have named her after one."

"It is her mother's favorite flower, not mine," Malachai said.

Shit. Had I miscalculated? My shoulders bunched together as I braced for a laughing pumpkin overhead. I decided to stick with my hunch. "No way. You would never cede that measure of control to another, not for something as important as your own blood. The hellebore is *your* favorite flower, not your wife's."

Malachai kept his eyes trained on me impassively. "You are correct." He swept past me as if I were a servant he had dismissed.

I let out air I didn't even know I was holding in. *Wow, talk about intense.*

I searched the diminishing crowd, hoping I hadn't lost my chance to corner Artur. I spotted him with his back to me. He was just finishing up a conversation with a blossom fae when I approached from behind. They were laughing as he turned around. When Artur saw me standing before him, his happiness melted into a sneer, like acetone washing away the paint of a false smile. I showed him my teacup and looked at his.

Artur raked his fingers over his face and groaned. "Of course he matched us up," he muttered.

His words landed home. *Ambrose had a hand in who I was paired with for this event.* To what end? Were these some of the people he considered potential suspects? *Malachai too? Could the king of the shadows have a reason to murder the head of the House of Dawn? They are rival houses. Could such a heinous act boil down to simple politics? It would have been nice of him to warn me, so I could've made better use of my time with the king. What about his son, though? What motive might Artur have for wanting to see his father harmed?*

"There's been a rift between you since you lost your father's silk holdings to the Court of Shadows," I realized aloud.

Artur recoiled from me, aghast. He quickly checked around us to see if any others had heard. The surrounding fae were too preoccupied with their own battles of wit to eavesdrop on us. Artur leaned in closer. But where Olan had leaned in for a cordial exchange of pleasantries, Artur's words were sharp and harsh.

"You tell my father that he knows full well I was duped." He said, then speaking to himself and muttering under his breath he emitted a string of anxiety riddled questions. "What do I have to do to make it up to him? Should I grovel at his feet in front of the whole realm? Am I to be punished eternally for a single mistake?"

I thought carefully before continuing. "You lost the silk holdings quite recently."

Artur painted a wretched smile. "Well, we can't all be as perfect as his dear sweet Cyan. Perfect daddy's girl swooping in to save us all with her money."

"Cyan is helping Ambrose recover from the financial hardship you brought upon the House of Dawn," I gasped.

Artur didn't catch my tone. He was too preoccupied with glancing over my shoulder at the object of his ire. Cyan was behind us, engaged in her own question with a shadow fae. She wore a translucent violet jumpsuit with purple lacing that barely concealed her most tender regions. Delicate strands connected the sleeves to her lace gloves. Swoops of sheer fabric connected her elbow to her waist in an elastic web. The ensemble should have made her look like a badass base jumper, one that would plummet rather than glide, but on Cyan it looked like the height of fashion and sophistication. Rows of gold bracelets jingled around her slender arms and matched her gold stiletto heels. It was a wonder her teacup never spilled, as she spoke quite animatedly. She was the picture of haute couture, setting trends where they never needed to go but always inevitably must. I felt a twinge of jealousy that she could pull off such a ridiculous outfit.

"So, Cyan bailed out the House of Dawn..." I repeated my disbelief that the self-indulgent woman could do anything kind for another living being.

Artur waggled a finger in my face with a smug smirk. "Ah, you see. Father thinks he knows everything, but he didn't know that one."

I had to be careful with what I said. Artur was under some delusion that Ambrose had sent me to spy on him. To what end, I had no idea. But he was being awfully useful, spilling his guts. Ambrose would need to watch his son more carefully in the future. He was a walking liability.

I was wondering what I could say to keep him talking when I discovered the answer was simply to keep quiet.

"He really thought the rice paddies brought in a cash overflow this season." Artur snorted. "They barely pay for themselves, let alone turn a profit. That injection of cash came from his darling little girl, going against the wishes of our overproud father."

"But you let her funnel money through you," I surmised.

Artur waved his hand dismissively. "We both knew he'd never take a handout. You tell him that, though—it was *both* of us who put the scheme together. Not just his baby girl. I helped just as much as Cyan."

"Cyan wasn't partially to blame for losing the silk holdings, though."

I've never seen someone scowl with every part of their body before. The righteous indignation from Artur was palpable. Even the fae around us, wrapped in their own little bubbles of conversation, seemed to sense it and shift away from us. The loss of the silk holdings was a major source of contention for him.

Enough to murder his own father over?

For a moment I worried he might attack me, with the way he glared with glassy eyes. I decided to hold my ground. I remained silent, leaving that space between us for him to fill.

It worked. Suddenly there was a shift in his stance. It was as if he were a piece of paper that crumpled in on itself. His teacup clattered to the polished wood floor. It was a marvel the porcelain didn't shatter, put the liquid splashed on both our legs. He buried his face in his hands, sobbing. Despite my stoic front, I sidled up to him and patted his back.

Nearby fae were beginning to stare at the commotion. "Have some respect," I snapped at one woman ogling us. That did the trick. The fae quickly put some distance between us and went back to their own business.

"It's alright, Artur, just let it out," I whispered as I rubbed his back just beneath his folded wings.

A laughing jack-o'-lantern head appeared over Artur. He was, naturally, disqualified for spilling his tea. Both Persa and Silas had said I wasn't allowed to drink my tea until after I'd been involved in six conversations or true or false.

"He never trusted me. All my life, I just wanted to make him proud. Wise old man Ambrose, keeper of the domain. You can't imagine what it was like to grow up with that cold-hearted bastard. It was the honor of my life to have him finally give me a tiny scrap of the House to run. Cyan has her fashion empire, Alegra her royal ·duties as librarian, and even Geraldine has the run of the staff, and he's not even blood.

"But I failed him. How could I have fallen for their schemes? They lied to me. They crafted the hole around me, then put the shovel in my hands and offered to help me climb out. I thought she was my friend... but I was so stupid. Of course we had other options. How could I have been so foolish?"

So the Court of Shadows deliberately set Artur up to fail, then "bailed him out" by buying up the silk holdings for a fraction of their cost. Big surprise. (That was sarcasm.) The whole scenario sounded no different than what some equity firms did in the human realm. In the nineties, they still called it a hostile takeover. These days it was just business as usual. The strong are always preying on the weak. And given how easily Artur broke down, I surmised he had always been "the weak."

I didn't feel guilty, because I didn't feel I'd pushed him very far before he broke. However, no matter how irritating Artur was as a person, I did feel bad for him. I knew too well what it was like to have a parent who looked down on everything you did. Though his mistake was monumental, Artur was still a person with feelings.

"Not everyone is good with business," I coaxed him. "And not everyone needs to be. I think you should go to your father and tell him how you feel about the whole situation. Better that than keeping this all bottled up inside."

Artur sniffled, dabbing his eyes with a handkerchief. They all seemed to possess handkerchiefs, as if they expected to cry at some point during the day. Was that fae-centric or a House of Dawn tendency? And if the latter, why were they crying all the time?

"Did he tell you to say that?" Artur asked. "He never changes. How can I face him when he won't even speak to me himself?"

"It's better than bottling up your emotions until you explode in front of a total stranger," I insisted.

"Really, Arty," Cyan said as she cut between us, purposefully shrugging my arm away from her brother. "Are you crying again?"

Artur looked down at the floor, mortified.

"Now's not the time," I warned her.

Cyan ignored me, keeping her eyes trained on her brother. "Show some backbone. You're sniveling like a brownie in the middle of the Wyld Hunt, for fuck's sake. Geraldine, help my brother get cleaned up, won't you?"

Geraldine swooped in out of nowhere, his sharkish nose raised in the air. He hooked an arm around Artur and spoke with a tenderness I didn't know he was capable of. "Come, Master Artur, let's get you cleaned up somewhere more private."

Artur was like a lost puppy. He mumbled and stared with a faraway glazed look in his eyes.

"You know, your daughter is very intelligent, Artur. Perhaps in the future you could consult with her when making business decisions," I offered.

He snapped his head toward me with a sneer. "What do you know about anything?"

"Come now, Master Artur," Geraldine prodded, turning Artur away from me. "Everything will be alright."

"I've spilled tea on my pants," Artur said pitifully as he let Geraldine lead him away. I watched them disappear into the thinning crowd before turning my attention back to Cyan.

"I didn't mean to upset him," I said.

"Artur has been throwing tantrums since he was eighty-five," Cyan said. "But let's not pretend you came to the hunt for anything other than to spy on us. I understand daddy wants to ensure Artur's little mishap doesn't repeat itself elsewhere. Still, I'm not sure it was wise to hire a…" She made a point of looking at my shoulders.

"A half-breed?" I offered. It was clear she was looking at my lack of wings.

"A *warden*," Cyan snidely corrected.

"You find the concept of a warden distasteful?"

"Perish such a thought. I simply think there is a time and a *place* for a warden. And this is not it. I find the world operates more smoothly when everyone knows where they fit."

She couldn't be blunter than that. Cyan saw me as a second-class citizen. I didn't belong in the palace, rubbing shoulders with the other nobles. I belonged on the lawn, in the tents, making my merry with the other *low-breeds*. She was a deplorable excuse for a human being.

I chastised myself. The people I interacted with, though they seemed similar, were not human. The fae were a different people, and I needed to stop measuring them against my knowledge of human behavior. Still, for someone who represented the height of fashion, Cyan was a disgusting person. I wondered how many fae would still look up to her as an icon if they saw the real person beneath the fancy clothes and flawless skin. Would that Cyan hold up to their scrutiny?

"You're speaking the truth, at least as much as you believe it is so. It's interesting to me that you are so beautiful, yet your behavior is hideous," I said.

Cyan laughed. "Please, don't act as if you've unraveled my persona in the five seconds we've known each other. You're nothing but a little girl grasping at greatness and praying it makes you unique. It's to be expected with you *wardens*. I've heard all about your life among the humans, Lady Alacore. How ghastly. To have lived around those stinking creatures… What can someone like you know about a woman like me?"

She might be a rude bitch, but she isn't entirely heartless, I reminded myself.

Cyan was funneling money into her father's house to save his economic empire. Although, part of that decision was surely rooted in self-preservation. Cyan's popularity in fashion circles would surely deteriorate if the House of Dawn fell to ruin. Surely someone as nasty as she was had amassed a long list of rivals by now. But there was something else there as well. It was the way I'd seen her look at Ambrose. The way she'd blocked the woman on the steps yesterday.

I didn't believe she was capable of hurting her father. What was it Artur had called her? *His darling little girl.* She worshipped the man.

Then what was the whole spectacle between her and that other woman about?

I gazed up at the imperious woman in awe as the answer hit me. "You're having an affair."

Cyan's carefully manicured façade faltered. I caught a glimpse of shock and fear. Her teacup rattled in one hand as the other pressed to her bosom. If I had any doubt about my revelation, it was dispelled by her eyes which quickly darted back and forth over my head, realizing the mistake she'd just made.

"There won't be a laughing pumpkin," I said with more confidence than I felt. "You already asked your question earlier and I answered that you told the truth. But really, you shouldn't have asked me what I know about you. That woman yesterday, she's your lover. She was going after your father on the stairs."

"Please, keep your voice down," Cyan begged.

"You needn't worry," I said, pointedly looking around. "There's barely anybody left to hear us."

It was true. There were maybe twenty or so fae still beneath the rotating ranunculus mirage. And those that remained were too busy quickly trying to ask and answer questions to pay us any mind. Cyan's gold bracelets jingled as she pulled me to the side of the room, toward the closed doors of the balcony.

"Litari wasn't *going after* my father," Cyan whispered. "Not in the way you're implying. Does he know? Oh, of course he does. Why else would you be here tormenting me like this?" Her ivy hair and vanilla flowers blushed a violet that matched her dress.

Even embarrassed she still manages to look radiant, I thought. Cyan was deeply distressed over the prospect of her father knowing she was having an affair. I didn't see what the big deal was. Tae had told me Cyan flirted with everyone she met.

"I heard rumors you and Isabo shared lovers."

"Isabo has a tenacious appetite for sensual delights. I can hardly keep up with her."

"Yet you're screwing around behind her back with this Litari woman," I pointed out.

Cyan huffed. "That's different. What we have is… Litari gets me on a whole other level. We're bonded."

I gasped. Bonded meant that the two of them had declared true love, a soul binding so that if one died, the other would too. It was an archaic practice only followed by moony romantics and lovesick tweens. To get out of it, Cyan would need to beseech the court. One look at her told me she had no intention of ever getting out of it.

"I still don't see what this has to do with your father."

Cyan paused and eyed me shrewdly. "He doesn't know about Litari?"

"Not that he's mentioned to me."

She straightened her posture and mussed her hair, flipping it over her shoulder with her free hand. Once she was composed, she spoke again. "What is it you want from me? Is it money? Of course it's money. Your kind never ceases to amaze me. Well, out with it then. Tell me how much this is going to cost so I can get on with my day."

"Are you offering me a bribe?" I snickered despite myself. "You're ridiculous. I'm not shaking you down." *Shut up, Lanie. This woman's rich. Take all the money she'll throw at you!* I screamed inside. But it didn't matter, both me and my inner bullshit knew I would never stoop so low.

Cyan was thrown off. Her perception of the world was teetering on the precipice of uncertainty. "Is it some task you require of me?"

"Would you knock it off," I said, annoyed.

"Are you going to tell my father?"

"I wasn't planning on it. And it can stay that way if you help me understand the whole picture. But if you're going to call me nasty names and stick your nose in the air, then maybe I won't be able to stop myself from mentioning it when I meet with Ambrose tomorrow afternoon." I felt low making the threat, but I needed information.

She huffed. "*Fine.* I met Litari three years ago at a show in Ruby City. Isabo was feeling under the weather, which means she had taken too many pills that morning, so she stayed back at the villa. We connected instantly. It was like walking into a room and finding your other half. That is what she is to me, you must understand, the missing piece that completes my being. From the moment I met her I knew how much trouble I was in. How could I love anyone this deeply? My relationship with Isabo is a prop, a flashy affair that everyone buzzed about. 'Cyan has taken the top model of the Deep as her lover.' The gossip was in all the headlines. What would those same headlines say if I came out with a shadow fae on my shoulder?"

"Litari isn't a water fae?"

Cyan arched a perfectly angled brow at me. "You saw her with your own eyes, though I don't know how. Nobody can see a slyph unless they will it." I saw her searching inward for understanding. "Unless she wanted you to see…"

I quickly shook my head. "I've never even met her before."

Cyan sighed with relief.

I was still missing something. Why care that Litari was a shadow fae? *Surely fae from other Houses have fallen in love before. Haven't they?* I searched my mind of all the fae I'd met. In the province there were many cross-species relationships. But since arriving at the palace, I hadn't seen any such pairings. Was that kind of comingling frowned upon enough to bring shame to Cyan? Surely the fae couldn't be that backwards in their beliefs. I refused to believe it could be so. There was something else at play behind Cyan's secrecy.

"You don't want to let your father down," I realized.

"He's very old-fashioned. Father believes that marriage is a sacred vow between lovers that should never be taken lightly. He pressed me terribly when I declared my engagement to Isabo. I assured him we were in love and would always be together."

"But you want to be with Litari."

"She is my everything."

Cyan was working hard to keep this secret from her father because she was ashamed of herself. Litari wasn't some assassin trying to get close enough to Ambrose to slit his throat. She was a desperate lover trying to break down the only barrier left to a life of happiness with the woman she loved. Once Ambrose knew, the bandage would be ripped off, and Cyan would be hers completely. Whatever fallout might come, they would endure it together.

Shit, that means she can't possibly be the murderer. Anyone this desperate to keep their father happy isn't plotting his demise.

"Will you keep this secret?" Cyan prodded.

"I'm not going to tell your dad who you're sleeping with," I said. "It's none of his business."

Cyan gawked at me in disbelief. All through our conversation, she had held out that I would demand something of her. She looked at me as if truly seeing me for the first time. Something shifted in the way she assessed me. Was it respect?

"But you do owe your wife an explanation," I added. "What you're doing isn't fair to her. You need to go to Isabo and explain everything.

Secrets like this aren't good for your soul, Cyan. You want to truly feel complete? Get this off your chest to Isabo, not to me."

To my utter surprise, she nodded sheepishly. "I know I need to tell her. I've been a coward putting it off for so long. I will speak to her tonight, after the Wyld Hunt, and explain everything."

"That's good."

"You really want nothing in exchange for keeping this secret." Cyan said it as if she was trying to understand the meaning of charity. "You're a very interesting person, Lady Alacore. I'm not sure I deserve your silence, but I am glad that you are working to help my father with whatever it is he hired you for."

I was shocked. She really meant that.

I had gotten both Artur and Cyan to open up to me somehow. That success should have left me feeling elated. After all, in less than thirty minutes, I'd made substantial progress on my investigation. But I was left feeling empty instead. None of what they'd provided helped me get closer to preventing Ambrose's murder.

Sure it did. Now I know neither of them are suspects.

I still felt gutted. Cyan had been one of my prime suspects. With her out of the running, that only left one other person who might be up to no good.

"Valia," I said under my breath.

"That's my name," Valia said as she closed the distance between us.

I instantly noticed two things. First, Valia held a teacup with an orange ranunculus on it. And second, Tae, who had promised to keep an eye on Valia, was nowhere to be seen.

17

ae sat on a crate with her hands demurely folded in her lap. "You'd think it would smell musty in here, but it's really quite lovely. It's a rather pleasant surprise, what with all the gloomy corners in this warehouse. You know, that aroma comes from the teak wood. Fantastic material for ships. I've always felt teak smells rather manly. It's got that bold spiciness to it that—"

"Would you shut your yap for five bloody seconds?" Rovio snapped.

Tae blinked innocently at him.

Valia's men had disagreed over what to do with Tae once they caught her. Rovio said they needed to figure out why she was tailing them, while Fexil was in favor of eliminating her so they could be on their way. He was a squirrely one. In the end, they led her inside the warehouse, told her to sit on a crate, and then huddled together in a series of whispers and over-the-shoulder glances.

There's no way they're going to let me go with a slap on the wrist, she thought, eyeing the dagger tucked into Fexil's belt.

"Did you know teak forests are practically gone in the human realm? Poor trees. The humans harvested them right out of existence. I guess that's why—"

Rovio broke away from his partner and raced up to her. He raised the back of his hand for a slap.

Tae didn't flinch. To do so would be to invite fear into her heart. Fear was the enemy of her natural talents. Instead, she shot her doe eyes up at Rovio. He didn't realize he'd walked into her trap. The whole time they were debating how to get rid of her, Tae had been letting her magic loose around her. Succubus magic was a fantastically potent substance. Like a light fog, it exuded from her pores with the pleasing aroma of an earthy incense. Rovio walked right into her cloud of pheromones. The smoke quickly coiled around him like the tendrils of a squid.

Rovio was breathing hard in his agitation. All the better for Tae's magic to enter him. In her secret line of work, she'd found it was easy enough to rile up petty thugs such as Rovio and Fexil, men for whom violence was a tool of their trade. She smiled coyly at Rovio as he inhaled her pheromones.

A cloud of confusion crossed his face. He gaped at her, then looked at his raised hand in befuddlement. "What was I…?"

"You said something about showing me how good it feels to be spanked," Tae said.

Fexil stitched his brow together and stalked in behind his companion. "Oh shit, she's a damned succubus. I told you we never should have brought her in here alone with us. Get away from the witch before she puts you under her spell."

Tae squeezed her fists tighter, spilling out a denser cloud of magic. The smoke ran up Fexil's thighs. He slapped at it as it circled his waist, but it was futile. The smoke slid up his chest like probing hands and penetrated his mouth, leaving him glassy-eyed.

"Silly boys, it was *my* idea to come inside." Tae held up a teasing finger. Her finely manicured nail caught their eye. It was perfectly uniform with a glossy sheen that mesmerized them.

"It was?" Fexil asked dumbly.

Both men looked intoxicated, swaying in place and staring at her with dopey grins.

"Don't tease me now," she fake pouted. "You know how much I wanted this." She slowly moved that manicured finger like a hypnotic snake, careful to ensure they were both watching it like fish with a worm on a hook. She brought it down to the collar of her blouse. One flick snapped away the top button.

Rovio bit his lower lip in anticipation. She flicked her finger again, releasing the next button. The third popped open on its own, gravity taking over and spilling her cleavage out enough that her captors could get an ample view of her black lace bra.

Fexil clutched his partner's arm and whimpered. "We're under her spell."

"And why shouldn't you want to be?" Tae asked innocently. "How can anything this sweet be bad?" She slid her legs apart so they could get a generous view of her naked thighs and the promise hidden between the folds of her skirt. "Don't you both want to take me here on this crate?"

"You want *us* to take you?" Rovio asked with uncertainty.

Tae's magic clogged the air around them. "Who wouldn't want such virile men to ravish her?" She snapped her fingers.

The men had a simultaneous flash of insight that she projected. Mouths sucking on nipples, fingers stroking their rigid flesh, ragged breathing as they thrust inside of her. They stood like zombies, transfixed in their lustful fantasy. Fexil was the more resistant of the pair. His hands were large and meaty, with fingers twitching as he fought her spell. His pinky finger gave him away, though. It stroked Rovio's thigh.

They're lovers, she realized. Nothing she couldn't work with. "Show me how you play with each other first," she offered.

Fexil finally succumbed to his desire. He let out a moan as the pair of them fell on each other. They kissed passionately, Fexil's thicker lips engulfing Rovio's. Tae had them trapped.

She chanced a glance at the warehouse door. *I should make a run for it.* The men making out with each other was turning her on. Rovio undid his partner's belt and thrust his hand down his pants. Fexil moaned loudly.

Tae slid silently off the crate, careful to continue spilling out her miasma of pheromones. Better to keep them preoccupied with each other as long as possible. She needed to get far away from that warehouse.

However, it was hard to walk away. Between her magic and their passion, Tae was getting worked up in her own right. Such raw lust wasn't easily ignored by a succubus. She concentrated on keeping her feet moving toward the door, but she couldn't help watching the men as Rovio tugged his partner down to his knees. She bit her lower lip.

And walked right into a stack of wooden crates. Her shoulder cracked against the corner of the crates, and she yelped in pain.

"Wait…," Fexil mumbled.

"Eh?"

Tae turned back in time to see Fexil chasing after her. His head was lowered like a charging bull. Rovio was left standing by himself, holding his cock for his missing lover. But Fexil wore a look of determination. He was fighting her magic with every fiber of his being.

"Get back here!" he shouted.

"Sorry, time to skedaddle," Tae called. As she ran around the stacked crates, she threw her shoulder into them.

Fexil had just enough time to shout his surprise before the crates tumbled over him. His head hit the floorboards with a loud crack. She peeked around the mess. There was no blood on the floor, which was good. Tae wasn't built for killing people. She was a lover, not a fighter—literally. Generally, she tried to avoid violence at all costs, but she wasn't going to stand around and let someone hurt her either.

Rovio cried. "Fexil, oh no, what happened to you?" He knelt beside his incapacitated partner and stroked the hair from his brow.

"Your friend's taken a little tumble," Tae said. "Stay here with him and I'll go get a healer."

Rovio nodded numbly. "Yes, you go get a healer. I'll stay here." He was still in her trance. She thought about asking him to show her the box he'd taken from Valia, but she couldn't risk it. These were dangerous men to toy with.

Wow, I was in that warehouse longer than I realized, she thought as she left the building. The sunlight was already fading below the horizon. She checked her bracelet to ensure the dweomer was still active, masking her features so no one could identify her, and then set off down the alley.

The warehouse door slammed shut behind her. "Where'd you go, you bitch?" It was Rovio, and he sounded very much awake.

Tae ducked into the alleyway across from the warehouse, behind a stack of wine barrels. She could see Rovio from between the barrels. He held a dagger and was gritting his teeth.

Shit, he's pissed. Waking up from the trance to find his lover knocked out beneath a stack of crates had enraged the thug. He was out for blood. He was so angry, in fact, that he didn't pay any heed to the telltale silhouette of the dragonfly resting on top of the warehouse roof.

Tae saw the dark outline of the insect and shuddered. She wisely made herself smaller against the wine barrels.

"I know you're hiding around here somewhere," Rovio shouted. "Come out and face me."

Oh sure, why don't I just go out with my hands up and let you stab me? Tae thought. *That dummy better stop waving his arms around before the dragonfly notices him.*

Rovio shoved over a pile of crates at the corner of the warehouse. "You're not going to be able to hide from me long."

The dragonfly twitched its body around at the commotion. Rovio threw his arms up in anger and shoved another crate to the ground. When he found nothing behind it, he screamed in rage and walked out into the center of the street. The dragonfly turned its body so its bulbous eyes were facing him. Rovio stopped in the center of the street, and his eyes landed on the wine barrels where she hid.

"Ah, there you are," he growled.

The dragonfly zipped off the rooftop, its wings droning so close it hurt Tae's ears. Rovio turned and threw his arms up in terror as the monstrous insect swooped down at him.

Tae tackled him in the midsection, hurling the pair of them into the pile of crates he'd knocked over. The dragonfly hit the dirt, then zipped off into the air with an angry drone. It had missed its opportunity. Tae had saved Rovio from a horrible death of being eaten alive by the insect.

He lay in a limp pile beneath her. His temple had hit one of the crates when they went down, knocking him out clean. Tae quickly got to her feet and cursed. The collision had damaged her enchanted bracelet. One of the gemstones was gone and with it her disguise. She searched the dirt for the stone, but it was nowhere to be seen, and the sound of the returning dragonfly came from the west.

Tae hooked her hands under Rovio's armpits and dragged him closer to the wall of the warehouse. Dragonflies react to movement, but they can also track their prey through memory and smell. If she left Rovio out in the open, the insect could still find him. Pressed against the warehouse, with a pile of crates between him and the road, he would be safe. And when he woke up, she'd be long gone.

At least I can get a gander at that package Valia gave him. She fished around in his jacket pockets until she found it. It was an ordinary-looking wooden box.

"Let's see what all the fuss was about," she grumbled.

The wooden panel slid free quite easily.

Tae gasped at what she found inside. Valia Medi'tu, duchess of the Court of Shadows, was peddling shimmer.

18

"You look a bit flushed, Valia. Are you feeling well?" Cyan asked, feigning concern.

"Nothing I can't handle, just a bit of business. You know how it goes. I was running a little behind and rushed to get here. How fortunate for me that we were matched, though. I only have one question left to answer."

Rushed? I wondered. *Why was she late? And where's Tae?*

I scanned the thinning crowds around us but there was no sign of my friend. The gathering was almost dispersed. Only a few pockets of stragglers like us remained under each flower, everyone else having moved on to snack on refreshments at the center of the atrium and finally drink their tea until the next phase of the hunt began.

"I'm afraid I'm all done," Cyan said. "Lady Alacore answered my last question. Such a pity, time is running short. Perhaps you can help one another?" Cyan lifted a questioning brow to me.

Shit, I hope not, I thought. *The last thing I want to do is talk to this uptight bitch. How many do I have left? Silas and Malachai answered two of my questions. Olan and Cyan asked me theirs, and Artur disqualified himself, but I think that still counts in my favor. That means I still need to ask one more question to complete the challenge. Of course, just my luck.*

I sighed in defeat. "I have one last question to ask."

Valia turned up her nose as if the prospect of speaking to me was an odor she'd rather not be around. She looked between me and Cyan several times in disbelief. I could see her mentally willing for the situation not to be happening.

"Well, if either of you wants to remain in the running, you better get moving," Cyan said as she departed. "The bells will be going off soon."

Once the bells sounded, the first challenge of the hunt would be over. Anyone who hadn't accomplished their task by then would be disqualified—laughing pumpkins and all that. Valia and I sneered at each other with as much open hostility as I've ever felt for another woman. Neither of us wanted to be near the other.

"Guess it's either talk to each other or quit," I conceded.

"I can't dream how you can say that as if I were the one putting you out. Hurry and ask your question so we can be done with this."

Hmm, what to ask the queen of uptight bitches? I know nearly nothing about her. Tae said Valia's family is a military might in the Court of Shadows. I didn't think that meant Valia herself was much of a fighter. I remembered how she'd cowered when I was about to slap her that night at the lunar party when I was searching for Charlie.

Still, she does have a weird deadly edge to her. She reminded me of a scorpion waiting to sting its prey when they turned their back. I imagined she was the type of person who liked to pluck the wings off baby birds. Of course, that idea could've stemmed from jealousy. Did I really care that much who Lucien hung out with? Valia and he had been friends, or whatever they were, long before I came around. And the two of us weren't exactly a couple. More like fuck buddies.

"Are you just going to stand there and grin at me like a dope?" Valia snapped. "Ask your question."

I decided there was something far more calculating and cunning about Valia when she wasn't around Lucien. Did she put on the show of flighty mean girl for his benefit? And why was she running late to the hunt? What business could she possibly have during a spring celebration?

"It was you," I said.

Valia stared at me as if I'd lost my mind.

"You're the one who tricked Artur into giving up his silk holdings. That's why he's so familiar with you."

"What of it?" Valia shrugged. "It's not exactly a state secret. I can't help it if Artur doesn't know how to handle his business affairs. I mean, he couldn't have made it any easier. Why do you care, anyhow? What's it to you if the House of Dawn has a financial misstep? Don't you have a soap shop to run or something?"

"It's an apothecary," I corrected her, though it was obvious she knew what kind of business I ran and only said that to get a rise out of me. "It's a dirty thing to swindle someone out of their livelihood."

Valia laughed. "I knew you were a naïve little strumpet, but I had no idea you were a sentimentalist to boot. Oh, Lanie, this world is going to positively gobble you up."

A loud voice rose over the gathering. "Participants have two minutes remaining to complete the tea ceremony."

My heart skipped a beat. It was now or never. I had to ask Valia something so I could figure out whether she was lying or telling the truth.

"Quickly, ask me something," Valia urged.

"Why don't you like me?" *Ugh, kill me now.* How could I have asked such a lame question? There was something about the moment, the urgency of it, that made the first thing that popped into my head come stumbling out through my lips.

Valia flinched like she'd been slapped. She blinked at me. A dead silence hung between us for an ocean of time.

"One minute remaining," the voice warned.

Valia finally blinked again. "Because I'm jealous of you."

I felt numb all over. "But you're so beautiful. How could you possibly feel threatened by me?"

"I didn't say threatened," Valia corrected.

I saw it clearly. She was lying. Valia was threatened by the relationship she perceived was developing between me and Lucien. I wanted to reassure her that there was nothing going on between us, but I couldn't. I certainly didn't love Lucien. I just didn't want to walk away from him yet. Lucien had something I couldn't get anywhere else. Someone as perfect as Valia could never understand what it was like to be trapped underneath my curse, to never be able to feel intimacy with another living being. Her face shifted from cruel mockery to shame. It physically pained her to admit she was jealous of me.

"You're telling the truth," I said. "You're actually jealous of me. No wonder you're always so mean. You're worried I'm going to take Lucien away from you."

"Don't mock me," she warned.

"I'm not. I would never. Not about that. I just don't think you need to worry about someone like me stealing Lucien away from you."

It was the wrong thing to say. My moment of pity and her millisecond of weakness dissolved in her glaring eyes. Valia looked so enraged that I took a step back from her. Her bare shoulders trembled, and she gritted her teeth.

"Why would I ever need to worry about someone like you? You're nothing. You're an insignificant *slut*. Do you know how many drooling women I've seen flash their cunts in Lucien's face over the years? All you are to him is a place to rut. You know that deep down too. You're a good-for-nothing piece of trash that nobody is ever going to love. You strut around here like you're better than the rest of us. 'Oh, look at me, I'm the dumb bitch who grew up around humans. I don't know any of our customs, tee hee.' The sight of you makes me sick to my stomach. You're beyond worthless. Tell me, Lanie, am I speaking the truth this time too?"

Her verbal assault relented when the bells overhead chimed, signaling the end of the tea game. I wanted to lash back, to sting her where it would hurt most, the way she'd done to me. I told myself to be strong like Deedee would've been. But I knew if I opened my mouth I would start crying. I felt the promise of it like a lump in the back of my throat. I turned away from her and fled with my head held high. I refused to give her the satisfaction of seeing me upset.

She's a petty girl saying nasty things to salve her own wounded pride, I told myself.

Logic didn't matter. Most of what she'd said hit too close to home.

At that moment all I wanted was for someone like Lobo to hold me. He let me do that once before. I'd cried into his chest as he held me, and I never felt safer. Valia didn't know about my curse, but she was still right. That was the kind of life that would be forever denied to me. As long as the curse had a hold over my body, I would never be able to have a normal relationship, I would never find love, never find someone to share my life with.

An irrational panic gripped me by the chest, squeezing my heart and leaving me breathless. I left the atrium for the far corner of the balcony. Clutching the wooden parapet helped steady my body. I gazed out at the swelling crowd below. The "lesser" races were relegated to the palace grounds, but Ambrose had ensured their festival was every bit as grand as the one inside. Drobas and satyrs rubbed shoulders with brownies and pixies. They laughed in merriment, children running between their parents and lovers teasing one another. It was another reminder of all the things I would never have in life.

A smothering gloom enveloped me.

"Are you alright, my lady?" Silas sidled up to me, his teacup in one hand. He studied my face intently.

I was mortified. He was so achingly beautiful, and I felt like a grotesque creature that needed to crawl back out of the sunlight. I couldn't stand the thought of his eyes on me, and the last thing I needed was to be mocked. "Just go away." I winced at how sullen my voice sounded.

He bowed graciously. "I am sorry to have disturbed you. I only wanted to warn you that a moment ago a sprite tied your shoelaces together."

Sure enough, my laces were knotted together. I searched for Bella, but she was nowhere to be seen. "That little…"

Silas chuckled. "They can be merciless in their pranks. Now I will leave you to your own devices."

His smile disarmed my anger. I suddenly felt very guilty for rebuking him. "No. Please, stay."

"Are you certain?"

"You were only trying to help, and I was being rude. I just…I thought maybe you were…"

"Trying to poke fun at you? Someone was unkind to you," he surmised as he handed me a handkerchief.

"Is it that obvious?"

"Just a dab around the eyes. You're leaking a little."

"You must think I'm awfully pathetic."

Looking into Silas's eyes was like staring into the open ocean. "Quite the contrary. You seem to be the only genuine person I've met in ages. I can see it in the way you look around at the palace in wonder. Your eyes light up, whether you are taking in the majesty of Starfire's boughs or delighting in the flight of a starling overhead. There's nothing pathetic about that level of enthusiasm for the world around you." He waved a dismissive hand toward the atrium, his other perfectly poised, holding his tea saucer close to his chest without spilling a drop. He was a far more graceful creature than I was. My tea had spilled onto the saucer a bit. "These nobility…they can be quite barbaric."

"Aren't you one of them?"

He scoffed at the notion. "Surely you've heard by now that I am the fallen angel."

"What makes you think I've asked around about you?"

He laughed at the look I must have given him.

"Why did Ambrose kick you out of the family?" It felt like too forward of a question to be asking, but there was a vulnerability connecting us that I couldn't deny.

Silas glowered at the crowd below us. "You can't blame Ambrose Amaryllis for my fate. The happy owners of that invention were my parents, father and mother alike."

I stayed silent. What could I say that would mend the sorrow so pungent in his voice? I was determined to be his dutiful listener as he had just been for me. I liked watching Silas speak. He was very animated, with his hands constantly waving about to emphasize his words. And anyway, it gave me an excuse to stare at his chiseled jaw and bright eyes.

"They abandoned me. That's the sad truth of it. My parents left me so they could go fight in that miserable war." He said it with bitter regret.

"The one between the giants and the fae?"

"Heavens no. That was four centuries ago. Do I really look that old?"

I giggled nervously. "I can never really tell with fae."

"No, the conflict they entered was nothing so lofty as saving the realm. Like a good deal of others at the time, my mother and father defied the edicts of our Great Houses to pick up arms and join the cause of the humans. They called it World War Two, a conflict that engulfed the entire human realm."

"I didn't know the fae fought in human wars."

"They don't. Not usually. But this war was too much for my mother and father to bear. I was only a child at the time, but I still remember the sound of my mother weeping. My father, Perseus, argued with Ambrose that the entire fae realm needed to get involved. Perseus insisted that if the humans learned of our existence, it would unite them into stopping the evil encroaching on their realm. This was before the Americans joined the Allies. The Third Reich was wiping out entire lineages. It was genocide. My mother argued that once the Nazis claimed their inevitable victory, given how deeply interested Hitler was in the occult, it would only be a matter of time before they discovered our realm."

"Wow. So they defied their parents and joined the human war to stop the Nazis?" I marveled. "That sounds like a noble cause to me."

"At what cost? It's easy to say that, but you didn't lose everything because of their decision. I miss them so desperately. Each day I can still hear my mother's laughter. I find myself thinking about the times she would chase me through the palace gardens. When I look in the mirror, I see my father looking back at me. He's there in my own face, in my eyes, his memory so fresh it pains me. To the point that I wear this glamour just so I don't have relive that daily reminder.

"After they died, I lost all rights to the House of Dawn. If Perseus hadn't openly defied grandfather's orders then he could have spared me, but as it was… No, I'm not one of the nobility. I'm something else to them. A passing fancy, the foppish nephew who gallivants with rich humans and throws wild parties. I'm here because they have no choice, and I know exactly how cruel these people can be. Cyan has been tormenting me for years. I think she sees it as her duty to punish me for my parents' transgressions. You don't deserve that sort of treatment."

We both realized he'd been resting his hand over mine on the balcony rail. His grip was warm and strong. I stared at his hand.

"I'm sorry." Silas laughed nervously. "It seems I've forgotten myself." He snatched away his hand and averted his gaze to the floor as scarlet colored around his tanned cheekbones. Cold air replaced where his hand had been, and I longed to feel his fingers back on my skin.

"You have nothing to apologize for," I assured him. "You're a very nice person, Silas. I was feeling rotten and mired in my own melancholy when you came over. Thank you. I mean it. And thank you for sharing your story with me."

His smile returned, but that scarlet glow around his high cheekbones and sturdy jaw remained. "I don't know what got into me. I don't usually open up to people so quickly." He studied me for a moment. "I see now why you were chosen to take the trials to become warden of your province."

Hmm. That sounded like a line. There might be some truth to it, but the practiced smirk Silas put on felt like another mask he desperately tried to slip over his open emotions. Mask or not, I found myself transfixed by his smile. His lips looked thick and strong. How would they feel pressed against my own? As if reading my mind, his eyes lingered on my open mouth. An uneasy yet heady energy radiated between us.

148

I suddenly cleared my throat. "Should we drink our tea and see who we're matched with?"

Silas looked relieved to have the tension broken. He lifted his cup to his lips and paused to wink at me. "Maybe I'll get lucky and get paired with Lady Alacore."

I giggled despite how corny he was being. *It would be pretty cool to be matched up, though.*

"I'm afraid I've beaten you to the punch, my good friend," Lucien said, overhearing our conversation as he strutted out onto the balcony. He looked dashing in his form-fitting suit with a tight mandarin collar that called attention to the pale curve of his milky-white throat. His silver-hammered eyes drank me up and then shifted to Silas as he turned his teacup at an angle so we could see the bottom. The tea leaves had settled in an amalgamation of my face.

"Prince Lucien!" Silas greeted enthusiastically.

"You know each other?" I asked, unable to conceal my surprise.

The two of them embraced, each patting the other's back the way men do when they're showing affection but want to establish their manliness. It almost made me roll my eyes. But then Silas kissed both of Lucien's cheeks.

"Silas and I are old friends," Lucien replied cheerfully.

"You're in a friendlier mood than usual," I said. "Could it be because I haven't seen your handler around? Where is the knuckle-dragger these days?"

"I'll remind you that knuckle-dragger is my cousin. Finnely is conducting my affairs in the provinces, freeing me up to attend the spring festival with my father." He shot me one of his lopsided smirks as if everything between us was business as usual. I resented the way my chest fluttered. Part of me was excited to be in his company with him speaking to me as I was used to. The other part wanted nothing more than to slap him in the face for thinking he could be so rude to me one day and then waltz up the next as if nothing had happened.

Silas chuckled, more amused by our exchange than uncomfortable. "I've known Prince Lucien since our days at the academy together. Just how do the two of you know each other?"

"Lanie and I...*bump* into each other from time to time," Lucien said without breaking eye contact with me. "You know how it is, old boy."

Silas arched a brow. "Indeed, I do."

I winced at Silas's tone. I didn't want him to think I was, how did Valia put it, just someone to rut around with in bed. When his eyes brushed across me again, I blushed. Why did Lucien have to be so crude? I suddenly felt naked, trapped between those two gorgeous men. I crossed my arms over my chest and glared at Lucien. He only laughed.

"I think the lady is upset with you," Silas pointed out playfully.

Lucien finally turned away from me. "I'm afraid I may have behaved rather boorishly yesterday afternoon when she interrupted my father's conversation with your cousin Cyan. I shouldn't have been so cold. It is hard to remember sometimes that Lanie is not purposefully attempting to be rude." He closed the distance between us. His eyes searched mine for something. "She was raised around humans, after all."

What is he saying? Did I unknowingly overstep my bounds at the banquet? I thought back to my encounter with his family. They had been wrapped in conversation with Cyan and her wife at the time. Had anyone else approached them? Was it seen as poor manners for a commoner like me to walk up to high nobility and strike up a conversation? Put in that context, and through the lens of my embarrassing choking spectacle, courtesy of Bella, I started viewing the situation differently.

Perhaps that was true, but Lucien's cold indifference toward me still needled like a splinter stuck beneath my skin. "What do you want, an apology? Did speaking to a commoner embarrass you in front of your big important daddy?"

Lucien had the good sense to look stunned. His cocky demeanor gave way, and for the slightest of moments I caught something else. *Is that shame?*

Silas laughed. "Oh, she's got you there, prince. Lady Alacore, I had no idea you could be so feisty."

Lucien smiled wistfully and gazed knowingly at me. "Yes, she's practically feral at times."

I felt embarrassed. Was that really how he saw me? My shoulders sagged as I wilted.

Lucien put a hand on my arm. It was a reflexive gesture to console me. I saw uncertainty pass over him as he realized what he was doing. Silas didn't catch on to the movement.

MICHELLE MURPHY

Lucien was torn. I had forgotten what his life was like. He wore the weight of his station for all the world to see, as a dutiful son to one of the most powerful families in the fae realm. But that wasn't the real Lucien. The Lucien I knew took pleasure in sitting by the river and watching children play. He was a man who rose to my defense when the chips were unfairly stacked against me, even though it would earn his father's ire and potential ill will with his court. I felt my anger uncoil, replaced by an uncomfortable awkwardness.

I wasn't sure where to look or what to do, so I gulped down my tea. To my surprise, the tea was still hot. Not piping enough to scald my tongue but that perfect temperature I like so it warms me down to my toes. The flavor was remarkable, like fresh squeezed oranges and cardamom, with the sweetness of vanilla root. I drank all of it down, then set the cup on the saucer.

Sure enough, Lucien's face was formed in crushed tea leaves that clung to the bottom of the fine porcelain. I couldn't help grinning.

The bells chimed across the atrium and out onto the balcony.

"Remaining participants, please gather your partner and head to your appointed meeting spot," Geraldine's voice commanded.

Silas made a strangled sound. "I better go find my partner. Good luck to the two of you." He leaned in, one hand on my back, to give me a half-hug, then departed.

It was so sudden and yet intimate that I caught my breath. Silas's skin smelled like musk, and it lingered on my dress, the heat of his fingertips still etched onto my bare back. Lucien noted my reaction and shot me a sly grin.

"How do we know where our appointed spot is?" I quickly asked, desperate to shift his attention to something else.

"It should be on our cups somewhere." He lifted his teacup from the saucer and inspected the bottom of it.

I followed suit, but the bottom only had an insignia of the House of Dawn. The saucer was plain. I rotated the teacup, hoping to find the name of where we were to head next. Amidst the curling vines and budding flowers were vertical patterns set in even rows from top to bottom.

"Are those books?" I asked.

"Let me see." Lucien leaned in close so he could peer at my cup.

151

I pushed him back a step. "Back up, sucker. You're not out of the doghouse yet."

"Doghouse?" He frowned.

Normally his confusion would have made me laugh, but I was still annoyed with him. "I guess it's a human saying. It means *boy who was rude to me yesterday doesn't get to cuddle up against me today.* Now, stay focused. Books?" I held out the cup for him to see.

Looking only slightly chagrined, Lucien turned his attention back to the teacup. "They could be books. Mine is different. It has a small dress on it with a jagged hem."

Sure enough his cup had no books. A dress was caught in the intertwined ivy wrapped around the porcelain. "Where have I seen that before?" I felt a bolt of excitement. "The library!"

"Shh, keep it down," Lucien warned, looking over his shoulder. "We don't want to give the answer away to everyone listening. Who knows how many other fae have the same scavenger hunt as us."

"Oh, is that what this part is?"

"It's literally called the Wyld Hunt. What did you think we were going to be doing?"

"I've never been on a scavenger hunt before," I said, too thrilled about the prospect to let his condescension bring me down. "That dress looks just like the one I saw the palace librarian Nuala wearing the other day. And with the books…"

"Brilliant," Lucien intoned before bowing and gesturing for us to head out.

We cut across the atrium, past other fae inspecting their cups or still looking for their partners. How much of a coincidence was it that Lucien and I were paired up? If it had been any other fae, I would still have been scouring the crowd for their face. As it was, we were already off to our first clue, up the steps to the second floor, when I caught a glimpse of Valia. She was by herself, scowling at me and clutching her teacup so tightly I thought it might shatter.

She's seething that I'm with Lucien.

I felt a touch of satisfaction at that and grabbed his arm as if I needed help climbing the steps. Lucien's hand naturally circled around my waist and pressed my lower back. His icy fingertips permeated through the thin fabric of my dress, sending a delicious wave up my spine. Valia's lips moved. I didn't know what she said, but judging by the way the sun fae walking up to her suddenly gasped, it had to be bad. I knew it was petty to antagonize her. It still felt good.

Lucien confidently navigated through the palace.

We soon arrived at the library to find an underbutler blocking the double doors. "I apologize Prince Lucien, the library is closed to the public today."

"Here is our invitation." Lucien handed them his teacup.

The underbutler turned it slightly, then nodded and held out an open palm for my cup. Once they had both, they nodded and stepped aside. "Your path has taken you to a point of a circle. Ellipse the edge with poise, and you will find your next steps."

Lucien strode through the doors like a baron returning to his mansion. It was so abrupt and imperious that it left me startled for a moment.

"Thank you," I said to the underbutler, embarrassed by how callously Lucien had dismissed him. I scurried to catch up to Lucien, then scowled at him. "Why were you so rude to them?"

Lucien was taking in the library with an appraising eye. "Rude? To whom?"

"That poor underbutler. You didn't have to be so dismissive."

Lucien looked perfectly confused. "Their purpose was to allow entry to riddle holders and to pass on the next clue. What more should I have done? Should I have groveled at their feet for doing such a *tremendous* job?"

"It's called common courtesy." I didn't feel like arguing over the point. "Was that our second clue?"

"Yes, but what does it mean? Circles by their nature are pointless." He chuckled to himself. "There are no sharp edges to be had…unless it is a circular blade they were referring to. Could that have been what they meant? The point is the edge of a circular blade?"

The library was empty. Either we were the first participants to arrive or someone else had breezed through this step of the hunt. I thought over the clue phrase once more. "They said our path has taken us to a point of the circle, ellipse the edge with poise." Lucien was right. Circles aren't known for having points. Arrows have points. Circles are smooth. They are the embodiment of grace. "But grace and poise are two different things. Poise is more in how you stand, right?"

Lucien tucked his long hair behind his ear. "Poise and gracefulness can be one and the same. When I think of poise, I think of how one bears themselves."

"Right, like a dancer," I agreed.

Lucien's silver eyes practically glowed as he snatched my hand and grinned. "That's fantastic, Lanie. A dancer. They didn't say point, they said pointe."

"Like ballet?"

Lucien cut across the library, tugging me by my sleeve like an excited child. "Exactly. Now, what kind of ballet involves ellipses?"

"Nuala," I called.

A sparkle of light above us fluttered like a disco ball. Nuala floated down out of the light on her faerie wings. "Lady Alacore, what a pleasure."

"Hullo! I was wondering what books you might have on ballet ellipses," I said.

"My, you are a clever pair." Nuala smirked. "I expected my riddle to take a *little* longer to solve, at least. You'll find a book on Matthew Hindson's ballet *Ellipse* in row IV, third rack on the left."

Lucien turned to go, but I snatched his arm and dug my nails in just hard enough to give him pause. He tugged his arm away and frowned at me.

"Thank you, Nuala. I hope you have a splendid evening," I said pointedly. "Lucien?"

He rolled his eyes at me and sighed. "Yes, thank you for your assistance, librarian."

Nuala tittered and zipped back into her strobing light, disappearing to wherever she had been before I called her. When I looked down again, Lucien was already turning the corner to aisle IV. I zipped up beside him to catch up.

"Was that so hard?"

He groaned. "I don't see why you're making such a big fuss. Surely the librarian was happy enough to have been helpful."

"It never hurts to make others feel valued," I insisted kindly. I had to remind myself that Lucien was a prince. That was the lens he lived his life through, for better or worse. To him the world was populated with people waiting to serve his every need. How could I blame him for behaving that way? He wasn't outwardly rude to either of the palace staff we'd encountered. Maybe I *was* being silly, as he thought?

"Here it is." Lucien pulled a green leatherbound book from the shelf. "Ah, a page is marked." A satin bookmark was attached to the book. Nuala had left it pulled through the spine, marking page eighty-five. The right page was dominated by an elaborate illustration of a ballet duo.

I didn't need to read the caption. "That painting is in the palace art gallery."

Lucien clapped the book shut and slid it back onto the shelf. "Best partner ever," he intoned gleefully.

I warmed under his praise and bit my lower lip to keep my grin from taking over my face. Lucien grabbed my hand and led me out of the library.

Our next clue *was* in a painting. Not the painting of the ballet duo, but across from it. The gallery had a very different feel fully lit. Underbutlers stood on either side of the entrance, with several more sticking close to the walls with their hands folded behind their backs. They were all courtesy and charm, though I was certain their duty was to ensure disorderly guests didn't damage any of the artwork on display.

It was easier than I expected to find my way back to the ballet painting. The piece was more a study of movement than realism, with the energy of the man's arms as he lifted the ballerina carved out in oil colors. Her legs were flung upward in a graceful pose. It was a masterful illusion, at first glance seeming effortless, but the longer I stared, the more I saw each careful brushstroke, made with an energetic fervor, to convey even the details of the woman's splayed fingers.

"I think this placard is our next clue," I said.

Typically, a placard will denote information about the art piece, what type of mediums were used, a little about the artist, maybe even the inspiration behind it. The one beside *Ellipse* was written out like a poem.

Lucien read it aloud. "Who is to say where our feet rest? Can it be a shifting veil, the smile from a gale? Ballet requires nimble feet, but to look upon them is replete. Rather, the dancer must gaze ever outward with pep, to convey confidence in every step." He frowned.

"Well, it's no Keats," I said. "But I think it means we need to follow the ballet dancer's eyes."

Her gaze was pointed over my shoulder. I turned to find a familiar row of statues. My skin crawled in an involuntary shudder. I could still feel the gaze of my shadowy stalker lingering around those same sculptures. Even lit, there was a feeling of wrongness clinging to them.

I forced myself to shrug it off and inspect them closer. I closed one eye and used my finger to trace a line in the air from the ballerina's gaze to the statue of the little girl I'd seen before.

I moved in closer, inspecting her for the next clue. I kept finding my eyes drawn to her face. My skin crawled. She felt so real that every time I glanced away, I was sure her eyes followed me. There was a hint of a smirk in one corner of her mouth. Yet at the same time she had a look of shock about her. As if she hadn't expected to be carved from the stone that birthed her. I had an urge to touch her curls, convinced I could run my fingers through their stony permanence.

Why did the artist put crow's feet around her eyes? I wondered. It was an odd choice for a statue of a child. And yet it suited her. I couldn't imagine that cherubic face without the wrinkles. I leaned in closer, inspecting behind the statue. Her hands were folded behind her back, the fingers fully detailed and intertwined like a nervous child might twiddle.

A nearby underbutler cleared her throat.

"Oops, sorry." I quickly moved away from the statue.

"I think this is it," Lucien called. "The riddle isn't about her eyes, but his. Why should she need to keep an eye on her feet? She's in the air. *He* must stand firm to gracefully balance her."

"You're right," I exclaimed. There's nothing like solving a puzzle to pump up my serotonin. Lucien had followed the ballerina's gaze to a colorful painting on the wall at the end of the row of statues. I gaped. "Is that Van Gogh's *Almond Blossom*?"

"Indeed." Lucien studied the piece with his arms folded over his chest. "But what does it mean?"

The placard beside it informed me of the medium and dimensions, but nothing else. "Why would the House of Dawn showcase human artwork? I thought all things human are abhorred by the fae?"

Lucien chuckled. "Imagine that. Van Gogh, a human. Next you'll be saying David Bowie was human too."

I was double confounded by that revelation. I'd certainly heard that some of the most artistic and influential humans were in fact fae, but it stunned me nonetheless to discover the man who played King Oberon in *Labyrinth* was actually a fae. What house did he belong to?

Lucien snapped his fingers. "Of course. Almond trees. There is a whole grove of them in the forest behind the palace," he said, already heading back the way we'd come. "Hurry up. We're off to the stables."

I had to trust that he was right. I knew nothing about the woods behind the palace. Either way, I was eager to escape the gallery and leave the creepy statue of the little girl behind.

I'd never been near a real-life horse before. The closest I'd come was spotting a ranch while driving down a country road. There weren't exactly a lot of horses roaming around New York City. Okay, I'd seen a few mounted police around Central Park, but that was a far cry from what happened next.

The stables were located behind Starfire, on the edge of the forest. We had to leave by the main palace entrance and circle around her massive trunk to reach them. There was an odd tree on the way, close to the stables, with leaves that lit up the night with an inner golden glow. I made a mental note to revisit the tree, as I'm always interested in learning about new plants. A pair of riders was just leaving as we arrived at the stables, which were large enough to house at least thirty horses. A palpable odor hit me when we entered. It was hard to place, somewhere between fresh hay, animals, wood, and a musk from the horses that was sweet like a rose. It was a surprisingly pleasant smell.

"Here we are," Lucien announced stopping before a stall door. A sleek black stallion stuck his head out to greet Lucien. The stallion had clear eyes and a shiny coat. "Interesting, they've put Alastor's bridle on." He glanced at the opposite stall. "Arion too. Well, that seals it. We're definitely on the right track." He stroked the stallion as he opened the door and led him out. "You can ride Arion. Alastor's not partial to more than one rider."

"Sure thing," I said, trying to hide my panic.

Arion turned her head to the side to gaze at me with her knowing hazel eyes. She was a beautiful mare, her coat a golden champagne color and her mane chocolate brown. She shifted hoof to hoof, eager to join Alastor for a run in the woods. I reached a tentative hand out to her, and she pressed her head against my open palm.

The connection between us was instantaneous. One second, I was standing, hand outstretched for her, and the next I was nuzzling my equine muzzle against the unicorn faerie standing on the other side of my stable door. This fae smelled different than the shadow fae that usually came around. She was almost horse-like, sweet, but with a jasmine pungency that clung to my coat. It was jarring.

I stumbled backward. "What in the world was that?"

"Come on," Lucien called from the exit. "We better get moving."

I gaped back at Arion. Her eyes glistened with recognition, and she gave me a low-pitched nicker. I inherently understood it was meant to be a greeting, an invitation, and a recognition that we were kin. "Is this...did I just feel what you were feeling?"

Arion nickered again. She raised her head and playfully shook her chocolate mane from side to side. She was raring to go. Alastor was already outside, and she wasn't about to let him get the better of her. He spent enough time showing off for Valia's kin.

Hurry, silly unicorn girl, we need to go.

It was confounding. I understood what she was thinking. Not in words, as I would have communicated with another person, but in clear pictures and sweeping emotions that threatened to engulf me if I lingered in them too long. I reached a tentative hand for Arion, hungry to submerge myself in that roiling feeling of oneness once more.

She loved my touch. I was kin. She was eager to let loose, to leave the stables behind. I was worthy of joining her. She embraced my warmth. I saw myself as she did, a brilliant light muddled by something at my core but radiating all the same.

So that's what my curse looks like to a horse, I realized in wonder.

We felt each other from the inside out, exploring the world through each other's senses. Her vision was remarkable. Details hidden by the shadows of night were clear as day to Arion's superior vision. Where I smelled the stables, she could pinpoint each strand of hay—some musty, others ripe. She could tell the difference between each horse in the other stalls by their scent alone. It was an uncanny way of experiencing the world around us.

Is this what it's like for Lobo? Werewolves also had a heightened sense of smell far above that of a human.

"You're very comfortable with her," Lucien complimented.

I hadn't even realized I'd left the stables with Arion, let alone mounted her. The connection between us was still there, a powerful sense of dual minds, but Lucien's words centered me. I crawled back inside my body, slipping the feeling of myself back on like sliding into a glove. It was disorienting, but there was that feeling of rightness about it.

"I've never ridden a horse before," I said distantly.

Lucien scowled playfully. He didn't believe me. "We'll take that path ahead into the forest. Just keep close and follow me. I know the way to the almond grove."

Alastor carried him away like a sleek shadow. The dirt path they chose was well used, wide enough for wagons and horses to trot alongside each other. I imagined it was a trade route to the nearest towns to the Tides. Arion squealed. Her champagne body felt like one giant muscle between my thighs.

I want to go. It's time to gallop. Alastor was getting too far ahead.

"Then go after him," I insisted.

I almost flew off her as she jetted forward. The earth shook beneath her hammering hooves. My body rocked back and forth, careening on the verge of spilling off her back. I clung to the reins for dear life.

Silly faerie girl, we move all wrong.

"Well, I don't know what I'm doing," I snapped.

Arion bristled. She was annoyed with me. *Soften, you are too stiff. You will fall.*

The thought of tumbling onto the rocky road only made me more rigid. Arion bristled. All she could think about was how much farther ahead Alastor was than us.

Because you are stiff. Move your seat, unicorn. Feel our rhythm, match it. You sit like you are a lifeless lump of stone. Here, let me show you. I felt a dizzying sensation as Arion reached inside my being. It felt like her head was nudging my back, rubbing against my hips, coaxing me into a matching rhythm. Soon I was swaying my hips back and forth to match the beat of her movement.

Don't squeeze me, put your weight in your heels.

This time I did as she bade. It was like releasing the pent-up energy of a corkscrew. My thigh muscles relaxed, trusting in the gravity of my heels to keep me in place. I felt far more balanced as I bounced in beat to her trot and gyrated my hips to match the steady movement of her muscular legs.

Arion sighed a blast of air from her nostrils. If we weren't connected, I might have been alarmed, but I could feel her own tension ease. We were moving as one, which allowed her to pick up her pace.

I'm riding a horse! I thought excitedly.

I am letting you ride with me, she corrected.

I leaned into her trot, knowing the truth in what she felt. She was the master of this dance. It was a privilege that she allowed me to come along. The forest sped past faster and faster in a heart-pounding way that made me feel more alive than ever.

I always hated running even though I was quite good at it, faster than most. Still, I never saw the point of people who did it for sport. What fun could there be in purposefully getting all sweaty, achy, and out of breath? Now I realized what I had been missing out on. The wind cut through my hair, tossing it back like a smaller twin to Arion's chocolate mane. Galloping like this was freedom, it was power in shaking the earth, in cutting through the wind, in sheer speed as the world whizzed by.

Arion, you're wonderful! This is what I was meant to do my entire life, I thought. I had never felt more like a unicorn than in that moment. Arion proudly accepted my compliments.

Lucien chuckled as we came up alongside Alastor. The black stallion teased me, the sense of him on the edge of my being. He marveled that I had joined them and urged me to get off Arion and run alongside them. Arion scoffed at him and pushed ahead. Lucien's laugh was pure joy in our wake.

I eased along with Arion, copying her movements, leaning with her. We cut around a bend and she suddenly leapt across a fallen tree. It was pure bliss.

And then it was over. I knew we'd reached the almond grove minutes before we entered the clearing. The intoxicating vanilla-almond aroma of the trees hit me tenfold through my connection with Arion. Hummingbirds zipped around the boughs of the trees, suckling the nectar of white flowers amid their budding spring blossoms. Shepherd hook-shaped posts were spaced at intervals, glass globes hanging from them housing immaru bug habitats to light the woods. The clearing was wide enough for Arion to gallop in a full circle before slowing and bringing us back down to a trot toward the middle. An underbutler sat on a tree stump in the center, a circle of turned earth around her. She clapped at Arion's show of speed. Arion nickered low and came to a stop.

"What a beautiful mare," the underbutler complimented as she hopped to her feet with a carrot in hand. She offered it to Arion, at the same time taking hold of her reins. I felt the carrot crunch in her mouth, tasted the sweetness of it light up her palate. She was jubilant that her magnificence was recognized.

"I've never seen Valia's mare move like that," Lucien commented as Alastor pulled up next to us.

You're Valia's horse? I thought, astonished.

I belong to no one, Arion corrected offhandedly as she enjoyed her carrot.

"Nobody can own a horse," I corrected Lucien.

"Tell that to our ranch," he snickered. "You're right, though. Technically speaking, she belongs to my family. Though the only person who ever rides her is Valia."

I leaned down and whispered in her ear. "I'm glad you're not Valia's. She's a jerk."

Valia has a stronger core than you, Arion pointed out. *She's better at riding.* It wasn't a slight. Horses had no need for such pettiness. I understood that on a fundamental level. What Arion shared was, to her, simply a point of fact. *Unicorns should have stronger muscles. You'll need to make them better. We will ride together more. I will help you get stronger.*

I should have been annoyed. Horses didn't think like humans. They didn't think like fae. There was no uncertainty to their views. There was only room for understanding of the world around them. That understanding could be shaped by new information, and until it was, there was a conviction of rightness bred from experience. Humans would call it callous and stubborn. I could feel the wrongness of labeling it so. My connection to Arion was strong and true, and what she conveyed was born from a place of love. She pitied me that I had waited so long to learn to ride, but also believed I was capable of becoming exactly what she said. In her mind there was no doubt that I would become a stronger rider than any fae. I wanted that to be true. I wanted to be worthy of her esteem and become the best rider I could.

It was an interesting thing to be so suddenly thrust upon a yearning need that only minutes before hadn't even been an idea in my orbit.

Thank you, I would love that, I conveyed to her as I leaned forward and stroked her chocolate mane.

"Well, what is our next clue?" Lucien impatiently asked the underbutler.

"Ah, yes, of course." The woman bowed. "Wise we watch with wide eyes as under the boughs of life will you journey. Look beyond our bright feathers, look on to the next, ever deeper into our heart of hearts. There you will find the end of the beginning."

Once the poem was recited in full, she bowed reverently and turned her back to us. That was our clue given and delivered. The underbutler resumed her seat on the tree stump and turned her eyes to the sky. Perhaps, if Lucien hadn't been so curt with her, there might have been more conversation. She reminded me of a tulip rapidly curling up its petals for the evening.

"Wide eyes…" Lucien repeated under his breath as I dissected the clue in my mind.

"And the feathers," I said. "So, a bird…one that sits in the boughs of a tree. Which is every bird in the forest."

"Not every bird," Lucien noted with an upraised finger. Alastor crunched his carrot delightedly and sidled up to brush against Arion. Her body heated up, and I felt a matching passion stir inside me as my own thigh brushed Lucien's muscular leg. I caught my breath at the powerful surge of it, amplified through my connection with the animal urges of the horses. I hadn't realized Arion's need for competition with Alastor stemmed from a baser desire. She showed me what she would win from their courtship, and I blushed deeply.

That's right. He will not catch me. I am faster than Alastor. But if he can finally catch me, I will let him take me, and we will share our bodies.

Lucien chuckled. He had a devilish glint in his eye that told me he was interpreting my red face as a reaction to his leg brushing mine. In some ways that was true, but his assumption spoiled it.

"There are many hummingbirds around the grove," he pointed out.

I shook my head. "Hummingbirds have tiny eyes, and you never really catch them sitting in a tree." I gazed around the clearing, searching for other birds that might be out. An azure blue was washing over the sky.

The brightest stars were poking through as day finally succumbed fully to the evening sky. "Nighttime," I said. "Wide eyes…they're owls."

"I think you're right," Lucien grinned. His eyes sought the surroundings with a feral intensity. Deep in concentration, he clenched his jaw. His face was all angles, strong features, and chiseled bone. It must have been the horse's passion seeping into me, because I had a sudden urge to lean over and rub my face against his hard jawline.

It is not us. Arion corrected matter-of-factly. *You will want to mate too. He is a good partner. Excellent for you to rut.*

I covered my mouth to hide my laugh.

"There. At the edge of the grove," Lucien said. "There's an owl in the boughs watching us. Come on, Alastor."

They fell into a quick trot away from the underbutler. I urged Arion to follow, and soon we were stopped again at the northeastern edge of the grove. A white owl sat contentedly in the boughs. When we first arrived, I'd thought the grove had only one entrance. Now that I looked around us more carefully, I saw a dozen similar openings, with roads snaking into the forest.

"Then owls mark our path," I said.

Lucien nodded and led the way. We left the grove and its faerie lights behind. The forest was dark but in a lovely way. Spring had the newly budding trees mingling with evergreens and rustling in the thinning breeze coming up from the cliffs far behind us.

"This path is awfully smooth for a forest bed," I remarked. The road was an even layer of short, trimmed grass with no divots or stones on which Arion could twist her hoof.

"I suspect these paths were created for the sole purpose of this evening's festivities."

"They dug new paths through the forest just for the Wyld Hunt?" I said in disbelief. "How can that be? I haven't heard of any work happening in the forest. It would take weeks to pull off something like that. And this grass doesn't look new. Plus, where are the tree stumps?"

The trees rustled as if appalled by the idea of tree stumps.

"I'd be careful what you say in these woods," Lucien cautioned but with a glimmer of mischief in his eye so I couldn't tell if he was being serious or not. "The trees might not take too kindly to your threats."

I snickered and rolled my eyes at him.

"You still think like a human," he said. "Fae do not dominate a land in the way humans do. We are one with our realm. It shows a good deal how much the forest respects Ambrose Amaryllis to move aside for him. You see, we do not cut down and burn to make our spaces. We ease the forest to open up for us, so that we might come in to play for a while and admire her majesty."

"Are we still talking about the forest or my thighs?"

Lucien flashed me a devilish grin and shrugged. Before I could say more, we happened upon another owl. I almost missed it, as I was focused on Lucien's eyes. The only way I noticed the jet-black owl was because of my connection with Arion. Her night vision was far superior to my own. I pointed the owl out to Lucien, and we turned off the path onto a narrower one that wound through the forest in a serpentine bend.

"That was a good catch," he complimented.

"Thanks. So, how are things back in Willow's Edge?"

"Same as usual, minus the kidnappings and murders. Free house is as bustling as ever. I drove by your shop the other day. You really ought to fix that front window. It's an eyesore."

I winced. "I'm going to get it taken care of as soon as I get back."

"And when exactly is that? How far along are you in your trials?"

I didn't want to admit I had no idea when Uriel was going to let me return. In fact, I might be kicked out of the trials soon. The manticore trial was in the morning, and I didn't have the first clue how to proceed.

"Soon, I think."

We walked past another owl, Arion pressed me. I could feel her impatience. She wanted to gallop. All this trotting was for mules. She hated it. I ran a hand down her neck, feeling it soothe her as if I were patting my own coat. I informed Lucien we had just missed an owl, and we turned around.

"How do you know we missed it?" he asked.

I talk to horses.

Horses don't talk, unicorn, Arion reminded me.

I snorted. *Yeah, good thing too. Don't go telling anyone I'm a unicorn. You're going to get me killed.*

Arion whined. She didn't like the idea of me being harmed.

"Arion senses the owl," I finally replied.

Lucien took it in stride. "I've been wondering what your magic can do…" He let the thought trail off, leaving space for me to fill in the blanks.

"Keep wondering," I replied with a grin.

Arion pulled up short under the tree. The owl stared ahead as if we didn't exist. It was another jet-black cousin of the last we'd seen. And a path even narrower than the one we were on cut around the owl's tree.

Arion pushed in front of Alastor. *I am lead. Alastor didn't smell the owl. I did.*

That gave me an idea. I leaned close to her head. *You can smell the owls? Is that how you're finding them? Can you lead me to the others that way?*

Of course I can. She nickered and blew out her air proudly. *But it would be faster to go directly to the cat.*

Cat? The clue didn't say anything about a cat.

The cat waits in the center of the owls. It has other things with it. That is where we will go. I will gallop now.

I had a fraction of a second to discern what she meant and grip the reins. Arion broke into a gallop. It was both terrifying and exhilarating. The path was so narrow that I was forced to shift to the side to avoid swiping branches.

Not stiff, Arion reminded me. *Move with me.*

I pushed my weight back into my heels and relaxed, focusing on moving with her rhythm once more. It was an intoxicating thing, to be fully in the moment. My thoughts were solely focused on moving my hips, letting my body fall into the flow of Arion's gallop.

Lucien laughed behind me and assured me that I was a maniac. He was probably right. No sane person would open up a horse like this on a secluded forest path they'd never been on. But this was different. I wasn't opening Arion up. She was the one in control. I was the one trusting in her. I let the world fly past me in a dizzying blur that left me feeling heady, and I could not stop smiling. I grinned so hard that my face was beginning to hurt, but I couldn't help it. I felt so alive, so free.

After many twists and turns, we came to another grove, this one half the size of the almond grove. Arion slowed to a trot as we entered the clearing. Like the earlier clearing, there was an underbutler at the heart. He wore a smart coat and dress pants that cut off at the calves. Inside the suit was a cat person. I'd heard of the sheibas but had never seen one. He held a wooden serving tray in one hand with the other perfectly folded behind his back. Arion came to a stop a few feet from the cat. Alastor was only a few seconds behind her.

The sheiba bowed his head to us. "Congratulations, you have completed the Wyld Hunt. The House of Dawn rewards your efforts and ingenuity with a small token of our affection." He spoke with a purring lilt to his Rs that warmed me from the inside. I'd always loved cats, but it was impossible to find an apartment in the city that would allow me to keep one. The sheiba was no different, with his dappled grey and black fur and orange eyes that glinted in the light from the immaru bug globes.

He removed the lid from the platter and brought it close enough for me to lean down and take one of the prizes.

It was a magnolia flower. The wood that it had been carved from was seamless. I ran my fingertip over the magnolia's petals and was greeted with a fresh aroma that was lightly fruity and calming. "Thank you, this is exquisite," I gushed.

The sheiba purred in pleasure over my gratitude. He blinked orange eyes at me, and then Lucien took his prize. We cantered away from the sheiba as a pair of walkers we'd passed earlier came into the clearing.

"That was a lot of fun," I said.

"You're speaking as if our night is over," Lucien said. "Surely you're not ready to call it a day just yet?"

"I have an early morning to prepare for. And anyhow, I don't think it'd be wise to linger around you longer than I should."

"You act as if I'm trouble to be around," Lucien balked, feigning offense.

The game is over, Arion said to me. *You are the victor. You can let him take you now.*

Lucien caught my blush and grinned sharply. He reached across the space between our horses and stroked his cold hand down my arm. "At least stay long enough for me to show you one thing."

"I already know what you want to show me." I laughed.

He shrugged. "I'd be lying if I denied it."

I felt myself stir inside.

"But that's not what I meant. There's something I want you to see, as only Lanie Alacore can."

I was intrigued. Plus, the idea of going somewhere secluded and letting Lucien ravage me was powerfully tantalizing, thanks to my bond with Arion. She was ready for Alastor. I felt her longing deep inside me and had to fight down the urge to pounce on Lucien.

I fought off a devilish grin as I decided what to do next. "Lead the way."

The horses had a blast galloping through the woods. They maintained a steady pace alongside each other until we came to Lucien's destination, and he called for them to stop. We were on a dark dirt road. It was unlike the tidy grass pathways the forest had created for the Wyld Hunt. This route had been here a long time. A pale blue light lit the forest up ahead, where the path curved.

Lucien was already off Alastor by the time Arion came to a halt. I felt her heavy breathing between my thighs. "We'll walk from here," Lucien called as he turned to head further down the path.

"Wait, I don't know how to get down," I said in a panic. I didn't even remember getting on Arion. It had happened sometime during our first dizzying connection with each other. The ground seemed to be miles away from the back of a horse.

Arion shook her mane. *It is time for you to leave. I will let Alastor mate with me now.*

Lucien chuckled. "Would you stop that? It's obvious you know your way around horses."

"It was my first time riding," I said sheepishly. Did I dare to further explain the extent of my connection with Arion? It didn't seem like a good idea. My grandmother had been gravely foreboding when she warned me to keep my legacy a secret. I worried that Lucien might make the connection between my ability to connect with Arion and my unicorn heritage. It was too big a risk. "Just tell me how to get down."

He crossed his arms and shot me a bemused look. Arion rocked from side to side and snorted. She was raring to go.

"Please?" I said.

Lucien rolled his eyes and sighed. "Fine. I'll play your little game. Lean forward and slide one leg over Arion's backside. Gravity will do the rest."

I leaned forward so that my face was pressed against Arion's neck. "Thank you for letting me ride with you today," I whispered. I slid my leg slowly across her backside as Lucien had instructed and then yelped as I slipped off. The ground rushed toward me. I almost grabbed ahold of her reins again to stop from falling, but my body recoiled from the shared mental image of it jerking her head to the side and hurting her.

Lucien caught me before I hit the dirt feet first. I felt silly, realizing how close to the ground I'd actually been. He held me tight as my heart hammered. We stayed like that for a moment, firmly pressed against each other, my blood pumping hard, his silver eyes penetrating me.

I cleared my throat. "Told you I wasn't messing around."

"Riiight." He smirked as he set me down. "Come on, you have to see this."

I felt his absence as he pulled away, as if the world grew chillier. Which was a funny sensation, considering Lucien's skin is perpetually cold.

Arion reared up behind us and whinnied. I turned in surprise to see her already beating her hooves back the way we had come with Alastor close on her heels. "Oh no," I gasped. "Will they be okay on their own?"

Lucien snorted. "They're horses, Lanie. They will do what they wish, and when they are done, they will return to the stables to be pampered and cared for."

"Oh, right," I said lamely. Then another thought hit me. "But how will we get back to the palace?"

He playfully tugged at the sleeve of my dress. "We'll walk back. Starfire's much closer than you think."

I followed him down the path. I felt like a moth being drawn to the blue light ahead of us. I was dying to look around the bend, but nothing could have prepared me for the spectacle awaiting us.

We came to a small clearing surrounded by white willows that were speckled with pink dots. A large glowing pond dominated the farthest side.

"I didn't know trees could have freckles," I said in a low voice that belied my awe.

Lucien smiled knowingly. "It's from sharing the earth with the armillari caps. Can you feel the way they feed the land here?"

Pastel yellow mushrooms grew against the trunks of the trees like cascading fungi shelves. Toadstools large enough to sit on ringed the blue glowing waters of the pond. They had wide caps in bioluminescent pink and purple hues that reflected off the surface of the still pond. Thickets of cattails ringed the pond in places, their stalks glowing the same pale blue as the water. A palpable energy moved through the air of the clearing. I closed my eyes and let it wash over me.

"They're…communicating," I said.

I could feel a vibration working between the mushrooms and willows. Deep beneath my feet, a network of nerve-like tendrils originating from the larger mushrooms grew around the roots of the willows, each nurturing the other, allowing them to harness the magical energy in the air around us. This was an ancient place, a place of power. I felt humbled to be allowed in their presence, though they paid as much notice to us as we would to butterflies. We were something pretty but inconsequential to plant minds that had lived for eons.

"Lucien, what do you know about manticores?" I asked as I stared at the glowing fungi.

"Dreadful things," he said behind me. "They have quills on their tail that can poison their prey. Make them foam at the mouth and go into convulsions. They like to eat you alive."

A splash of water broke my reverie. I turned to find Lucien wading into the pond. He was fully naked, his clothes folded neatly in a pile underneath the boughs of one of the larger willows that skirted the pond. His skin was so pale that it too seemed to glow as well. Perhaps it was the bioluminescence reflecting off him. I traced my eyes down his back, across his sleek and muscular body, fit as an Olympic runner, down to the curve of his bare ass. He looked like a polished statue brought to life, a perfect specimen of man. Something let loose inside my gut, and I bit my lower lip.

He was hip deep when he turned back to me, wearing a wry grin. "What are you waiting for? Come join me." He playfully flicked the pond's surface. "Don't worry, the water's warm." Rings of blue light, much brighter than the mushrooms, rippled in his wake, lighting up his face and the boughs of the willows around the clearing.

I giggled. "An iceberg would probably feel warm to you."

He shrugged, still grinning, and disappeared beneath the water. I did feel sweaty, and the air was suddenly much warmer than it had felt a minute before. It would feel good to soak my sore muscles for a bit. I kicked off my sneakers beside Lucien's tidy pile. The ground was covered in a thick layer of moss that felt like heaven on my aching heels. I wiggled my feet in it and relished the feel of the cool moss between my toes.

Tiny glow bugs fluttered over the pond, swooping just above the surface and then spiraling into the air. The light of the pond reflected off Lucien's eyes like twin stars as his head broke the surface to watch me.

I met his gaze and grinned. I turned my back to him as I unzipped the side of my dress, then slowly bent forward so that the dress pulled tight against my ass. He sucked in a breath and held it in anticipation. I peeled the dress down, shimmying my hips, then stopped at my waist.

I peered over my shoulder. Lucien was watching me like a dog that sees a treat. I watched his lips press together as if he were dying of thirst.

I tugged the dress down more, revealing my pink lace panties, then down over my thighs. Lucien blew out his breath and splashed his face with water. I giggled and stepped lightly out of the crumpled dress. I wasn't wearing a bra, which I'm sure was obvious to him when we rode the horses. Yet his evident appreciation of my raised nipples was no less flattering.

I pulled my hair back behind my ears and then let my fingers linger around my mouth. Lucien watched as I slowly brought them down between my breasts, circled my belly button, then inched slowly into the elastic band of my panties. They were pink with white lace around the hips. I tugged at the strap, bringing it down just enough to show off the top of my bikini line.

Lucien looked ready to swallow a hat at that point. It thrilled me to see him so worked up. I was already wetter than the pond water could ever make me. I carefully pulled the elastic band as far as it could go. Lucien's whole body leaned forward in the water. He couldn't wait for me to pull my panties down.

I let the band snap back into place and hopped into the water with a splash.

The pond was deep enough to tread in place. Lucien wasn't lying either—it was warm as a hot tub and deliciously refreshing on my aching thighs.

"You're incorrigible," he laughed.

"You like calling me names today, huh?" I teased. "What was it you called me earlier? Let me see... oh yeah, I remember. You said I was *feral*!" I splashed water in his face.

Lucien winced and dove underwater. His head popped up behind me seconds later, and he tugged me hard against his body. "I meant every word of it," he said earnestly, his mouth pressed against my ear. He nibbled on my earlobe, and a ripple of heat washed through me.

I turned my head to let him kiss me from the side. I fell into that kiss, relishing the feeling of our bodies pressed against each other in the glowing water. Lucien was already hard, stabbing into my thigh. I turned my body to face him and wrapped my arms around his neck. His tongue was like an icy peppermint in my mouth. The tip of his dick nudged me through my panties, and I let out a moan.

"I missed this," Lucien insisted.

It was an astonishing admission. Before I could react, he kissed me again, exploring me with his icy tongue. Shivers of pleasure radiated from my core. I'd missed him too. I wanted to give myself to him so badly it hurt. I met the intensity of his kiss. His frigid fingers found their way to the band of my panties and slid inside.

"Not in the water," I said and gently pushed away from him.

I backstroked to the edge of the pond and climbed out as he chased after me. We tumbled into the mossy bed beneath the willow and rolled around, exploring the taste of each other's bodies. Lucien laid me on my back and slid between my thighs. His rigid cock brushed against me through the thin wet layer of my panties and sent hungry shivers through my core. I moved to meet him, but he pulled his waist away teasingly. He shook his head as he hovered over me. I could feel the strain he was putting into holding back from devouring me.

He fell on me and kissed my throat with his icy lips. The sensation they left behind was ice followed by a burst of heat, each kiss a stinging pleasure. Soon there were so many it was hard to think. He ran his tongue over my stiff nipples. I felt his ice magic pierce my flesh and tear through my body. I was soaking wet by the time his tongue traced a path down to my belly button. I couldn't wait any longer. I grabbed his head and shoved it down farther, thrusting my hips up to meet him.

That was when I saw Silas watching us.

He had the look of someone who had just stumbled upon something embarrassing and was turning to leave when we locked eyes. I had a strange sensation then. It should have been shocking to see the man I was so attracted to catch me having sex with his friend. I'd seen enough movies to know my proper reaction was to yelp and cover my breasts. I didn't. Spotting him had the opposite effect entirely. In fact, I felt a strange thrill to find Silas's eyes on me.

I think he read that in my expression. He was at the edge of the clearing as Lucien was nibbling on my thighs. Suddenly, he made the decision to duck behind one of the trees.

He's going to watch us! That pervert.

I wanted to tell him what a pig he was and that I wasn't that type of girl, but Lucien's mouth was doing an excellent job, and I found that having Silas's eyes on me were making me even hornier. By the time Lucien pulled my panties aside and flicked his tongue over my clit, I'd already given in. I wanted Silas to watch me. The idea of him hiding in the trees and lusting after me was intoxicating. I felt drunk with ecstasy.

Lucien sucked on my clit, rubbing the nub with his thumb in between pressing his lips to it. I moaned and pushed myself hard against his eager lips. His fingers entered me, sliding into my slickness, teasing my insides as he suckled on my swollen clit.

Silas bit his lower lip.

I came hard.

My eyes slammed shut as a wave of euphoria exploded from my core without warning. A burst of rainbow color haloed around us. I lost all sense of who I was and what the world was, existing only in that moment of pure pleasure.

When I opened my eyes, I found that I had flipped over on my hands and knees. Lucien grabbed my hips from behind and pulled me toward him. His throbbing cock pressed against my pussy. I was dying to feel him inside me and pushed my ass back to meet him as he eased his thick cock inside me. My pussy stretched to fit him.

Lucien groaned as he entered me. We worked together, rocking my hips back and forth so he could fit inside. He felt even bigger from behind. I moaned as he rode me harder and harder. It was so good. I wanted more. But I couldn't see Silas anymore.

"Let me ride you," I insisted, quickly pulling away so that Lucien's cock slid out of me. I felt empty suddenly.

I twisted around and threw myself at him, slamming him down to the ground. He sat up with his back to Silas. I pressed my breasts in his face, letting him suck on my nipples in turn as I positioned myself over his hard cock.

I quickly found Silas again. The blossom faerie's eyes were ravenous as they took me in. He watched me with the longing of a dying man in the desert who spots an oasis. An electric thrill of excitement worked through me. Lucien's hands were at my waist. I imagined they were Silas's hands.

I told him that with my eyes. *This could be you.*

Lucien held my panties to the side as I lowered myself onto his hard cock. He was still slick from being inside me. He stretched my pussy, touching every piece of me as I slowly and deliberately eased him all the way in. I felt another orgasm already building in my core. I met Silas's eyes and slammed down hard, letting Lucien fill me to the hilt. It was harder than he expected. He cried out in pleasure.

Silas was licking his lips. I couldn't see his hands behind the tree, but I knew he was jerking off.

Is this what you'd like? I thought. *You want to fuck me like this?*

As if he heard my thoughts, Silas nodded, urging me on.

When I saw his arm moving faster, I felt turned on beyond control. I rammed Lucien inside me, pumping up and down as if in a fever dream, just wanting to scratch that itch, just wanting Silas to see me fuck his friend beyond belief. Lucien was moaning as I jammed him in as deep as I could take. His cock rubbed against every inch of me. It was delicious. I wanted to eat him up. I bit down on his shoulder.

Lucien yelled, but he loved it. Suddenly he thrust me off him and flipped me onto my knees again. He shoved my head into the moss and tore my panties apart. His cock slammed into me from behind, and he fucked me hard. Harder than I ever thought I could take. And every inch of it made my body shudder. I rocked my hips, starving to meet each thrust. Everything inside of me was on fire, tight, swollen, slick, and wanting, my core building like a time bomb.

I couldn't see Silas anymore. I didn't care. I could feel his eyes watching me get fucked. I imagined it was him behind me, imagined my curse was gone and I could take any lover I chose. I tried to see myself from his vantage, the curve of my ass, the quiver of my body as I moaned with every fervent thrust. Lucien reached around me and rubbed my clit as he slammed in and out as hard as I could take it.

That was it. I screamed as my core exploded. Rainbow light poured from my open lips, working across my naked flesh. When it touched Lucien, he screamed in ecstasy and let loose inside of me. I felt his cock pulsating, throbbing as he filled me to the brim. It was like being in the center of an explosion.

We collapsed in a heap, then rolled onto our backs beside each other. We were both laughing, our hands still rubbing each other's arms, chest, thighs, wherever we could touch, our skin tingling with pleasure.

I looked at the spot where Silas had been. There was nobody there. I wasn't sure if there had ever been. I told myself it could have been my mind playing tricks on me or the bend of the light from the pond.

"I really did miss you," Lucien admitted.

Guilt stirred in my belly like butterflies. There was never a point where I had missed Lucien since I arrived at the Tides. It wasn't until I saw him come down the stairs to the banquet that my mind even lingered on us being together. If anything, I'd found myself all too often daydreaming about Lobo. It didn't seem fair to Lucien. Then, to add salt to the wound, while we were just fooling around, it was Silas I was thinking about.

"I missed you too," I said. I realized I meant it. Lucien gave me something nobody else in the world could provide while the curse still had a grip over me. It wasn't just that, though. I had a good time when I was with him. When we were alone, that is.

I lay with his arm around me for a while, both of us quietly watching the starry sky. Glow bugs swirled overhead. A gentle breeze kicked up from the nearby ocean, stirring the willow branches. One of them tickled my naked toes. The air smelled fresh and clean. I let the gentle evening breeze wash over my naked body and sighed in bliss. What I'd just done was so unlike me, so naughty. It was deliciously wicked. I couldn't wait to tell Deedee all about it.

I felt as if someone had punched me in the gut. Poor Deedee. Not only was she trapped in a coma, but now I'd abandoned her as well. I had told myself she would be alright while I was away because Tae would be checking on her. But now Tae was here with me, and Deedee was left alone.

What if she wakes up to find herself in Free House? How scared will she be? I wished beyond hope that she would wake up. I missed her voice, her laugh, her steady confidence.

"What's troubling you?" Lucien asked softly, his fingers twining my hair.

"Oh, nothing," I said breathlessly.

"Sounded like more than nothing," he prodded.

"I didn't say anything."

"No, but you moaned. It was one of those soft everything-hurts-inside moans. Don't try to deny it, I'm an expert on moans."

"Yeah, you are," I teased.

"Seriously, Lanie, if there's something troubling you, I want to hear about it."

A silence opened between us. It stretched uncomfortably long before I spoke again. I hated how soft and timid my voice sounded. "I'm not sure you'd understand."

"Try me."

"A few months ago, when I first came to Willow's Edge, I was attacked by a changeling. He was the one who killed my grandmother."

"Yes, I've heard all about that attack. I think everyone in the province has."

The idea that everyone in the province knew anything about me at all made me wince. "Well, that night a very good friend of mine was injured. The changeling...he tortured her." The words came out smaller and smaller, like a strangled whisper that caught in my throat.

Lucien held me tight. His arms were strong, and I felt shielded beneath his icy embrace. "That's horrible, Lanie. I'm so sorry."

"Deedee was an amazing person. Listen to me. *Is,* not was. She never should have been there alone. I left her at my shop while I went off to find a weapon to stop the changeling. I should have been there with her, Lucien. I should've helped her."

"Did you know the changeling was coming?"

"I had a hunch he might, so I left Doule there with her."

"She had a werewolf there? Then how could you have known the changeling could've hurt her? You can't blame yourself."

"You don't understand. If the shoes were reversed, Deedee would never have left me in danger. She would have fought tooth and nail to keep me safe. She always did, ever since I've known her. If I could just…"

I let my words falter. I'd almost told Lucien about my curse! I couldn't bear to share that shame with him. That was my secret to keep and mine alone. Plus, if he knew he was the only person I could have sex with, then he'd also know that I was aware of his own secret. I'd worked it out weeks ago. My curse made me black out at the faintest whiff of erotic pleasure with any other person. It was the same reason my magic was able to trickle out when Lucien gave me an orgasm. I was convinced Lucien's magical power was to dampen the magic of others. He was like a walking anti-magic cone.

"I know what it's like to have a loved one hurt," Lucien confided. "My brother died years ago. That sort of pain is something you can never quite escape from."

"How did he die?" This was the first time Lucien had ever opened up to me about his life, at least in a meaningful way.

"The fool went off to prove himself as some hero of the ages." He puckered his lips as if he tasted something sour. "He wasn't the only one. A whole gaggle of them, high and mighty in their beliefs, went off to fight. In a human conflict, of all things."

"World War Two?"

Lucien sneered. "World war. Only a human could come up with something so preposterous. As if the world was only what revolved around their stinking cities. They're parasites, the lot of them, leeching away at the earth. They're no better than a cancer."

It stung me to hear Lucien's rancor for humanity. The fae had no love for humans. I knew I wasn't a fae, but in many ways I still felt human. I was an outsider dipping her toes into the fae realm. So it still felt personal when I heard how disparaging they could be about humankind. It felt unfair. In many ways, both races were the same, although the fae would never like to admit that.

I kept my mouth shut. Lucien was opening up to me in a way I had never expected he was capable of and I didn't want to ruin it.

"When I was little, Siriden used to take me to the woods to hunt—at least that's what he'd tell my father. What we really did was climb trees and jump in streams. Sometimes we'd even play hide-and-seek. That was the sort of thing I could never do back at the palace. If my father ever caught us horsing around, there would have been hell to pay. 'Life is duty and honor.' There's no place in that sort of thinking for childish whims. Siriden knew that because he experienced it first, when he was the only child. He used to let me win too. He'd pretend he couldn't help himself and he'd giggle when I came close to his hiding spot, but I knew he did it on purpose. There was nobody greater in the whole wide world than my big brother.

"I was sad when he left to go do his service to the royal family as our House's firstborn. But at least I was still able to visit him. Then those humans infected his mind, just like they do everything else they touch. And now he's gone…just like your friend."

"She's not gone," I whispered. It was hard to see Lucien in so much pain. I rubbed his smooth chest. "I can still save her. She's in a coma." If I could break my curse, then I could use my magic to heal her. It had worked in Sam's farmhouse. All those fae were cleansed of their wounds when my magic was unleashed. It had to work for Deedee too.

Lucien placed his hand over mine. "If you say you will, then it will be done."

His conviction startled me. "How can you be so sure?"

He snickered. "Lanie, I've not known you very long, but one thing I've learned is that if you say you're going to do something, then it gets done."

I grinned and nuzzled my face into his chest.

"Anyhow, is your friend hot?"

I laughed, refusing to take his bait. "Men drool when they see her."

"Oh, then you simply must help her out of the coma. I must meet this woman," he teased.

I couldn't help laughing at the silly look on his face. I didn't have the heart to tell him she was human. Not after he'd opened up about losing his brother. Instead, I pretended to punch him, and we laughed.

"You know, you're a lot more fun to be around when you're not acting like a stuck up noble."

His body stiffened. "What is that supposed to mean?"

"Don't take it the wrong way. You know what I mean. You spend so much of your time trying to pretend you're something you're not. It must be exhausting. Honestly, I think if more people got to see this side of you, they'd like you better."

He pulled his arm out from underneath me and sat up. "Interesting. I wasn't aware I'm such a horrible person to be around."

This was going all wrong. "No, you're not. Don't be stupid, it's only when you're being fake that you're—"

"What the fuck, Lanie?" Lucien stood up and started getting dressed.

An uneasy silence hung in the air. I felt completely exposed, sitting there naked. I found my dress and pulled it over my damp skin.

"Listen, maybe I misspoke," I said.

"What could you know about my life? I was born into responsibilities you could never fathom. I have to be there for thousands of fae every single day. What kind of responsibilities do you have? Feeding an imp? You'll never know what it's like to have that kind of weight hanging over you, the expectations my father has... You don't even *have* a family." His words were sharp and meant to sting. They were aimed directly where they needed to be.

"Fuck you," I said.

Lucien looked shocked at his own words. He knew he had gone too far. "Lanie, I—"

"Shove it up your ass. If you weren't so concerned with what everyone else thought, maybe you could live a life where you were happy instead of behaving like a sanctimonious resentful prick. And how dare you bring up my family? You're not one to talk, with Daddy Nightmares-a-Lot. I'm sorry I brought it up. Why would I want you to be happy? You should stick to being exactly who you are, the dutiful prince that hides in his father's shadow and does whatever he's told. Subservient is the right shade of bullshit for you anyhow."

I stomped away, too angry to care whether I was walking toward the palace or away from it.

Lucien didn't try to follow me. Which was good, because I was so angry with him that tears blurred my vision, and if he saw them, I would probably try to scratch his eyes out.

How did the night turn wrong so quickly?

I woke up the next morning with a feeling of gloom. Bella was nowhere to be seen. The previous evening fell on me like a ton of bricks. Why did I have to say anything to Lucien? We were having such a good time. It was no secret he was an asshole. Why couldn't I have been content with what we had?

Then I remembered his barbed sting about me not having a family. I'd always felt completely loveless. How could anyone ever care about me if my own mother didn't want me? That kind of stuff didn't just go away because you get a bestie. Deep down you always knew you were a piece of shit.

"Can't wallow in bed all day," I grumbled. "Got a big day ahead of me. Have to get eaten by a manticore."

Even the sight of butterflies sleeping on the wall garden couldn't cheer me up. I washed up and tossed on jeans and a long-sleeved green Henley. It was a far cry from the dress I'd worn the night before, but I suspected the manticore wouldn't care if I looked pretty or not. And I was going to need to be able to move fast.

I shouldn't have wasted my time with that jerk, I thought. If I'd been more focused on my responsibilities and less on getting fucked, then I might have been better prepared for that day's trial. As it was, I'd gathered next to no new knowledge about manticores. There wouldn't be enough time to go to the library. By the time I located it, found the right book, and learned about manticores, it would be past the hour to arrive at Uriel's. That was if the library even had a book on manticores.

Hmm, what do I know about manticores? They have a face like a man but with rows of razor-sharp teeth, the body of a lion, and a tail with poisonous stingers.

I'd sprouted an idea the night before on how to deal with this situation. If I could concoct something to put the manticore to sleep, I might have a chance. I rummaged through my luggage until I found some of the apothecary supplies I'd brought along. I set my mortar and pestle on the floor, then rolled open the leather tool belt I'd packed. A dozen glass vials held ingredients of my trade. I found my valerian root. It was a fantastic remedy for sleepless nights, and the valerian that grew in Willow's Edge was potent stuff. That would do the trick...*if* the manticore had insomnia. I emptied the vial into the mortar.

It's a start, but I need something that packs a bigger punch, I thought, tapping my lower lip.

I sifted through the contents of my backpack until I found what I was looking for. Buried deep in the bottom was a bottle of motion sickness pills. I'd brought them along when I found out I was going to be journeying on a flying sailboat to the Tides. The label on the bottle read, "Adults take one pill before your activity. May cause drowsiness." One pill had knocked me on my ass for the bulk of the voyage.

A grown manticore would need fifteen? No twenty. I poured them into my mortar, then added a bit of bergamot oil. The citrus scent would help cover up the valerian root. Also, bergamot helps reduce stress, slowing heart rates and lowering blood pressure.

It was a decent concoction. I would never give anything like it to a customer, of course. There was no finesse, no safety measures. Still...did I want to trust my safety to *decent*? I needed something to push the mixture over the edge.

I had a carefully wrapped package in the side of my backpack. I opened it. The lumeria petals were still intact. Before the incident with Charlie, I'd been using them regularly to help a fraction of my magic seep past the curse. They worked as an amplifier. I'd stopped after Lucien warned me they were considered sacrilegious to use, since the flowers only grew from the soil of deceased fae.

"Sorry if this is sacrilege, great spirits," I mumbled. "I respect you and all, but staying alive myself is kind of my top priority right now."

I crumbled four of the petals into the mixture and used my pestle to grind it together. As I did so, I focused on what I was trying to achieve. I pictured the manticore drifting off to sleep and focused on that thought. Miniscule drops of sweat fell from my brow into the mortar, each one a translucent rainbow color that glowed as it hit the ingredients. After some effort, it all turned into an even powder. I put on my leather glove and flattened out a piece of rice paper from my toolbelt. I set an empty glass vial next to that, along with a paper funnel. I lumped a third of the mixture into the glass vial and the rest onto the rice paper, then rolled it into a ball.

With that done, I was ready to face my trial and die. Because there was no way I was going to trick a manticore into eating that shit.

Maybe if I had some food to slip it inside? There might be something useful in the palace kitchens.

Butterflies fluttered around my insides. I had completely forgotten about my run-in with Chef Henri. I could still see the troll's wounded expression when I'd lashed out at him. How many times had I been the butt of similar treatment growing up? Who knew better than me how bad a sharp word could sting? How it could linger in the mind for long hours into the night? I felt miserable to have inflicted such treatment on Henri. Whether there was food I could use or not, I owed the troll an apology.

I stuffed the rolled-up ball and the glass vial in my jacket pockets and went in search of the kitchen. It took me less time than I expected to find my way to the basement. Halfway down the steps I bumped into Gizmitt. He nuzzled my ankles and purred.

"Morning, fluffy butt," I said, kneeling and stroking the ferillo's segmented body. He flopped onto his back and showed me his kittenish belly. When I petted his tummy, he wrapped his six paws around my hand and purred loudly. I laughed. "Wish I could pet you all day, buddy, but I have to find the palace kitchen."

Gizmitt unwound and rolled over, shaking his little head back and forth excitedly. He zipped away down the hall. When he saw I wasn't following, he scurried back to me and nudged my heel.

"You want me to follow you?" I asked. "Sorry, I have to find Chef Henri."

Gizmitt meeped and jumped up and down, then nudged my heel again. I realized he wanted to show me the way to the kitchen and eagerly followed.

Before I could worry that I might be delusional for following a ferillo through the palace, we came to the stairs I'd fallen down the day before. Gizmitt zipped down the stairs and disappeared around the corner. I only needed to follow my nose after that. The aroma of fresh pastry dough and sugar lured me down the dark halls into the base of the great tree.

Henri was busy working over his stove. He rocked a frying pan over a fire, flipping two pancakes as he whistled a happy tune. The troll wore a chef's hat that flopped over on one side and a white chef's coat that was as immaculately kept as Starfire's bark. His kitchen was smaller than I'd expected for a palace. Besides his large six-burner stove, there was a full-size proofer and four-tier oven for baking breads, sweets, and pizzas. Several wooden tables with shelving underneath stored various pots and pans. There was none of the stainless-steel human chefs surrounded themselves with. It was all wooden countertops and magic fire.

I found Gizmitt in one corner of the kitchen, happily slurping up a bowl of something Henri had left on the floor for him.

One of the tables was laden with leftovers from the banquet. Food that would be used for that day's festivities or doled out to the staff. Nothing would go to waste. That wasn't the fae way of doing things. Everything needed to have a purpose. Beyond that, hanging from a cord, was a feathered pheasant that had to weigh at least thirty pounds. No pheasant in the human realm could ever match its size.

"Oh," I gasped.

My gasp startled Henri, who hadn't heard me come in. His eyes were ringed with fear as soon as he took in his guest. "Lady Alacore, my apologies. I didn't see you enter the kitchen."

He twisted his wrist to slide the pancakes off the frying pan, joining a dozen others on a wooden platter, then set the pan down. He looked to his feet as he nervously wiped his hands on his apron. "What is it I can do…? Um, that is…"

"Please, I don't want to disturb your work," I said. "I only came down to apologize for my behavior yesterday."

For all his girth, Henri looked like a startled deer. "Oh no, there's no need. I understand. Usually I know better. I shouldn't have come up on you like that."

"Don't make excuses for me. It's not right. The things I said to you were inexcusable. Why I reacted the way I did, the things I've experienced, none of it gave me the right to treat you that way. I am sorry. Truly. And I hope that you can accept my apology, because you seem like a fine person to know."

Henri was clearly not used to receiving such esteem. I could see he was, by nature, a very shy person and that it took a great deal of effort for him to meet my eye. "I can't help it that I look this way," he said, and it broke my heart.

"There's nothing wrong with the way you look," I said more sharply than I intended.

Henri flinched and began wringing his hands faster on his apron. "That's kind of you to say, but I see the way everyone stares at me. Fae poke fun at me. Children get scared when they see my face. That's why I like to make tasty food. When folk see my dishes, they ooh and ah. I can bake pretty pastries that sing on your palate. As long as I stay hidden, I can watch folk as something I made makes them light up in a way I never see when they know a troll is in the room."

I crossed the kitchen and grabbed hold of his hands. They were calloused from work. I gripped them tight, forcing him to meet my eyes again. "You are a wonderful person, Henri. There is nothing ugly about you, and anyone who says so must have a stain on their soul or wool over their eyes to think so. Don't you let my poor behavior, or anyone else's, shake that truth from that big green head of yours. The truth is I was running away from someone. I don't know who they were, but they were chasing me through the palace. When I stumbled into you, I thought they'd caught me."

Henri gripped my hands firmly, and his face changed to worry. "Someone was trying to hurt you? In Starfire? Have you told Master Ambrose?"

"That's not the only reason I was mean to you," I admitted. "Just a few weeks ago, I had a run-in with a different troll. We were friends, I thought. But he tried to…he was going to…" My body shuddered as I remembered Droll shoving a gag in my mouth. I could still hear his table saw, still feel the rope binding my ankle. I shook my head stubbornly. "So you see, nothing about that reaction was your fault. It's my own baggage to deal with, and I took it out on the wrong person."

Henri gave me a toothy troll smile and lifted my hands in his. "I forgive you, Lady Alacore. Trouble yourself no longer over this burden."

I sighed my relief. We stood smiling at each other for a few moments. The pancake platter smelled divine, and my stomach must have been on full alert, because it suddenly and quite audibly growled.

"Do you like pancakes?" Henri asked sheepishly.

"I adore them." I beamed.

Henri used a spatula to pile three on a ceramic plate for me, with a pat of fresh cream on top. He placed the plate on one of the wooden tables deeper in the kitchen. "Please, eat up. I was just preparing for the breakfast banquet."

It felt rude to eat in his kitchen while he was trying to work, but I knew it would have been ruder still to decline his hospitality. The pancakes tasted as heavenly as they looked, fluffy with a touch of vanilla bean. Each bite melted in my mouth.

"These are incredible. In fact, everything I've eaten since coming to the palace has been on a whole other level."

"A whole other level," Henri repeated, then giggled as he poured more batter onto a freshly heated pan. "I've never heard that phrase before. I like it."

"Huh, it's funny the number of things I take for granted. I grew up in the other realm, and I suppose some of things I say are distinctly human."

"Wow, that's wild. You truly lived among them? I know many fae spend time in their realm, but you grew up there? It must have been awfully scary. I could never dare."

I forked another mouthful of pancake, speaking between bites. "I'm sure there are many humans who would say the same about faerie folk. It seems a common theme of our world is to be scared of that which you don't understand. It's actually quite funny when I think about it, because I see so many similarities between the fae and humans."

"Oh, the purebloods wouldn't want to hear talk like that," Henri warned. "How do you like the Tides? Does it compare to the human realm?"

"I think they both have their charms. That's not to diminish the beauty of a place like the Tides. I think I'm starting to get the hang of being around so many fae."

"Well, if there's anything I can do to make it easier, just let me know. Especially if it has to do with delicious food."

"Actually, I was wondering about one of those pheasants you have hanging there. Do you think you could spare one for me?"

Henri shot me an incredulous look that was saturated with approval. "You want to eat an entire pheasant?"

"No thanks, I'm already big enough," I teased. "It's for a trial I'm participating in this morning."

"Ah, for your wardenship." He nodded knowingly and flipped the pancakes.

"You know about my trials to become warden?"

"One does not get invited to stay as a guest at the palace without having their name and story spread around the staff like wildfire, my lady. If the pheasant will help you in your trials, I would be honored to offer it to you." He whistled happily, then added the pancakes to the platter stack.

I plopped another forkful of pancake into my mouth and eagerly leaned over the prep table. I grabbed one of the pheasants off the hook, snaring it by the twine that bound its feet together. This would be perfect for my needs.

"This is great. If I can—"

Gizmitt made a retching noise.

"Do armadillo cats get hairballs?" I asked as I peered over the prep table at him. My blood turned to ice. For a moment I could do nothing but stare in horror. Gizmitt was lying on his side in a puddle of blood.

"Henri!" I shouted, finally able to find my voice. "Something's wrong with Gizmitt!"

The troll tossed his pan down on the stovetop and ran over. I felt like I was moving in slow motion as I followed close behind. It was hard to see around Henri's broad shoulders. He knelt over Gizmitt's still body.

"Is he…?"

"Dead," Henri confirmed.

"But he was just running around and playing," I denied. "I was petting him upstairs. He was so happy…"

Henri had tears streaming down his green cheeks. He tried to stand but lost his balance and staggered to the nearest prep table. He leaned his massive weight against it with his head bowed as he sobbed.

I couldn't bear to look at Gizmitt's body. My attention focused instead on his bowl of food. It was filled halfway with a familiar liquid.

"Henri…what was Gizmitt drinking?"

"Huh?" Henri was firmly out of it, lost in his despair. He waved a green hand. "Just Master Ambrose's special tea."

"Why would he be drinking Ambrose's tea?" I asked as a niggling thought burrowed into my brain. I tried to quiet it. This question was important. I needed an answer. Henri stared dully into the void. "Henri, why was Gizmitt drinking Ambrose's tea?" I shouted.

Henri flinched. He looked scared, his eyes flashing to the tea and then the blood. "What? Master Ambrose always has his special tea this time of day. It helps his constitution. Sometimes Gizmitt comes around 'cause he knows I've made it, and I give him the leftovers. He likes it. He…"

"Oh, fuck me," I said as that niggling idea slammed home. "Someone poisoned the tea! Shit, this isn't good. When did you send it up to Ambrose?"

"What? No, the tea can't be poisoned. I made it myself. I would never—"

I grabbed Henri's massive arms and tried to shake him out of his stupor. It was like trying to move a stone wall. "Not you, Henri. Someone else must have slipped something into the tea leaves! When did you send the tea up?"

"Just now. Just before you got here. Master always has his tea at—"

I was already running. If the tea had just gone up, there might still be time to save Ambrose. He had an elaborate ritual about drinking his tea. I prayed it would give me enough time to get there and stop him.

"He's in the crystal pagoda!" Henri roared from down the hallway.

I was already up the steps to the first level when I digested his words. Ambrose was past the hedge maze. "Of course he is," I huffed.

I threw everything I had into that run. Servants screamed as I flew past them at a dizzying speed. When I say I can move faster than most, it's no exaggeration.

When I reached the balcony, I thought for a second of jumping over the rail, but the fall would shatter my ankle. That would be silly. Instead, I threw myself on the stair rail and used it to slide all the way down, then leapt from it and sprinted through the atrium.

Malachai and Minerva were there, speaking in hushed tones with Valia.

"What is that foolish girl doing now?" Minerva gaped.

I didn't have time to hear Valia's response. I was already on the lawn. I hopped over tent ropes. Frightened children screamed as they got out of my way. I ignored a nasty remark from a satyr. None of them mattered. All I could picture was poor little Gizmitt lying in a pool of his own blood.

I failed Ambrose. Why oh why did I spend the night fooling around with Lucien when I should have been trying to prevent Ambrose's murder?

I knew why. Because I never truly believed it would happen. Somewhere inside I had held out this certainty that Ambrose was overreacting and we'd find out it was some other ill intent, some hostile business takeover or a scandalous political fiasco.

"Stupid, fucking bitch, Lanie," I chided myself.

My vision blurred with tears as the image of Ambrose lying in blood assaulted me. I knew in my hollowed-out heart that I was already too late. I screamed my denial like a banshee as I entered the hedge maze. My feet never moved so fast in my entire life. I almost fell sideways trying to cut around the corner of the maze. It forced me to slow my pace as I hit each turn.

Screw the turns, I thought and leapt straight through the hedge wall. The brambles tore my skin, fine papercut-sized lacerations that stung with the stickiness of the evergreen hedges. I roared out another scream and threw my head down as I tackled the next hedge in my way.

Geraldine gaped at me as I burst out the other side. He was reaching for a sword hilt at his side when I ran around him in another burst of speed.

Ambrose was lifting the teacup to his lips. I wanted to scream for him to stop, but I was panting too hard to say anything. Instead, I ran straight for him.

The cup touched his lips. I threw my body into him, slapping the cup away as we both fell.

The teacup shattered on the floor of the crystal pagoda.

I lay there panting for air. My lungs felt like they were going to explode. My heart was beating a million miles per second.

Ambrose lay on his side next to me, staring at me in bewilderment even as Geraldine's rough hands seized hold of my collar from behind.

I looked down to find the pheasant still in my left hand and let out a deranged laugh.

22

There was no time to celebrate. After Geraldine was called off by Ambrose, and before he could wring my neck, we witnessed the effect of the poisoned tea. It had spilled from the shattered cup across the floor of the crystal pagoda and over the side, where it rapidly reduced an azalea to a withered husk. Whatever foul ingredients had been slipped into Ambrose's tea were powerful. Geraldine's estimation of me was finally elevated. I had saved Ambrose Amaryllis from an assassination attempt.

"What a relief that it's over," Geraldine said, brushing nonexistent dust from Ambrose's coat as he fussed over his lord.

Ambrose shooed him away. "It is not, I am sorry to say, *over*."

"But, Master, the assassin's plan has been foiled. Surely they would not dare to pursue further aggression now that their hand has been revealed?"

This was a perfect portrait of fae thinking. They were not human. The fae are a people who would never dream of mortal violence against each other, at least not pureblood to pureblood. To Geraldine, the murderer's attempt being subverted meant that the danger was over.

"They'll most certainly try again," I said. "In fact, I think the next attempt will be even more clever. If what I know from books and television is true, which it might not be but my gut says is, assassins take great pride in their craft. To find out their attempt failed will twist like a thorn in their side. We'll need to be ever more vigilant in protecting Master Ambrose until we can determine the identity of our killer."

Geraldine stood taller; his shoulders squared. "No one will harm Master Amaryllis." He pulled his sword from the sheath and bandied it across his chest in salute. "I will cut down any who attempt such violence."

"Maybe," I said with a shrug. "But I made it past you and got to Ambrose. I have no doubt you could have cut me down once you caught up, but if I had wanted to, I could have shot him dead before then."

Geraldine blanched at that, then scowled angrily at me. I had questioned his capability, and he was not finding it amusing.

Ambrose put up a hand to stay his man's fury. "You *are* quite fast, Lady Alacore. I would say a great deal faster than any fae I've ever met, since I sense you weren't using any enchantments."

"Which means it's not impossible that there might be others out there like me," I said.

"Oh, I doubt that's true," Ambrose said with a hint of knowing mirth in the corners of his eyes.

Why would he say that? I panicked. *Could he know my secret?*

If he did, he wasn't letting on past that simple remark. He quickly moved the conversation along.

"The best we can do now is use the time Lady Alacore has gifted me to our advantage. If the assassin believes their plan successful, then they will not bother setting up another attempt," Ambrose said.

"If you can stay out of the public eye until we gather everyone together, maybe we can root out our culprit when you show up alive and well," I said.

"They'd have to be a devilishly talented poker player not to have a reaction when it's revealed Master Ambrose is still with us," Geraldine agreed.

"It's a good plan," I said. The only one we had, but good nonetheless. Geraldine would sneak Ambrose back into the palace, and that evening, before the masquerade ball began, he would make an appearance while Geraldine and I watched the crowd for any reactions.

"Agreed. I just have one question," Geraldine said. "Why in the world are you carrying around a dead pheasant?"

With our plan laid out, I had just enough time to go up to my room and wash some of the cuts from the hedges away. I was just heading out of the palace again when I heard someone call my name.

"Lady Alacore."

I turned to find Cyan coming out of the palace behind me.

"I'm just heading out for my warden trials," I said. I didn't feel like getting into a pissing match with her this early in the morning.

Cyan's entourage milled by the palace entrance. She motioned for them to stay put as she closed the distance between us. Her smile was disarming. "I won't keep you long," she promised in a low voice. "I just wanted to thank you."

"You wanted to what now?" Did I hit my head when I was running to save Ambrose?

Cyan laughed and waved a hand in the air. "I know I can be a bit much. I thought you should know I've decided to take your advice. No more secrets. It's unhealthy. I'm going to tell my father the truth at the masquerade tonight."

"And Isabo?"

She nodded in concession. "And Isabo. You were right, it doesn't do anyone any good to live a lie. I just wanted to thank you for helping me find my way."

"Oh, well, I'm very happy for you," I said. Cyan's entire demeanor was off-putting. She was softer around the edges, less intimidating. Stress could do that to a person. Cyan was still a bitch in my book, though. Hiding her relationship with Litari was no excuse for how she treated Persa. "I really do need to get going, though."

She nodded. "Naturally. I wouldn't want you to be late for your appointment with the gladewarden. The woman's a beast to be on the wrong side of. Anyhow, thank you again."

It didn't matter if I approved of Cyan as a person. It was good that Isabo would learn the truth. I hoped she could find a partner she deserved. She had to be able to do better than self-centered Cyan. It felt satisfying to know I'd helped the three of them. Freeing Isabo from Cyan's influence while also allowing the couple to live on their own terms felt right. Love shouldn't have to hide for anyone.

My run to the woods was nothing like the mad dash I had thrown myself into to save Ambrose. Instead, it was a normal "shit I'm late and I better hurry" run. I only had until sunset to retrieve the chŏra from the manticore's tail. I checked the contents of my jacket pockets with my free hand, nervous that I had damaged one of them while playing linebacker with the hedge bushes. Thankfully both were intact, though my arms couldn't say the same. The hedges had left razor-thin cuts on my tender skin. I knew my face was similarly scratched, but this was no time to worry over minor scrapes and bruises.

If I fail to reach the manticore's lair in time, I'll lose my chance of becoming warden. Then again, if I succeeded, I might end up being eaten alive. It wasn't the best prospect to keep me motivated.

I made my way down the cliff steps, through the town, and deep into the Whispering Woods, all the while heading toward the general area Uriel had marked on my crummy map. It was surprisingly easier to find than I expected.

I guess when you're an apex predator, you don't worry too much over who can find you as much as how well they can hide from you, I thought.

Silence was my ally. Once there were no signs of birds, no scurrying of squirrels, no slithering of snakes or buzzing of bugs, I knew I was heading in the right direction. Any animal with a lick of common sense would give the manticore's lair a wide berth.

I stopped and knelt to work on the pheasant. Fortunately, Henri hadn't cleaned the bird yet. I figured a wild creature like the manticore would prefer their meal to be more complete. Not much call for roasted bird out in the wild. I was careful to tuck my mouth underneath the collar of my henley while I worked. No sense in knocking myself out with my own sleeping powder.

I'm sure the manticore wouldn't mind if I screwed up. Then it could have pheasant for an appetizer and unicorn for lunch, I thought morbidly.

I pulled the stopper from my sleeping powder and gingerly sifted the contents over the pheasant. I shook out every drop of it, then rolled the pheasant in the dirt to mask some of the powder. I lost a little in the process, but there was plenty remaining to get the job done.

I retrieved my specially seasoned pheasant by the neck and pressed deeper into the woods. The trees earned their moniker, whispering as the breeze from the nearby coast brushed the magnolias against their hollow trunks. Once in a while, a loose petal twirled down from one of the trees, their color catching in the thin rays of light spilling through the canopy.

Geez, this would be an idyllic stroll if there wasn't a ferocious beast waiting for me somewhere close by. Even the bugs know better than to come into this part of the forest. I must have lost my mind to agree to do this. I probably had. I didn't remember ever being a particularly stubborn person. Then again, I couldn't recall ever wanting something as much as I did the wardenship.

The sun was high overhead by the time I found the manticore's den. It must have already been midday. Time was going by way too fast. The forest ended abruptly at a rocky wall shaped like a horseshoe. The silver- and charcoal-colored surface towered over the forest ahead.

Is that a mountain? The striated stone looked so interesting in its marbled colors. I craned my neck to try to make out the top of it through the forest canopy. There was none in sight. *I don't remember seeing a dead end on the map,* I thought morosely. *Leave it to a man-eating beast to live in a dead end.*

I snorted, but the laugh died in my throat as my eyes landed on a black opening in the side of the mountain. It was the entrance to a cave. I knew instantly that was where I would find the manticore. My heart started beating as hard as the rushing hooves of a stallion.

I felt each thud of it in my chest as I crept closer to the cave. The only thing I'd learned that might be useful was that manticores slept during the day.

Maybe it's a super sound sleeper, I thought, knowing full well my luck was never that good. The manticore's snoring echoed off the walls of its dark cave. It was already asleep. *Is that good or bad? If it's sleeping, should I even wake it to take my bait, or am I better off trying to sneak inside its lair and pluck the quill free from its tail?*

I pondered it for a few minutes, listening to the steady snoring. *No, that way would be suicide. Better to drug the monster before I try to get up close and personal.* For that matter, could my sleeping dust even keep the manticore knocked out enough not to wake when I pulled a stinger free?

It doesn't matter. I'm here. The time to act is now. I could have backed out yesterday, but I took this trial, and now it needs to be completed. I gazed down at the pheasant I was pinning my entire future on. *What am I talking about? Of course I can back out now.*

I was too scared to turn my back on the cave entrance, certain the moment I did the manticore would leap on me from behind. I pictured my path back through the forest. That way led to safety. To fae laughter, good food, new friends, and a masquerade ball planned for that evening. Anyone in their right mind would have turned around then and there and forgotten all about that stupid trial.

I laid the pheasant down in the grass before the cave entrance, then turned on my heel and dashed away through the forest. I ran about forty yards away before scurrying up a tree as high as I could go.

Last chance, Lanie, I thought. *There's still time to hop down and run back to town.*

With one arm wrapped around the trunk of the tree, I leaned to the side, cupped my other hand to the side of my mouth, and shouted my best impersonation of a bird squawking. It sounded at best like someone was strangling Donald Duck. I let out three more "birdcalls," then pressed the bulk of my body behind the tree trunk.

I watched the cave entrance with bated breath as beads of sweat rolled down my forehead. The cave entrance was a black gash in the mountainside, an empty void waiting for the devil himself to step forth and wreak havoc upon my world. Time seemed to pause, dying in the stillness of the shadows.

Then I saw movement.

The manticore's shaggy mane came first as it shuffled lazily around the corner of the cave entrance. The beast was everything I had heard and more, a beautiful creature of death. Its face was a mixture of man and lion, with overwide lips that stretched from one ear to the next. Its mane was scarlet, while its hide was gold as a honeycomb, distinctly leonine and muscular, with wide paws that I was certain housed vicious claws. The detail I hadn't expected was the presence of wings. The manticore's wings were bat-like, with a fleshy purple color to them, and folded against its spine.

It's beautiful, I thought in awe, even as I realized my perch in the tree was no longer the brilliant hiding place I'd thought it was. *For that matter, can lions climb trees? Panthers do. Why did I think climbing a tree would keep me safe from that thing?*

The manticore took in the still forest with sleepy eyes. It yawned wide, displaying rows of teeth, each longer than my forearm and glistening wetly with saliva. It smacked its lips lazily as its sleepy eyes continued to search the forest. Its nostrils flared, and it looked down at the present waiting on its doorstep. With complete disinterest, as if the pheasant was something it expected to find waiting, the manticore slapped a paw over it and dragged the dead bird back inside its lair, swishing its bulbous tail languidly as it disappeared back into the shadows.

Yes, he took the bait, I silently celebrated.

Now all I had to do was sit tight and wait for the manticore to eat my Trojan Horse. Trojan Bird? Did that analogy even work? Whatever, either way I simply had to wait.

Time, however, was not on my side, and the longer I waited, the more anxious I became.

The sun was past its zenith by the time I gathered enough nerve to come down from the tree. I crept slow as a snail as I neared the cave entrance for the second time that day. The beast's musk hit me like a pungent slap that stung my eyes. Air whipped out of the cave entrance, then sucked back inside to the beat of the behemoth's snoring. The sleeping sounds were more pronounced and far heavier than they had been earlier.

My powder knocked it on its ass, I thought proudly.

I cleared my throat loudly to test out that theory. Would it have been a better idea to make loud noises from the tree cover instead of right on the manticore's doorstep? Absolutely. And if I had thought of that at the time, I would have done so. Remember, I'm no professional hunter. I was winging it and doing the best I could with what I had.

So I listened closely as I cleared my throat. The manticore's rhythmic snoring never broke a beat. It was a heavy snore in, followed by a deep windy exhale out. Its breath hit me in the face, the foul musky odor laced with something like rotting meat.

I covered my mouth with one hand and crept inside the cave. I paused just inside the entrance, closing my eyes and reopening them to try to adjust to the absence of light. There were a couple of smaller openings inside the cave, higher up on the same wall as the entrance, which let in a foggy haze of light. The manticore's lair wasn't big, only slightly larger than a master bedroom, but the cave ceiling was higher than I could make out. The manticore's bulk took up most of the space, but there was plenty of room for me to walk around it. The cave floor was scattered with a bed of reeds.

That's odd. I expected to find half-eaten skeletons lying all over the place, but the manticore keeps a tidy den. Maybe it's a clean freak, I joked in an attempt to calm my frayed nerves. It didn't work.

I crept closer. The manticore lay on its belly facing away from me. That was good; if it opened its eyes, it'd have to turn all the way around before it could spot me. I planned on being far away from the cave before something like that happened.

Pheasant feet stuck out from underneath its paws, which were tucked under its head like a cat clutching a prize. I couldn't see how much of the bird the manticore had eaten, but it was clearly enough to knock it out.

I sidled around behind it and peered through the gloom, looking for its tail. The barbed stinger was curled up close to its hind legs. Goosebumps pricked my arms as I took in the ghastly appendage. It looked like a lion tail where it came out from the manticore's body, but halfway down it bubbled larger and fleshy. The fur gave way to charred raw skin that ended in a bulb covered with beige quills. Each was as long as my hand from wrist to fingertip.

How in the world am I going to grab hold of one of those without pricking myself on another one? I got down on my knees to get a better angle.

That was my second mistake. My first was entering the manticore's lair to begin with.

I spotted a turquoise quill sticking up from the reedy bed. *What luck! That has to be the chŏra. It must have fallen out while the manticore was sleeping.*

Even as I reached for it, I sensed how screwed I was.

The cave moved. Really it was the manticore unwinding its body and twisting around, but the sheer size of the beast and the speed with which it moved was dizzying, hitting me with an optical illusion that the entire earth suddenly spun in a circle. I didn't even have a chance to stand before the manticore's furry side brushed against me as it ran around my body.

A face from a nightmare loomed in front of my own. Two intelligent brown eyes took me in with glee as that all-too-human yet wrongly deformed mouth grinned. I was wrong about the manticore's teeth. They weren't in overlapping rows. Two complete sets of needle-sharp teeth, a longer row the size of my forearm and a smaller in front of those, filled its mouth.

"A visitor," the manticore purred, hitting my face with its gross carrion breath. "And a very rude one at that. Not even a knock before you enter my home? Is that how your parents taught you to behave?"

I opened my mouth to speak, but the words, if I had any, died in my throat.

"Not even a greeting for me?" The manticore grinned cruelly. One bite from that mouth, and I was finished. Saliva dripped from between its teeth.

"You're so big," I managed to mumble.

The manticore feigned a wounded expression. "That's not a nice thing to say to someone you only just met," it pouted.

It leaned in closer so that my face was inches from that giant maw. I was suddenly reminded of circus performers who stuck their heads inside the open mouths of lions for show. I always thought that was the height of stupidity, until that moment.

"I was an idiot to ever come here," I croaked.

The manticore greedily smacked its lips. "Don't beat yourself up over it. I've found through the years that so many fae are as foolish as you. It's in your nature, you see. You humanoid types often feel that you're the rulers of this world. Because you walk upright and reason over things that matter to nothing, like philosophy and art. Not that I don't like pretty paintings. They're fine and dandy now and again. The problem is that your kind thinks because you can paint pretty colors on canvas, you must be so smart. That arrogant certainty of self is why you so often underestimate me. For example, did you really think I would be stupid enough to eat your poisoned bird?"

The manticore shook the powdered pheasant with its giant paw, then tossed the bird against the cave wall in a burst of feathers and powder. I cringed at the force of it.

"No," I managed to whisper.

"No?" the manticore repeated. "First you sneak into my den like a common thief, then you have the audacity to lie to my face and claim you didn't think I'd eat your trap?"

"No, I really didn't," I insisted. "That's why I brought a second one."

I threw the sachet of sleeping powder that I'd retrieved from my other jacket packet directly into the manticore's gaping maw before it could react. A burst of powder came out of its nostrils even as I was already running out of the cave. The manticore managed to roar a strangled sound of protest as the powder went down its windpipe.

The ground trembled as he chased after me. I was fast, faster perhaps than I had been that morning, but the manticore was larger, with powerful muscles that propelled its body and claws that rent the earth in sprays of dirt.

I spied my tree and immediately gave up any notion of climbing to safety. Instead, I circled the trunk. The manticore couldn't slow fast enough to turn and ended up rolling in the grass. It thudded into a tree so violently that a shower of flower petals and twigs shook loose.

I ran back toward the cave. The manticore found its paws and chased after me. Its roar shook the forest. I knew that I was dead. Running was futile, and my muscles already ached from earlier in the day.

I spun around to face my death head on and roared back at the monstrous beast.

The manticore was right at my heels. Its eyes went wide as I spun around. It opened its fanged maw wide to swallow me.

The mouth clamped down on empty air as I dashed to the side. The manticore's face slammed into the rock wall. Its whole body followed, crumpled like a lifeless ball as it crashed headfirst into the mountainside.

The impact was so violent that I was tossed onto my ass. It was like seeing a steam train crash into a mountain, except there was no explosion. There was no blood either. That was how powerfully built a manticore was. If any ordinary person had hit that mountain, they would have split open like a melon.

I scrambled to my feet not daring to take my eyes off the manticore. It staggered upright on shaky legs. Its eyes were glassy and confused as it turned to find me. It took two steps in my direction, then crumpled into the grass. Its side rose and fell in the slow unmistakable rhythm of someone who was fast asleep. My sleeping powder might have taken a bit to take hold, but it *had* worked!

I wasn't about to do a dance to celebrate. I dashed back to the cave entrance. With one last look over my shoulder to ensure the manticore was still lying there, I entered. The cave was too dark for me to make out anything properly at first. As my eyes adjusted, I saw that the bed of reeds had been tossed around by the manticore's violent struggle to spit out the sleeping powder. Dust particles floated in the air. I tucked my mouth into my Henley and began my search.

It took some time for me to uncover the turquoise quill. I had to be careful not to prick myself as I was brushing aside the reeds, since I wasn't certain how much poison might still be inside the stinger.

Once I had my prize, I wrapped it in the length of fabric I'd brought along and tucked it inside my back pocket. I peered around the exit. The manticore was still knocked on its ass, right where I'd left it. I ran as fast as I could muster, not slowing until I reached the perimeter of Uriel's fire pit.

She was poking her fire to stoke the flames when I entered. There was an entire side of deer roasting on a spit over the fire pit. If she noticed my disheveled state, she didn't care. "You took long enough in getting here," she complained. "You better have my chŏra."

"I got it right here." I fished the packet free from my pocket.

"Hurry now, you silly girl," she snapped. "We haven't time to dawdle. The sun is setting soon. We must perform the incantation before it does, or you'll have wasted our whole day."

I unwrapped the fabric and presented her with the quill. Uriel scowled at me and waved an impatient hand. "Don't hand it to me. Go use the mortar."

Her stone mortar was the size of a stool. I dropped the quill inside and began to grind it with the heavy pestle. Uriel met me there and bent over my work. "Good, that is good. Grind it down to a fine powder. Yes, the oil is freed." She sprinkled an herb into the mortar as I worked the quill down to dust. A green twig followed from her other hand. "Keep grinding," she insisted.

I worked at the pestle until sweat was rolling down my face. It dripped into the mortar. "Good, yes, just like that. You're a natural, girl."

It was the first time I'd heard anything remotely pleasant come out of Uriel's mouth. I found it disarming.

Perhaps that was why it was so easy for her to suddenly seize my hand. She wrenched it away from the pestle and flicked a blade across my finger. I yelled in shock, but she held me like a vise, pulling my hand over the center of the mortar. "Stop squirming," she snarled. She squeezed my finger until three drops of blood fell inside before finally letting me go.

"You cut me!"

Uriel's eyes widened as she looked at the sky. "Quickly now, keep stirring. The last rays of the sun are almost gone!"

There was a fervency in her voice that defused me. I found myself ardently stirring the pestle to grind the ingredients until they became a paste. Uriel bent down like she might be sick. Her face was almost inside the mortar, making it difficult to keep stirring. She began to chant. They were low words in a language that I didn't recognize. The words sounded more like pictures, the sounds like they came from an instrument. It reminded me dimly of the water syren's song.

There was no flash of light, no puff of smoke or gonging sound to signal that the spell was complete. One minute Uriel was chanting, the next she was finished.

She stood up and nodded to me. "It is ready," she proclaimed. "Fetch the vessel."

I followed her pointing finger to a clay pot on the ground beside her rocking chair. It was three-quarters full of lime-green loamy soil. I carried the pot over, having to use both hands to balance its weight.

"Geez, what do you have in here, a dead body?"

Uriel snorted. I hoisted it onto the wooden table beside her and stood back as she dug her twisted fingers inside. The gladewarden carved a hole in the center up to her knuckles. "Add the poultice."

I maneuvered the heavy mortar so it was over the top of the vessel, then slid the paste out with a wooden spoon so that it filled the hole she had made. Uriel grunted and grumbled for me not to waste any. I scraped the pestle until every drop of the mixture was inside the clay pot. Uriel covered the hole with the dug-up soil, patting and smoothing it until it was as if the hole had never been there. She hobbled over to her basin and washed her hands.

"Now what do we do?" I asked.

"The task is complete," Uriel said cryptically.

"Then I passed the trial?" I asked.

"She should be disqualified." The voice was familiar, and the hairs on my neck rose as it spoke. The manticore rumbled as it came around the side of Uriel's cottage. "She hit me."

Without even looking over her shoulder, Uriel waved a dismissive hand. "Oh, you big baby. The girl retrieved the quill. You lost. What's done is done, Marik."

My body was frozen in place, numb as my mind raced to process what was happening.

Marik whined like a cowed pup. I wouldn't have imagined the great beast could ever make such a noise. "But I'm starving. She made me run all over the place."

Uriel dried her hands on her apron and rolled her eyes. "I've got a roast on the spit for you."

The manticore skipped to the fire like an excited cat. He circled it, brushing his body against me as he went and forcing me back a step. Massive paws swiped the roast deer, and Marik fell on his meal. I watched in horror as his teeth made short work of the haunch. Bones snapped as if they were brittle as straw. In seconds he had the entire side of deer wolfed down. Uriel smiled over him and rubbed the fur behind his ear, and he purred, kicking his hind leg.

"Wait…so the two of you are friends?" I asked, finally able to find my voice.

Uriel shrugged. Marik ignored the question.

"Oh, it's sprouting," Uriel said.

Marik sat upright and gazed at the clay pot in wonder. An aura of light lifted off the green soil like a miniature fog. Something disturbed the surface, as if a bug burrowed just beneath the soil. Then it poked its head out, the tip of a sapling. I gasped as it twisted its way free, growing higher and higher until it was a foot tall, a spiraled plant that thickened until its center was bark-like. Tiny magenta leaves grew from lengthening branches. We all watched in awe as it continued to grow until the glowing fog dissipated. What was left looked like a bonsai tree.

"It's magnificent," I whispered.

"You've outdone yourself, Uriel," Marik agreed, nudging her shoulder with his forehead.

I scowled. "You should have told me the two of you are pals."

"What business is it of yours who I have over for tea?" Uriel asked coldly as she rubbed the fur between Marik's ears.

"It became my business when you sent me to fetch his quill. Do you have any idea the morning I had? You're a twisted bitch. You could've just asked your buddy for one and saved me the hassle." I glowered.

Uriel waved a hand at me as if she were shooing away a gnat. "A manticore's chŏra is not some bowl of sugar you go next door to borrow.

It is a prize. One that must be won in fair contest. Only a champion can fulfill such a task. This is a once-in-a-lifetime opportunity, and you stand there scowling like some ornery brat."

I felt properly cowed but wasn't ready to back down. "Still, it was pretty rotten of you, both of you. I was terrified today."

Uriel tsked as if she felt sorry for me. "And would you have put everything you had into the pursuit had you known Marik and I have been acquaintances for centuries?"

I thought about it. "Probably not," I admitted. Had I known Uriel was friends with Marik, I doubt I would have approached the situation with as much gusto. "I would've known there was no real danger to me, so I probably wouldn't have been able to retrieve the quill because I wouldn't have wanted to risk hurting Marik."

"No real danger?" Uriel scoffed. She looked to Marik and they both laughed, her cackling and him rumbling. "She thinks because *we* are friends she wasn't in any danger."

Marik grinned at me with all his teeth displayed. "Uriel promised that I could eat you if you failed."

23

"Wait, so the manticore would have eaten you?" Tae balked. "Surely they must've been pulling your leg?" She sat on the edge of my canopy bed, looking like a goddess thinly veiled behind the delicate silk drapes. Bella flitted around the ivy wall, whispering to the butterflies she came across. Her little voice sounded like the tinkling of tiny bells.

"He seemed pretty serious about the whole thing," I said as I paced back and forth in front of her. "If I messed up, he would've eaten me without thinking twice." An involuntary shudder worked up my back at the memory of Marik's teeth tearing apart the deer flank.

"That's got to be it then, right? Tell me you're finally done with that horrible woman."

"I wish. There's one last trial tomorrow. Apparently, I must help the plant reach full maturity. We're going to be putting together fertilizer from ingredients around the forest. It sounds boring, but at least then my trials will be over." I sighed and gazed out the open window. Starfire's boughs were already lit by the rising full moon. There was no grander way to see the moon rise than over the horizon of an ocean. It soothed my nerves.

"Well, that's a relief," Tae said. "We're all looking forward to having you back home again. I can't believe you saved Ambrose too. No, that's the wrong way of putting it. It's the fact that someone tried to poison the old man that I can't believe." She shook her head. "You've had a hell of a day."

"It was scary," I admitted.

"And you really don't think it could have been Cyan?" Tae asked.

"She might be the world's biggest bitch, but she's no killer. Cyan was more scared of Ambrose finding out about her affair than anything else. If she didn't care what her father thought about her life choices, then she might be a suspect, but there's a clear level of respect for him ingrained in her. It's not a respect built from fear either. Cyan loves her father."

"Too bad she doesn't love her wife as much." Tae frowned. "Poor Isabo. She's going to be heartbroken."

"And it can't be Artur," I continued. "He's a spineless coward, all bark and no bite."

"Plus, Valia duped him into losing the silk holdings," Tae pointed out. "I don't see someone like him being clever enough to pull off an assassination."

"Or brave enough," I agreed. "I still don't understand Valia, though. Why would someone of her societal status have shimmer?"

It was a dirty thing to be trading in. Shimmer was made from the ground bones and wings of fae. It was an outlawed practice that was punishable by death, something the long-lived purebloods took very seriously. The drug would enhance the user's magical abilities or, if they were human, give them access to a sort of third eye so they could see the fae. That Valia, a highborn noble, would be using the stuff was mind-boggling.

"I've given that a lot of thought," Tae said. "It could be that Valia is in league with the underground market that's peddling shimmer. That would directly connect her to that business with Sam last month. If that's the case, there might be something else going on here that we don't fully understand."

"Which would still place her at the top of our list of suspects," I said. "What we don't know about this shimmer business could be the piece that connects Ambrose to it all."

Tae pondered that. "From what I understand, the House of Dawn *was* one of the loudest voices in the movement to eliminate the drug from our society. His own daughter, Cyan, was known to use it and had a bad time of kicking the habit. You could be onto something there."

"I can sense there's an *or* coming," I said.

"*Or* it could just be that Valia was having some drugs shipped back home for a party. It wouldn't be unheard of for a pureblood brat like her to be caught doing shimmer."

"That's disgusting."

Tae shrugged. "I'm sorry, but I don't think we should discredit looking further at Ambrose's family. What about Alegra?"

"She's kinda scary, honestly," I said. "But what would her motive be? What could be so bad that it would make her want to murder her own father?"

"Has to be tough being the firstborn of a great house," Tae reasoned. "Maybe there's some unresolved issues there from being carted off to live in exile at the royal palace when she was just a kid."

"What a crummy deal," I said. "Then again, I know what it feels like."

"Oh yeah, your mum sent you away to that human boarding school when you were a kid too."

"I hate her guts for it," I admitted. "But I've never daydreamed about murdering her over it. Still, Alegra's worth looking into."

"Alegra's sad," Bella said as she swooped past the bed.

"Mind your own business, you little snoop," Tae said, swatting Bella away.

"Hang on," I said. Not that Bella needed my help, since she effortlessly zipped around Tae's hands while giggling. "Bella, what do you mean? What do you know about Alegra?"

Bella hovered in front of my face with her arms crossed. "Alegra loved Gizmitt. We all did. He was fun. She's under my tree right now, crying."

I didn't understand what she meant. I looked to Tae for guidance.

"All sprites are born from magic, *pure* nature magic. I think Bella is saying her magic was in the form of a tree and that it's somewhere on the palace grounds."

Bella nodded enthusiastically. "Just outside the grounds, on the edge of the woods, by the stables," she said, pleased as punch.

"If you have your own tree, why do you live inside the palace?" I asked.

"Why do you live here?" Bella kicked back. She opened her arms wide to gesture at the room around us. "Bella likes this better. There's a hot bath, scrummy food, tasty drinks, and now I have my pillow too." She pointed at me as she said *pillow*. Which made sense in her childish brain, since she slept on top of me every night. "Plus, I bring part of my tree here so Starfire can connect us." She flitted to the ivy wall and let loose a sparkle of glittery light in her wake as she ran her fingertips over the waxy leaves.

I hadn't realized how much of that room truly belonged to Bella until that moment. "All this time you've felt like I've been intruding on your personal space," I realized. A tiny part of me felt guilty for the pranks I'd played on her.

Bella shrugged and giggled. "Lanie girl is fun. You can stay, but don't think Bella will take it easy on you." She flipped her curls over her shoulder and winked at me, then zipped out the open window and disappeared into the branches, off to whatever trouble she was planning to get into next.

Tae snickered. "She's still a little pain in the ass."

"Okay, we have a couple of hours left before the masquerade kicks off," I said. "Let's use that time wisely. We should go down to Bella's tree and see what we can find out from Alegra."

"What are you going to wear?"

I shrugged. "I'll figure it out when I get back. I'm pretty sure I saw Bella's tree yesterday when we went horseback riding. I need to get a better read on Alegra, and this might be our only shot to get her alone."

"I'm going to sit that one out."

"Oh?"

"I'm famished. Probably going to head downstairs and snack on the appetizers."

She was lying to me. I didn't know why she felt the need to keep something from me, but I trusted Tae enough not to press the point. "Okay, then let's meet back here before the masquerade."

Tae wasn't sure why she'd lied to Lanie. Perhaps it was because Lanie had so much on her mind already, and Tae didn't want to add to that burden. She doubted very much that Alegra was the assassin. Carted off to the royal palace or not, she wasn't the type. Unfortunately, that was the problem with psychopaths. They could be anyone. Heck, if someone had told her a year ago that Droll—funny, foppish, old Droll—was a serial killer, she would have been sure they'd drunk too much of Drys's mead. Still, Alegra murdering her father? That theory rang hollow.

Something had nagged Tae ever since Lanie told her about the stalker in the gallery. Lanie was convinced the stalker followed her through the palace. Tae's gut said that was wrong. *I bet Lanie stumbled on the creep doing something. But why would someone be lurking in a dark gallery in the middle of the day?*

That was exactly the question she was hoping to answer on her little rendezvous. If she looked around the gallery a bit, it might provide some clues.

The palace halls were mostly empty. It seemed like that quite often. Starfire had an air about it like a place lost to time. She could imagine these halls bustling with life and laughter, a fae paradise.

Likely those days ended the night Ambrose's wife, Criscilla, was bitten by the spider. Tae was convinced Criscilla must have been the heart of the Amaryllis family. With their matron gone, the palace was only a stark reminder of loss. Tae only saw one underbutler on her way to deliver folded blankets to someone. The woman nodded at her as they passed.

Word had spread that Lady Alacore's succubus friend was visiting. *Still, you'd think they'd give me a little more than just a how-do-ya-do. No wonder someone was able to slip poison into Ambrose's tea so easily. There's practically no security here.*

I don't get Ambrose. It's not like the House of Dawn doesn't have an army at its disposal. There's got to be a few hundred guardians and thousands of knights among their military. Is he that worried having guards crawling all over the palace will make him look weak? Seems stupid. The Court of Shadows has no compunction stealing his holdings right out from under his son's nose. Perhaps the talk around the realm is right and Ambrose is getting soft?

She found the open archway to the palace gallery. It was dark inside, as none of that evening's festivities would take place in the gallery.

Tae pulled the nub of a candle from her jacket. She liked carrying it in case of emergency. The candle was special. It had a self-lighting enchantment that flared to life when she snapped her fingers over the wick. The shadows retreated in long angles away from her as she marched inside the gallery. Even Tae, with all her experience, felt a twinge of anxiety rustling in her belly.

Maybe I am hungry after all, she thought. *Lanie said she felt like she was being watched when she was here. I kinda do too. I bet Ambrose has a dweomer around his gallery to make trespassers feel uneasy. It probably goes away once the place is lit.*

That kind of spell wasn't uncommon for wealthy merchants to use on their markets. The idea was that if the trespasser felt uneasy, they might get scared and turn away. Most thieves wouldn't even bother with the attempt. It might explain some things. In fact, Lanie might not have had anyone chasing her at all. If Ambrose had a spell like that over the gallery, it could have made her see things as well.

A sound cut into her thoughts like shards of broken glass.

Tae blew out the candle and fell into a low crouch. She held her breath and listened. The gallery was still.

Must have just been a—

There it was again. A rustling sound, like cloth against cloth. Tae hurried toward it, focusing her weight on her toes to avoid the clacking of her high heels. She reached the end of the aisle. The sound came from just around the corner. She peered around a statue of the famed knight Akotar, dressed in dragon scales and holding a trident diagonally across his chest, careful to hide her body behind its marbled bulk.

There was nothing there.

Bullshit, she thought.

Tae could feel the stalker's presence. He might be hidden, but she could smell his male sex. Pheromones exuded from him. She picked them out as surely as a non-succubus could smell cologne. She remained crouched, waiting for her eyes to pick out where the man was hiding.

Tae mentally traced the contour of each statue down the long aisle. There was a satyr offering grapes to an unseen sun. After that was a proud water fae, her staff held up, flowers blooming from her robes. Next was a small girl, her hands folded behind her back. After this was a statue of a robed woman with a long beard and pointy ears meditating.

Wait. There he is, she thought, snapping her eyes back to the statue of the little girl. The unmistakable outline of a figure hunched at the girl's feet.

What's he doing?

The man was fidgeting with something. The fabric of his hooded cape rustled as he tugged. But on what? She needed a better angle to make out what he was doing. She leaned in closer, tightening her eyes to try and make out some detail around his hands.

The statue in front of her was lighter than she'd realized and shifted on its pedestal. Tae squeaked as it teetered. She threw her arms instinctively around the legs to stabilize it.

The figure gasped. He rose in a swirl of fabric and shadows to face her.

"Shit," Tae said. She hadn't thought to activate her disguise bracelet. Whoever he was, she hoped he couldn't see in the dark. His own face was hidden in the shadows of his cowl. "What are you doing in here?" she brazenly demanded as she settled the unbalanced statue back in place.

As soon as she spoke, his body jerked. He snatched something large from the base of the statue and tucked it inside the folds of his cloak. It disappeared into the clearly enchanted fabric. Before Tae could say another word, the man was on the move.

"Wait," Tae ordered.

Shit, he's not waiting. She groaned.

Tae hated running in heels. Why hadn't she planned this better? It was unlike her. She chased after him, listening more than seeing. He breathed heavily as he ran ahead of her. Her heels clunked on the wooden floor, slowing her progress.

She cut around a corner of the gallery, worrying over possibly breaking her heel, and almost missed the painting flying at her head. She ducked as it went by and cursed. *That bastard almost took my head off! I'm going to punch him right in the balls when I catch up to him.*

She caught a glimpse of his cape as she regained her stride. It slipped inside a nearby wall. Her brain felt scrambled, trying to process what that meant. *Teleportation?* No, if he was a blink fae, then there would have been a puff of smoke. She ran up to the spot where he'd been, feeling dumb.

A large oil painting of the ocean depths dominated the wall where she last saw the cape fluttering. It hung slightly ajar; the left side pulled away from the wall as if it were on a hinge.

It's a secret door!

Tae tugged at the painting, and sure enough, there was the outline of an entrance behind it. She quickly slid behind the canvas and through the opening into a dank corridor. A network of spiderwebs stretched across the dirt ceiling, broken by the ivory and silver roots of the great tree. *I'm underneath the palace,* she realized. The temporal displacement left her feeling heady, but she determinedly pressed on down the carved corridor. She heard footsteps beating through puddles up ahead.

Tae rounded the corner in a sprint. The hall was lined with open windows. The view was a mindfuck. She was sure that the hall was located underground, but the windows looked out from Starfire's highest boughs. *This damn place,* she cursed. *Up is down, left is right, one minute I'm on the first floor, the next I'm—*

"Oh fuck," she cursed when she spotted the man standing before an open window at the end of the hall. One of his boots was on the windowsill.

He heard her curse and snapped his head around. His hands were up before she could get a good look at his face. A torrent of rain burst from his palms. Wind whipped up from the storm spell. Tae had just enough time to throw herself flat to the ground before the surge of rain blew past. The wind pushed her body, but she was too low for it to get a grip.

When the last drops had soaked her hair, she looked up in time to see the man leap out the window.

"No!" she screamed.

Tae bolted to the open window, already knowing she was too late. She braced herself for the grisly scene she would surely see below, of the man's broken body on the ground.

The view was dizzying. It was still hard for her brain to process that she was both underground and hundreds of feet in the air. Starfire was so tall that the people milling around the ground below looked like little toys.

The broken body she'd expected to see wasn't there.

But how could that be? Unless…if he's a pureblood, then he could've flown away on his faerie wings. She leaned out the window and turned her neck to look up at the sky. A pebble rolled down from the rooftop and caught in her hair.

That slippery weasel is on the roof!

Sure enough, there were wooden steps affixed to the closest bough to the open window. If she climbed outside, she could easily put her foot on it. Tae sighed. She couldn't let the man get away, not if he could be Ambrose's assassin.

Why would he be running if he was innocent? Damn it, these are my favorite pumps. She grumbled as she kicked off the heels, knowing even as she straddled the windowsill that she'd likely never see them again.

The wind behaved differently at this height. Even on a clear night, without a cloud in the sky, the gusts of wind were powerful. She steeled her resolve and found purchase on the first wooden step. Tae clambered up them quickly, eager to be off the precarious footholds.

The rooftops that greeted her were a strange assimilation of thatch and wooden shingles. It looked more like an amalgamation of nests than a proper roof. *Why does a tree even need a rooftop?* she wondered in frustration.

She pulled herself up the side and over the edge. The roofs combined had to be at least the size of a field, with leafy spokes of Starfire's branches poking through like towering fingertips. The man was slowly crossing the rooftops.

He heard her climb onto the roof and spun around in a swirl of cape, cursing.

Damn wind, I can't even hear what he's saying. "There's nowhere else for you to run," she called, "and I'm not going away. Now, just stay there so we can talk."

Annnnd he's running again.

She snarled and sprinted after him.

Tae soon discovered why the man had been walking so carefully before. He tripped on a bump in the thatching, and that bump reared up its head and raised an angry fist at him. Other heads rose all around them.

Tae realized there were scores of little people living in the thatching and shingles. They were kodama, small humanoid tree spirits with oblong heads disproportionate to their tiny bodies. Their faces looked like wooden masks with big round eyes.

She was gawking at them when her toe smacked into a tiny table. She watched in confusion as the table flung into the air, throwing a deck of mini playing cards wide. The cards scattered in the wind.

The tiny spirit people hollered at her.

"I'm so sorry," she said, even as she tried to catch up to the running man.

An acorn pelted her on the forehead.

"Ow, knock that off," she said.

More kodama rose from the thatch. They were chasing her, a stampede of tiny angry people. Acorns rained at her from all directions. Tae flinched as one came close to stinging her eye. Her foot caught on something, and she tumbled sideways with a yelp.

She flailed her arms in panic as she rolled over the edge of the roof into the open air.

24

I was completely unaware of Tae's plight as I cut through the forest. Bella's tree was right where I remembered, a short distance behind the stables, just off the main path. It was the birch with glowing golden leaves I'd seen during the Wyld Hunt. As beautiful as the tree looked, my attention was focused on its visitor.

Alegra was busy digging a hole with her shovel. A rolled section of silk the size and shape of a ferillo rested on the ground beside the hole. My heart lurched to see Gizmitt's dead body. I wish I could erase the memory of his limp body from my mind.

"Miss Alacore," Alegra said with her back to me. Instead of the dry, uncaring sarcastic tone I expected to match my wits against, there was clear pain etched in every syllable she spoke. And she sounded like a woman who hadn't slept in weeks. "Why are you here?"

Why was I here? My mind raced to remember. Suddenly I felt like the worst intruder. What could I possibly say to this woman to justify why I was imposing on what was clearly an event of mourning? "I came down to question you," I admitted.

"I know," Alegra replied, digging pitifully into the dirt.

"You know?"

"Cousin Persa told me all about how father believes someone is trying to murder him." Alegra sighed.

"Wow, I don't know what to say." My mind raced. "How did Persa find out that's what I was here for?"

"Geraldine."

"Damn butler," I mumbled before I could think.

Alegra pushed the tip of the shovel into the dirt and used it to balance her weight. I noticed a sheen of sweat on her lean arms. Her eyes were puffy from crying, and her hair, usually kept perfectly pulled back, was frazzled. It was the look of someone genuinely in pain. My heart went out to her.

"You mustn't blame Geraldine. He has a heart of gold, you know. He's one of the only lights in this horrid place, truly. He practically raised us. After the assassination attempt this morning, he saw it as his duty to inform us. You couldn't expect him to know there's danger coming and not caution us to stay safe."

"And how would the rest of the family be in danger?" I asked carefully.

"Whatever silly superstitions my father may have, none of his family would harm him. I believe he's finally losing it after all these years. He is ancient by anyone's estimation. How could he think one of his own children would harm him?"

"Someone tried to take his life this morning," I reminded her, my eyes accidentally going down to the rolled silk by her feet.

Alegra stifled a sob. It was heart-wrenching. I moved without thinking. My hand pressed the top of Alegra's back. *Lanie, you're supposed to be interrogating this woman, not consoling her. She's a suspect!*

Alegra looked at me in confusion.

"I'm sorry about Gizmitt," I said.

"He was my only friend," Alegra sobbed. "You don't know what it was like to grow up in this place with these people."

"I might have a better idea than you'd think," I said.

"That's right." She wiped the tears from her eyes with her sleeve. "I asked around about you when I found out why you were here. I never knew your grandmother, but I've heard stories about Rosalie Alacore. She has a hefty reputation. Why did she send you off to live with the humans?"

"She didn't. That was my mother's doing. Thacinda is an emotionally bankrupt crone who would rather throw herself into her business affairs than be saddled with a brat like me. I think the closest she ever came to maternal instinct was ordering others to take care of me."

Alegra snorted. "Sounds like my father."

"Really? Ambrose seems like a kind enough person."

"He is. Oh, he's kind in spades. That is, if you're one of the thousands of fae living beneath his rule. There's so much you don't know, you poor innocent girl. You really shouldn't be here. These people are going to eat you alive."

"I can handle myself just fine," I said curtly.

Alegra shook her head at my foolishness. We both knew I was wrong, but she let it end there. She held her head high and composed herself. "You came to ask me questions. Ask them."

That was the opening I was looking for. But it was all wrong. I wanted answers, but not like that. "Not with Gizmitt's body lying here. I never should have come out here like this. It's wrong. Let me help you put him to rest."

A look passed over Alegra's face. It could have been respect. It was hard to gauge. She nodded and handed me the shovel. "We'll take turns."

We spent the next hour doing exactly that. We dug in silence. I lost myself in the work. It felt good to exercise my muscles at first, but soon every movement was aching across my back, through my shoulders, and even in my knees. While one of us dug, the other moved larger rocks out of the way. We dug and dug until finally Alegra declared the grave was deep enough.

She hopped down into the hole, and I lowered Gizmitt's silk-wrapped body down to her. She placed him on the dirt at her feet as tenderly as a mother would move a newborn, then unwrapped him for a moment.

"My little Gizzie," she whispered. She caressed his fluffy head as she spoke, and tears fell from her face onto his limp form. "You always loved to chase squirrels in the woods. You didn't deserve this. Go play now, Gizzie. Go run in the woods of the afterlife, the Great Lady is calling you."

With that said, she wrapped him back up. I reached down and helped her out of the grave. When the first dirt was poured over Gizmitt's body, she let out a wail of agony.

I held her for a while as she cried. No one deserved to be left alone with that kind of pain. We took turns filling the grave back in after that. Once the dirt was back in its home, we stacked the rocks on top of it as a cairn.

Alegra placed the final rock, then stepped back to take in the grave. She smiled affectionately, then pressed her fingers to her lips and blew a farewell kiss to her lost friend.

"Let us walk back together," she said.

I nodded.

We walked in the woods for a bit before she stopped and sat with her back against a tree. "Actually, I'm too tired. Ask your questions, Lanie."

I knelt in the grass beside her. "Are you sure? We can do it later."

"There will be no other time," she said, and somehow I knew she was right. "Actually, before I answer your questions, I must tell you about my life here. You need to understand the full picture."

"Okay." What else was there for me to say? She was going to spill the beans. I should have been excited for the breakthrough, but a part of me felt heavy, as if I'd taken on the weight of the world.

"Starfire is where I grew up. There were only the three of us in the beginning, before the other children were born. Even then, Ambrose was distant. But my mother was an amazing woman," she said wistfully. "You should have seen her. The way her flowers lit up when she laughed. She was achingly beautiful. I know what you're thinking. 'The apple must've fallen pretty far from the tree.'" She laughed ruefully. "No sense in denying it. I know I'm plain looking. I inherited too much of *his* blood. But my mother, she never made me feel less than. She treated me as if I was the queen of the world."

Her eyes turned dark. "When she died...it was..."

She choked up, and I let her sit in silence for a few minutes until she was ready to go on again. "Ambrose never mourned my mother. Not the way he did when Criscilla was bitten by that spider. Geraldine always said it was because she was his second wife, that losing two wives was too much for him. That's not the truth, though. Geraldine says fancy things because he has an infantilized view of the world. He could never see any wrong in Ambrose. The man's a god to him. After all, Ambrose was the one who saved him when Geraldine's family turned him out for wanting to marry Carson."

"They disowned him for being gay?"

Alegra crinkled her nose at me in disgust. "What? No. Our kind doesn't judge sexuality in the way humans do. What business is it of mine who wants to do what in their bedroom? No, it was because Geraldine was of noble lineage. Carson is of lesser blood. Such marriages are frowned upon. Anyway, the point is Geraldine can never see anything wrong in Ambrose. He has always made excuses for why Ambrose was so cold to me, why he was so cruel in the things he'd say, how he'd rather do anything than share a moment with his daughter.

"I grew up wishing that time could fly by, waiting for my chance to leave this place and join the royal family. I made excuses to myself back then that it was just his nature to be cold. Until I saw him with his new family. The first time I witnessed him playing with Perseus, I thought I'd lost my mind. Surely, I must have suffered a mental break. Play with his children? Not my father. Not Ambrose Amaryllis. Then the twins came along, and it was the same, Ambrose doting over his sweet little Cyan and Artur. Criscilla was always kind to me, but how could I grow close to her and her children?

"He robbed me of that. No matter how much I wanted to love my siblings, there was always this wedge of jealousy. Because he loved them more than me. What was so wrong with me that my own father didn't want me?"

Alegra's words hammered at my heart. It was as if she took the details of my childhood and laid them out in the grass before me. I knew exactly what it felt like to ask myself those same questions while lying in bed at night. How could my mother abandon me? Why didn't she want me? What was wrong with me that I was so unworthy of love?

Alegra held my hand. She knew. I didn't need to speak the words for her to understand. We were kin in our fractured childhoods, two lost souls wandering through the abyss.

I had to ask her the question that loomed between us. I didn't want to because I was certain she wasn't the murderer. Still, the words had to be spoken, or there would be that lingering doubt.

"Alegra…did you try to murder your father?"

"Never."

I believed her. The air came out of me, and I suddenly felt my exhaustion in every aching muscle, the sore soles of my feet, and in fingertips that felt scraped raw from my run in with Marik and the long labor of Gizmitt's burial. I felt the exhaustion behind my dry eyelids, which burned red-hot when I closed them. But I couldn't sleep. There was still the masquerade to attend, still a killer waiting out there for their opportunity to strike down Ambrose.

"Even after all that, he's my father. I may not like him very much, but I do love him. I could never harm him."

"What about your brother and sister?"

"Are you serious? Could you really picture Artur murdering someone? And Cyan would sooner die than go against a single thing my father said. No, it's not someone in our family."

"What about someone from the Court of Shadows?"

Alegra arched her brow. "You have a suspect in mind."

"I might."

"They would be at the top of the list of fae wanting to damage my father's reputation. Ambrose has politically out maneuvered them many times over the years. No doubt Malachai sees my father as an obstacle. But enough to murder him? I can't imagine even Malachai would stoop so low. Murder among nobility is unconscionable."

"So, they'll steal his business holdings and try to destroy his reputation, but murder is a step too far?" I summarized. "Because the nobility are purebloods?"

"Their bloodlines are sacred. They are the direct descendants of the first children. Each Great House can trace their lineage to the same source, Queen Titania and King Oberon."

"And nothing could rattle that allegiance?"

"Bloodlines mean everything to our people."

They didn't to my mother, I thought.

Whether I agreed with Alegra's estimation or not, she was unshakeable in her certainty.

It's got to be Valia. She was my last and best suspect for this crime. If I could figure out why she was moving shimmer, it might lead me to the missing clue I needed to complete the puzzle.

"Ugh, I have to go," I groaned as I pulled myself to my feet.

"Yes, we mustn't upset father by being late to the masquerade," Alegra said.

The full moon looked down at me with foreboding. I had to meet Tae and get ready with less than an hour left. *Oh geez, I hope Tae hasn't been waiting for me for too long.*

Tae screamed as she tumbled over the side of the roof. Her feet kicked open air. Her fingers clawed at the thatch for dear life. They dragged through the thick bramble as her body weight inexorably pulled her farther and farther over the edge.

Great. This is it. After all the insane scrapes I've been in through the years, this is how I die.

She'd always envisioned her death differently. Perhaps dying of old age surrounded by loved ones. Or even better, in the act of having an orgasm so complete, so perfect and unyielding, that she simply ceased to exist. A fine way to go out for a succubus. Not by stubbing her toe on a tree spirit's head and falling off a rooftop.

Her legs dangled uselessly in the open air. Tae looked down and immediately regretted it. The ground seemed to be miles away. "Wait, I'm not falling," she said. "I'm not falling?"

Tiny hands held the cuff of her jacket. Tae watched in shock as others joined it. The kodama were saving her! Dozens of tiny hands reached out for her fingers. They tugged and heaved, their little voices groaning with the exertion. More joined in to grab her wrists. Soon she was back over the ledge. She clamped down, digging her fingers into the thatch to help support her weight as the kodama continued their rescue effort. A mob of them were lined up like an army of ants, bracing each other, lending strength to the group. Their little bodies moved in unison as if they were playing tug-of-war. They didn't stop until Tae's legs came over the ledge.

The man was still there. He watched the scene unfold, his face an expressionless mask of shadows lost beneath his hood. "Sick bastard stuck around to watch me fall," Tae grumbled. "I'm going to tear his head off."

The man stiffened.

One of the kodama came up to Tae's face. She was an older woman with a shawl wrapped around her knobby head. She stroked Tae's forehead tenderly and said something comforting in her reedy language.

"Thank you," Tae breathed. "You saved my life."

The old woman nodded appreciatively. Then she raised her finger and proceeded to chastise.

"I know," Tae said, feeling properly cowed. "I'm sorry I caused so much damage to your homes."

The crowd of tree spirits was suddenly in a tizzy. Tae followed their pointing fingers back to the man. He stood on the edge of the rooftop. With one final glance over his shoulder, he leapt off.

Tae found her feet in a huff and dashed to the spot where he'd been. She peered over the ledge to find the man spiraling downward. His cloak burst outward to reveal extended faerie wings. They caught on the wind and pulled him upward like a parachute. In a dizzying display of speed, he turned his body around and zipped back inside the tree. He disappeared, escaping through some open window not unlike the one she'd climbed through mere minutes ago.

25

The gallery felt colder than it had the night I was with Lucien. The art was no longer fanciful to me but more of a backdrop to Ambrose's false image. It was hard to hide my resentment toward him after hearing of the loveless childhood Alegra had endured. He seemed so gentle, so kind and caring toward the world at large. I wondered if he even realized the emotional impact his failure as a father figure for her had wrought.

"And you say the man was crouching before this statue?" Ambrose was decked out in a fantastic coat that hung down to his ankles. The fabric had a rainbow gradient, purple at the bottom and shifting through the colors to a bright red around the shoulders. Woody vines grew from the fabric, with green leaves that had rainbow veining draping down over his shoulders like miniature tree canopies. He was dressed to impress for that night's masquerade.

Tae's outfit was far more disheveled than I was used to and contrasted greatly with his fine attire. The last time I'd seen her in such a state was the night the changeling hunted us down. Except that time she had a look of terror circling her eyes instead of the anger that centered them to tiny points.

"He was definitely messing with the statue of this little girl," Tae confirmed for the third time.

Geraldine was inspecting all angles of the sculpture, carefully running his fingers over the surface in search of something.

"And you're certain you didn't get a good look at his face?" Ambrose prodded.

Tae shook her head, allowing her frustration to bubble to the surface. "I already told you, he had on some sort of magical cloak. The hood obscured his face in shadows. Even when we were outside in the moonlight, I couldn't get a good look."

"The kodama are in an uproar over the damage you caused," Geraldine said from behind the statue.

"I am sorry about that," Tae replied. "I'll try to be more graceful next time I'm chasing down an assassin trying to murder you."

I held back a snicker at her sarcasm. "Where did this statue come from?" I asked, hoping to move the conversation away from whatever responsibility they were trying to allude Tae owed to the tree spirits. "Can you think of any reason someone would be interested in it?"

Ambrose frowned placidly. He reminded me of a melancholy monk deep in thought. "The statue is a recent addition to my collection."

"Who gave it to you?" I pressed.

He looked sideways, torn over revealing the person's identity.

"This is stupid," I said. "We're trying to save your life here, sir. If you can't trust me enough to reveal who gave you this statue, then how am I supposed to help you?"

"It was a gift from my daughter Cyan," Ambrose said softly. How must it feel to speak aloud your fear that your own daughter might be trying to murder you? I couldn't imagine it.

I sighed. "Cyan's not behind your assassination attempt."

"How can you be certain?" Ambrose pressed hopefully.

It sickened me to hear the desperation in his voice. Would he sound the same if he suspected Alegra as the murderer? "I already vetted Cyan. She's not out to get you. Your daughter worships you. If anything, she's more scared you'll learn—"

I clamped my mouth shut before I accidentally revealed Cyan's affair.

"I'll learn what?" Ambrose pressed.

I shook my head. "It's not my place to intervene. You'll need to speak with your daughter about it. All I can say is, I'm certain it's not her."

"And the intruder was not concerned with this statue," Geraldine said.

"I'm telling you I definitely saw the man in the cloak crouching down right there," Tae insisted.

"I believe that you did," Geraldine said from the other side of the statue. "You were correct about where he was standing. Just off on which statue was involved."

He stepped out from behind the sculptures, directing our attention to, not the girl, but the statue beside her. It was of a robed woman holding a staff up to the sun. Bursts of blooming flowers were carved all around the hem of her robe, where they met the earth and became one. Geraldine was gesturing to a spot halfway down the sculpture's side, partially obscured by her raised hand clutching the staff. A small cylindrical device was stuck to the stonework there.

"What in the hell is that?" I asked.

"A trap," Tae said in a low voice.

Ambrose produced a twig from his coat. He murmured a command, and a rush of water spit forth from the tip of the branch. His spell enveloped the cylinder in a perfect sphere of water. With a flick of his wrist, the sphere plucked the cylinder free from the statue. The water swirled faster and faster around the sphere's surface as Ambrose, his eyes closed, concentrated on the spell.

He finally stopped chanting and opened his eyes. "The succubus is correct." He bowed deferentially to Tae. "Someone has placed a poison trap on the statue of Lady Nisang."

"Ah, of course," Tae said.

"But why would they do that?" I asked, feeling lost. "What am I missing?"

It was Geraldine who filled in the blanks for me. "The water fae before you, depicted so grandly, is the original blossom faerie, Lady Nisang Amaryllis. She is the mother of spring. It is an annual tradition for the House of Dawn to bring her statue out for Master Amaryllis's closing speech. This is the moment that marks the true beginning of spring."

"When I stood before Lady Nisang," Ambrose finished, "the trap would've sprung, and the toxin inside utterly destroyed me. I have disarmed it."

"Holy shit," I said. The three of them cringed at my bad manners, but I was too excited to be embarrassed over my faux pas. "This is great news."

"You believe that the assassin utilizing the symbol of our Lady Nisang in an attempt to murder the head of our Great House at the height of our most sacred celebration to be *good news*?" Geraldine said dryly.

"Yes! I mean, not the trying to murder him part. But don't you see what Tae's discovery means for us?"

Geraldine looked like he'd tasted a sour lemon.

"The killer may not know that we have found this," Ambrose explained.

"But they will surely know that the succubus has alerted us to their trap," Geraldine reasoned.

"Her name is Taewyn, Geraldine, not *the succubus*," I said. "And the killer might think so. But really, we hold all the poker chips here." I waved away Geraldine's next question before he could open his mouth. "The assassin will assume Tae has told us where she spotted them. They won't be able to resist coming back here to see if we've removed the trap. All we need to do is put it back in place and wait. The killer will do the rest of the work for us."

"We can have some of our guardians hiding in the gallery, waiting to capture him," Ambrose agreed.

"But what if they don't suspect the succu—err, *Taewyn* of discovering their trap?"

"Either way we're covered," I said. "If they don't come back to the gallery, then we'll be watching for them during the speech. Only the assassin should have a reaction when Ambrose steps beside the statue and lives. If we're clever enough, we'll be able to spot them in the crowd. It's a good plan, and a godsend since *someone* accidentally leaked our last one."

Geraldine looked at the floor with stooped shoulders.

"I'm well aware that Geraldine told the children of the poisoning," Ambrose said. "He may have gotten a bit overzealous in ensuring none of them had drunk the same tea."

I didn't feel like pointing out that Geraldine could have just asked Chef Henri who the tea had been served to. It looked like whatever punishment Ambrose had doled out had properly cowed the head butler. "Well, either way, this plan is going to work. All we need to do is wait for the assassin to walk into *our* trap."

Ambrose nodded approvingly. "And until then, the danger to me has been lifted. I will place the disarmed trap back on the statue. This way it will look as if we haven't found it. In fact, we should remove Cyan's statue from the gallery instead. This way the killer will think they've duped us, thus making the lie all the more credible."

It was an awesome plan. "We're finally going to catch this bastard."

When I returned to my room, I found a gown, mask, and shoes waiting for me on my bed. Geraldine had had them delivered while I was consoling Alegra and Tae was chasing down the assassin. It was funny how much could change in just an hour.

Tae couldn't wait for me to try it on. The dress was sublime, with delicate tulle skirts that shifted from a blue as deep as the night sky to tinges of purple and then back to a light turquoise. A smattering of beads throughout the dress made it sparkle when I moved. It was the prettiest thing I'd ever worn, like something out of a dream. To my delight, it fit perfectly. The silk bodice hugged my body as if it were a second skin.

"Damn, Lanie, you look sexy as fuck. And your shoulders look divine exposed like that," Tae purred. "Let's see it with the mask."

The mask was made from twilight-purple lace. It was a domino mask that covered my eyes and nose. The top of it rose to a point over my forehead, where a lone amethyst was affixed. There were no straps. If I'd bought something like it in the human realm, I would have to glue it on to keep it in place. The fae mask needed no adhesive. When it came close to my skin, it tingled and sat perfectly in place.

It was like someone else was looking back at me in the mirror.

"I look beautiful," I gasped.

"You always look beautiful, sweetie," Tae said. "Tonight, you look stunning as well. You're just missing one thing." She rummaged through her bag and produced a length of white satin. "Stand still."

Tae's arms draped my shoulders from behind as she snaked her hands around my throat and tied the satin choker. I was going to point out the difference in colors when she tapped the center of the choker. In an instant a twilight purple color spread through the fabric of the choker like seeping ink until the fabric was completely dyed.

"It accentuates your gorgeous neckline," she said as she helped me fix my hair into a waterfall braid.

Once it was done, I slipped into the sparkly purple flats while Taewyn poured herself into a gorgeous trumpet dress smothered in gold sequins. The dress barely clung to her. The sleeve on her left arm ended in a v at her wrist, while the other arm was sleeveless. The center of the dress swooped down at an angle, revealing an ample view of the curve of her breasts. Another slash worked around the side, from the hem all the way up to her ribs. The train came down to her ankles but was cut with a third slit that showed off her legs and upper right thigh.

My face grew hot looking at her. "Tae, you look...," I stammered, trying to find the right words to express how exquisitely sensual she was. The dress looked like it was painted on her more than worn.

"*We* look," Tae corrected, turning me so we faced the mirror together. She purred over my shoulder.

I saw us standing together, looking our best, and blushed. "We really do."

And I felt it as we walked down the steps into the masquerade ballroom. I was no longer Lanie Alacore, the wilting flower who hid in the backroom. I felt like a princess, my head held high.

The ballroom was magnificently decadent. The ceiling soared overhead, a dome of overlapping ivory branches and silver leaves. There were no windows. I realized we were in the heart of Starfire, below the atrium.

Starfire's heart literally floated above us, directly in the center of the ballroom. It was a thirty-foot sphere of pulsating light beating to the rhythm of the music being played by a string quartet. Archways to either side of the ballroom housed hundreds of round tables laden with food and drink, fancy plates, tea sets, and finely carved wooden forks and knives. Lush foliage blanketed the walls, ivy threaded through with waxy flowers, overlapping white roots, and giant clinging light lilies, their petals opened wide.

Floral topiaries were set all around the ballroom, towering over the dancers in a full celebration of the spring bloom. There was a majestic dolphin topiary cresting a wave of bluebells and creamy hyacinths, a tangle of two hands intertwined like lovers erupting from a fountain of rose petals in a spray of colors, and another topiary of the great dragonflies that made their home on the reef.

The fae in attendance were dressed in an array of fashions for the masquerade, every one of them looking like something out of a dream. One man wore a mask that looked like a crescent moon overlapping a sun, and another looked like a diamond-encrusted face with dove wings at the edges.

Persa stood at the top of the stairs, greeting newcomers in an orange dress that shifted at the top to an eye-piercing yellow that could've come from a ray of sunshine. She wore a yellow mask that covered the skin around her eyes and swooped down to points around her cheekbones. It looked lovely against her plantlike hair, pinned up with a dangling bit of orange ribbon.

Minerva floated through the ballroom below on Malachai's rigid arm. He wore a classic tuxedo while she dazzled in a crimson spaghetti-strap dress with black embroidered raven wings running up her curvaceous hips. Her mask was more of a headdress, with black feathered wings framing her ruby eyes. The top of the headdress was encrusted with a cornucopia of emeralds and diamonds that sparkled as she moved.

"Everyone looks amazing," I said.

"It's the spring masquerade," Tae replied, as if that was a forgone conclusion.

"What I like most is how happy everyone seems, and nobody is going out of their way to get attention."

"The fae have a deep respect for new life," Persa explained, overhearing us as we approached. "Tonight, that is what we're celebrating."

"Yes, we are," Tae agreed heartily. She leaned in close to whisper in my ear. "Since you and Ambrose have everything wrapped up, I'm going to go find myself some trouble to get into."

"Have fun," I giggled.

Tae kissed me on the cheek and cut into the ballroom. Before I looked away, she already had three fae vying for her attention.

"You look so beautiful tonight," Persa said.

I curtsied. "That's exactly what I was going to say to you."

Her eyes darted demurely to the floor. She laughed nervously and asked me if we could talk for a minute.

I let her pull me off to the side, into the shadow of the stairs where no one could see or overhear us. She suddenly looked so troubled I thought she was going to start weeping.

I put a hand on her shoulder. "What is it? Did something happen to Ambrose?"

"Yes—I mean, no," Persa stammered. "But I heard what happened to him this morning, and I…"

What a relief. Ever since Alegra broke the news to me that her family knew what I was here for, I'd been expecting this. "You had me worried for a second there," I said. "Your grandfather is fine. I got to him before anything bad could happen."

"But poor Gizmitt," Persa said. "We're all so lucky you made it to grandfather in time…but I can't help worrying. What if they try something again? How can you be certain my grandfather is safe?"

It was just like Persa to be burdened with these thoughts. She was clearly distraught. Her eyes were bloodshot, and I could see bags beneath them through her masquerade mask. Her hands were shaking like leaves in the wind. I grasped them and squeezed reassuringly.

"Persa, listen to me. You can stop worrying over this. We have everything under control."

"Then you caught the killer?"

"Well, no. But we stopped them, and that's all that matters right now."

Persa shook her head, unconvinced.

"Please, you're going to have to trust me."

"I do trust you," she said. "But…how can you be certain the killer won't try anything again? I don't know why grandfather insists on continuing to be here. The celebration can go on without him. Surely it would be better to get him somewhere safe. And what about you? You're no warrior. Don't get me wrong, I believe you to be a highly capable woman. But aren't you worried that if you confront this killer, you're going to get hurt?"

"Yes, of course I am. Recently I've had several run-ins with vicious creatures. Just this morning a manticore tried to eat me in the Whispering Woods. To be honest, I'm scared all the time. However, I refuse to allow fear to rule my life. Because if I do, I might as well crumple into a helpless ball in the corner and just wait to die. As you said, I'm no warrior, but I won't turn my back on your grandfather. When I find the killer, I'll confront them and do everything in my power to stop their evil plan."

It was alarming to hear myself speak these words. My days of being a shrinking violet really were over. I hadn't let the changeling end me, and I hadn't let the "prince" end Charlie. Perhaps it was the dress lending me false confidence, but in that moment, I felt made of sterner stuff than I could have ever dreamed possible half a year before.

That wasn't what Persa wanted to hear. If anything, I only added to her already overwhelming anxiety. "I don't want anything bad to happen to you," she said, "but I thought you'd say something like that. You're too bold to back down from danger." She paused to think, then added, "I wish I was more like you."

"I'm actually not bold at all."

"If you could see yourself as I do, you wouldn't say that. Here, I got this for you." She pulled a two-inch crystal out of the inside pocket of her dress. "It's an echo crystal. Have you ever used one?"

It looked like an ordinary piece of clear quartz. "No. What does it do?"

"It's for communicating over long distances, like a human telephone," Persa explained. "They're quite rare."

"Are you sure you want me to have this?"

"I need you to," she insisted, pressing the crystal into my palm. "I can't stop you from throwing yourself into danger, but at least I can help. If you find out where the killer is or get a lead that you think might be worthwhile—anything with even a whiff of risk—I want you to use the crystal."

"What can this do against a trained assassin?"

"You can communicate with me, and I will immediately send House of Dawn knights to your location."

"I don't know." The whole thing seemed ridiculous. We already had an airtight plan put together. I thought about coming clean with Persa, but I couldn't. If our plan was to work, I had to ensure not a whisper of it got out. And besides, I would've felt like a hypocrite after I gave Geraldine such a hard time for sharing our earlier plan.

"Please, Lanie, I'm begging you," Persa whined. "If anything happens to you, I could never forgive myself. You must accept my help in this."

"Fine, stop shaking," I said. "I'll use it." Anything to calm the poor girl down. Besides, it couldn't hurt to have some backup. Why was I being so stubborn, anyway? I'd only survived all my encounters with danger by the skin of my teeth. A little extra help couldn't hurt.

Persa threw her arms around me and thanked me repeatedly. "I'm so relieved. I feel like a weight has been lifted off my shoulders."

"Good, because this is a celebration." I beamed.

"Something my little cousin needs constant reminding of," Silas said as he came around the corner of the stairs. "I saw her ferret you away and knew she'd be talking your ear off about family business."

I shot Persa a quick look. She replied with the slightest shake of her head.

Silas didn't know what was going on. He wasn't considered part of the inner circle. That was just as well. I didn't want to spend my night reassuring one Amaryllis after the other. Not when we had everything locked down. This evening, one way or another, the killer would be revealed. Until then, I just wanted to have some fun.

So when Silas asked me for a dance, I quickly accepted his arm and let him lead me to the dance floor. I felt hidden behind my mask. As if wearing it shielded me from the knowledge that Silas had watched me have sex with Lucien under the willow tree. He wore a cream-colored suit with a vanilla flower growing from the fabric around his lapel. The collar of his jacket cut a wide V, showing a jade dress shirt beneath that brought out the green in his eyes. His white-and-gold mask covered his face from forehead to just under his nose, leaving only his eyes, mouth, and strong jawline exposed.

We smiled at each other as we cut our way through dancing fae. I spotted Valia scowling at me. She looked ravishing in a dress of black feathers and blue lace. Where was Lucien? I felt a twinge of jealousy but then noticed he wasn't with her.

Why should I care? I have a dashing man whisking me away to dance. Lucien's nothing but trouble. I realized how much I had been attracted to danger in the past. First with my werewolf, Lobo, and then the dark prince of shadows, Lucien. *Are cold brooding bastards my type?*

Silas pulled me close with his palm against my lower back. Our fingers intertwined, and our feet moved to the music coming from the string quartet that played in the center of the dance floor. The dancers twirled around them in a dizzying spectacle of grace. I let Silas sweep me away. He was nothing like my past crushes. He was warm where Lucien was cold and open where Lobo was a sealed vault.

"I loved watching you yesterday," he whispered in my ear.

My back stiffened as I felt the blood rush to my face. I feigned innocence. "You did?"

Silas twirled me out and then pulled me back toward him. "You were on your horse, riding away from the stables," he said. "I've never seen anyone so excited to be riding. It was like watching a wildflower caught on the breeze."

"It was my first time."

"That's interesting," he said, tightening his hand around my waist. I felt the heat of his body through the satin and silk. He moved his lips close to my ear. "The way you ride made me jealous of the horse."

Oh fuck. I felt dizzy. Silas was turning me on with just his words. I needed to stop before I blacked out, but I felt intoxicated, poised on the precipice between my curse and desire. It made me angry. I wanted Silas. I wanted him to throw me on the ground and do whatever he desired, to let me ride him the way I did his friend yesterday. Unfortunately, the curse ruled my life, trapping me into obedience. Lucien was my only lifeline, my one sole opportunity to subvert its hold over me.

All of that and more ran through my mind as I processed his words and their double meaning. I turned my face just enough so that my lips were near his as I spoke. We were so close I could practically taste him. "We should go riding *together* some time," I teased, unable to control myself.

"Excuse me, Silas," a man laughed jovially. "If you don't mind, I'd like to ask the lady for this next dance."

It was Olan. The music had stopped between songs, and Silas and I were standing still, staring at each other.

"I would be honored," I said to Olan.

Silas's eyes searched mine for confirmation. I bit my lower lip. I knew I couldn't have him, but I could still play at the dream of it happening. Silas grinned like a rapscallion.

He politely backed away and bowed to us, though I caught the look he shot at Olan's back.

"I hope I wasn't interrupting," Olan apologized, his cherubic eyes twinkling in Starfire's pulsating light.

"Not at all," I insisted. The truth was the old man came at the perfect moment. A second longer with Silas, and I would've pushed things too far. Blacking out on the ballroom floor didn't seem like a good idea, though it would have been in line with my previous track record at parties. But I could hardly count this as a party. This was a grand ball.

The music picked back up, kicking into a faster waltz. Olan respectfully held me like he would his own daughter.

"Do you have children?" I asked.

His face twitched in surprise. "Why, no, I have never had the good fortune of fertility."

"I'm sorry, that was a rude question."

"Not at all." Olan smiled kindly. "No offense taken. Though no child has been born of my direct bloodline, I see all light fae as my children. In my service to them, I get to carry on the celebration of life."

"That's a lovely way to think," I said.

Olan smiled, pleased I thought so. Starfire's heart pulsed brightly.

"Oh, it is beginning," Olan laughed.

Before I could ask what he meant, the ballroom shifted. A sound of delight rippled through the dancers as Starfire's heart beat faster. The air around me changed, a golden glow of tiny specks emitting from the tree's core. I suddenly felt much lighter and realized my feet were no longer on the floor. The dancers around us glided through the air, continuing their dance steps in the ballroom's anti-gravity field. My feet touched the air as if it were solid, leaving behind a ripple of golden light that dissipated as we moved on.

Olan gave me a playful spin, and I laughed like a little girl. He pulled me back in for the steady rhythm of our dance. For a man likely twenty times my age, he was quite graceful on his feet. I felt happier than I'd been in a long time.

Olan's eyes twinkled as he took me in. "You look just like her when she was your age," he reminisced.

"My grandmother? Please, tell me about how you met?" I asked hopefully. "What was she like back then?"

"Ah, it was so long ago, but often I think of those days. One's formative years are such an interesting part of your life, with so many things happening for the first time. The world seemed larger back then, a mysterious place filled with wonder at every turn. True to her legacy, the day I met your grandmother was the day she saved my life."

The music faded into the background for me as I found myself entranced by Olan's words, our feet gliding several feet above the ballroom floor.

"I was raised on the Sommerset Isles, same as Rosalie, but we were from different sides of the archipelago. That was when we were teenagers, on the cusp of our second decade, practically zygotes when you think about it. The isle is home to many species of flora and fauna, fantastical creatures you can't find anywhere else in the world. My parents were positively obsessed with having company over. Every day there was another visiting dignitary or wealthy merchant coming to stay with us. The parties they threw for these guests were as legendary to the grownups as they were boring to a teenager.

"More often than not, I found myself sneaking away to wander the jungle. You see, I was far more interested in bugs and begonias than haughty nobility. One day I spied a dappled horse. It was the size of a puppy; unlike any creature I'd heard of. I followed that horse like a hound dog, obsessed with getting close enough to pet it. Of course, there was no horse. It was a gremlin in disguise, up to its dirty tricks. The little bugger led me right into a trap. It was a roper, a vicious plant that looks harmless, with a budding flower as large as a bush. The roper's petals are a bright orange-crème that catches the eye pleasantly. All the better for the carnivorous plant, because while your eye is taking in the majestic flower, it's vines slither in the grass and snatch you up."

He said the last with a snap of his teeth that made me flinch. "How did you get away?"

"Well, the roper was happy to dangle me upside down until it was ready to eat. They've vines powerful as a giant's hands. It was sheer luck that the plant had only that morning caught an unlucky bongo and was digesting her in its sack.

"The gremlin changed forms on a high branch above us and danced around the roper, hooting. Soon two of its brethren came to join in their japes. How rough it felt not only to be disillusioned of innocence but also to have my imminent death celebrated. That was a feeling I could never shake, even after all these years.

"I must have hung by my ankles for hours, all the while being mocked by the gremlins for my stupidity. One of them was in a long diatribe about the hundred ways light fae are stupid when a rock hit the little fellow directly in the center of his forehead.

"Ha! You should have seen the look on his face. The gremlin's eyes crossed, and he fell straight down from the tree into the roper's territory. Within seconds he was wound up by one of the roper's free vines. The plant shuddered in excitement over its bounty. What a day to have caught not two, but three meals.

"Before the other gremlins could react, two more stones were shot, one for each of them. Now this is the important part. Ropers only have three appendages, but like a squirrel with a nut, they find new prey irresistible. It snatched the second gremlin but had to release me to snatch the third. I sat on the ground, rubbing my forehead, puzzled as to what had just happened.

"'Well, c'mon, you nincompoop,' Rosalie chastised me. 'Hurry out of there before the plant changes it's mind.'

"I scrambled toward her voice, cutting through the chest-high grass until I was face to face with the most beautiful girl in all the realms. We saw each other and laughed, for we knew instantly that we had found a kindred spirit."

"She took out all three gremlins to save you?" I asked in awe.

"Oh, nothing of the sort." Olan shook his bushy white beard. "Rosalie and I went back later that afternoon and rescued the poor saps. She gave them a firm scolding for what they'd done, just as if she was their elder. It was a sight to behold."

"What was she like back then?" I asked.

"Alot like you, really. I saw much of Rosalie in you that day in court. She was headstrong and obstinate, but also with a frenetic love for the world. Rosalie was a confident and capable woman who would rest at nothing to keep those around her safe."

"I don't feel like a capable woman," I admitted.

Olan thought that was hilarious. "My dear girl, in the short time you've been with our people, you've put an end to a changeling, stopped a trafficking ring, and thwarted a serial killer. How much more capable must one be than that?"

As much as it embarrassed me to receive it, I glowed under his praise. "Thank you for sharing that story. I wish so much that I had a chance to know her better."

"What your mother did to you was cruel." Olan's face darkened.

My heart skipped a beat. "You know my mother too?"

I noticed Lucien staring at me from the other side of the ballroom. I let Olan turn me in a circle as we danced through the air.

"I've known Thacinda since she was practically a guppy," Olan said. "She never had any business keeping you away from your family like that. What a nasty thing, to be forced to grow up around humans with no knowledge of your true heritage. Honestly, I can't understand how any fae would intentionally spend time over there."

"It wasn't so bad," I said weakly. Lucien was still staring at us. "Ugh, I think he's going to come over here."

Olan glanced over his shoulder, and sure enough, Lucien was already making his way through the dancers toward us. "Prince Lucien, eh? Is the lad troubling you? I'll make him go away."

"No," I said a little too loudly. Then in a lower voice, I added, "I mean, please don't. I wouldn't like to cause a scene, not on such a lovely night. I think instead I'll take my leave."

"As you wish," Olan let go of my hand and took a step back. He took me in from head to toe with that twinkle in his eye and a shake of his head. "Exactly like Rosalie."

"Thank you again for sharing your story with me," I said and curtsied.

"It was my pleasure. Anytime you'd like to hear about Rosalie, or for that matter should you need anything at all, please come and find me. Lanie Alacore is always welcome at the Blackberry Estate."

"That's a kind offer." I smiled half-heartedly because Lucien was almost to us.

"I mean it, Lanie. Anytime you need anything, I'm at your disposal." He nodded.

I waved goodbye as I retreated toward the other side of the dance floor. I shouldn't have left Olan like that, floating alone, surrounded by dancers. It was awfully rude after how sweet the old man had been.

There was just a look about Lucien, like a cat raring to fight. I didn't want to get into another argument with him. Not tonight. I just wanted one evening where I had no responsibilities, no commitments, no arguments—just dancing and forgetting my troubles.

It was hard to make my way across the dance floor. The air felt firmer when I was dancing. Now it gave with every footstep, throwing me in an awkward rush that left me unbalanced. A golden trail of light marked my wake as I hurried down from the floating aura to the dance floor. On top of that, dancing couples kept blocking my path.

Still, I managed to make it all the way to the edge of the dance floor and back to ground level before Lucien suddenly stepped out in front of me.

26

"How did you do that?" I gasped through my annoyance.

Lucien glanced at the scrape on my forehead. "You've injured yourself."

"What do you want, Lucien?" I said impatiently.

"I only wish to speak with you," he implored.

His tone was far more pleading than I'd expected. It stifled my anger. He took my silence as acquiescence and stepped closer. His mask was silverwood, with two ravens pointing beaks at each other over his forehead and a full moon between them. It made his eyes of hammered silver look even more alien.

"You said everything you needed to yesterday," I said haughtily.

"Yes, we both said a lot of things last evening," he pointed out. "And the truth is your words stung me."

"Oh, boohoo. Poor prince had his feelings hurt. That doesn't give you the right—"

"Please, at least allow me to finish apologizing before you cast further aspersions. Yes, your words stung me, but I realized that was no excuse for what I said to you. And I didn't mean it anyway. The truth is I very much like being around you, Lanie. I overreacted to a slight that only had the teeth I gave it. I know you meant well, and you're right. I am much happier when I'm being myself."

Dancers were starting to look down at us. I wondered how many of them could hear what we were saying over the loud music. On impulse I leaned in close and placed a hand on Lucien's chest. His heart was beating fast. This admission was scary to him. We stared into each other's eyes. That was all that needed to be done. Sometimes words aren't enough, or too much. We saw each other's truth, and it was alright again between us. He placed an icy hand over mine, holding it to his chest.

Over his shoulder I caught a glimpse of Malachai and Minerva. They were dancing lower to the ground, their gazes fixated on us. I could practically feel Malachai's scowl of disapproval beneath his full mask.

"Are you sure about this? I'm not sure your father will be thrilled to see you talking to a commoner."

Lucien winced at the jab. He quickly recovered and pulled me closer. "To hell and back with what my father thinks."

That was it. Lucien passed the test I didn't even know he was taking. I didn't want to be around someone who was embarrassed to be seen with me. I'd spent my life in the background, and I never wanted to go back. I let him lead me deeper onto the dance floor, his arm around my waist as we ascended into the air once more. I scanned the crowd for Valia, but she was nowhere to be seen.

Instead, my eye caught on Cyan. She was cutting across the dance floor in a showstopper of a dress. It reminded me of a Victorian-style princess gown, made of delicate peach-colored fabric. The skirts beneath were black, along with the lace corset. A long peach-and-black colored train followed behind her, but the real eye candy were the enormous peach-and-black butterflies that rested on either shoulder. Another pair of them sat on her puffy skirt, happily fluttering their wings to the music. They had to have had a wingspan of at least two feet. She wore a spectacular headdress with teal-and-lavender butterfly wings framing her face. Elaborate pearls dangled from the headdress over her forehead.

The dress was something out of a fairy tale, but the look in Cyan's eyes was so deadly serious that, for a moment, I was convinced I'd messed everything up.

She was heading directly for Ambrose, who was dancing with Persa.

Oh shit, she is the killer after all, I thought in a panic, my body suddenly numb.

Cyan's lower lip trembled as she neared her father. Her eyes were filled with a wavering resolve. There was too much uncertainty there for a killer ready to strike. She was making her move, but hurting Ambrose wasn't on the agenda. There was someone else who would be wounded that night.

"Oh shit, she's going to tell him," I said.

Lucien followed my eye. "Tell who what? Do you mean Lord Ambrose?"

"You'll see," I said. It wasn't my place to speak until Cyan shared the news formally with her father.

Ambrose stopped dancing. He let go of Persa as he watched his daughter stalk toward them.

"Cyan!"

It was the call of a desperate woman. Cyan's back stiffened at the sound. Her footsteps faltered.

Many heads turned to see what the commotion was all about. I expected to find Isabo chasing after her wife. Instead, my eyes landed on Cyan's lover. Litari looked as if she'd been crying. Geraldine's men were blocking her entrance to the masquerade. "Don't do this!" she screamed.

"Why wouldn't she want Cyan to tell her father about their affair?" I whispered.

Lucien snickered. "I think you're misreading the situation."

Cyan stood frozen in place as Litari pelted her back with heart wrenching pleas. Geraldine's men dragged her away from the ballroom. Cyan had a decision to make. Turn around and go to the woman she loved or keep moving forward and do her duty for her family. As much as I didn't like her, it was an unbearable decision to have to make.

"She's torn, though," I whispered. "She's not sure she's making the right choice. It isn't too late. She can still turn around and chase after Litari."

Cyan's gaze shifted tentatively over her shoulder.

Ambrose called her to him. His voice was clear and commanding. Cyan caught my eye and quickly averted her gaze. I read shame in that glance. Ambrose held a hand up for his daughter. She took a deep breath and went to him. He took her in his arms and pulled her close, a father and daughter sharing a dance. The rest of the attendees fell back into their own conversations, most blissfully unaware of what had just transpired. For his part, Ambrose didn't look the slightest bit bothered.

"Because he already knew," I said in shock. "She must have told him before the masquerade began. That's it, then. Cyan really turned her back on her true love."

"Why do you sound so surprised?" Lucien grinned, pulling me closer to him. "Cyan is a member of the House of Dawn. You could scarcely believe she'd forsake her family's lifeline for a little rut in the sack."

That was when I learned the truth.

Lucien explained it all to me in detail, filling in the empty spaces as we danced in the air. Cyan's wife Isabo was from a wealthy family of water fae nobility that lorded over the Deep. Their marriage was one of arrangement, where both families stood to benefit. Isabo's family secured their legacy by marrying into the House of Dawn, and in return their daughter brought a veritable fortune into the Great House. Regardless of what Cyan felt in her heart, she had obligations to her family to uphold. She could no sooner turn her back on them than she could cut off her own hand. It was a depressing quandary to bear.

I told myself that Cyan wasn't a very good person. She probably had this coming, karma and all. Who was I to say that what Cyan was doing was the wrong thing, anyhow? Ambrose had not only the livelihood of his immediate family but tens of thousands of fae to look out for. The money Isabo's marriage provided would help keep the House of Dawn in power so they could do exactly that. So what that it was at the cost of Cyan's happiness? There were plenty of people out there living day to day in a job they loathed, sacrificing the things they dreamed of doing, all in the name of taking care of those they loved. How was Cyan's plight any different?

It wasn't. And that was the problem. Instead of focusing on that, I'd made it about me. Why was I worrying over Cyan's problems? I had enough of my own: my best friend was stuck in a coma, my mother abandoned me, someone was trying to murder my employer, I had no money, and I didn't know if I could keep the apothecary open for even another couple of months. To top all that off, I was trapped beneath a curse that cut me off from having the relationship I dreamed of. That was enough to handle without also taking on Cyan's self-induced problems. Perhaps if she was a little nicer of a person, it would have been harder to fool myself into turning a blind eye to her plight. Because no matter how much I tried to justify it, I knew deep down that what just happened was wrong.

In the end, I couldn't rationalize which decision was the correct one. Not that it mattered. It was Cyan's decision to make. Not mine.

I threw myself into my dance with Lucien. I wanted to be present, to have a night where I could let loose and to hell with the angels. That was a saying I'd heard before. I had no idea what it meant, but thinking it made me feel like a badass.

I danced with Lucien for the next few hours. Nobody dared cut in on the prince, and I never saw Silas on the dance floor again, much to my disappointment. I wasn't sure where Tae had snuck off to, though I was certain she was enjoying herself. No one knew how to have a good time more than a succubus.

I glided over the ballroom floor, spinning and dipping, waltzing and trotting, surrounded by laughing fae in masquerade masks. We soared higher and higher until the room warped to fit all the fae. The floating field wrapped around itself in a bubble of antigravity. Fae were soon dancing on the ceiling upside down and on the walls around us. Twirling sideways in the air left me feeling giddy, as if I'd drunk too much champagne.

Lucien held me close. His icy body through the layers of my silk dress was a stark contrast to the way Silas's had felt only a few hours earlier. I wanted him to keep holding me, to guide me through the air and keep laughing together.

When we finally finished dancing, I was giddy and still feeling light-headed from the antigravity dweomer. We floated down off the dance floor, arm in arm.

Lucien leaned sideways. His lips grazed my earlobe and sent a shiver coursing through me. "Come with me, I have a surprise for you."

I thought of the lagoon and warmed inside. We left the ballroom and entered halls that were packed with masked fae celebrating the coming of spring. They were drinking and laughing in revelry.

Soon we moved through a doorway into a wider hall.

I was rooted in place by shock. Crushed velvet couches and chairs, floor cushions and silk sheets furnished the hall. And they were filled with scores of squirming bodies and moans of pleasure. I'd stumbled into my first fae orgy.

A woman with a strap-on was riding another woman doggy style over the arm of a chair by the wall. In the central area four fae were simultaneously fucking in a ring. It was an overload of naked flesh, fluttering wings, quivering bodies, and sucking lips.

"I don't think I can do this," I said, backing away.

Lucien laughed. "Not here. I've got a private room all set up for us down the hall."

A wave of relief flooded over me. The truth was I was soaking wet at the sight of all that carnal pleasure. I just couldn't picture being brave enough to join in. Although, it seemed half the fae in the palace had descended upon that hallway to engage in the orgy.

Lucien led me farther into the hall. I caught a glimpse of Minerva through an open doorway on our right. She was lying on a bed with a man thrusting between her legs and two more standing on either side of the bed. A naked woman with a mask on saw me looking and slowly closed the door.

Lucien smirked at me and shrugged. We walked past ten more closed doors before we stopped at our room. Lucien pulled me close and nibbled on my neck. His cold lips felt delicious on my hungry skin. I wanted him to gobble me up. I palmed his hardness through his pants.

"You're going to love this," Lucien promised. He opened the door and stepped aside for me to enter.

A dozen candles lit the room, with the space in between the flickering light filled by flowers. The canopy bed was draped in red sheer silks and the bedposts carved to look like giant sun daisies tilting down toward the floor. It was a more romantic gesture than I'd ever expected from someone like Lucien.

Then I saw him.

My heart stopped. There was someone else sitting on the bed, wearing a mask. I was ready to turn from the room when I caught a glimpse of the man's jawline.

"Silas?"

Lucien laughed playfully. I turned to him. His face was inches from mine. "You enjoyed yourself so much while Silas watched us yesterday, I thought why not invite him to join us?"

"You knew he was watching?"

Lucien grinned.

Silas sat against the headboard; his muscular arms draped over the pillows on either side of him. His dress shirt was unbuttoned down to his navel, exposing the coppery skin beneath. He was in great shape, not as defined as Lucien but all muscles regardless. He sat with his legs out straight and ankles crossed. He still wore his mask, eager jade eyes watching me from behind the silk curtains like some dream.

Will it work? Can Lucien's ability to negate my curse carry over to Silas? Was it a ranged magic or something that had to do with touch? My mind was racing. The idea of being with both of these men at the same time stole my breath away.

"Don't leave me," I told Lucien, gripping his arm tight.

"I wouldn't dream of going anywhere else." He smiled, and I let him press me down to the bed. The back of my head rested on Silas's strong thighs. He bent over to look me in the eyes through his mask.

"Hi," he said as he caressed my hair.

"Hello." It was the first time we'd spoken since I entered the room.

Silas ran his fingertips across my earlobe then down the curve of my jaw, sending sparks of electricity through my brain. I nuzzled his hand and kissed his fingers. He delicately traced the shape of my lips.

I looked down to find Lucien smiling at me from the foot of the bed. He gently parted my legs and bit his lower lip.

Silas bent over me and pressed his lips to my mouth. I opened my lips and invited his tongue to meet me. Lucien's icy hands worked up my dress, stroking and massaging my legs up to the thighs. As I tasted Silas, Lucien sent his ice magic in whirls of chill air that penetrated my flesh. I felt dizzy with anticipation. I slapped a hand down to meet his, gripping him tightly to make sure he didn't let go of me.

With my other hand I tugged my panties down and shimmied them down to my knees. Silas held my throat as we hungrily kissed. It was a sensation overload that left me hot as a furnace ready to explode. I was so turned on that when Lucien brought his cold lips to my pussy, I bucked my hips to meet him, and my body trembled. Lucien licked around my swollen lips, his icy tongue flicking inside my hot center. Silas leaned down far, using his fingers to massage my clit in tight circles while Lucien sucked on my pussy lips. To have both men touching me left me feeling like I was spinning in ecstasy. A moan spilled from my lips, which encouraged Lucien to slip his tongue deeper inside me.

Silas used his other hand to pull down the front of my dress, releasing my breasts and shifting his attention from my aching clit to my nipples. He alternated sucking and nibbling on my breasts, kneading my flesh with his strong hands. I reached up into his open shirt and I stroked his bare chest. His skin was hot where Lucien's was cold, and the dual sensations worked wonders on my libido. I massaged his chest upside down as he moved further and further down my stomach, his lips suckling my flesh. I wrapped my thighs around Lucien's head as he worked me from below. I could feel the orgasm tightening inside my core, ready to explode.

Silas's waist hovered above me. He was bulging with desire. I finally let go of Lucien so I could use both hands to unzip Silas's trousers. His cock throbbed to greet me as I released it. I wrapped my hands around the shaft and gave two tentative strokes, admiring the length of it. Silas's desire was muffled by his lips as his mouth made its way down to my clit. He had a beautiful cock, bulging at the top, with a thick shaft. I rubbed the head with my thumb as I tugged him down to me. He groaned as I wrapped my lips around the tip to taste his precum. I slid my forefinger down the shaft and played with his balls as I let him slide further inside my mouth.

Lucien's fingers entered me as Silas started to slowly pump in and out of my mouth. The pressure in my core grew as Lucien's fingers filled my soaking wet pussy and pressed against my swollen g-spot. It sent a burst of pleasure through my core.

"Let me get a taste," Silas said lustily as I moaned on his cock.

"Oh, please do," Lucien purred back. His cold lips left my pussy and met Silas's. Silas sucked on Lucien's lower lip then his tongue, tasting me off his friend's mouth. His cock throbbed and swelled inside my mouth as he did.

Then they were both there, Silas's hot lips sucking on my clit as Lucien's icy fingers stroked against my g-spot. Lucien alternated from using his mouth to explore the sides of my pussy to meeting Silas at my clit where their tongues would cross.

It was more than I could take. Suddenly I was bucking my hips hard against Lucien's face as my pent-up orgasm let loose in an explosion of color. It came out like a lightning bolt, charging the room. I screamed in ecstasy, letting the light ripple from my core and blind my partners. Silas spasmed and filled my mouth with his cum. His scream matched the intensity of my orgasm, but he never stopped pumping his cock inside my mouth as I rode the wave of my orgasm.

Silas pushed up onto his knees beside me, breathing hard. "What was that?" he asked in stunned disbelief and glee.

"That's my Lanie," Lucien answered, sitting up between my legs. "Isn't she wonderful?"

I bit my lower lip. "I want more," I growled.

Lucien's cock was sticking up like a lightning rod between his thighs. I shimmied out of my dress as he climbed on the bed. He was fully naked except for his mask. He laid flat on his back.

"Are you ready for me to ride your friend?" I asked Silas. He watched me with hungry eyes as I climbed on and sank Lucien's thick cock into me. I was already slick from their tongues and my desire, but it still took some work to ease his girth into my pussy.

I shuddered as he slammed his hips up, jamming himself into my core. I stayed on my knees, with him fully inside, and gyrated against his icy body. Silas got behind me and wrapped his arm around my waist. He reached down and slid his fingers between me and Lucien where we met, then let loose water magic to create a thin layer of lube. It was like a hot spring, a sublime contrast to Lucien's icy girth. Silas worked my clit with one hand while using the other to grab me by the hair. He tugged my head back and kissed me.

"You like watching me fuck your friend?" I asked.

Silas locked eyes with me. He bit his lower lip and nodded. I rubbed myself against Lucien's body faster. He slammed his hips up, jolting my insides like a lightning bolt. I let out a scream of pleasure. Silas jammed his fingers in my mouth for me to suck on. I greedily sucked them with our eyes locked on each other.

Silas grinned. He pulled the fingers slowly out and down my lips as I rode his friend. He pinched my nipple then brushed his fingers down my spine until he made it to my ass. His magic let water flow down my cheeks, across Lucien's thighs.

"Is this ok?" Silas paused and squeezed my bouncing cheeks as Lucien thrust up again.

"Oh my god, yes," I rasped, my desire growing even higher with the thought of what was to come.

His fingers explored my asshole, massaging it with the tips in a way that made me dizzy. Water magic lubricated me as his finger slid into my backdoor, and I moaned.

Lucien slammed his hips up to meet my gyrating. He was stretching my pussy, rubbing against all the right spots inside me in exactly in the way I needed. I already felt another orgasm tightening in my core. Silas fucked my ass with his fingers from behind.

"I feel so full," I moaned.

I bent my head back so we could kiss. He nibbled on my lower lip. I reached down between his thighs to find him hard once more. The tip of his cock was dripping with more precum. I jerked him off as Lucien moaned beneath me. He was ready to cum. I jerked Silas faster, and Lucien tore me apart from the inside with harder and harder thrusts.

Suddenly Lucien's whole body locked up and he exploded inside my pussy, his seed spurting into my core. I was on the verge of another orgasm, riding a wave of euphoria. I couldn't stop. I kept sliding up and down his slick cock. Silas was filling my ass with his fingers as Lucien stretched me to my limits from the front. I felt like a runaway train, desperately grasping Silas's cock from the side less I tumble away into the cosmos unmoored.

"Oh fuck," I yelled as my orgasm let loose. My body quivered as I collapsed on top of Lucien. My vision blurred. I didn't know such pleasure was possible. After what felt like an eternity of orgasmic bliss, I fell to the side, off of Lucien. The soft sheets felt like heaven against my tingling body.

"Oh no, you don't," Silas said. "We're not done with you yet."

He slid between my legs and pressed the length of his rock-hard cock between my pussy lips. My body trembled from the sensation. Lucien's hand reached down to grab his friend. He rubbed Silas's cock up and down my swollen slit as I moaned, then held the tip over my opening.

"Are you all stretched out and ready for him?" Lucien asked.

"Please," I begged.

"Good girl." Lucien's cold lips kissed me as he guided Silas inside.

Silas's cock wasn't as thick as Lucien's, but the curve of it slid deliciously against my g-spot. He grabbed my ankles and pinned them far back so he could thrust all the way inside. I was already tingling from the fucking Lucien had given me, but this was on a whole other level. Silas slammed his hips down like a jackhammer, making me scream with pleasure. His cock pressed into me deeper and deeper until I could practically feel him in my belly. Water poured from his skin, deliciously hot and steaming where it met my flesh. Everywhere the magic water touched me felt like an explosion of erotic pleasure.

Lucien moved behind him, his head over Silas's shoulder. He massaged Silas's chest with one arm over him, grinning as he watched me getting fucked beyond belief, and whispered in Silas's ear. Silas nodded and smiled as he continued his long deep strokes. His jade eyes devoured me as if he was trying to memorize every second of this. I bucked my hips up to meet him, feeling a jolt of ecstasy each time he slammed into my core.

Suddenly Lucien came around to my head and grabbed my ankles away from Silas. He held them back as Silas gradually picked up his pace until he was panting with each thrust.

"You like how good he's fucking you?" Lucien asked.

"Oh yes, fuck me harder," I yelled, unable to contain myself.

Silas obliged with slamming thrusts that lit up my core. I could feel his cock throbbing inside, almost ready to burst, and it pressed my own pent-up explosion toward the edge.

"You heard her," Lucien said to Silas. "Harder than that. Make my Lanie cum all over your cock."

I almost felt that I could take no more, the pleasure was so intense. The harder I screamed the more powerful Silas's cock seemed to penetrate me. I thought I might explode.

And then I did. Rainbow light burst from my open lips, rippling down my sweaty body. When it touched Silas he instantly let loose inside me. The light kept traveling, wrapping around my legs until it hit Lucien's hands at my ankles. He quivered and pulsated inside above me. My body trembled uncontrollably under the euphoria of it. We fell in a heap of tingling bodies, laughing and moaning as our hands massaged each other's overstimulated muscles.

"You are amazing," Silas complimented me. "I don't even know what that was. It was so wild."

Lucien chuckled. "I told you. She's positively feral."

I laughed and ran my fingers down Lucien's naked chest to his hard shaft. "You're the one still ready to go."

Lucien mumbled something incoherent as both men fell over me, the three of us sharing a kiss.

27

There have been few times in my life when I felt happier than that evening. After a while of laying in each other's arms, the three of us left our private paradise to rejoin the masquerade. Ambrose's closing speech would begin soon, and none of us wanted to miss it.

Lucien slipped off into the bustling ranks of fae nobility that only a few hours earlier had been occupied in orgiastic glee. I walked beside Silas, the two of us sharing sideways glances. He grinned sheepishly, and I blushed. Something more than sex had transpired between us in that room. A deeper connection resonated like a pulsating thread between our hearts.

I dared to dream of what that meant for my future. *I could be with him. Lucien would have to be the conduit between us to make sex work, but the rest of the time I could be with Silas.*

It's a pipedream, I told myself. *There's no way someone like Silas would want to have a relationship with someone like me. He's an aristocrat, jet-setting across the world in designer suits and languishing in palatial estates. What could a guy like that have in common with a girl who can't even afford to get the front windows of her apothecary fixed?*

We squeezed past a group of fae engaged in conversation. The back of Silas's hand brushed against my own. I giggled nervously.

"Sorry, that guy bumped me," I said as an excuse. *Why are you berating yourself for liking this guy? He just had his cock down your throat. I'm pretty sure he's into you.*

Silas's hand brushed mine again. This time there was no denying it. He was trying to hold hands with me. I wasn't sure how to handle that. He looked meaningfully at our hands. I could see his hesitation, that he wasn't sure if *I* wanted to hold *his* hand.

I spread my fingers apart, allowing his fingers access, and my heart soared. We entered the ballroom all smiles, and I felt as though I was floating on a cloud.

The shape of the ballroom had changed while we were gone. Starfire's heart still floated in the center over our heads, but the floor had become more like a stadium, curved on a decline to the far side of the ballroom, where a stage had been set up. Curtains obscured our view of the stage.

The room was rapidly filling up as fae returned, each of them unmasking for the final ceremony. Silas tried to lead me to a spot at the front of the room.

"Actually, I need to stand to the side of the stage," I said. I needed a good vantage of the crowd if I was going to spot the murderer's reaction to their botched assassination attempt.

"Then I'll join you," he said without missing a beat.

I pulled him by the hand through the crowd. I found a perfect spot in the farthest corner of the front row, where it curved around the side of the stage. From there I would have a good view of all the guests. By now the ballroom was overflowing with fae nobility. Ambrose's speech would be projected by an echoing spell to the lawn, so the so-called 'lesser bloods' would see it as well.

As the room continued to fill, I began to worry about our plan. How could we be certain one of the nobility was even involved in Ambrose's assassination attempts? In theory it made sense. Such an attempt required access, money, and resources that some of the non-pureblood fae simply didn't have. But if I'd learned anything over the last half year, it was that villainous fae could be quite resourceful when they wanted something badly enough.

"There's Valia," I mumbled. She was in the center of the front row, tucked between Lucien and his father. Malachai scowled at Lucien, then forced his attention to the stage. I was grateful for my positioning to the side of the room, as I could get a full view of Valia's face.

"Never mind that silly shadow fae," Silas said. He squeezed my hand affectionately. "She wouldn't dare try to bully you tonight. I'm right here with you." As if that weren't enough to melt my heart, he lifted my hand to his lips and kissed my knuckles.

The crowd of fae broke out into a raucous round of applause. For a single mortifying instant, I thought they were reacting to Silas's show of affection. Then I saw the curtains dissolving into a burst of blue butterflies and flower petals, spreading out over the heads of the onlookers and then up to the ceiling to rest. It was a dazzling display of life and beauty, fitting for the celebration of spring.

Ambrose took center stage. The stage was overflowing with peony bushes, their blossoms as large as my head. Between them were the five statues from the palace gallery. The knight and mermaid to the left, the girl with her hands behind her back and the satyr with grapes to the right, and in dead center, the star of the show, Lady Nisang. Displayed on the stage of the ballroom and surrounded by healthy peonies, the statues became monuments to spring.

He's brought all five statues out? I wondered. *I see what Ambrose is up to. He's going to draw it out, make the killer watch in anticipation as he strolls past each statue. They'll be practically salivating by the time he touches Lady Nisang.*

Ambrose lifted his hands to quiet the crowd. "Thank you, thank you, my friends, my family, people of my people, blood of the earth."

The crowd fell silent. A palpable energy worked through the room like an electric current. How much magic was housed in this ballroom?

Ambrose paced back and forth across the stage as he spoke, the whole room hanging on his every word. I watched the crowd. Particularly Valia. She stiffened when Ambrose's pacing brought him before the Court of Shadows representatives.

"This has been a festival for the ages. So many fae gathered in one place with a singular focus. The celebration of life, in all forms great and small. The sacred balance of nature unites us."

Valia looked practically ready to jump out of her skin. But why? I still couldn't understand what her motive could be. Had Ambrose discovered she was transporting shimmer through his territories? I should have shared what Tae discovered so I could have gauged his reaction.

Ambrose took a step back until he stood beside the statue of the grape-offering satyr. He placed a hand on it and continued. "It seems ages ago now that Peliu shared his bounty with the fair folk. Each spring we learn anew what that gift meant. It shaped our people. His act of charity fostered a new generation of fae into the realm. It gave us the roadmap for how we treat one another, to live in balance with chaos and strive toward a peaceful society."

Malachai bristled at some double meaning that was lost on me.

Ambrose moved on to the next statue. Valia's eyes tracked his movement like a dog waiting for a bone. He backed up between the statues of the little girl and Lady Nisang. This was when the trap should have sprung, but nothing happened.

"I know exactly what you have done," Ambrose declared.

My gaze flew back to Valia, but her expression hadn't changed. "She's not reacting," I whispered.

Silas's grip tightened. I felt like the room was closing in on me. If Valia wasn't the murderer, then who? I couldn't think with Silas pawing me. I gently shook him loose and heard him gasp.

I looked up to apologize.

Beads of sweat rolled down the sides of his forehead. His face was white as a ghost, drained of color as he stared wide-eyed at Ambrose. I snapped my head back to see what I'd missed. Did Valia make her move?

Valia was still standing between Malachai and Lucien. To be honest, she looked more bored and annoyed than like a maniacal murderer. Ambrose remained between the statues of the girl and Lady Nisang, his shoulder brushing purposefully against the nullified poison dart trap. I couldn't focus on his words as he continued his speech. I scanned the crowd for a reaction.

Shuffling fabric told me Silas was moving.

I stared after him as he cut through the crowd for the exit. The ballroom felt like it was constricting around my throat. My vision tightened into a dwindling tunnel, blacking around the edges of my disbelief. My heart was beating too fast. I was panting.

Am I having an anxiety attack? I thought calmly, even as my brain panicked over what I was witnessing.

It finally struck me.

"Oh my god, Silas is the killer."

My mind was still racing to process how I could have missed the warning signs as I followed Silas through the palace. I moved like a woman possessed, numb to the world around me as we zigzagged through the halls. Silas was lost in a state of panic so deep he never even noticed me following.

Of all the people Ambrose had wronged over the years, Silas, perhaps, had the most cause to hate him. Ambrose had abandoned Silas as a child, excommunicating him from the family for the transgressions of his parents. In Ambrose's eyes, they chose the plight of humanity over their own Great House. That was an unforgivable betrayal in his eyes. He disinherited Silas and sent him packing to fend for himself. What harsh judgment to pass on an innocent child. Ambrose had pushed Silas out of their life, out of his legacy as heir to one of the four Great Houses.

This was never about trading contracts or gaining power. It was just petty revenge.

I was disgusted with the whole situation. There was no doubt that Ambrose was wrong for what he'd done to Silas as a child. But that did not—could not—justify murder. I refused to embrace that.

I thought it would be harder to follow Silas once he left the palace through the front gates. Surely out in the open he would notice me tracking his movements. He didn't. He was moving like a man deranged. He was babbling something mad and incoherent to himself that I couldn't make out across the distance between us.

Our gambit had broken him. Gone was the rogue stalking through shadows and leaping off rooftops. He stumbled as if drunk, sometimes cantering sideways.

Then, suddenly, he tossed off his jacket and leapt from the cliffs. His faerie wings bore him down into town far faster than my dash down the cliffside steps could take me.

I almost wailed in fury when I lost him. I ran full tilt down the steps and into town, heading in the general direction I'd seen him land. I knew it was hopeless, but I pressed on anyhow, trusting in my uncanny speed to help me catch up to him. The streets were silent. Everyone in the Tides was up at the palace celebrating.

Ambrose would still be giving his closing speech.

I should have said something to him, told him where I was going, I thought. *What would I have said? I think your grandson did it because he started sweating?* That was me making desperate excuses so I didn't have to confront the cold brutal reality. *I saw the look on Silas's face when Ambrose moved near the statue. He freaked out as soon as Ambrose touched it.*

A door slammed to the east.

I switched directions and ran toward the sound. Silas's hideout was hard to miss. The towering seashell houses stood like lone watchers in the night, their silhouettes draped in darkness. Even the glowflowers were still bundled up in their shiny leaves. Silas's was the only thing lit on the entire street. The front window was an oval of candlelight spilling onto the front path like a beacon.

I hid in the shadows of the house across the street from it, watching with bated breath. What could I do now? Why had I followed him this far? All the town guardians were at the palace.

I need to go back up the cliffs and get help.

But I wasn't moving. Because I didn't want to believe it was true. There had to be some mistake, some other reason for Silas's erratic behavior. Then I saw the girl on his couch. Her face was framed by candlelight, and I recognized her in an instant. Those still serene eyes forever frozen as they watched Silas pace the living room.

What the shit? It's the statue of the little girl from Ambrose's gallery. But why was that statue on Silas's couch?

It can't be. I just saw it on the stage in Ambrose's ballroom.

Silas was ranting and raving to the girl's still, stony form like a madman.

Unless… A series of thoughts rushed me. It was common knowledge that Silas had a gambling problem. The statue had been lost in a bet to Cyan. Except what if none of that was true? What if Silas staged that problem specifically so he could maneuver that very statue into Ambrose's palace? We were all checked for weapons when entering the palace. What better way to sneak a poison trap into the Starfire undetected than by having it lie in wait months in advance?

Silas must have had two identical copies of that statue produced. One of them had a secret compartment where he hid the device. Tae must have caught him when he was switching out the statues. Could she have missed him carrying something that large? She said he had pushed something into his cloak, like through a magical portal. Could that portal have led directly to his secret apartment in town?

I shook my head in anger. How could I have missed all of this? It didn't matter how he did it. The only thing that mattered was stopping him before he hurt anyone else.

I pulled the echo crystal from my dress and whispered Persa's name.

The tiny stone immediately flared to life, the energy from its awakened core warming my palm.

"Lanie? Is that you?" It was Persa's voice. I could hear a crowd of people speaking in the background.

I winced at how loud the crystal was and pulled back into the alley, out of sight from Silas's front window. Except when Persa spoke again, I realized her voice was inside my mind rather than touching my ears. We were speaking through a telepathic connection!

"Where are you?" she asked. "Grandfather is very upset. He's worried something happened to you. Why is he so worried, Lanie?"

"There was a device planted on Lady Nisang's statue," I explained. "It was Silas. He planted the trap."

"That can't be true," Persa said, mortified. "Cousin Silas couldn't hurt a fly."

"Persa, shut up," I snapped. I didn't have time for her skittishness. "You must tell Ambrose that Silas is the assassin right away. You said you can trace me based on where the echo crystal is, right? Ambrose needs to send guardians down here right now before Silas escapes."

Persa was silent on the other end. All I could hear was the crowd of people in the background. It was strange to hear a crowd through someone else's ears.

"Damnit, you told me if I needed help you would send it," I hissed. "I know this sounds crazy and I know how much you love your cousin, but I'm asking you to trust me right now. Do you trust me or not?"

Persa sucked in her breath. She was thinking. I could feel her worry through the crystal. She finally made up her mind. "I trust you."

I sighed and peered around the corner. Silas wasn't in his living room. "You better hurry. He's trying to make a run for it."

"I'll get Grandfather right now and have him send soldiers to your location."

"Thank you. Have him send some to the harbor too, just in case," I added.

"Stay where you are and don't put yourself in any danger," Persa pleaded.

"I won't," I lied.

The crystal went dead even as I was already walking toward Silas's house to confront him.

28

hould I have waited for House of Dawn guardians to back me up? Obviously. But Lanie Alacore in her infinite wisdom burst into Silas's apartment. How I wish now that I could rewind time and do things differently. I was such a fool.

Silas was pacing in the living room, still ranting to his statue, when I rushed through the front door. He jumped and tried to run to the fireplace, where he had a sword resting on the mantel. I dashed between him and the weapon, blocking his path.

Silas's eyes finally centered on me, and he froze in place, confused. "Lanie? What are *you* doing here?"

"Don't play me for a fool, Silas," I snapped. "You know exactly why I'm here."

Silas looked at the floor, and his shoulders slumped. "Of course. How could I be so stupid? That's why Ambrose hired you, isn't it? You're his agent."

"Right, like you didn't know I was working for Ambrose on this. Did you really think you'd be able to get away with it?" I raised my voice.

"Lanie, you have to understand—"

"How could you use me like that?" My voice broke. "Was that your plan? Get stupid Lanie to fall for you so you could go behind her back and accomplish your dastardly deed? I can't believe I bought that whole sob story about your parents. Well, that's me, twice the fool and three times the sucker." I clapped my hands in mock applause. "Congratulations, Silas, you pulled it off. You fooled me good. Hurray for you."

"It wasn't like that, Lanie." He groaned. "If I had known you were working to stop me, I never would have—"

"What?" I yelled. "You never would have what, Silas? Fucked me? Pushed my best friend off the palace roof?"

He wilted guiltily. "I didn't *push* her. She tripped on one of the kodama."

"And you stood back to make sure she fell."

He shook his head in denial. "I would have rescued her. The tree spirits had her, though. She didn't need my help. I would never have hurt her. You have to believe me."

I snorted. "Why on God's green earth would I ever believe a single thing that came out of your mouth? After everything you've done? You want me to believe you never would've hurt Tae while at the same time you've been plotting to murder Ambrose. Geraldine told me how deadly that bomb you left was. It would've reduced your grandfather to a steaming pile of guts if we hadn't disabled it, so drop the 'I'm such a nice guy' act. You're a creep and a murderer, and you're going to pay for what you've done."

Silas worked his mouth open and closed. He smacked his lips, staring at me. "Lanie, what are you talking about?"

"You're a fucking murderer, Silas," I repeated, louder and angrier.

"Master Silas?" The voice was tiny and afraid.

We weren't alone in the room. I cursed and jumped to the side. Other than me and Silas, the room appeared to be empty. Flickering candles rested on either side of the sofa, where the statue rested. Silas had some suitcases stacked in one corner and a sword on the mantel over a cooking fireplace behind me. It wasn't until he moved to the sofa that I saw the truth of it.

"Wait…is that statue sitting?" I asked.

"Everything is okay, Pepper," Silas reassured the statue that was no statue at all. She was identical to the girl's statue that I'd seen in the gallery, but her cheeks were rosy and her eyes, though a serene grey, were quite alive. Her stony hair was now curls of red that matched the freckles dotting her nose and cheeks.

The girl wrung her hands nervously in her lap as she looked from me to Silas with wide eyes of worry. "Is this woman telling the truth? Have you hurt someone, Master?" she asked in the innocent voice of a child.

"Not at all. Lanie is confused, I assure you."

She shot him a doubtful look.

"What's going on here?" I asked. "Are you that depraved? Did you get a little girl to help you with your plan? That's beyond twisted." I put my hands to either side of my head to keep the room from spinning. I felt sick to my stomach. "First Droll and now you? Wow, I really am the world's worst judge of character."

Silas stood beside the sofa and sighed. "Lanie, this is Pepper. She's not a little girl. I know she must look like one to you, but she's actually a moon lily."

"A moon lily?" I repeated.

Pepper smiled serenely at me. There was a placid quality about her person, as if she was either eternally stoned or meditating. "I work for Master Silas," she said.

"You have a child working for you?"

"She's not a child. How can I explain it? Pepper is a moon lily. Her people are a very rare breed of fae that were practically wiped out during the war. Ten years ago I captured Pepper in the Jasper Woods while hunting. It's a long story. The point is she's been working for me ever since. However, I'm afraid I've been a poor master to her. You see, I have a bit of a gambling problem. When I'm up, I make a decent living of it, but when I'm down…"

He sighed and raked his fingers down his face. "Ugh, I'm not making any sense. It was Cyan. She tricked me. She's always been cruel to me. I know how everyone sees me in the family, the child of the derelicts. Well, she must have caught wind of how bad things were going for me. She can be like honey when she wants to. A spider, that one is. She waited until I was down to my bones in debt after a three-week-straight game of cards. Then she swooped in for the kill.

"The offer was simple. She would help me get out of the hole I'd dug myself in exchange for my fae estates. What a tyrant to steal from her own blood like that. Of course, I gave in to her demands. What else could I do? I couldn't raise the amount of money necessary to appease my creditors before they took their pound of flesh. So, I signed them over to her, all the land titles I had left to my name from the fae realm. But that wasn't enough for Cyan. She said there would be no deal unless I also gave her Pepper."

"She took the girl from you?" I asked, still trying to catch up with all that he was saying.

"I was angry at first. What sort of a person trades other fae like they're some commodity? That wicked friend of hers Valia would, sure. She's a shadow fae. They don't think twice about the cost of another living being's soul. I was going to fight her on it, but then I realized Pepper would be better off. Cyan is surrounded by luxury everywhere she goes. Her whole life is one big party. What was the worst she could do, overpamper

Pepper?" He snorted. "How wrong I was. I forgot who I was dealing with. That bitch had her pal Valia turn Pepper into stone. Then the two of them laughed about it as if it was just some silly prank.

"I spent the last six years trying to get her to sell me back Pepper. I don't gamble anymore. I've earned quite a fair sum in the human economy that I offered her, but she wouldn't budge. She loves lording it over me that she owns Pepper."

"It was horrible," Pepper said. "I could see everything all that time. I could hear it too. And my body was so heavy...always so heavy."

Silas fell to his knees before the girl and interlocked his fingers as if in prayer. "I'm so sorry, Pepper. Please, you have to forgive me. I never would've done it if I'd known she would hurt you. I've spent so many nights trying to play it back in my mind. I should never have taken you away from your woods in the first place. I had no right. I'm a horrible person, and I'm so sorry."

Pepper watched him as if stunned. When he was done, he dropped his head in her lap and cried. She continued to watch him for a few seconds, then smiled and stroked his hair. "It's okay, Master Silas. I'm better now. You saved me."

Silas sat up and hugged her. "Oh, Pepper. I'm so sorry. I'll never do anything like that again. We're going to get far away from here. I'll take you back to your woods where you can be free again."

Pepper frowned. "I don't want to go back there. I want to stay with you, Master Silas."

Silas put a hand on either of her shoulders and looked her in the eye. "No, Pepper. I am not your master. I set you free. You are free. The bond has been broken. I severed it a few years ago in the vain hope it would free you from the contract I had formed with Cyan. You're your own person again. You can do whatever you'd like."

Pepper nodded. "I already know that. I want to stay with you."

"Wait," I said louder than I intended. "Just hold on. Rewind a bit. I'm confused. If Cyan is the one who wronged you, then why try to murder Ambrose? What does your grandfather have to do with all of this?"

Silas shook his head and chuckled at me. "Lanie, you really are confused. I never tried to do anything to harm Grandfather. He's a cad, but that doesn't mean I'd want to hurt him. What a ridiculous thing to say. Cyan is the one who involved him.

"She told me she was gifting Pepper's statue to Ambrose and that now I would never get it back. She thought she was so smart, gloating over me. Except I finally had an idea of how to free Pepper. I paid good money to have a replica of the statue made. You almost caught me that day when I switched the statues in the gallery. I confess you spooked me so badly that I dropped my sack near the statues when I was fleeing the palace with Pepper.

"The night the succubus came by, I was retrieving the sack so there wouldn't be any evidence of my ruse. I figured by the time the festivities were over and Cyan realized what I'd done, it would be too late. I'd have Pepper back in her woods and free. I needed to make sure I retrieved that pouch so nobody would look too closely at my forgery. I told you I have rotten luck. When grandfather announced, 'I know what you've done' from the stage while he was touching the forgery, I knew they'd already caught on to my ruse. I didn't expect he'd be as angry as he is. Please, Lanie, I know you're just doing your job, but you have to let me get Pepper out of here."

A pit opened in my stomach. "Oh my god, what have I done? You're not trying to kill Ambrose at all."

"Lanie, again with this foolishness. For the last time, *nobody* is trying to kill my grandfather."

"Look at her, Master," Pepper said. "Can't you see she's not here for me?"

Silas frowned and furrowed his brow. I opened my mouth, and out came the entire story. I spilled everything to him, recounting it all the way back to my first meeting with Geraldine outside my apartment. "So you see, someone is indeed trying to kill Ambrose. And I've been a fool. When I saw you run off, you can see how it looked…"

"But that means the killer is still up there in the palace with my grandfather right now."

"And Ambrose is sending his guardians down here to apprehend you," I said.

Silas's eyes darted to Pepper in alarm. "No! If they take Pepper back to the palace, then Cyan will know what I've done. She'll turn her back into a statue."

"But when Ambrose hears how Cyan tricked you, surely he won't make you hand her over?"

Silas scowled at me. "Have you learned nothing of your time with the fair folk? A deal is a deal, never to be broken on the words of a bond."

"Then we have to get her out of here." I grabbed Pepper's hand and helped her off the couch. She was a slight thing, a wisp of a girl.

"Not through the front, they'll be coming that way. Follow me, there's a door out back. We'll never outrun the guardians though. I'm going to have to go back with them. Please Lanie, you must get Pepper out of here in the meantime. Get her to the Whispering Woods. I'm certain the gladewarden will shelter her until I can explain everything to my grandfather. I'll be in a lot of trouble, but it'll buy us time. You'll need to stay with Pepper and get her on the first ship out tomorrow."

"But the murderer?"

"I'll not leave Ambrose's side until I figure out who is vying to hurt our house," Silas vowed.

I let him lead us down the hall. There was a back door off the bedroom. We had just entered the room when a shadow moved past the bedroom window. Silas held up a hand for us to stop moving.

"Goddess be damned, they're already here," he hissed. "Quickly, get Pepper and yourself in the hall closet. Keep her out sight until we leave."

"But if I explain—"

Silas shoved us into the closet. "Lanie, please, you have to keep her hidden." He slid the closet shut and then stopped halfway. "Wait, the echo crystal. Give it to me, or they'll be able to track the two of you. I'll tell them we argued and you went back up to the palace."

I fished the crystal out from my dress and pressed it into his palm. "Be careful," I whispered.

"Don't worry. I'll sort this out with my grandfather in no time." He leaned forward and grazed my lips with a kiss, then slid the closet door the rest of the way shut.

Glass broke in the living room. I flinched and pulled Pepper deeper into the closet, behind the hanging suits, until our backs were pressed against the wall. She clung to me.

"Master shouldn't go out there alone," she whispered worriedly.

"What are you doing, breaking into my home like this?" Silas asked imperiously.

"Silas Amaryllis?" The voice that spoke was guttural and oily. It wasn't like any frogman I'd ever heard. The sound of it was like a stain on my mind.

Boots creaked across the wood floor. I leaned forward and peered through the closet slats. Two huddled shapes, like smears of black ink, stood just inside the doorway, with a third standing sentry outside. Their glowing red eyes beat through the shadows.

"You don't work for my grandfather," Silas said.

The men laughed, a choking sound of spittle and phlegm. It grated against my nerves as I finally realized what I was looking at. *They're vampires!*

"Us, work for Ambrose Amaryllis? How can we work for a dead man?"

"How dare you threaten the head of the House of Dawn?" Silas growled. "I'll flay the skin from your unholy bones, you demonic abominations." His hand went to his belt to pull his sword free. But it wasn't there. It was still on the mantel because I'd cut him off from retrieving it.

"The warden's not outside, Ralic," the other vampire said.

The first one growled. "Klas, go get eyes on her. We can't have any witnesses."

"Gladly," the vampire sentry said as he disappeared into the night.

Silas laughed scornfully. "Have you ever seen how fast she can move? You'll never catch up to Lanie. I guarantee she took one look at you idiots and ran to get help. She's probably halfway to the palace by now. When the House of Dawn finds out what you're doing, they'll send every guardian in the Tides down on your heads, you miserable fucks."

"He's lying," Ralic said, trying to gauge Silas's reaction. "Check the house."

Silas tackled the second vampire without warning. There was a flash of inky movement, and I flinched back behind the coats. Something heavy hit the living room wall. One of the vampires screamed like a banshee. I clutched Pepper close to my body, covering her mouth with one hand to keep her screams muffled.

I thought about bolting from the closet. If I ran fast enough, I could intercept Ambrose's guardians and bring them back to help Silas. It was no good. I had no idea how fast Pepper could move. It was unlikely she could keep up with my speed and I couldn't risk the girl getting hurt. If only I could use my unicorn powers, maybe I could help Silas.

Damn this curse. Damn the world for making me like this.

"You'll never catch up to her in time," Silas insisted weakly.

The sound of tearing flesh is a ghastly thing. Silas howled in agony. The vampires laughed as they fell on him, and the struggle ceased. All I could hear was the sucking sound of them draining his blood. Those vile bastards. I was helpless to stop them. Pepper pressed her face into my stomach, her whole body shaking like a leaf.

"We need the woman," the other vampire said wetly.

Ralic stopped his drinking. "Are you sure she wasn't outside?"

"Her crystal is here, in the dead man's hand," the other said.

"What if he wasn't lying? She could be running back to the palace to warn that toad, Ambrose."

"That's okay. I love a good hunt."

They shared a knowing laugh.

Their shadowy bodies spun around the room, tossing things aside and smashing vases. The closet door rattled when one of them brushed against it. I had to bite my fist to keep from crying out. Then they were gone, out the front door and howling into the night. I clutched Pepper to me for some time, still locked in a paralysis of fear. Those things were outside hunting for me, heading back to the palace. I could get Pepper to safety. I just needed to head to the Whispering Woods like Silas told me.

"Silas," I croaked.

I threw the closet door open and rushed to him. He was crumpled on the floor in a pool of purple blood.

"We need to get him to a healer," I said.

When I rolled him over, I thought for a fleeting moment that it was a different person. That Silas had tricked them. He'd escaped and replaced his body with a double, much like he'd done with Pepper's statue. Then I remembered the truth of it. The man I was looking at *was* Silas. The glamour he'd used to make himself appear more human was gone now because he was dead. His body was a withered husk, stretched wrong over his bones after being drained by the vampires. His blond hair was a tangle of brown leaves, curled and crumbling. He looked more like a bloom, but still very much my Silas.

I cradled his head in my lap and wept. Pepper knelt on the other side of his still body and rested her head on his chest as she sobbed.

I heard the banshee howl of one of the vampires in the distance. This wasn't over. There was no time for me to dwell in despair. The vampires were heading to the palace. I had to warn Ambrose before it was too late.

Although he didn't know it at the time, it was Silas's dying wish that I get Pepper to the gladewarden and lay low. How I wanted to be worthy of his faith in me. But I couldn't. There is a part of me that is off. I realize that now. I'm not built like other people. It's a wonder I never thought to become a first responder when I lived among the humans, because nothing in the world could have stopped me from trying to save Ambrose's life from those vampires.

I left Pepper on the path to Uriel's cottage.

"The gladewarden lives just up ahead. All you need to do is stay on this path," I said, bent over with hands on my knees to speak to her at her level.

Pepper stared wide-eyed up at me, and I felt ashamed of abandoning her there. "Is she a nice lady?"

"Not very," I said. "But she does like children, I think. You'll be safe with Uriel for the time being. Just explain everything that has happened."

"Can't you come with me?"

Her plea tugged at my heartstrings. I wanted so badly to go with her, to hide in Uriel's cottage until the break of dawn, when the vampires couldn't roam the land. "I can't. I already failed Silas. I won't do the same for Ambrose."

"He needs your help?"

"He does."

She pondered that, then nodded. "Okay."

I ran before I could lose my nerve. My mad dash through the town and up the cliffside steps was a blur. All I can remember was a feeling of impending doom. Last time I'd made it to Ambrose before he could drink the poison. Would I have any hope of doing the same against murderous vampires?

There were no guards at Starfire's gates when I arrived. I felt a lump in my throat. Was I already too late? There was no sign of conflict. Perhaps they went with the guardians Ambrose had sent into town to apprehend Silas. What would they think when they found him there, his body all torn up and ruined?

My shoes clapped against Starfire's white floor, leaving dirty footprints in my wake. The atrium was cleared out of most guests. A few lingered here and there, pockets of fae still inebriated from their night of revelry. Wary eyes followed me as I dashed across the atrium. I was aware of them as if in a trance. The sound of the babbling waterfall, birds chirping overhead, and whispers about the scandalous fae girl running through the palace. I could only imagine what I looked like to them, my hair disheveled, bags under my eyes from crying, my eyes wide with alarm.

I stopped at the foot of the steps to the second floor. Where would I find Ambrose? I had only paid him visits in his private garden, but it was long past the time for that daily routine. Would he be in the library? In his rooms? Where were his rooms? How could I warn him? How would I ever find him in this giant palace?

"Ambrose!" I shouted in desperation. "Geraldine!"

The few fae remaining put space between themselves and the mad woman screaming in the atrium. A commotion rippled through them.

"The woman's deranged."

"Can't hold her drink."

"How uncouth."

"Someone call the palace guards."

"The palace guards?" I repeated, scanning them wild-eyed. "Who said that? Yes, do that. Call the palace guards! Ambrose! Geraldine!"

"Lanie!" Persa ran down the steps. I met her halfway, already on the move.

"We have to get to Ambrose! He's in grave danger!"

Persa grabbed both my hands and tried to stop my shaking. "Lanie, what happened? I've been trying to get ahold of you for an hour."

"They killed him." I choked on my words, tears streaming down my face. "Those monsters. They cut him to pieces!"

"What's going on here?" Lucien dashed down the steps.

I fell on him, sobbing. "They murdered Silas."

His body stiffened. I felt his heart hammering underneath the layers of his suit.

"That can't be," Persa said in disbelief. "The soldiers, they never would have—"

"Not the soldiers," I said wildly. "They were like shadows. Smears of ink—"

"What is she talking about?" Lucien asked.

"I don't know."

"Oh, to hell with this," I yelled. "We must warn Ambrose now! They're coming for him!"

Lucien's body instantly uncoiled like a panther ready to hunt. "Where is your grandfather right now, Persa?"

She wilted away from him. "In his study, most likely."

"Then get us there!" I shouted in her face. I couldn't waste time worrying about how it hurt her feelings to be yelled at. We needed to act.

Persa flinched and then nodded resolutely. She turned and ran up the steps. We followed her quickly through the winding halls.

"Someone's been trying to murder Ambrose," I explained to Lucien. "That's what he hired me for. I've been here trying to root out the killer."

"Through here!" Persa called, stopping at an arched doorway and flinging open the door.

I bolted inside the room. One look told me this was Ambrose's office. A large mahogany desk adorned the side of the room by an open balcony. There was a velvet sofa and behind that a wall of shelving stacked with leather-bound tomes and horned scroll holders. The room had all the markings of a stuffy old man's study, but it was missing the most important ingredient: the old man.

"He's not in here," Lucien said.

"The bookshelf. Slide the copy of *Burning Winds* to the right to open the secret corridor," Persa said from the doorway.

I dashed to the shelves and started pulling every book I saw to the right. My mind was in too much disarray to discern one title from the next. "Where is it? It has to be here. Which fucking book is it, Persa?"

The back of Lucien's hand tapped my shoulder. "She's lying, Lanie."

His voice cut through my madness like a rusty blade. Gone was the whimsical, sardonic prince I knew. This was the voice of a man who knew he had walked into a trap. We both had.

I turned to find Persa standing before the closed door. She locked it with a skeleton key, then showed me the key and dropped it to the floor.

"I have her with me," she said into the echo crystal in her other hand. The glow of it pulsed as the person on the other end replied to her mind. She shook her head at me as she slid it back inside her dress pocket. "You just couldn't leave it alone, could you?" She used her heel to kick the key back under the door, where it disappeared into the hallway. "I tried to warn you. This is dangerous business. But you just couldn't be stopped. I even told you not to go inside Silas's house. Why couldn't you have just listened to me?"

"You sick bitch," I growled. How could I have been such a fool? The killer had been right in my face the whole time. Sweet, innocent Persa. The scared, shy little blossom faerie who just cared so much about her mean family. All of it was an act so she could get close to me. "None of the other family members were remotely interested in getting to know me. But you, of course you must have realized why Ambrose hired me."

"It was pretty obvious," Persa said calmly. "I still don't know how the old man caught wind of it, though. I suppose that's the problem with mercenaries. They run their mouths too much."

"You murdered Silas? How dare you spill the blood of a true born faerie?" Lucien growled. "You'll never get away with this, you daft bitch."

"Oh, please." Persa waved a dismissive hand in the air. "Spare me your sanctimonious tirade. As if the Court of Shadows hasn't done far worse."

"But why would you want to murder your own grandfather?" I asked.

"The old man should have stepped aside five decades ago. Everyone knows he's been broken from the minute Criscilla died. Look at him. He's wasting away. We're all expected to just sit back and wither away with him. The House of Dawn is one of the great bastions of our realm. Should I leave its future to imbeciles like my father and that pathetic sniveling Cyan? This Great House needs a new order. Such things shouldn't be left to one man alone. We should be operating like a court, as both our shadow and light brethren have done. The House of Dawn is falling apart at the seams. And who is to blame for this failure? Look no further than the weaknesses of an old man dragging down an entire people with him as he clings to his outdated beliefs and superstitions. I mean, half the things he spouts are nonsense. Like 'nature's calling.' What a preposterous concept.

Do you know he lets those damned spiders live in his garden still? One of them killed his wife, and yet he can't bear to exterminate them. But his grandson, who has done nothing wrong, gets exiled from the family for something his parents did. What kind of a leader is that? Tell her, Prince Lucien. You understand."

"You're sick," Lucien snarled.

"That's a shame." Persa pursed her lips. "Your father will be very disappointed to lose another son. Poor prince Lucien, cut down struggling to subdue Silas after he tried to murder my grandfather. Lanie here tried to intervene, but how could anyone expect that a useless…what are you, even? That a *mutt* could survive between a battle of two titans?"

"Everyone saw me in the palace atrium," I pointed out.

"Yes. They saw a half-crazed guest of our house, with a dress covered in blood, running after Prince Lucien. I really did like you, Lanie. You're fun. I can see why the prince likes sticking his dick in you so much. The real shame, however, is that you've set my plans back. I can't kill Grandfather for at least another couple of months now. Not after the mess you've made of my careful planning."

Lucien snorted his contempt. "Your madder than I thought if you think you can overpower me."

Persa laughed as if he'd just made a joke at a dinner party. "Prince Lucien, you've such a sharp wit. You really think I would fight you? Why would I do something so reckless when I can have my agents dispose of you instead?"

A gust of wind came from the balcony, flinging the curtains in the air.

"Hmm, here they are now. Right on cue. I think even you can appreciate how hopelessly outmatched you are. They are ever-so-resourceful creatures. You took long enough, Ralic."

Dark shapes moved behind the billowing curtains, and my skin crawled. Glowing red eyes cut through the translucent fabric. Their mouths were overlong, stretched like jackals, with rows of fangs and long, hanging forked tongues. There was nothing romantic about these creatures. They were the stuff of nightmares, created for one purpose. To kill.

"Tell our patron we apologize for our lack of timeliness, Cezar," Ralic said. He looked like he was anything but sorry.

"It *is* a large tree," the other vampire explained.

Another gust of wind flitted the curtains as Klas, the vampire sentry, flew inside the room. He was bent over with his too-long arms and claws dragging on the ground. I couldn't believe I was ever attracted to one of those abominations.

"Ah, a shadow fae," Klas purred. "They are ever so tasty."

Lucien stood tall and imperious in the face of the three bloodsuckers. "This *shadow fae* is your prince. You threaten Lucien Erlkönig, prince of the Court of Shadows, master of your house and liege to whom you will show subservience."

If they were impressed, it was hard to see through their laughter. "You are not our liege," Ralic said. "King Malachai is the ruler of our House."

"You would raise arms against your prince?" Lucien balked.

Klas shrugged. "We are mercenaries with a contract to fulfill."

"Then you will meet my blade in this room, on my name and honor," Lucien proclaimed.

"I have an alternate proposal," Persa said. "Just let us dispose of the warden. There is no reason we should be enemies, Prince Lucien. I assure you we have a common goal in this. Stand aside and let us dispose of her, and we can all go on our merry way."

Lucien pulled his saber, Iceshadow, free in one fluid movement and pointed it at the trio. "Touch her and die." The deep blue blade sparkled like ice. Tendrils of shadow coiled up and down its gleaming surface.

Persa shook her head ruefully. "Kill them both."

I screamed when Klas fell on Lucien in a blur of shadow. Lucien's saber was up in a flash, throwing wide the fiend's splayed talons. He brought it quickly back down for a killing stroke, but Ralic was already there to deflect it with his claws. Lucien dropped down even as his blade struck the hardened talons and swept his leg out across the floor. Both vampires were knocked to the ground, but the third fiend, Cezar, leapt forth with claws slashing for Lucien's chest.

Lucien caught the vampire's arm with one hand, as if he'd already anticipated the move, and was coming back up to meet it. He grabbed a firm hold and countered Cezar's weight with a twist of his body, flinging the monster over his head. The speed and strength of his attack shocked me. I knew Lucien was muscular, but to see him in battle was another thing entirely. My heart soared when I saw the deft maneuver was successful.

That celebration was short-lived. The flung vampire turned into a smear of inky movement, its body dissolving into vampiric magic. Cezar reformed again, standing behind Lucien, and slammed a fist into his kidney. Lucien staggered forward from the blow, right into the arms of the recovered vampires.

"Lucien!" I screamed.

At least I tried to. My voice was cut short by the water whip that wrapped around my throat from behind. Persa tugged the whip, throwing me on my back. She towered over me with the magic whip in one hand. She was going to kill me, and no one would ever know she was Ambrose's assassin. I'd failed him as surely as I'd failed Silas.

When was I going to learn to keep my nose out of other people's business? Ever since I'd found out I was a fae, I'd been running headlong into trouble, all in the name of my grandmother's legacy. What had any of that earned me? Deedee was stuck in a coma because of me. Silas was murdered, and now Lucien would be too. All my meddling only amounted to me lying helpless on the floor, knowing the cruel woman towering over me was going to choke me to death with a whip made from water.

Persa shook her head as if she pitied me. "I told you this was too dangerous to stick your nose in."

ater magic can be devious. I had always thought of it as an element of life that offered healing and nurturing. But water can also destroy. Tsunamis have wiped out entire towns. Even mighty mountains bend to water's will, eroding as it sculpts them anew. Persa harnessed that power of destruction, using her magical ability to tighten the water whip around my throat.

I grasped at it futilely. How do you get a firm grip on water? For every fingerhold I achieved, the water melted away and reformed under my hands. My vision was blurry and dark around the edges as oxygen was cut off from my brain. The only way to break such a spell would be with another spell.

But I had no magic. I might have stood a chance if I could access my powers. I probed for them even as my head began to pound from the lack of oxygen. There was nothing there. I had no control over my abilities. The few times I'd used it were with assistance. First when I held the relic, which negated my curse, and then when I ate the lumeria while being shot at in Sam's farmhouse. Both times I had no idea what I was doing. I was operating on impulse. It was a fight-or-flight response hardcoded into my DNA.

I need some hardcoding right about now, I thought as I desperately clawed at the water whip.

A dark smear flew overhead. I felt the impact of the vampire as it collided with Persa. She and the monstrous creature rolled to the floor. The whip dissolved into a puddle as her concentration broke.

Air stung my throat. My lungs ached to fill with the sweet stuff, but I couldn't hold it in. I hacked in spurts, trying to stop the room from spinning.

"You nitwit, get off me," Persa scolded the vampire on top of her.

Get up, Lanie, I told myself. *You're a sitting duck lying here like this. You have to move.* Sometimes the body didn't want to listen to the brain. All I could manage was a weak backwards shuffle on the floor like a worm after a heavy rain as I tried to catch my breath.

I managed to pull myself up to a sitting position with my back resting against Ambrose's desk. Lucien was locked in combat with the two vampires still standing, and it was only a matter of seconds before the third rejoined his allies. My vision was returning to normal as I blinked repeatedly.

Lucien took a blow to the chest in a spray of blood. His face was a mask of rage. He spun all the way around with the blow so that when he slashed Iceshadow, it was aimed right in Ralic's face. An arc of razor-thin ice shot out from the slashing saber.

Sensing the danger, Ralic ducked just in time. The ice blade whizzed through the air directly into the vampire behind him. Klas grabbed his throat in terror. He could only gawk as Iceshadow's magic tore through him. For a moment the room seemed to stand still, time slowed in infinite detail. I could see the realization on Klas's face, his impossibly long gaping maw hanging in shock. The tightening of Lucien's eyes as he knew he had scored a fatal blow. Persa's snarling lips as she pushed up off the floor.

Then time slammed back into fourth gear. Ralic rammed Lucien headfirst in the midsection, tackling them both over Ambrose's reading sofa. Klas's eyes darted around the room even as his decapitated head slid off his shoulders.

And most importantly, Persa was back on her feet.

I threw a hand up toward her and screamed.

My magic refused to come out to play. I could feel it thudding to be let loose but blocked by my infernal curse.

"Damn it, work," I yelled hoarsely, each syllable stinging my throat.

Cezar had recovered from his collision with Persa and swooped over the sofa to join his comrade.

Persa cracked her whip. I rolled to the side just in time as the whip knocked Ambrose's desk back a few inches.

I scurried on hands and knees to the side of the sofa. Lucien was straddling Cezar, his hands pinning the wicked creature to the floor. I didn't know where Ralic had gone. Iceshadow was on the ground between us. The vampire snarled like a rabid animal, quaking and bucking his body to free himself from Lucien's grasp. Cezar craned his neck and gnashed his teeth in Lucien's face.

Lucien pulled his head back and cracked it down like a sledgehammer. His headbutt dazed the vampire and broke some of its fangs.

Persa's water whip cracked against the sofa, knocking it to the side. I scurried to get back behind cover. She cursed me and whipped again. This time it landed a stinging kiss on my ankle. I screamed at the pain of it, certain that my foot was severed. I pressed a hand to the laceration. It was wet with blood, but a surface wound at worst.

Ralic returned in a blur of oily black and grey, a smear of rending teeth and claws lunging at Lucien's back as he straddled Cezar.

"Behind you!" I yelled and kicked the pommel of his blade. It skittered in a haphazard circle across the floor.

Lucien released the dazed vampire and scooped up Iceshadow. He managed to get it overhead just in time to block Ralic's clamping bite. The assassin leader snarled and shook his head, trying to tear the blade from Lucien's hands.

But Lucien would not relinquish the weapon. Ralic's talons raked his back, tearing through fabric and flesh. Lucien gritted his teeth, but still he refused to give up the blade. I was dodging another of Persa's attacks when I saw the real danger. The dazed vampire Lucien straddled had recovered. No longer pinned down, Cezar sat up and sank his broken teeth into Lucien's chest.

Lucien cried out in shock.

Persa's whip cracked over the sofa. I stumbled sideways, throwing my weight into the three of them. Cezar slashed his grotesque talons at me, but I was too fast. My attack did nothing to hurt the vampire, but at least it forced him to stop drinking Lucien's blood. I had to admire the man, he never released his hold on that sword. Both he and Ralic tumbled sideways. In a quick slash, Lucien's saber scored Ralic's lips, forcing the fiend back on his heels.

I pummeled Cezar with my fists. I might as well have been a child battering against a giant for all the good it did. The vampire was more annoyed with me than anything. He snatched me by the collar of my dress and tossed me across the floor. I slid until my back hit the wall.

Lucien was on his feet beside me in an instant, swinging his blade to keep the stalking Ralic at bay. Persa marched between her hired assassins, her wicked water whip dragging on the ground at her feet.

"You both make me sick," she snarled. "Look at you. You're worthless. Some *Prince of Shadows*. You can't even stop a few of your own House's creations."

"I'm still standing, aren't I?" Lucien huffed. He held Iceshadow in front of him with steely determination, but he was limping, and blood poured from his chest wounds.

I managed to get to my knees while Persa was talking. She swiveled her fiery gaze to me. I put my palms on the wall and used it to help leverage myself back to my shaky feet.

"And you, *Lady* Alacore," Persa laughed, "some warden you turned out to be. You're both finished here. By this time tomorrow, everyone will be mourning the loss of Prince Lucien and Silas Amaryllis. Not a single fae will mention or even remember your name, Lanie. I expected you to put up a little more of a fight, at least. It's depressing seeing you squirm around on the ground like that." She tilted her head to assess me, realization coming to her. "You don't even have any magic, do you? What kind of a pathetic fae are you, anyway?"

"That's been your biggest mistake, Persa," I rasped. "You think I'm some helpless woman? The truth is you don't know a damned thing about me."

I slammed my hand down on Lucien's arm.

I felt it immediately. Lucien's dampening magic loosened the shackles of my curse the same as it did every time we made love. His dampening field was strong enough to silence my curse, but there was something far more powerful beneath that, lying in wait. I could feel my unicorn power coursing through my veins, roaring to protect me. I reached for it deep inside. It was like trying to catch light with your hands.

"Lucien, close your eyes," I whispered.

God bless the man. He was facing two ferocious blood-sucking vampires and a half-mad water fae. Yet, for all that, he glanced at me sideways and gave a tight nod. And he closed his eyes.

"You want to see what kind of fae I am?" I yelled. "Let me show you!"

I threw my hand up and screamed my rage. It was anger for everything bad that had happened to me since I'd learned of the fae. Fury for poor defenseless Gizmitt, who had drunk Persa's poison; rage for the torture Deedee had endured at the hands of the changeling; rage for Silas, my dear poor sweet Silas, murdered in cold blood.

Persa laughed at me, for earlier I had done the same thing with no result. But the vampires weren't laughing. They knew they had fucked up.

A burst of blinding light coalesced across my skin. The vampires howled in agony as my power burned into their unholy forms. My light grew bolder and bolder until it was as if they were standing in front of a blazing star. Cezar clutched his face as his skin lit on fire. Ralic spun around, shifting into an inky blur, but he was on fire too. He fled for the fireplace and disappeared in a howling plume of smoke.

Persa wasn't laughing anymore.

My spell exploded.

A rainbow of light burst from my open palm. It fused into the form of a unicorn head, charging with its horn down. The unicorn slammed into Persa, carrying her across the room and across Ambrose's desk. She hit the floor beside the balcony curtains with the loud cracking sound of bones breaking.

The light faded, and I slumped toward the floor.

Lucien caught me around the waist. "Lanie! Are you—?"

"I'm okay, just…it takes a lot out of me," I said weakly.

"But…how did you…?" He gazed around the room. Smoke billowed out of the fireplace. All that was left of the first vampire was a smoldering mass of bones and gore where it had been standing.

"I used my magic," I said plainly.

"That's impossible," Lucien said.

"Because of your power to negate magic?" I whispered with a wry grin.

Lucien looked as though he'd seen a ghost. It was the first time I'd admitted I knew about his power.

"Don't worry, I would never tell anyone about your secret magic."

"Nothing can get through my dampening field," he insisted.

"You never noticed my magic when we slept together?" I asked. The dizziness was fizzling away. I stood a little firmer beside him, patting his hand thankfully.

"That must have been lost in the throes of passion." He shrugged, and I realized he'd not actually thought about it before. Silly man.

"There's nothing more passionate than not wanting to die," I said with a chuckle.

Lucien assessed me with an astonished grin. "You really are amazing."

Persa groaned from the other side of the desk.

Lucien helped me cross the room with his blade held out in front of him. Persa was on her knees. A line of blood trickled from her nose. Her right eye was swollen shut, and a gash marred her crown. She was trying to produce magic. It sputtered from her palms in fizzling sparks and driblets of water.

"You broke her wing," Lucien said in awe.

Sure enough, Persa's right wing hung limply, having snapped when she collided with Ambrose's desk. Purebloods derived power from their faerie wings. With Persa's broken, so too was her access to her abilities, at least for the time being.

But that wasn't all my magic had done to her.

"I'm blind," Persa moaned. "What have you done to me? I can't see anything. You bitch, you deplorable low-blood skank. I'll have your eyes ripped from your head for this."

"The fight is over, Persa," I said with a sad shake of my head. "We need to get you to a healer."

"Don't you talk down to me, you simpering cow," Persa snarled.

Lucien let go of me. He leaned down and pulled Persa to her feet. "Lanie's right. It's over. You'll face your grandfather and justice, but be glad she let you live."

Persa howled. She twisted free of Lucien's arms. We'd sorely underestimated her resolve. She came at me in a flurry of slashing nails like a stark-raving mad monster. I jumped to the side, out of her furious path, and Persa tangled in the balcony curtains. She thrashed around as they ripped free from the rod. I tried to get to her in time, but I was too weak from casting my magic, too slow.

I was too late.

Persa tumbled headlong over the side of the balcony.

"No!" I screamed. I reached out for her as I bent over the rail.

She was already on the ground. I would never be able to erase the image of her broken body from my mind.

31

mbrose sat behind his desk, calmly watching me as I finished recounting the events of that evening. We were in his study. His real study, not the room Persa had led us to, which apparently had been his late son's office. Ambrose had been deeply distraught over the damage the room had suffered and Geraldine promised he already had servants working to set the room back in order.

Ambrose leaned back in his chair and contemplated all that I had said.

"I tried to catch her," I repeated, the image of Persa tumbling over the balcony still as fresh in my mind as an open wound.

Tae patted my shoulder. She stood beside my chair. She'd come as soon as she heard the commotion in the atrium, but by the time she arrived, we had already gone. The palace was in an uproar over Persa's death. Such a thing—an open battle in the home of one of the Great Houses—was unheard of.

Geraldine waited patiently at his master's side, and Alegra stood in the far corner by the bookshelves. Ambrose had kept his other children out of the room, but he could not deny Alegra access, since she was the royal representative and would have to report back to Queen Titania all that had transpired that evening.

"And you are certain she was working alone?" Ambrose asked.

"I'm not entirely convinced," I admitted. "She spoke about everything as if it were part of some larger plan. It sounded like her ultimate goal was changing the House of Dawn into a Court of Dawn instead. I don't believe Artur was involved in any way, based on what she had to say about him. Persa was the mastermind behind the assassination attempts."

There was an unspoken acknowledgment between us. Ambrose's uncertainty wafted off him like a foul stench. Even if Persa had succeeded in murdering him, she would not have been next in line to take over the house. That would've fallen to the twins. And she had spoken about the need to turn the House of Dawn into a court, like their brethren of Summer and Shadow. Persa wasn't acting alone. She had help from someone powerful, but they weren't inside the House of Dawn. Some other agency was at play, making a move to alter the balance of power in the fae realm.

Lucien could have backed up my testimony, but once the Dawn soldiers arrived at the study and opened the locked door, he made an abrupt departure. I couldn't blame him. With his involvement, the whole ordeal would have become the fae equivalent of an international incident. What rumors would spread if the fae learned that the prince of shadows had been involved in the death of a member of the Amaryllis family?

"Lady Alacore, it would seem that you have indeed lived up to your end of our agreement," Ambrose said abruptly. "No matter how sloppy your work has been."

I winced at that.

"Hey, Lanie saved your life," Tae said, gripping my shoulder encouragingly.

"Indeed. However, the House of Dawn has been made weaker for her efforts. We've lost two of our direct bloodline in this affair." Ambrose frowned. "None of that is your concern, however. With Persa's death, our business together has concluded. Lady Alacore, I shall have your payment brought to your room, and Geraldine will arrange for your things to be taken to your lodgings in the Tides."

"So it's over?" I asked in disbelief. "Just like that? But how will you explain this to Persa's father? And what if whoever put Persa up to this has other plans?"

"I appreciate your concern," Ambrose said, "but those are House of Dawn problems, and as such we will handle them ourselves."

It was fine for Ambrose to throw me in harm's way when I was saving his life, but now that the danger was averted, he was carting me off like used trash. "You've got some nerve," I seethed.

Tae gripped my shoulder tight. I looked up at her, and she gave me a short shake of her head. She was right, this wasn't the time or place for my indignation.

"Excellent. If that is all—"

I cut Ambrose off. "That is not all. I told you before I no longer wanted the money. You said you would answer my question."

"Ah, yes, of course. The nonsense about the Sphynx. It could be nothing more than superstitions and old wives' tales, you know. Are you sure you wouldn't rather have the money we outlined in our first meeting?"

Well, not when you put it like that, I thought, squirming in my seat. But the Sphynx could lift my curse. What could be more important than that? After my run-in with Persa, I was particularly set on removing it. That was the fourth time I'd found my life in danger since I learned about the fae. If that was any sort of measurement, there would be other dangers in my future. My hand went to the sore skin around my throat. I had felt so helpless when Persa was choking the life out of me.

"I won't be a victim ever again," I mumbled.

Ambrose leaned forward with both hands on his desk. "Speak up now. Tell me what's it going to be. Wouldn't you rather have the money that will guarantee your apothecary's success over answers to the whereabouts of a creature from bedtime stories?"

"Tell me where the Sphynx is," I said.

"Very well." Ambrose shrugged as if he'd warned me.

He walked to the balcony and gestured for me to join him. I motioned for Tae to stay where she was and stepped out into the cool night air, tentatively eyeing the balcony railing. We weren't as high up as his son's study had been, but it was still a decent drop through Starfire's ivory boughs to the ground.

"What you ask is no simple thing," Ambrose explained. He seemed taller than he had over the last week, towering beside me with those unreadable grey eyes boring into my soul. "The Sphynx is an ancient creature. One that is ruled by neither the realm of fae nor that of man. I would have gladly given you the money you asked for. The knowledge of the Sphynx's location is no boon to you at all."

"You gave me your word," I reminded him impatiently.

Ambrose sighed. "And I will fulfill that obligation. Though after all you have done here, I could never forgive myself if I did not go a step further. You have heard stories, no doubt, of the Sphynx's power to gift you that which your heart desires. I am sure this is what you seek. However, what fae do not speak of is the cost of that gift. The Sphynx will not give you what it has to offer freely. You must prove yourself worthy in its eyes. You will be tested in the Sphynx's temple."

I couldn't help groaning. "Just my luck. What is it with you people and trials?"

"The trials will not be easily overcome. The Sphynx will put before you a dangerous path. I urge you, Lanie Alacore, to turn back from this. Go to the gladewarden. Complete your training and become the warden of Willow's Edge. Forget this folly of the Sphynx. It's not too late. I will gladly honor the financial reward we first discussed."

I was touched by Ambrose's genuine concern for my well-being. Then I saw Alegra's uneasy face over his shoulder. She was outlined in the light of the open doorway, curtains billowing behind her into the room. I saw how his compassion toward me stung her. There was no ire for me. She simply longed for that sort of compassion from a father who was never there for her. It made me think of my own mother. How much would I have given for her to look at me even once as Ambrose did now?

"I think I've had enough of the safe road to last me a lifetime," I said.

He deflated. "I am sorry to hear that."

"I've made my decision." I tried to put as much finality into those words as I could muster.

Ambrose sighed once more. He looked at the moon as it sank toward the horizon. It was almost dawn. The monstrous dragonflies buzzed over the reef. The seaweed fingers of the Lamina's Light stretched long shadows over the lapping waves. "The location of the Sphynx's temple is on the highest peak of Mount Temenanki."

"Really? I said, hope blossoming inside of me. "That's only a few days from the Tides. I can head there as soon as I finish my training with the gladewarden."

"You misunderstand." Ambrose shook his head sadly. "To visit the Sphynx will require a sacrifice. Now that you have been told the whereabouts of the temple you must offer your sacrifice before the next sunrise."

"But that's only a few hours away." Why was this happening? Why couldn't anything ever be easy?

"It will need to be something of the utmost value to you," Ambrose continued.

"I don't have anything of worth to give," I balked. My shoulders slumped.

Ambrose frowned.

He hadn't said I had to give up something worth money. He said it had to be of the utmost value to me. The thing that was worth the most to me at that moment was in the Whispering Woods.

"Sacrifice my opportunity to become warden?" I said meekly. "But today is my last trial with Uriel."

"Then go," Ambrose beseeched me. "Make it to that meeting and become a warden. You can live a happy life without whatever it is you believe the Sphynx can offer."

That was easy for Ambrose to say. He didn't have to live trapped beneath a smothering curse. I resented the way he buried his emotions. If I could live without my curse, I could be with whomever I chose. I could use my magic to make my potions stronger for those who needed healing. I dared to hope that it would even allow me to wake Deedee from her coma.

"I have to try. Can I use one of your horses to ride to the mountain?"

"The House of Dawn cannot offer you help in this," Ambrose insisted.

"When will you get your head out of your ass?" Alegra said to him. "After all this girl has done, you deny her assistance. Why? Because the great and powerful Ambrose Amaryllis knows better than all those around the realm. Get over yourself."

Ambrose blinked in shock at his daughter's verbal assault. I imagine it was the first time she'd spoken her mind to him in all the years she'd been alive. "Alegra, I-."

"Don't," she warned him then turned to me. "You won't need a horse from the House of Dawn, Lanie. I'll fly you there." She stepped from the doorway onto the balcony and blew on a whistle she'd pulled from the bun in her hair. The high-pitched sound carried over Starfire's boughs and across the cove below. A disturbance rustled the canopy of the Whispering Woods. Alegra blew on her whistle once more. The rustling burst into a spray of leaves and twigs.

It was a sparrow, but unlike any I'd ever seen. The sparrow was larger than a horse. Its puffy white-feathered cheeks contrasted brilliantly with the chestnut brown of its crown and wings. The giant sparrow crossed the distance and alighted on the bough just beneath Ambrose's balcony.

"Hello, Row-Row," Alegra called down to him.

The sparrow chirped and lifted its head over the rail so she could pet it. Alegra laughed as she stroked his feathers.

"What's going on?" Tae called from the doorway as Geraldine blocked her path.

Ambrose waved for his man to step aside and let her out on the balcony.

"It's alright," I said. "I'm going to see the Sphynx."

"Then I'll go with you," Tae insisted.

"Row-Row is a strong sparrow, but I don't think he can manage more than the two of us," Alegra said apologetically.

"It's okay, Tae, really," I said and gave her a heartfelt hug.

"I wish I could go with you," Tae said.

"I can't believe I'm really going to lift it," I said, trying to suppress my excitement.

Gerladine arched an eyebrow inside the room. I'd still need to be careful what I said. Best not to forget that man's uncanny hearing.

Tae held both my hands and beamed. "You've got this, Lanie."

I took a deep breath. Everything I wanted was about to come true. It was a lot to take in. "Just do me a favor and stop by the gladewarden's. Let her know I'll be by to retrieve that 'package' I left with her."

Tae gave me a slight nod. I'd already whispered to her all about Pepper before Geraldine and Ambrose interrogated me.

I unintentionally glanced over at Ambrose, worried he would see through me and learn about Silas's broken contract with Cyan. He bowed with a royal solemnity. "I do wish you all the luck in the realm, Lanie Alacore."

Alegra sat on the railing and dropped down onto Row-Row's back. She grabbed the bird's reins and offered a hand to me. I climbed on the sparrow's back a little less gracefully, but with Alegra's help, I managed to shimmy in front of her. I felt secure between her legs and pressed against the warmth of the giant bird.

My heart seized when Row-Row hopped from the bough without warning. For a moment we were free falling, and then the sparrow spread wide his massive wings. They caught on the air, and soon we were climbing higher and higher into the sky.

I took one last look over my shoulder at all I was leaving behind and had no regrets. I'd made my decision. I was going to see the Sphynx.

32

I highly recommend sleeping on a sparrow. Row-Row's feathers were softer than a downy comforter. Between his fluffy feathers and Alegra's warm body pressed against me from behind, I felt snug as a bug in a rug.

I awoke to a dizzying view, soaring above a pink-hued lake. A fisherman worked the water on his skiff. He and his craft looked surreal from our airy height.

"Ah, you're awake," Alegra said over my shoulder.

When I sat upright, the wind blew my hair back. "Sorry, I guess I was pretty tired. I think that's the first time I've had any good sleep in the last week."

"Well, I'm glad you managed to get some rest. If any of those stories about the Sphynx are true, you're going to need it. Anyhow, we're just about there." She reached over my shoulder and pointed ahead.

A snowcapped mountain lay directly in our flight path. The air around the mountain was clear of clouds, and yet it crackled with spiderwebs of multicolored light. I could feel that I was gazing at a place as old as time, where both realms met and became one through nature's will. "Mount Temenanki," I said with wonder.

"I can see the temple on the top peak," Alegra shouted over the wind.

As we grew closer to the mountain, I saw it too. Polished golden columns wound around the mountain, leading to the highest peak. Each one gleamed in the sunlight wherever the surface peered out from underneath the clinging snow. Among them were stone arches marking walkways and domed structures buried beneath snowdrifts.

I raised my voice to be heard over the growing wind. "That must be the path pilgrims walk to reach the summit."

The air crackled around us as we closed in on the mountain. The hair on my arms stood up as if it were charged with static electricity. There were no clouds to be seen, and yet snow pelted me in the face, forcing me to bury my nose in Row-Row's neck.

Row-Row opened his wings wide to catch an air current, taking us in a complete circuit of the temple. Closer, I could see it was carved from the mountain itself, a dominating structure supported by colonnades that led to recesses of darkness. Thick layers of snow covered the peak as if someone had dipped the mountain in icing. The snowdrifts stopped short at a promenade that led to stone steps that ran the length of the temple.

Row-Row alighted on the promenade as gracefully as a swan. Alegra slid off first and helped me get down. The frigid air was a stark contrast to Row-Row's warm body. I wrapped my arms over my chest in a fit of shivers as Row-Row preened his feathers.

Alegra appraised the temple with a scholar's eye. "Looks like they're expecting you." Her breath came out in a plume of vapor as she spoke.

The sound of grinding stone carried down the steps to the promenade. Massive double doors slowly opened inward past the colonnades, though I could see no fae operating them.

"Will you come inside?" Now that we'd arrived, I was feeling queasy about entering the temple.

"Row-Row isn't one for cold climates," Alegra said. As if to accentuate her claim, the sparrow sneezed. Alegra laughed. "Oh, stop making a fuss, you big attention whore," she teased, sliding her pack over her shoulder and reaching inside with both hands. She came out with hands cupped under a mound of seeds that she offered to Row-Row. The sparrow whistled and dug into the bounty. "He'll be fine once he eats a little, and then we'll head back to that lake we passed. I'll keep an eye out for you until tomorrow morning. After that, we'll have to head back to the Tides."

"Are you sure you don't want to come inside with me?" I asked. "I bet there's a lot of interesting things in there. Maybe even enough that you could write your own book and add it to that royal library."

Alegra laughed. "I never said I didn't want to, but I wasn't invited," she explained. "Only those who sacrifice something can enter. I wish I could stay longer, but I can't miss my ship out tomorrow. The queen will be waiting for my report. Besides, my library is probably a mess with me being gone all week."

"I understand. And thank you for flying me here." The cold was seeping into my bones. "I couldn't have made it here without you." I couldn't believe I was going to attempt traveling to the mountain on horseback. By flying, we had made it to the temple around the same time I was supposed to be arriving at Uriel's cottage for my last trial. If I'd taken a horse, I wouldn't have made it until the next day at the earliest, thus missing my appointment. And I couldn't sacrifice that which I'd already missed.

"You'd better head inside before you freeze to death," Alegra said as she climbed back on Row-Row and took his reins.

Row-Row shifted his feet and then leapt into the air. The power of his beating wings forced me back a step. I stood in the wind and the snow for a few minutes and watched as they flew over the edge of the mountaintop.

I guess I'm alone now. I eyed the snow-blown steps that lay before me. The dark shadows of the colonnade were broken up by flickering torchlights inside the open doors. I hurried up the steps and inside. The wind stopped howling in my ears as soon as I crossed the threshold. The air inside was a musty combination of dust, old scrolls, and beeswax, but it was far more inviting than the freezing mountaintop. I brushed snow from my shirt and shook the already melting flakes from my hair.

"Lanie Alacore, your trials await."

I shook at the sound of that voice. A small, hooded figure stood before me. His brown robes covered him to his ankles, revealing sandaled feet. He looked like a monk if monks had a full head of hair. His forked black beard reached down to his stomach.

"You're a human," I said.

"I am known as Sigar." He bowed with hands clasped together under heavy sleeves. "Welcome to the Temple of the Sphynx. Please remove your shoes." He gestured to my feet.

There were plenty of religions and cultural customs that expected as much. I slipped out of my heels, then noticed there were several piles of shoes by the entrance. "Guess you've got lots of visitors today," I said with a nervous laugh.

"No new pilgrims have visited the temple in over a decade." Sigar had a very monotone and yet matter-of-fact way of speaking that unnerved me.

"Is that where I should put mine?"

Sigar smiled as if he pitied me. "You can leave them on the floor. I will add them to the others… should it be necessary."

A shiver worked down my spine that had nothing to do with the frigid air fluttering in from the open doors. The difference between our clothing was ironic. I wore a fancy ball gown, brilliantly colored and made of the finest materials in fae. Yet it was torn from my fight and stained with blood, making it hang awkwardly from one shoulder. Compared to Sigar's humble yet practical robes, I looked ridiculous.

"You probably don't get too many visitors wearing ball gowns, huh?"

"You are the first."

"I was at a masquerade," I said lamely.

"Please step up to the dais. We are almost ready to begin. Once your challenger arrives, we shall get the trials underway."

I barely heard him as I took in the temple ceiling. It soared far overhead, lost in a shadowy abyss. A central path inlaid with gold led to a raised platform with stairs on all four sides. There was a small gold bowl on top of a pedestal at the center. Rows of identical statues peeked out of the shadows on either side of me, men with plaited beards holding a scepter in one hand and a blooming lotus on the upturned palm of the other. A curb bordered both sides of the gold walkway, its surface etched with runes. The runes looked familiar, but I was no expert at paleography.

And then there was the most imposing structure of all on the far side, just past the pedestal. It was a statue of the Sphynx.

The statue watched me with blank eyes. Her mane was braided with gold beads, her human face a stony condemnation meant to induce fear and awe. She had a leonine form, resting with her hind legs tucked underneath and to one side, while her front paws lay on either side of the raised platform. A gold headdress hung over her smooth forehead.

"Please, Miss Alacore, the dais," Sigar repeated, gesturing toward the pedestal.

I climbed the short steps to the pedestal. I had an uneasy feeling in my stomach. It appeared as if the Sphynx's eyes had shifted to gaze down at me, though I'd never seen them move. I felt tiny and insignificant under the silent weight of her judgment.

Another pair of monks appeared from the shadows, dragging an oval mirror the size of my body up the steps. They placed the mirror on the opposite side of the pedestal. Once they had the weight of it settled on the floor, they stood still, hands holding it upright from behind.

"Will I be able to speak with the actual Sphynx?" I asked Sigar.

"If you would please state your name and your purpose for coming today," he said, pointing to the statue.

"But you already know my name."

"Please, Miss Alacore, state your name and purpose for coming today." He directed me to the Sphynx's stony gaze once more.

I looked up at the statue and took a deep breath to calm my nerves. Her face loomed over me. "I am Lanie Alacore, and I have come to speak with the Sphynx."

The temple was silent.

The howling wind outside battered the mountainside.

One of the monks cleared his throat.

I was about to ask Sigar what I needed to do next when the Sphynx's eyes blazed to life. The empty orbs glowed, and twin beams of light shot forth from them onto the mirror. The monks shuffled backward, bracing the mirror's weight as the light pressed through the surface.

The glass rippled like water. I sucked in my breath when a foot came through the portal of light. It was followed by another foot and then the rest of a woman's body. She looked around, aghast.

"The Sphynx has chosen your challenger," Sigar explained.

I gawked at the new arrival in disbelief. "Valia?"

"What kind of stunt are you trying to pull now?" Valia snarled at me. Judging from her black blouse, tight leather pants, and bare feet, I guessed she wasn't planning on a trip to the temple this morning. She bared her teeth at me and reached for a dagger strapped to her belt. The blade disappeared.

"No weapons may be brought into the trials," Sigar proclaimed as he finished swirling his fingers in the air.

Valia shot him a look that could melt rocks, then pursed her lips. She tightened her gaze, taking in the temple. Her eyes lit up when they landed on the statue before us. "The Sphynx," she murmured. The acoustics of the temple carried her whisper to me, and she flinched. "Is this the real temple of the Sphynx?" she asked Sigar.

He bowed to her. "You have been chosen as challenger."

"Just a second. Nobody said anything about having a challenger," I protested.

"This is customary. Without adversity, there can be no true test of your worth," Sigar explained as his fellow monks carried the mirror back behind the statue of the Sphynx.

"But I sacrificed to be here," I said.

"And as such, you are allowed to take the trials." Sigar nodded. "If you prove your worth, then the Sphynx will grant you a single boon."

"And if Valia wins?" I asked.

She perked up, dreadfully interested in the monk's answer.

"Then Valia will be granted the boon. You will get nothing."

"But…"

"Blood has not been spilled. You can still turn back," Sigar offered, gesturing to the open temple doors. The wind outside was whipping up swirls of snow.

Would Alegra see me if I left now? I wondered. *Not likely. I'll be stuck hiking down the mountain trail with no gear and nothing between me and the cold but this flimsy dress.*

Valia snorted contemptuously. "If she forfeits, do I still get the Sphynx's boon?"

"I'm not forfeiting," I said quickly.

"Then the test of purity will commence," Sigar announced.

The two monks returned from the shadows. They walked up the stone steps so that one was across from me and the other across from Valia, with the pedestal between all of us. They each held a bone dagger. First they showed it to the Sphynx, then turned to face us.

"A single drop of your blood is all that is required to prove your purity," Sigar explained.

Valia faced me with leer and held her hand out for the monk. He pricked her palm with the tip of the dagger. She tipped her hand until a drop of her blood hit the gold bowl. The bowl sang. A swirl of shadows blurred the surface. When it was gone, the bowl was left immaculate once more.

"Valia Medi'tu is pure," Sigar pronounced. "She may undertake the trials."

She looked at me, smugly flashing too many of her teeth. "Your turn, Lanie." Her wings fluttered in anticipation.

That bitch. She knows I'm not a pureblood fae. I have no wings, so how can I be? My blood is the mixture of unicorn and whatever the heck my mother's side of the family is. To Valia's kind, that makes me no better than a mutt.

Panic seized me. What could I do? My blood would reveal I wasn't meant to be there. I eyed Sigar. He stood impassively, waiting for my offering. *Wait, why would it matter if I was a pureblood fae? Ambrose specifically said the Sphynx belongs to neither human nor fae.* And Sigar was undoubtedly human. The temple existed between both realms, which meant both races made pilgrimages here.

Maybe purity means something else. What? Like being a good person? If that's the case, Valia wouldn't have passed the test.

"Miss Alacore," Sigar pressed.

I took a deep breath to steady my resolve. *If Valia's worthy of speaking to the Sphynx, then so am I, damn it.*

I thrust my open palm over the bowl before I could chicken out. Valia noticed how my fingers trembled, and she snickered. The monk took my hand with her bird-like talons, ever so delicately turning it. The tip of the bone dagger punctured my palm. It felt like getting stung by an angry hornet, but I refused to flinch. They always made that look so cool in movies, the blood pact, the simple act of slicing a palm with a pocketknife. Well, that shit hurts. I watched the blood pool in my palm. Valia was practically drooling in anticipation.

I tilted my hand and let the blood slide down. A single drop hit the gold bowl. My blood steamed, and a swirl of rainbow light filled the bowl. Before it dissipated, Sigar spoke. "Lanie Alacore is pure. She may undertake the trials."

I became aware of a soft humming sound. It might have been coming from the bowl. You could have knocked Valia over with a feather, she was so shocked that I'd been admitted as pure. I felt a rush of exhilaration and met her scowling eyes. I made my mouth a mocking O, closed my hand, turned it upside down, and gave her the middle finger.

"Steel yourself, for the first trial is about to begin."

I realized the humming sound was growing louder. The Sphynx's eyes lit once more, pulsating with energy. A flash of light blinded me as twin beams enveloped the two of us. I screamed despite myself as I fell into the light and toward my first trial.

33

When the light faded, we stood side by side in a large chamber lit by braziers in all four corners. A balcony skirted the room on an upper tier. The monks watched us from the balcony as we regained our senses. The stone floor before me was made of massive hexagonal tiles, each with a different rune etched on its surface. Another statue of the Sphynx, as large as the one in the entry hall, sat in stony silence on the opposite end of the chamber, across the gulf of rune tiles. A giant hourglass was fixed to the outside of the balcony above the Sphynx. If there was a ceiling, I couldn't see it. It was as if the darkness above me went on forever. The longer I stared upward, the dizzier I became, until I was forced to cast my eyes back to the floor to keep from falling over.

"The first trial will commence," Sigar announced, his voice booming across the chamber. He bent over the rail and flipped the hourglass on its axis. The sand trickled from the top chamber down to the bottom.

"Oh great, it's a timed event," I grumbled.

"Only forward the humble may approach,
through the wizened path that winds the world,
to awaken the sight of the Sphynx,
and thus witnessed, worthy you will be."

As Sigar spoke, a tile in the center of the room opened. A stone bench emerged from that opening. It held twin gemstones atop a black velvet cloth. At the same time, all along the stone balcony, the rail lit up with runes that matched those on the floor tiles. Different colors of light illuminated the etchings—a cerulean blue, a starry yellow, a flickering crimson, a warm sage, a neon purple, and a deeper black than the shadows of the chamber. They reminded me of something that I couldn't quite put my finger on.

Their light reflected off the gemstones on the bench. I determined they were the source of the trial. I studied the Sphynx's statue for some clue as to what I should do next. The Sphynx's eyes were lidded, and she had a concave hollow atop each of her paws that was large enough to fit one of the gemstones from the bench.

It's a simple puzzle, I thought. *I bet they start easy and get harder as you go.* I shrugged and stepped forward. I caught Valia watching me and froze in place, my foot hovering inches before the first hexagonal tile. There was a look in her eyes that disturbed me, as though she were a feral beast, all but licking her lips in anticipation. When my foot stopped in midair, her whole body seized up.

She caught me looking and laughed.

"The tiles are rigged, aren't they?" I said, carefully watching her eyes for a reaction.

There was a twinge and then a casual shrug, but Valia couldn't keep that dark grin from her lips.

I brought my foot back down, away from the tiles. There were eight of them before me in a row, with seven more rows beyond that, all set up in an orderly pattern that dominated the center of the chamber. The only way to retrieve a gemstone and put it in the Sphynx's paw was by walking out onto those tiles.

"There're sixty-four of them," I mumbled to myself. "But which tiles are safe?"

I had an idea and looked around the room for what I needed. I retrieved a decent-sized rock. With a deep breath, I tossed the rock onto the tile in front of me.

A few things happened. First, the tile the rock moved over came to life. The rune on its surface glowed with a black light. I barely had time to register this as a fountain of flames spewed upward in a pillar that rose high into the air. At the same time, the entire following row of tiles burst into a flaming wall.

I staggered backward with my arms up, blocking the scorching heat. Valia stood firm, her arms folded across her chest. She shook her head at me. After a minute the flames burned down, leaving the tiles unmarred.

"Are you insane?" I shouted up at the balcony. Sigar and the other two monks watched us impassively. "You could have killed me. What kind of sick religion is this?"

"You have chosen to enter the Temple of the Sphynx," Sigar said plainly. "This is her first trial. There can be no triumph without—"

"Adversity. Yeah, I heard you the first time," I yelled, then mumbled to myself, "Sick bastards."

Valia snickered at my outburst. "Where do you think we are? Did you think you were just going to walk out there and get the gemstones?"

"Yeah, well, you can't fly to get them either," I pointed out. "The flames are too high to risk it, and they were triggered before the stone ever touched the tile."

Valia pursed her lips. She studied the puzzle before us anew, tapping her right foot.

"What's the matter, Valia? You look disappointed."

"For a moment I was hoping you'd fall in the fire," she said glumly. Then her eyes lit up wickedly. "Then again, I could always push you."

I backed away from her.

"Any purposeful sabotage will result in forfeiture," Sigar proclaimed.

Valia pouted and fluttered her wings. "Well, that's a boring rule."

I ignored her. Something Valia had said triggered a memory. Uriel came to mind. A flash of brilliance hit me. I realized why the runes looked familiar.

They were the same as those around Gladewarden Uriel's fire pit.

One night not too long ago, Uriel had warned me to be careful around the pit unless I wanted to fall in. *How could I have been so blind? The runes covering the balcony and the floor are the same that I've been staring at for weeks now as I toiled away at Uriel's stupid chores.*

Uriel. A pit opened in my stomach. All that work I'd done to become warden had been for nothing. I had been right at the cusp of earning the title. *But instead I came to this temple. I could have taken Ambrose's money to fix up the apothecary and become warden in the same day. What if I made the wrong choice?*

Doubt is a sly beast, creeping up and seizing me by the throat when I least expected it. I couldn't let it maim me. The sand trickled down the hourglass. I needed to keep moving. I had to trust that the Sphynx would remove my curse.

Once it's gone, I'll be able to use my magic to wake Deedee from her coma.

I could practically hear the story Uriel had told me about the runes. "In the beginning the book of time was opened and thus began the great winding of the universe. Then came the duality of air and fire, then a swirling soup of elements. From this came the heart of life, water, and thus nature was created to give birth to our being. Finally, there was death, and the cycle was complete."

Okay, so time came first, I thought. *I just need to start out by stepping on the tile with the time rune.*

I scanned the first row. There were two tiles with time runes on them.

Fuck me. Nothing can ever be easy. I scanned the second row and found that only one of the runes for time had a tile for air beside it. That had to be the right path.

Valia was watching me like a hawk. I tried to swallow the lump in my throat and stepped up to the tile. *No big deal,* I thought sarcastically. *If I'm wrong, my foot will be burned to cinders before my heel even touches the floor.*

I was wrong.

I realized it just as I raised my foot. Because of that, I was already falling back and scrambling across the floor like some backwards crab before the flames erupted.

Valia's eyes were wide. "If you can move that fast, why don't you just run ahead and snatch up the gemstone?"

"I thought of that," I said as I got back to my feet and brushed off my dress. "They did too." I gestured to the monks. "That's why they erupt in the next row as well. That way if anyone tries running, they'll hit a wall of flame."

"I don't get it," Valia grumbled. "What did you do wrong?"

"Be quiet. I'm trying to think," I snapped.

The sound of the sand falling inside the hourglass echoed across the chamber. It was an unnerving noise. And what happened when time ran out? Why didn't any of the past pilgrims reclaim their shoes from the lobby? A shudder worked through me.

"My sequence was right," I mumbled. I scanned the tiles again. The only time rune that connected to an air rune was the one I had almost stepped on. "The sequence was right," I insisted again. "So, if it's not the order that was wrong, then what? It must be something else."

I tried to replay the instructions Sigar had given us. Each word he'd said seemed to matter. How had the riddle begun again? *Only forward the humble may approach.* That was the key. I needed to approach the Sphynx showing humility. But how? I could bow my head. Do a curtsy? No, that was the polite routine of gentry. Half the time people didn't even mean it when they bowed or curtsied. I had to mean it. *I need to feel humble down to my bones. This is a religion, and the Sphynx is an idol. And what do you do before idols? You pray.*

I got down on my knees before the time tile. My brain knew this was logical, but my heart was thundering in my chest. If I was wrong, there would be no turning back. I was going to be crawling on my hands and knees over the tiles. There were no second chances if I chose the wrong one or if my theory was incorrect. I would be face down in the center of one of those fire pillars.

My hands trembled as I reached for the tile. I slapped my palm down on the time rune.

Nothing happened.

I let out my pent-up breath and crawled fully onto the tile. The rune glowed purple beneath my body.

"It worked" I said, feeling shaky and breathless. I glanced up at the hourglass. It was already a third of the way spilled.

I hurried to the next tile, air. The tiles were larger than they looked. Lying down, I could fit two of myself across one of them. The air rune glowed white beneath me as I moved onto it. I had three choices for fire next. Two led to a water rune. It was hard to get a decent look farther on my hands and knees.

I don't think I can go backwards either. Sigar had specifically said, "Only forward the humble may approach." That could mean that if I backtracked, I would re-trigger the flaming pillars. It was a risk I couldn't afford to take.

I crane my neck to try and see further. Only one of the fire runes led to a water rune. I quickly followed that path, taking a left down the row, then forward onto the next, then right along that row.

When I finally reached the bench holding the gems, I rested my head on the stone surface. I needed a break. The tension was too much. One wrong move and I was dead. The stone bench felt cool and refreshing against my clammy forehead. I tried to remember the last time I'd eaten anything.

"Good going, Lanie," I grumbled. "You made it all the way to the temple just to have a blood sugar attack."

"Giving up already?" Valia taunted beside me.

Her body slithered past me, pressing me tight against the bench. She snatched one of the gemstones and shot me a wicked grin over her shoulder. "See you at the finish line, sucker."

Shit. I hadn't even been paying attention to Valia. Why had I assumed she wouldn't follow me? She scurried off the bench tile onto the next death tile and then to a time tile before I even had the remaining gemstone in my hand.

It was harder to crawl with the stone in my palm, but the angle was all wrong to try to place it in my pocket. Rosalie's crystal pendant swayed from my neck as I shuffled after Valia on all fours.

She reached the final row before me. How did you overtake someone on hands and knees? Valia laughed triumphantly as she stood and slapped her gemstone into the recess atop the Sphynx's left paw.

A second later I placed mine into the right paw.

The sand stopped.

"Valia Medi'tu has won the first trial," Sigar announced. "The Sphynx has awakened."

Before I could curse my ill luck, the statue's eyelids opened, revealing glowing orbs that flashed beams of light over me and Valia. I found myself tumbling through the light once more.

34

he light that had stretched out for eternity coalesced into a flickering flame. I watched it in dumb fascination as my mind caught up with my body and that flame became two, and then twelve, and then a hundred. My disorientation was less pronounced this time. Perhaps I was getting used to being magically transported through the temple, or maybe the distance we had moved was shorter.

It took me a few moments to realize the light I was seeing was not residual but that of many candles all around me. They were arranged in votive stands against a stone wall, row upon row of lit wicks and melting wax.

The room reminded me of a church except it was a tight space. There were no vaulted ceilings or stained glass. The room was split down the center by what looked like vertical panes of glass. I placed my palm against one of the walls boxing me in, and an electric ripple passed beneath my fingers. It was like touching the side of a great beast and feeling it move as blood pumped through its veins and air entered its lungs. I snatched my hand away from the alien sensation of a living wall and filed it in the back of my mind under *things to worry about later*.

The hourglass was perched high above me in the center of the wall, where another observation balcony skirted the room. The grains of sand were trickling down, marking the ever-marching procession of time, ticking away the moments that remained for me to complete the Sphynx's trials.

I gathered myself, determined to get a better handle on where I was. To my left, past the glass wall, Valia stood in her half of the room that mirrored my own. We each had our own private votive candle empire. A cloying fragrance of beeswax and incense suffused the space I was in, but it felt false, as if it was only there to cover up another scent. I sniffed the air, channeling my inner Lobo, and caught a whiff of decay. My mind recoiled from that as surely as my body leaned back, as if by doing so I could escape the odor.

Another glass pane behind me blocked my escape from the tight space. I was in one quarter of a room, not half, and Valia in another, with the space behind us lost to shadows the candlelight could not penetrate.

Something was back there, waiting in the darkness. It was large and sentient, like a predator watching its prey through the boughs of a tree. Goosebumps pricked my flesh.

"The second trial will commence," Sigar announced. "This trial will require no wit, and yet your brain must be employed to complete it. Your task is quite simple. Determine which candle burns the slowest."

I had to think fast. Valia had already won the first trial. If she completed this one before me, I would be out of the running. I couldn't fathom that, after everything I'd been through the last few months, I could end up with nothing in the blink of an eye.

My mind raced to digest what Sigar had told us. *There must be a hidden meaning. He says no wit required, but that could be a reference to sharp commentary instead of using my brain. Wait, he did say I'd have to use my brain. Okay, think, Lanie. Which candle would burn the slowest?*

I studied the candles before me. There had to be over a hundred of them. Their flames produced a steady flicker. The heat of so many candles warmed my skin. There were all different sizes—fat candles with three wicks, taper candles, tea lights, and colored glass tubes filled with wax. And yet they all burned at the same pace. I tried to study the way the wax dribbled over the sides of the candles. Did they look different?

"This is stupid," I muttered.

I could hear each grain of sand taunting me as it hit the bottom of the hourglass. The steady inevitable beat mocked my ineptitude. "How can all these candles burn equally?" I grumbled. "They're obviously different sizes."

Wait, he said I have to use my brain. Not my eyes, my brain. What if the answer isn't to find the right candle but to make it the right one? Yes, that's it.

I had the answer. *What candle would burn the slowest?* I grabbed the closest candle, closed my eyes, and blew out the flame. I felt proud that

I'd so easily unraveled the second riddle. *An unlit candle would burn the slowest.*

When I opened my eyes, I was greeted with failure. The tiny flame was still flickering. I blew harder, annoyed that I had just let Valia see the answer to the riddle. The flame danced away from my breath, then snapped back into place. I'd only succeeded in guttering the top of the candle.

I cursed my luck. The candles were enchanted. This was how they burned at the same steady rate. I felt a moment of panic followed by a rush of annoyance. I played with the crystal pendant hanging from my neck as I tried to think.

If it's not a riddle, then what? I played Sigar's words back in my mind a dozen times, dissecting and unravelling their hidden meaning. In the end I came to nothing. I had to choose a candle. I fought down my mounting panic. I briefly imagined shattering the hourglass to shut it up. A well-placed candle thrown into the glass would do it.

Stop. Focus on what you're doing. The trial is not going away, and Valia is no dummy. I need to figure this out before she does. Sigar said I need to pick a candle, so I have to pick one. And I can't get it wrong because if I choose the wrong one, then... Wait.

Sigar had said I needed to choose the slowest burning candle but nothing about how many times I could try. I tested my theory. If I was wrong, I would go home—or worse, be given to whatever was lurking in the back of the room.

Gingerly, I lifted a random candle to Sigar. "This one is the slowest," I said.

Sigar frowned at me.

But that was it. Only a frown. No proclamation that I was disqualified, no tumble into darkness, no triumph for Valia.

I set the candle down and offered the monks above me another. "This is the slowest," I said.

A frown.

I looked at Valia. She was studying her candles with a curled lip and both arms folded over her chest. When she saw me looking, she rolled her eyes. She clearly thought I was a moron.

I chose another.

Sigar frowned.

Then I chose another and another and another. I was dogged in my determination. If I could choose as many times as I wanted, all that was left was a process of elimination. Time ticked away as I continued choosing one candle at a time. At one point, Valia howled and swept her arms manically across the votive stands. Candles spilled to the floor, rolling on their sides and dribbling trails of melted wax in their wake. Her frustration was infectious, and I felt the tangle of time suffocating me. And yet I continued. Only a tenth of the sand remained in the top of the hourglass by the time I finally lifted the correct candle.

"Lanie Alacore has won the second trial," Sigar proclaimed.

A beam of light erupted from the back of the room, cutting through the glass pane as if it didn't exist. Beyond the shadows, I saw the source of that bestial mind that had stalked us. It was the statue of the Sphynx. Valia cursed me as the light swept me away to the third trial.

I knew even before I arrived that I would need to make good use of my lead over Valia. She was no dummy. Now that she'd seen it work, she would employ the very same tactic with the candles.

I craved for the light to be gone, eager to hear Sigar's instructions for my next riddle. I was so close to victory I could taste it. All I needed to do was complete the next trial, and I would ask the Sphynx to lift my curse. Once it was gone, I would finally have my freedom. I could live and love on my own terms.

And most importantly, I could use my magic to help heal Deedee. My heart soared at the idea of her opening her eyes. How I missed her voice. There was so much I wanted to tell her.

My imaginary celebration was cut off at the knees when my vision cleared enough to make out the room I was in.

Because there was no room. Vertigo hit me hard, and I had to throw my arms out to keep my balance. I stood atop a flat rock, rounded at the edges, overlooking a yawning chasm. A score of similar platforms lay before me, leading across the chasm, each balanced on a stone pillar. Enormous metal orbs hung from the cavern ceiling, candles burning inside them to light the central area. Every direction outside their radius was pitch black.

"This is no trial," I gasped. "It's a nightmare."

"The third trial will now commence," Sigar proclaimed. A light bloomed on the other side of the chasm, revealing the monks as they stood before a statue of the Sphynx. I had no time to wonder how they could be there with me and back with Valia at the same time. "To pass the third trial, come to the Sphynx."

Sigar tapped the hourglass and began the trial with no pomp and circumstance. There was no riddle to be trifled with. I just had to cross the chasm.

I was moving before I could think about how terrified I was. I leapt across the void to the next perch. The rock beneath me wobbled so much that I had to push my feet out wide and flail my arms to steady my balance. Once it was reoriented, I leapt to the next perch. I used the lights above to guide my path, choosing only the largest rocks to continue across the chasm.

I was feeling quite sure of myself when I screwed up. It was a misfire of timing. I didn't wait long enough for my rock to settle before hopping for the next one. It was too much for the already teetering platform. It tipped out from beneath me as I pushed my body into the air for my leap.

My trajectory was off. Time seemed to slow. I felt the insatiable pull of gravity. The rock I'd leapt from wobbled on its stony spire, then spilled over the side. It struck a piece of the stone spire as it tumbled down, then bounced off into the void.

I hit the next platform all wrong. The bottom half of my body dangled from it with my legs kicking air as my fingers clawed the smooth surface, searching for traction. The stone tipped toward me, and my weight pulled me farther over the edge.

"No!" I cried out in panic, scrambling up the surface of the stone to the center. I pressed my body flat against it, spreading my weight along the surface to try to stabilize it. The rock platform wobbled just as the last one had before it fell. But this time it came to a shuddering halt.

I could hear my heart hammering in my eardrums. I clung to the stone, too terrified to move even an inch, lest I unbalance the platform once more. I realized I'd never heard the stone that fell hit the bottom of the chasm. Was there a bottom? What would happen if I fell off one of those platforms? Would I tumble in darkness until I died of hunger? I couldn't fathom such a ghastly way to die, and I shivered and clutched the platform with my face pressed against the stone.

Fear can be crippling. People underestimate it. They scoff at anxiety, but that is a beast with no heart.

"The third trial has already commenced," Sigar announced.

I twitched, wondering why he was telling me this again. Then I saw the blast of light back where I had started. Valia was standing on the first platform, her body limned in a halo of brilliant light. "This trial will be complete when the first competitor reaches the Sphynx."

Valia grinned wickedly at me. "Too scary out there for you, warden?"

Her wings stretched wide as she flexed them, and she jumped straight up and flapped them. Then fell right back down, her face a mask of shock and indignation. She hit the platform hard, and even I had to wince at the sound of her knee hitting the stone.

"No magic will work in this chamber," Sigar coldly explained.

"Looks like you'll have to beat me using your own two feet," I called. My challenge was given more to bolster my own resolve than to antagonize Valia.

She leapt off the platform onto the first rock. She screamed as it teetered and rebalanced herself. She was more graceful than I had been. Her quick recovery made me start moving. I slowly pulled my knees up underneath myself. By the time I was back on my feet, Valia had nearly caught up to me.

I scanned the path ahead. Two of the flat rocks looked decent. I leapt across and landed gingerly on one. My heart seized as it wobbled and then settled back into place. As long as I didn't get overconfident again, I would be okay. I fell back into a steady rhythm, focusing on scanning the path ahead, choosing the best rocks to jump to next, and waiting until each rock stabilized properly before moving farther.

Valia closed the distance fast. She leapt onto a platform to my left while I was waiting for my own to settle. She looked down at the rock I stood on and grinned wickedly. Her wings were spread behind her, evenly balancing her weight. They gave her a serious advantage over me.

She leapt onto the platform I was going to use next before I could.

"See you at the Sphynx," she taunted even as she was already moving on to another platform.

I swore and leapt to my second choice. Valia was already four platforms ahead of me and closing in on the last stretch to the Sphynx.

I don't know what fell over me. It could have been sheer stupidity fueled by stubbornness, or maybe just an unshakeable need to win. Either way I soon found myself in a headlong rush. No longer was I waiting for the rocks to settle before moving on. Instead, I leapt and staggered to the far edge of the next platform and leapt straight off before the rock could even decide what to do with me. The platforms in my wake tumbled over their spires. I couldn't think about how reckless I was being or about the fact that I was destroying the temple's third trial for future pilgrims.

Screw them, I thought ruefully. *Maybe this will force them to come up with something that doesn't involve pilgrims falling to their death for an eternity.*

I felt a rush of adrenaline when I overtook Valia. The look of unbridled rage on her face was enough to keep me moving in my headlong reckless dash. She picked up her pace, but now that I was ahead, it made things more difficult for her, since wherever I went, platforms tumbled into the abyss.

The Sphynx was just ahead.

Four more platforms and I was there. I'd done it. I completed the trial before Valia. I couldn't wait to see that smug look of hers wiped off by my victory. Soon I would have everything I wanted. My curse would be removed! Then I would know. Did I want to be with Lucien, or was my attraction simply because he was the only one I *could* be with? Could I be with Lobo? He'd have to give me a second chance. Once I explained it all to him, once he realized what I'd suffered and why I hadn't been intimate, it would all be forgiven.

Three more platforms to go. I'm going to save Deedee with my magic! Yes! I was almost there, and not a moment too soon. The hourglass was down to its last few specks.

Valia screamed.

It wasn't the strangling screech of a bitter bitch being a sore loser. There was fear in her voice. Fear I didn't know someone as cruel as Valia could be capable of. I stopped on my platform, spreading my feet out to let the weight settle even as I looked over my shoulder. To my horror, Valia's platform tumbled out from underneath her. She was scrambling up the flat surface as it careened over the edge of its stone spire.

Serves her right.

I winced. Had I sunk so low that I would delight in the possibility of another person dying? I was ashamed of myself. I watched in horror as the stone fell into the abyss, then screamed as I saw Valia's body flung into the air. She'd managed a desperate jump to the next platform. The platform I had just left was already gone, tumbling into the chasm.

I leapt to the one on my left and then from there sprang onto the next. Even as I ran, I saw the futility of my efforts. Valia hit the platform between us hard. It knocked the air out of her. Her hands grasped weakly at the stone as she slid off backwards, her waist and legs dangling from the opposite end.

"Stay still," I shouted. "I'm coming."

I leapt onto the platform. The extra weight caused the stone to careen, spilling Valia even further off the edge. We both screamed. I threw myself backward onto the opposite end, acting as a counterweight to Valia. The platform tilted back my way as it settled in place. Unfortunately, Valia was still hanging off the edge. I dropped to my belly and spread my legs and arms.

"Grab my hand!" I yelled.

Valia clawed at my palm. Our fingers locked, and she pulled herself onto the platform. We lay on our bellies facing each other, panting to catch our breath.

A gong went off, rumbling across the chasm.

"Time is up," Sigar announced.

"You came back for me?" Valia gasped in disbelief. "What a fool you are. You gave up your wish to save someone who hates you."

Her words stung. "It was worth it," I insisted. "I could never live with myself if I chose a wish over someone's life. Even if that person is a rotten bitch."

It appeared I agreed with Ambrose's ideas after all. I had never sought to become a ruthless person. Even when I fought Droll in his basement, I had never wished to harm him. All life *is* precious.

Valia's mocking smile turned genuine.

The planes of her face altered. The shadows swallowed her features, then spit her out in a burst of shimmering light that slapped me in the face. The light swallowed me whole. I fell for a time, and then I was there.

This time when I opened my eyes, I stood before the real Sphynx.

35

We stood atop the mountain's highest reaches on a plain of warm grass. A clear dome sheltered us from the howling winds and snowy temperatures surrounding the temple. I could see the pink waters of the lake below and the woods beyond that. Far in the distance, Starfire stood like a beacon of light. I finally understood why so many people spent their life in the pursuit of climbing mountains.

"It's so beautiful," I whispered.

"Did you take my trials so that you could come up here to enjoy the view?" When the Sphynx spoke, it was like thunder rumbling in my chest.

She was twice as large as the statues inside her temple. The weight of her presence pressed down on my mind. She stood behind me. It took an effort to face her. Her eyes gleamed with an intensity that felt both familiar and terrifying, but there was something else there. Respect. The Sphynx held me in esteem for having completed her trials.

"But I failed the last trial," I said, forcing myself to look up at her face. She stared with eyes that looked more like emeralds. The planes of her face were smooth as polished stone. It was interesting how she could look so human and yet undeniably bestial at the same time. Her golden mane ruffled in the air as if her hair were moving underwater. Her naked breasts hung below her gleaming mantle, each as large as my torso. I blushed when I realized I was staring, and when I looked up again, I found the Sphynx smirking at me, one of her fangs poking out between her thick lips.

"You know you didn't fail my trials," she said plainly, settling on her belly with paws raking the grass like the world's largest feline.

"Or I would never be here with you," I acknowledged. If I had failed the trials, I knew I would never have been anywhere ever again. My shoes would have been added to the pile in the entry hall. I shivered to think what I had risked getting to this moment. "And Valia? Will she be okay, even though she didn't win?"

The Sphynx stopped licking her paw to scowl at me.

"Right. Valia was never really here, was she?" I had known it somehow from the moment Valia smiled at me. It was a look so genuine and filled with such warmth that it never could have belonged to her. "So she was, what, a phantom that you plucked from my mind?"

"You ask many questions, Lanie Alacore. You are still a blind cub feeling its way through the world. But the time will come, soon, when you must finally open your eyes. The time of learning is passing. I will give you this last answer for free, as a kindness. There can be no test without adversity. Would you have come back to save Valia if you had thought she was not real?"

"Probably not," I admitted.

"And so you would have failed the trial. Tell me, child, what was the purpose of the trials you undertook?" She settled herself in the grass, paws outstretched in front of her, and leaned over me. My legs felt wobbly under her scrutiny.

"I think the first trial was to measure bravery and humility," I said.

The Sphynx tsked at me. It reminded me of someone else I knew. "Come now, girl. You must have more conviction than that in you. Why do you persist in pretending to be unwise? Have you been so addled by others that you must constantly fear to speak your own mind? She says *I think*..." She rumbled in annoyance, but there was a clear undercurrent of warmth to her lecture. "You think or you know? What was the first trial about?"

"It was about bravery and humility," I said firmly, even raising my chin a bit, though my whole body trembled under the Sphynx's hungry gaze. "I had to be brave to put my body on the tiles, knowing if I was wrong, I would die. Humility was obvious, since that was the key to the puzzle."

The Sphynx looked pleased. "And the second trial?"

"You were measuring my patience and maybe my perseverance too."

"Maybe?" The Sphynx growled.

"I *had* to persevere," I corrected. "If I didn't stay true to what I believed was right, then I would never have found the candle you sought.

Though I'm not sure I can't confuse that for stubbornness, a trait I've found I dislike in others."

The mountain shook beneath me when the Sphynx laughed, a rumbling of ice and stone. I threw my arms out to keep my balance until it was over.

"And the final trial?" the Sphynx asked.

"At first I thought we were being tested on our agility or even our critical thinking, since I had to be careful to choose the right stone platform to balance on. But now I see the real test had nothing to do with getting across the chasm. It was about selflessness."

"Very good," the Sphynx purred, the vibration of it hitting me in the chest. "You are wise beyond your years. A suitable pilgrim. You will be tested beyond belief in this world, but in the end, you and your friends may be all that can save it. It has been a long time indeed since someone has passed my trials. For this I offer you two things. You may not ask for more, and it is not within my power to give further. The first is a question." She paused at my expression. "Ah, yes, you see now your ignorance almost cost you a great deal. Perhaps now that you know our terms, you will choose your words more carefully. I will answer one question only.

"The second gift I will bestow is a boon. It is only within my power to give you a boon that is tied to your life in an intimate way. You may not ask me for world peace or to fly to Mars or any other such nonsense. Now I have laid out the terms of our compact. There is no room to alter them. Do you understand?"

I nodded, too afraid to speak in case I said the wrong thing and squandered my opportunity. The Sphynx seemed to accept that. She swished her tail lazily behind her. "When you are ready to ask your question, place your hands on my paw and proceed." She wore fingerless gloves with yellow diamonds the size of my head atop the center of each of her paws.

I could ask any question. This was an amazing opportunity. What should I ask? My mind raced to think of all the things that were important to me. Who was behind Persa's attempts to overthrow Ambrose? It was clear she hadn't been acting alone. Who stood to gain the most by her actions? The Sphynx could tell me.

No, that would be a waste of my question. There were so many things I wanted to know flitting through my mind like scattered butterflies. *Where is my mother? Could Lobo love me if he knew the truth? Could the Sphynx lift my curse?* No, that was the boon I'd ask for. I could ask for any boon, anything in the world. I could be rich. I could live forever. I could rule the world. Well, maybe not. She said it had to be directly related to me. But I knew she could give me power. The promise of it filled the air between us.

But in the end there was really only one question that mattered to me.

I stepped forward to her left paw and placed both hands on the diamond. It radiated warmth against my palm that traveled up my arms. It was an immense power that threatened to swallow me whole. If I closed my eyes, I would lose myself in her mind. It had happened before to many pilgrims. The Sphynx was neither sad nor proud of that fact. It was simply a thing that was true. If they were lost, then they weren't worthy to begin with. I felt her tell me this as I pressed my hands against the gemstone. I opened my mouth and asked my question before I could be swept away.

"Can my unicorn magic heal Deedee from her coma?" I spit out the words and broke my contact with the Sphynx. I staggered back a step and gazed up at her even though the world tilted dizzily for a few seconds afterward.

The Sphynx's gaze turned inward. The emerald stones of her eyes spun in a swirling vortex. We stood in silence for what felt like an eternity, until I was certain she had forgotten I was standing there at all. My legs were shaky from our brief connection, and my body felt as drained as a spent battery. I needed to sit down. Would it offend her if I did so?

Suddenly the Sphynx was back, her eyes centered on me. "Your friend might come out of the coma if you are able to use your unicorn magic on her. There is no certainty about this. I know this is not the answer you wished for, but not all things in life are simple. Her mind has retreated deep inside of her being to escape the horror of what the changeling did. Your friend saw the changeling for who he truly was, and such a thing is not easy for a human mind to comprehend. Deedee is deeply damaged. However, there *is* a chance your magic might heal her."

I staggered at those words as if they physically assaulted me. I knew the Sphynx was speaking the truth, but it shattered the hope I'd been clinging to for months.

"It's not fair," I said in a voice that refused to give weight to my words.

"Fairness is a concept created by those that would see it born," the Sphynx replied candidly.

"I don't agree with that."

"As if that changes a thing." The Sphynx bristled. "Come now. I tire of this conversation. Use your boon for what you came here to do. Ask me to remove your curse."

"I am going to use my boon to heal Deedee." I said the words before I could take them back.

The Sphynx tilted her head to look at me, and in that moment she reminded me very much of a curious housecat. "You would forsake yourself in service of this woman?"

"I will," I said.

"This is no trick. You are not being tested, Lanie Alacore. If you do this, there will be no second boon."

"I understand." I tried to sound stoic, but my insides were being torn apart. I was losing my dream to remove my curse. It was no easy thing to sacrifice.

"Then I must tell you the cost."

"What cost? You said I would be given a boon."

The Sphynx laughed. "All great magic comes at a cost. You ask me to do that which even the power of a unicorn is not guaranteed to perform. Your friend's mind is badly damaged. To heal this, we must take from another part of her. I will use that part to create the spell that will heal her."

"What will you take from her to do this?" I asked, already terrified to hear the answer. Would it be something small, like a pinky toe, or would Deedee lose an arm? Would she ever forgive me for doing this to her? Maybe I shouldn't. Maybe I should just have my curse removed and trust in my power to heal her. The Sphynx did say there was a chance it would work.

The Sphynx roared at me. I fell to the ground, covering my face with my arms.

"Do you dare interrupt me with a question? After I have already explained that you may only ask one? Perhaps I should eat you for breaking the rules, eh? What say you, girl?" She hovered over me, baring her fangs.

I would have peed my pants if I'd had anything to drink in the last twelve hours. If not for something in the way she said those words, I would have probably died of a heart attack. But they were so familiar. I gazed up into her eyes, and she saw my recognition. The Sphynx grinned at that. She pulled her face away from me and relaxed back down on her haunches.

"Sit up. You look silly cowering on the ground like that," she admonished me. "Now listen closely, and I will finish my explanation. But no more questions. If you ask another, I will be forced to devour you. Nod that you understand me, girl."

I stood up and nodded mutely, studying her expression closer. Her features, the shape of her eyes. It was all there. I knew who the Sphynx was.

"Time enough for that later," she said, as if addressing my inspection. "The cost will be great. It might be more than you can bear. To heal Deedee, I will cut away parts of her mind. It will take a great deal. She will retain all sense of herself, but a piece of her will be forever lost. To heal her, I will need to take away all the pieces of you. They have power I can use, and together we can repair the rift. With this, I can guarantee she will be healed. However, all memories she has ever had of you will be gone. This is the cost of what you ask."

My world rocked on its axis. "You can't ask that of me. It's too much. Deedee wouldn't remember me at all..." I sobbed. "Deedee is my best friend. Ever since we met, we've been inseparable."

The idea of living my life without her left me gutted. Someone might as well have come along and cut my heart out of my chest. To have her gone was as just as bad as if she'd died.

"But she wouldn't be dead," I said to myself. "Deedee won't be in my life anymore...but she'll be alive."

There was really no choice at all. I stepped forward and slapped my palms down on the Sphynx's right paw. The yellow diamond warmed beneath me as it flooded my soul. "I will use my boon to heal Deedee," I proclaimed.

Memories swirled around me. They were Deedee's. The Sphynx was slowly stripping them away from her mind. I saw myself through Deedee's eyes. The first time she walked in the room and found me, a mousy teenager, sitting on the bed reading a book. The two of us riding bikes through Central Park. Her watching me sitting alone under a tree, my nose buried in a book again, scared of the world.

I saw myself through her eyes, and my heart broke. Deedee never thought of me as the worthless, mousy shut-in I always knew I was. She saw a Lanie who was alive, bursting with energy and enthusiasm, yet desperately hurt and bottling those urges deep inside.

I was there with her as she held me tight, feeling her simmering anger that anyone would hurt me in the way Ted had after the first time I tried to make love and blacked out. I saw the memories from just after her father died. Deedee had been bedridden with depression for over two weeks, and I stayed by her side and took care of her. I felt her love for me, her dearest friend in the world. I was her only family.

It was a swirling thunderstorm of our lives; a dizzying cyclone being sucked down a tube. I grasped for those memories with clawing hands. I'd made a mistake. I didn't want Deedee to forget our friendship. The loss was too great for me to handle.

But it was too late. The memories were stripped from her mind. They left behind an emptiness so profound that I thought I might die in that moment.

The Sphynx wrapped those memories together, folding them like a baker works laminated dough. They spread flat across time. She spit her magic onto the surface, and the memories smeared. She folded them over onto themselves again and again, spreading them flat, spitting her magic and folding them more, until they were something new. Then she pulled a rainbow light from me that she used to coat the memories.

The spell was ready. The Sphynx applied it to Deedee's mind. She was lost to me forever, but she was healed. Surprisingly, the Sphynx held me in her arms as I wept for the loss of my dearest friend.

And in a tiny room in the back of Free House, for the first time in sixteen weeks, Deedee opened her eyes.

It didn't take me long to leave the mountain. Alegra was keeping a close watch from the lake below and picked me up on the promenade. We spent the flight back in silence. I couldn't bear to speak of what I'd lost. I only told her I was successful. And I was. Deedee was healed from her coma. I could feel it in my bones.

I returned to my lodging in the Tides. My belongings had been delivered from the palace. Taewyn was waiting for me on the doorstep. I told her everything that had happened, and she held me while I cried a second time.

I wasn't sure what my life was going to be like without Deedee in it. But I was eternally grateful to the Sphynx that she had been healed.

Tae took my luggage and went on ahead. She said she had some things to sort out in Willow's Edge. I planned to meet her at home. There was only one more thing to do before I departed. I needed to apologize to Gladewarden Uriel for missing my last day of training. Part of me just wanted to leave and be done with it, but there was something I needed to retrieve from her cottage.

Uriel sat out front, stoking her fire pit with a rod and grumbling to herself. Pepper sat cross-legged at her feet, chewing on a long piece of straw.

"You were supposed to be here this morning," Uriel said without looking up.

"There was something important I needed to do," I said. "I just wanted to come by and thank you. I appreciate all the time you spent with me, even if it ended up being for nothing. And thank you for keeping Pepper safe."

Uriel grumbled as she rose from her seat, holding her aching back and leaning on the rod for support. Her bones cracked as she settled upright and beckoned with her gnarled hand for me to come closer. Once I was standing in front of her, she looked up into my eyes.

"Do you really believe it was for nothing?" she asked me in that knowing tone.

"No." And I meant it. "I saved Ambrose and healed my best friend. Even if it meant losing her. My time here has been worthy indeed."

Uriel nodded in that shaky old-lady way she liked to pretend she needed. "Indeed it was. You do your grandmother's memory proud. You will make a fine warden for Willow's Edge, Lanie Alacore."

That was the last thing I expected her to say. "You're going to let me become warden? But I never performed the final rite."

"Didn't you?" Uriel prodded.

I knew somehow that she wasn't talking about our planned meeting to grow the chŏra tree. "The temple of the Sphynx was the final trial?"

"Not entirely," Uriel said. "Though anyone who can pass the trials of the Sphynx is clearly capable of taking on the mantle of a warden." There was that look again. That flash of light in her eyes. I knew where I'd seen it before. It was the real reason I came to see Uriel. Well, that and to get Pepper. I just had to know if I was right.

"You're the Sphynx, aren't you?"

Uriel smiled coyly. She reached up with her shaky hand and patted my cheek lovingly, then tapped my chin with her knuckle. I felt the immensity of her being in that touch and had to steel myself against it lest I fell over. "You are such a clever girl."

"That's why the manticore defers to you," I said. "He's scared of you."

Uriel chuckled. "Marik isn't scared of anyone or anything, I can assure you of that. I like to think he listens to this old woman because he recognizes wisdom when he hears it."

"But why the old lady act?"

"It's not an act. This is me. Just as much as the Sphynx inside the temple is me. Oh, I know that answer doesn't satiate your curiosity, Lanie. And that's just as well. You've a sharp mind. Never stop asking questions. That is what will make you a strong warden."

A strong warden? Could that be true? Now that I'd earned the mantle I'd been working for, I felt anxiety crawling over my skin. A thought came to me. "How come you're not trying to rip my face off when I ask you questions now? You said I only got one."

"That was inside the temple." Uriel smiled. "Now, let me ask *you* a question. What was the boon you were going to ask for? The one you originally intended to seek."

"It was just as you said on top of the mountain. I was going to ask you to remove my curse," I said, not daring to let myself hope she might. The disappointment would be more than I could handle.

"As I guessed. But why do you want that curse removed?"

"It smothers me. With this curse I have no freedom. I have no power."

"Oh, my girl, that's nonsense. You are a unicorn. You have so much power within you." Uriel tapped the center of my chest. "Right there."

"Are you offering me another boon?" I asked despite myself.

Uriel shook her head slowly. "There can only be one boon in a lifetime. And you've had yours. But you will overcome this curse. I can see that in you."

"How?"

"For a fae to remove a curse, they must go to the source. The originator of the curse is the key to its removal."

"But how can I figure out who put this curse on me?"

harred flesh was never a pleasant odor to wake to. Rotting flesh from a leftover meal, perhaps, but never charred. Ralic wondered what the ship's crotchety chef was burning this time as he uncoiled from the abyss.

Then he remembered the stink was him. That foul fae bitch had burned his face and arms with that light magic of hers. He'd often wondered what it would be like to look at the sun, jealous that so many other creatures got to bask under its rays. Well, he'd never wonder again. Normally his vampiric metabolism would have healed his injuries by now. He'd even managed to drain a droba from the harbor before setting sail. Damn frog blood was like oil but better than nothing. Yet his face and arms were still a grizzled mess.

He pried open his coffin lid and climbed out into his stateroom. Vampire services cost a pretty penny. He was well off. Now that Klas and Cezar were dead, he would keep their share too. That was just as well. It was going to be harder to find decent work with his partners gone.

He was sliding his coffin lid back into place behind him to keep the humors trapped inside when he scraped his battered forearm on the wood. He winced and tried to shift into his shadow form. Even that didn't work.

The door opened, and Valia slid inside like a snake. She took one look at him and scowled. "Gross. You look like somebody replaced half your face with ground beef."

If anyone else had said that to him, he would have drained them in a flash. But Valia was a special customer. She paid extremely well, well enough for him to put up with a few barbs here and there. Though at the end of this job, he might drain her just for kicks.

"Serves you right. I thought you three were supposed to be professionals," she said, dropping her bundle on the table.

"Nobody said anything about the prince being there," Ralic grumbled.

Valia shook her head in disgust. "I still can't believe you knuckle-draggers tried offing Prince Lucien."

Neither could Ralic. He knew how badly they'd screwed things up. In that moment, there was so much promise of blood. The excitement of draining a pureblood had been too enticing to resist. Mercenaries couldn't be held liable for the work they performed under contract. They had a duty to act on their employer's orders. Now Persa was dead.

"What's in the package?"

"I brought some ingredients to make you a healing tea." Valia unrolled the parcel, revealing tiny pockets for vials. One contained wriggling worms, another dried herbs, and there were some knives and other implements.

Ralic ignored the other rubbish and focused on the vial of thick crimson blood. "I don't like tea. How about I just drink this one instead?"

Valia snatched the vial out of his hands. "You'll like this tea, and if you don't, tough shit. I'm not going to work with you if you look like a chewed-up corpse. Now, go sit down. I don't like you hovering over me when I'm working."

Ralic didn't like taking orders from Valia. She was never polite. Maybe he should just drain her. Her pure blood would do wonders for his metabolism. But who else knew she was here? That wretched prince was on the airship with them. If he came looking for Valia and found Ralic, there was no question he would recognize his face, especially all charred up. He thought about Prince Lucien's blade, Iceshadow, shearing Klas's head off and shuddered. He begrudgingly took a seat at the table while Valia fell to work over the stove. She had a solid reputation for making potions. Whatever she made was bound to help.

"You guys really screwed this one," Valia complained. "Ten years of working Persa to get her to turn, all down the drain because you couldn't take on one stupid fae."

"And the prince," Ralic reminded her.

Valia shot him a withering look that made his balls shrivel.

"How upset is Malachai?" he asked.

"What do you think? He's pretty friggin' miffed. It's a good thing he doesn't know you're on this airship, or you'd be spending the rest of eternity in that nightmare cape of his."

Ralic quaked at the prospect. Malachai Erlkönig's Mantle of Nightmares was legendary. Not even a vampire spawn could survive the cape's insatiable appetite. Being torn apart and sent to the nightmare realm to be tormented for eternity was a punishment he wouldn't wish on his worst enemy.

"At least that stupid bitch is dead," Valia said. "With Persa gone, there's no one left to tell what really happened. With the plan blown to high hell, it's better to have no loose ends."

"The House of Dawn could always bring in a necromancer," Ralic pointed out.

Valia snorted. "Ambrose Amaryllis would never dare. The old man's too scared of that sort of magic." She poured the steaming water into a wooden mug and slid it across the table.

Ralic took the mug in both hands, cupping it to feel the tendrils of warmth slip into his withered hand. His was a lifetime of cold. He could never quite warm up. He sniffed the drink and stuck his tongue out in disgust.

Valia rolled her eyes at him. "Don't be a baby."

I'd like to suck those eyeballs right out of her head. The tea was sweet like honeysuckle. It made him want to retch, but he drank down a big gulp to shut her up. *How dare she serve me twigs and herbs? The nerve. After all the hard work I've done for this bitch. She could've at least brought me a human baby to drain.*

Valia was always pulling stunts like this. He hated that Malachai had put her in charge of this operation. Ralic came to a decision. When this job was over, he would definitely drain Valia. And he'd do it slowly. She was too big for her britches. He'd suffered enough indignities in her service. The bitch wouldn't know what hit her.

She eyed him suspiciously.

"So, what's the plan?" he asked coyly.

"You mean how do I recover from your bumbling failure?" Valia said scathingly. "Well, we still have our man working the House of Amber. At least everything is going to plan on that front. As for the House of Dawn, I think I can manipulate Cyan. She thinks we're chums, after all. Persa was a far better option, but I can work with Ambrose's stuck-up daughter if I must. There's a gala this month I plan to attend, so I can bump into her. If we can weaken her position financially, then we can effectively strip the Amaryllises from power. A cleverly timed accident for Ambrose, and I can manipulate Cyan into moving the water fae toward a court instead of a house, as we planned."

Ralic finished off the tea and licked the sides of the cup. Perhaps it was tasty after all. He could feel her magic already coursing through his system. "When will you need me to arrange Ambrose's accident?"

Valia blinked at him. "You? Why in the world would we want you to have any part in our future endeavors?"

"I'm under contract," he coldly reminded her. Even a pureblood fae couldn't break the terms of a contract.

She snickered. "You really are a useless prat. Are you this daft? You tried to murder the Prince of Shadows. Did you think Malachai was going to turn a blind eye to that?"

"But you said…"

"Don't worry, I'm not feeding you to Malachai's cape. We decided that was too good for you."

Ralic opened his mouth to protest, but a strangled gurgle worked its way up his throat. He clutched his neck as black blood began to spew from his mouth. His vision blurred as more blood seeped from the corners of his eyes. He looked at the mug then back to Valia in horror.

Poisoned?

Valia sat back and watched him die, studying the amount of time it took for all the vampire essence to drain from his body. He was an interesting case study. Although, not nearly as entertaining as the last vampire she'd tested her concoction on. She felt zero remorse as he turned into a gurgling pile of steaming flesh. Even his bones sloughed away, as his vampire metabolism tried desperately to burn whatever it could to fight the poison.

"Interesting. For all Ralic's boasting, in the end he's nothing but a steaming pile of offal."

When it was over, she stood and wiped her hands on the towel by the stovetop. She left the stateroom without so much as a backward glance. There was no time for sentimentality. Malachai's plans were in rapid motion, and Valia had work to do.

he fresh smell of spring was in the air as we drove in Doule's cruiser with the windows rolled down. Tae sat in front with the werewolf detective. I was disappointed Lobo wasn't with him. There was so much I wanted to tell him. I guessed we weren't there yet.

It had been five days since Deedee woke up in Drys's home. The dryad had taken special care of her, then sent her on her way, back to the human realm where she belonged. It tore me up that I never got to say goodbye. Drys explained it was just as well. How much worse would it have been to have Deedee look me in the eyes and only see a stranger?

"Don't tug at your blindfold," Tae warned. "I'm watching you."

I snickered. "I had an itch." She'd put the blindfold on me the second we left Free House. Apparently they had some big surprise in store for me back at the apothecary. I couldn't wait to be home. I missed making my potions. I missed my plants and Sacha's sarcasm.

The car brakes whined as Doule pulled to a stop.

"She's here!" someone said excitedly outside the car. The side door opened, and Tae's hands were there, guiding me out.

I clunked my head on the roof of the car, and we both laughed. I let her guide me, and then her hands held me still by the shoulders.

"Okay, are you ready?" She bubbled with enthusiasm.

I nodded. My grin was so wide it hurt.

Tae took off the blindfold. At first the light stung my eyes, and all I saw was her smiling face as she backed away from me with arms spread to the side like Vanna White. "Tada!"

The apothecary was stunning. Someone had painted the front of the building with swirling vines and bursts of colorful peonies. There were potion bottles and crystals threaded between the vines, with gemstones and vials of oil. The colors popped off the building in vivid detail. The mural had transformed my dingy storefront with its boarded-up window into a brilliant work of art.

Then I saw my friends. Sacha flapped his tiny imp wings in the air. He was dressed to impress in a three-button tweed suit. Charlie stood beside him in her paint-stained overalls with her hair tucked behind her pointed ears. Doule and Tae were on the other side of Sacha, beaming at me.

And just behind the imp stood Lobo. My heart leapt to see him standing there, his hairy arms folded over his chest, and his rough face quirked in a smirk. Perhaps there was hope for us yet.

"Was this you, Charlie?" I demanded.

She wilted for a second, and I realized my tone was all off. "Don't you like it?"

"I love it!" I screamed as I ran up to her and wrapped her in a big hug. Tae hugged me from the side, and Sacha laughed with Doule. I realized how much I'd gained in the last four months, and I was determined never to let it go again.

Speaking of which...

"Guys, I'd like you to meet my new friend," I said.

Pepper stepped out from where she was hiding behind me, wearing a timid smile. "Hello," she said softly.

"This is Pepper," I said. "She's going to stay with us a while."

Everyone greeted Pepper, and she grinned from ear to ear.

"Let me show you around," Charlie offered, gesturing to the front door to the apothecary.

"Hold up," Sacha snapped.

Charlie sighed. "Of course you're going to complain."

Sacha furrowed his brow. "Complain about a moon lily coming to live with us? Not likely. She's bound to be useful around the shop. But I'm Lanie's partner, so I should be the one what shows around new guests."

We laughed at the exchange, and Tae took me aside as everyone else went into the apothecary.

"So, Uriel said the person who cursed you can lift it?" she whispered. She'd been waiting for me to finish my story since we got off the train. "Any chance she told you who that is?"

"Do you think Uriel would ever give me a straight answer?" I snorted. "No. She only said, 'Don't ask me questions you already know the answer to.'"

"And do you?" Tae prodded.

I did. I'd known since the day I found out I was a fae. The day I learned my whole life had been a lie. I just hadn't wanted to believe it before now. Acknowledging the truth would mean confronting her depths of cruelty.

Because the person who put the curse on me was my mother.

Author's Note

If you enjoyed this story, it would mean the absolute world to us if you could please drop onto your favorite site and give a review of LIGHT'S WARDEN.

We wanted to take a moment and thank all our readers for the overwhelming support you've sent our way since we first published Light's Awakening. We love the world of Alacore's Apothecary and are truly lucky to have found readers who resonate with our fae heroine and her friends.

We are excited to bring Book:4 Light's Shadow to life. We've been hinting at a larger story happening behind the scenes of Lanie's adventure. In book 4 we finally get to bring it to the forefront. There are so many questions to answer. Who does Tae work for in her secret job as a spy? What is the Court of Shadows up to? What is Malachai planning? Where is Lanie's mother?

Join us in book 4 where we'll answer all of these questions and more. Lanie will uncover new lies, conspiracy, and deadly dangers as she travels to a new province, a fae casino, the human realm, and finally to the gates of Shadow Keep.

Preorder your copy of Light's Shadow today.

To stay in the loop on everything Alacore's Apothecary join our mailing list where we give sneak peeks, exclusive first looks, event alerts, and progress reports. **www.michellemurphyauthor.com**

Printed in the USA
CPSIA information can be obtained
at www.ICGtesting.com
JSHW020718240324
59623JS00001B/31

9 798988 641421